About the Author

❖

JOSÉ RAÚL BERNARDO is the author of two previous novels: *Silent Wing,* elected as one of the Best Works of Fiction in 1998 by the *Los Angeles Times Book Review,* and *The Secret of the Bulls,* now available in seven languages. A renaissance man, José Raúl Bernardo is also a celebrated architect, poet, and a noted composer whose award-winning symphonic works have been heard all over the world. He now makes his home in the Catskill Mountains of New York.

The Wise Women of Havana

✿

José Raúl Bernardo

An Imprint of HarperCollins*Publishers*

TO THE WISE WOMEN OF MY FAMILY

✵

Parts of this book appeared as a short story, "Happy Blue Crabs," in the book *Family: American Writers Remember Their Own*, edited by Sharon Sloan Fiffer and Steve Fiffer (Pantheon Books, 1996).

This is a work of fiction. The characters, incidents, and dialogues are products of the author's imagination and are not to be construed as real. Any resemblance to actual persons, living or dead, is entirely coincidental.

HarperCollins books may be purchased for educational, business, or sales promotional use. For information please write: Special Markets Department, HarperCollins Publishers Inc., 10 East 53rd Street, New York, NY 10022.

FIRST RAYO PAPERBACK EDITION PUBLISHED 2003.

Designed by Leah Carlson-Stanisic

The Library of Congress has catalogued the hardcover edition as follows:

Bernardo, José Raúl.
The wise women of Havana / José Raúl Bernardo.—1st ed.
p.   cm.
ISBN 0-06-621123-9
1. Women—Cuba—Fiction.   2. Female friendship—Fiction.   3. Havana (Cuba)—Fiction.   I. Title.

PS3552.E7275 W5   2002
813'.54—dc21   2001031848

ISBN 0-06-093615-0 (pbk.)

03   04   05   06   07   WBC/RRD   10   9   8   7   6   5   4   3   2   1

Acknowledgments

This book would never have come to fruition if not for the efforts of my friend and agent, Owen Laster, who believed in it from its very conception. His kind words of encouragement never failed to reach me, particularly in those moments of despair that apparently every writer must live through. Thank you, Owen.

In addition, I want to thank Robert Joyner, Betty Early, and my father, José Bernardo, who read the original draft of the manuscript and whose suggestions were invaluable. As I want to thank all the people at HarperCollins*Publishers* whose brilliant comments and editing made this novel come alive:

Carolyn Marino, Erica Johanson, Lydia Weaver, and René Alegría.

Finally, I want to thank a woman I've never met, Ellen Kanner, who gave me the title for this book. In her review of my first novel, *The Secret of the Bulls*—a book that deals with the sad affair of machismo in Latino culture—she referred to the women in my novel as being "wise." And then she wrote, "They may appear frail and tiny, but that's just a disguise. Underneath they are 'strong . . . powerful . . . able to command souls.'"

She was right. They are.

This book is an homage to those women.

Happiness cannot be found—it must be created anew every day.

RAQUEL PÉREZ REGUEIRA

PART ONE

Rape

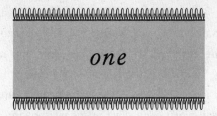

one

Even though it is the middle of February, when a thick, white shroud of snow covers vast areas of North America, and winter days are at their coldest, their grayest, and their most desolate, the weather in the city of Havana is simply as spectacular as it can ever be on this incredibly beautiful morning of 1938.

This magnificent weather of Cuba may be the only thing on the island that the Great Depression of the 1930s has not been able to wreck. Even as hundreds of thousands of Cubans starve—for unemployment has reached more than alarming proportions and almost nobody can get a job—the brilliant turquoise sky suspended above Marguita and Lorenzo as they begin to get off an old, clanking streetcar remains limpid and free of clouds, while gentle breezes insist on cooling the very hot midday Cuban sun, which is finding its way into the narrow and serpentine cobblestoned streets of the aged city.

For the last half hour or so, Marguita and Lorenzo have been riding on this badly battered streetcar that years ago must have been painted a gaudy yellow but that by now the ardent tropical sun has turned a chalky ivory, its wood-clad walls heavily pitted by the salty sea air and its well-worn cane seats way past showing their age. This ancient streetcar has taken the newlyweds from their brand-new home—a tiny two-room apartment located in Belascoaín, on the outskirts of the city—to the very center of Havana: *La Habana Vieja*—Old Havana—the sixteenth-century part of the city that still stands, fairly worn but mighty proud, by Havana Bay. And yet, though the trip has taken a lot longer than they had anticipated, neither Marguita nor Lorenzo, still honeymooners, thoroughly enjoying each other's company, has minded it in the very least. On the contrary, once she and Lorenzo get off the streetcar and breathe the heavenly scented ocean air coming from the bay, Marguita looks at her handsome young husband and they smile at each other in utter contentment.

It doesn't take but a few minutes for Lorenzo and his pretty wife to walk the few short city blocks that lead them from the streetcar stop into what in the late eighteenth century was the most fashionable neighborhood in all Havana—but which has long ago gone to seed and is now in an almost dilapidated condition. Elegantly dressed, the newlyweds are both wearing their Sunday best, which is exactly what they wore to their wedding two months ago. She, a bias-cut silver-gray dress—made by herself—that has a calf-length hemline, long sleeves, and high neckline, and that gently accentuates her well-rounded, womanly figure; and he, the better of his two suits, made of unbleached linen, and freshly ironed by Marguita herself.

Once they get to their destination in the middle of the block, Lorenzo knocks at a tall, narrow paneled wood door once painted a dark turquoise blue, now severely faded and peeling.

As they wait, Marguita turns to her husband, Lorenzo, he with the thin mustache, the unruly dark hair, and the deeply set dark-brown eyes she loves so much.

"How do I look?" she asks, her voice suddenly slightly on edge.

Lorenzo looks at her and admires what he sees: a bewitching young woman with short, light-golden hair, an oval face that is deeply tanned, a tiny nose, full, sensual lips, and pencil-thin plucked eyebrows that delicately frame her sparkling pale-blue eyes.

"As beautiful as ever," he answers gallantly, meaning every word.

"Oh, Lorenzo, please," a nervous Marguita replies. "I'm really serious. Do I look all right?"

This is the first time Marguita has been invited to Lorenzo's parents' house for a meal, and she is very tense about it, for she does not want to make a fool of herself.

Marguita has seldom seen Lorenzo's family.

During their three-year engagement it was always Lorenzo who would trek all the way across Havana to keep company with Marguita at her family's home. In fact, Lorenzo's and Marguita's families have seen each other only three times—and each of those times just for a few brief minutes. The first time, at the engagement party at Marguita's family's house, where the two families met; the second time, when Marguita and her parents went to Lorenzo's house for a very short and very formal early evening visit, as required by Cuban custom; and the third time at the actual wedding. So Marguita is extremely uneasy about this invitation to Sunday-noon dinner—her first ever at her in-laws'.

Lorenzo is about to say something to his apprehensive young wife when the door opens and Lorenzo's mother, Carmela, welcomes them warmly.

"Perfect timing," the petite, toothless old lady says as she adjusts a few loose strands of her completely white hair, which is tied in a tight bun at the back of her neck and worn in the severe Continental style of her Spanish homeland.

Thirty-six years ago, in 1902, the very same year Cuba achieved its independence from colonizing Spain, Lorenzo's parents, Padrón and Carmela—who were peasants back in Spain, where they had to work somebody else's land—came to Havana looking for a better life. Here, through a lot of hard work, Padrón eventually became a prosperous wine merchant until a few years ago, when his business totally collapsed due to the Great Depression—but not before they had five children, of whom only four survive, Lorenzo being Carmela's baby. However, though thirty-six long years have gone by since Lorenzo's parents came to Cuba, their way of life has not changed in the least, remaining as solidly and as rigidly Continental Spanish now as if they still lived back in Spain.

Smiling broadly, the thin and stooping sixty-two-year-old Carmela lets her son and her daughter-in-law in and closes the door behind them.

Dressed head to toe in the black of the most severe mourning, black stockings and all—what she has been wearing since her daughter Lucinda died seven years back—Carmela leads Marguita and Lorenzo into her home, going first through the music room and bypassing Lucinda's piano, a black upright covered with a black mourning shroud, and then across the long, narrow patio, until they reach the large dining room in back of the house.

As Marguita walks through the patio, which is paved with square terra-cotta tiles and already almost entirely in the shade even at this time of day, she begins to feel much more at ease, for both Lorenzo's family home as well as her own family's are what Cubans call *criollo*-style homes, that is, dwellings built by *criollos*—as people of Spanish descent born and raised on the island are called—to suit the challenging demands of the tropical climate of Cuba. These dwellings are long, narrow, one-story town houses sandwiched between other similar town houses, where most rooms face a fully enclosed, elongated, rectangular side patio. But unlike Marguita's family's home, a plain, simple structure located in Luyanó—the poorest barrio of Havana—Lorenzo's family's home, centrally located in Old Havana, is more like a mansion, having many rooms, all of them quite large and with very high ceilings that make them seem almost palatial. Marguita looks at this once-magnificent house with admiring eyes, realizing that everything is immaculately clean, even polished, though the structure seems to be badly in need of repairs, Marguita tells herself, when she notices that plaster ornaments and moldings have partially crumbled, and that many of the floor tiles in the patio are either broken or missing.

The moment Carmela and the newlyweds get to the dining room, the old lady says, "Just make yourselves at home. I'll go check on the food," and then she rushes into the kitchen.

Marguita takes a deep breath and smiles with anticipation. The air is filled with a wonderful aroma coming from the kitchen.

"That smells like *caldo Gallego*," she comments to Lorenzo, knowing that this thick, Spanish peasant soup, made with simple and the most inexpensive ingredients—collard greens, white beans, and bits of Spanish blood sausage—is one of Lorenzo's favorite dishes; one Marguita herself has never cooked, for she has been told that no Cuban woman can ever cook this Galician soup the way Spanish women do. After all, they've been cooking it for centuries, if not millennia.

It is then that Loló, the oldest of the two of Lorenzo's sisters still alive—eight years older than Lorenzo—comes into the dining room.

Loló is not dressed in the black of mourning, like her mother.

No. Not in the least.

Instead, she is wearing a tight, form-fitting, bias-cut white dress sprinkled with tiny red polka dots, which Marguita immediately notices is not homemade like her own dress, but store-bought at some fancy boutique.

"I'm sorry I cannot shake hands with you," Loló says as a way of greeting, showing Marguita and Lorenzo her beautifully manicured hands, "but I just finished retouching my nails and they're still wet." She playfully flutters her fingers at them as she takes her place at the table.

Although they have only seen each other on three occasions—and very briefly at that—Marguita has admired Loló's clear complexion from the first time they met, for it is almost pure white, flawless and unlined, even though Loló, who is much older than Marguita, is already past thirty. And then, to top it off, that immaculately white face of Loló's looks a lot whiter because it is framed by long, glossy, jet-black hair that she wears just like her mother's, Continental Spanish style, in a tight bun behind her neck. Loló is not exactly a beauty by Cuban standards, for she takes after her father and is too tall and too thin for Cuban men, who prefer their women to have voluptuous, well-rounded figures such as Marguita's. And yet, Loló cannot really be regarded as ugly, either. True, she does have a narrow face, a long, straight nose, and very thin lips. But she certainly compensates for those minor flaws by having exquisitely shaped black eyebrows and long, black eyelashes, which provide a magnificent frame for eyes so dark and so mystifying that they look as if they belonged on the face of a Gypsy woman.

"Where should I sit?" Marguita asks Lorenzo, for she doesn't want to take anyone else's place at the table. Lorenzo pulls up a chair and offers it to his wife.

"Right here," he says, smiling at her.

After Marguita sits down opposite Loló, who is sitting in her place directly across the large table from Marguita, Lorenzo sits by the side of his wife, which is the same place he used to sit before he and Marguita were married. Moments later they are joined by Lorenzo's father, Padrón, a tall, thin man, completely bald and with a long aquiline nose on a long horselike face who is much older than his wife, Carmela, and who, since the death of his oldest daughter,

Lucinda, has worn only black. After he greets his son and his new daughter-in-law with a barely noticeable nod, Padrón silently sits at the head of the table. Within a few minutes they are joined by Lorenzo's older brother, Fernando, a tall, skinny man, only four years older than Lorenzo but already balding, like his father. He wears a gray seersucker suit and a navy-blue bow tie, and the moment he comes into the dining room and sees his brother, he rushes to him, vigorously slaps Lorenzo's shoulders in a rough, manly way, and then, after heartily welcoming Marguita into their house, he sits on the other side of her.

No sooner does Fernando sit at the table than Lorenzo's other sister, Asunción, who is deaf and who, like both her parents, is also entirely dressed in black, carries from the kitchen a large, obviously heavy white tureen containing the *caldo Gallego* she has been working on all morning long. Though Asunción—who also takes after her father—is tall and thin and looks a lot like her older sister, Loló, the two women cannot be more different from each other. While Asunción's large, hazel eyes are always clear and crystalline, reflecting her kind, quiet personality, Loló's dark, gypsy eyes are always veiled and secretive, even cautious, as if hiding something behind them.

Welcoming Marguita with a warm, gentle smile, Asunción places the large tureen on the table, which is covered for the occasion with a white lace tablecloth that must have been quite beautiful when new, though it has since been patched many times. She then serves the soup to her father, Padrón, and waits patiently by his side until the old man tastes it and approves of it, as is the custom. It is only then that the *caldo Gallego* is served to the rest of the people at the table and eaten by all in absolute silence, as monks in a refectory.

At first this silence puzzles Marguita, for in her family's home a meal, no matter how plain, is always a celebration, where everybody seems to talk at the same time. But then she remembers that her mother, Dolores, warned her that Continental Spanish families are generally very stern, very cold, and very formal, and thus very different from Cuban families, which are just the opposite—as relaxed and as warm and as informal as any family could ever be. So Marguita, who already feels extremely ill at ease in this so-strange-to-her household, but who doesn't want to call undue attention to herself, eats her soup in silence—like the rest of the people at the table—and dares not utter a word.

Moments later, Asunción helps her mother, Carmela, clear the table. And then . . . nothing. The soup is followed by nothing. Not a thing. A watered-down coffee is soon served by Asunción, the deaf sister.

Marguita is also very puzzled by this.

In Cuba, the noontime meal is the heaviest meal of the day—especially on Sundays. During such a meal, a soup is followed by a main dish, which is generally served with an avocado salad and accompanied by ice-cold beer, and which is then followed by one or more desserts. And yet, today, the *caldo Gallego*—a soup—is followed by nothing. Not even dessert.

Maybe this is what Spanish families have for Sunday dinner, Marguita thinks.

Carmela comes back from the kitchen, takes her seat next to Lorenzo, her son, and then, all of a sudden, grabs his right hand and encircles it with her two hands.

Lorenzo is taken aback by Carmela's gesture.

And so is Marguita.

This clasping of his hand by his own mother is obviously something Lorenzo was not expecting, Marguita can read it in his eyes, for he does not know what to do, where to look, what to say. His eyes catch Marguita's but he says nothing. Then he looks at the empty table in front of him. And so does everybody else. Marguita. Carmela. Padrón. Asunción. Fernando. Even Loló, who for the moment has stopped admiring her bright fingernails and also looks at the worn white tablecloth.

Still clasping Lorenzo's hand, Carmela raises her eyes and stares intently at Padrón, her husband of so many years, hoping that he will say something. But the old man, as usual, says nothing, his expression a total blank as he gazes back at Carmela.

Not long after Padrón lost his business to the Depression, his firstborn, Lucinda—Lorenzo's oldest sister, who was not quite twenty-six—died of tuberculosis, then called consumption. Her death, together with the loss of his business, totally broke the old man's spirit. Since the day Lucinda was buried, Padrón has done little but take long morning walks, going by what once was his wine store on the way to the cemetery, and when he comes back home, he sits on a chair, hardly saying a word as he keeps gazing blankly into the far distance.

After a few tense moments go by, Carmela, still holding Lorenzo's hand within hers, finally breaks the ominous silence. "We . . . we've been thinking," she says, and again her eyes shift back to her husband, as if for help. But Padrón remains silent, almost aloof, as if carved from ivory. Carmela goes on. "Things are not so good around here," she says, and points to the huge, empty dining table where the scarce meal has just been served. "The way things are, we barely can put food on the table. And . . . well, we thought that, perhaps . . . if you were to move back in here . . . well, you know, the money you are paying for the rent of your apartment . . . we could use it, and . . ." She pauses and looks at Padrón, her husband, still an ivory statue in his black suit and tie. "Come, look," Carmela suddenly adds, as she stands up. "Look what we've done." They all stand up. Carmela, who has been talking exclusively to Lorenzo, completely ignoring Marguita, leads her son by the hand, and, bypassing Marguita, the old lady walks into what used to be Lucinda's room.

They all follow her, Marguita the last.

Lucinda's room is so clean it is sparkling, like the rest of the house—even though both walls and shutters are so old that they seem to be crumbling.

The room is also totally empty.

Gone are the large oak armoire, and the tall chest of drawers, and the dressing table, and the heavy oak bed. Gone are the two old dolls with frozen gray eyes staring out of pale ceramic faces, dressed in long dusty-rose birthing gowns, which used to sit propped on the bed. And gone, too, are the three Spanish black lace fans painted with pink and blue flowers that were hanging diagonally on the humidity-stained plaster wall above the blue and white tile wainscoting—though their silhouettes are still discernible on the bare wall. The tall, shuttered doors leading to the patio are wide open and the little bit of brilliant sunlight reaching into the old house stretches into the farthest corner of the room, bringing to it a certain kind of happiness, the kind of happiness the room has not experienced since Lucinda, pretty Lucinda who loved to play the piano, died, over seven years ago.

"This could be your room," Carmela tells Lorenzo, trying to sketch a smile. "It's right next to the bathroom," she quickly points out. "And I'm sure your things will fit in here easily."

Lorenzo looks anxiously at Marguita, who looks back at him, not saying a word.

It is only then, when she catches Lorenzo's glance at his wife, that Carmela looks at Marguita—the first time since they entered Lucinda's room. "It's much larger than it looks," the old lady tells her daughter-in-law. "And besides," she adds, "it's just for a little while, until things get better." Carmela faces Lorenzo again. "We used to count on you," she tells him, her soft voice on the point of breaking, "on the money you gave us when you lived here. And we all thought we could manage without you, we honestly did. But . . ."

Carmela faces Marguita again, and as she does Marguita realizes that this old woman probably never wanted to part with Lorenzo, just as she never wanted to part with any of her other children, all of whom are silently standing around her, none of them married—except for Lorenzo, Carmela's baby.

There is a pause. A long one.

"It's been hard," Carmela finally tells Marguita, as she lowers her eyes. "Really hard."

Surprised by Carmela's words, Marguita feels deeply embarrassed by this admission of need, which is particularly touching because it comes from a family of Spaniards, who Marguita has been told are always so aloof and always so proud. Then, not really knowing what to do or say, Marguita looks at Carmela, a toothless old woman dressed all in black with white hair tied in a tight bun at the back of her neck, still pensively staring at the worn, white marble floor.

Suddenly Marguita realizes that this Spanish family is now her family, too, especially now that she is expecting—something only she and Lorenzo know. So maybe, just maybe, moving in with them would not be such a bad idea after all, just to have somebody around should she need any help. But . . . she sighs. No. Involuntarily she shakes her head. *Quien se casa, casa quiere.* The old Cuban proverb comes to her head: "People who get married want a place of their own." Something undefined, something in the air, tells Marguita that it might be a great mistake to move into this old house in Old Havana, with its dark, narrow streets that let little air and little sun in, and live in a room with musty walls where chunks of plaster have fallen off, surrounded by all these people whose ways are so completely different from her own. Again she shakes her head, unaware that she is doing it.

"You don't think your things will fit in here?" asks a concerned Carmela, anxiously looking at Marguita, and misunderstanding Marguita's gesture.

Marguita suddenly realizes that she has been shaking her head.

"Oh, no, no, it's not that," she replies, embarrassed, as she faces Lorenzo and asks him, "But I thought you were giving your parents some money every month—"

"Oh, he does, he does," immediately interjects Carmela.

"But . . . of course, it's not as much as he used to give us, and we are so many, and . . . well, now, with just two people working instead of three—Fernando and Loló—they contribute as much as they can, but still it's not enough. Loló has to dress well, she has to look good at work, and, well, so does Fernando. They cannot give us as much as they would like to. Maybe after Loló finds a better job . . ." She looks at Loló, mare-faced Loló, who is standing apart from everyone else, admiring again her perfectly manicured, long and sharp, brilliant red fingernails.

Lorenzo looks at Marguita.

Marguita can read perfectly what is in his mind.

They have been so happy in their apartment, an apartment they can barely afford that they found only after months and months of looking and trekking all over Havana: a tiny apartment that came, not with an icebox but with a small electric refrigerator, and not with a coal stove but with a gas stove, where it is almost magic the way the burners light up on their own at the touch of a knob, and where Marguita has been doing her great Cuban-style cooking. Oh, yes, they've been so happy in their tiny apartment!

But a son must do as a son must.

And so must a son's wife.

Marguita knows that she would not even think about it twice had it been her parents doing the asking—even though she knows her parents would never have asked for anything like this. There is such a thing as Cuban pride. If bread and onions is all a Cuban family can afford, well, then, that is all there is. And if that is all there is, one learns to eat it day after day and to enjoy it. And how well do such things taste to an empty stomach! She and her family have had many a meal just like that in the last few years, Marguita recollects. Many.

But then she looks at Carmela and sees in the old woman's eyes a silent plea.

It is then Marguita realizes that there is nothing to be said.

This is now the family of her unborn child, and if they need help, well, then, help must be provided.

She turns around and looks at the room that used to be Lucinda's. "I'm sure our things will fit here, don't you think so?" she says, putting on her best smile as she turns and faces Lorenzo, who has not said a word.

"Oh, sure, sure," says Carmela, the words almost a long sigh. "And what doesn't fit here we can place in one of the other rooms," the old lady adds, now relaxed and smiling. "In the music room. Or in the living room. No one ever uses that room."

"But I thought you all went there to listen to the radio," interjects Lorenzo, opening his mouth for the first time, happy that his wife made the decision for both of them.

He knows how Marguita feels because he feels the very same way.

But . . . what must be done must be done.

"Oh, no," says Carmela. "The radio is now in our room. Didn't you see it as we went by it?" She lowers her voice. "Your father, he doesn't hear so well anymore, and last week the neighbors complained that the radio was too loud, so now we have it in the bedroom, next to his side of the bed. You know how much he likes listening to that radio." Carmela turns to her husband and raises her voice. "I'm telling Lorenzo how much you like the radio he gave you," she says and points to her son.

"Oh, yes," says Padrón. "A lot, *a lot.*"

Lorenzo looks at Marguita, and with his glance he asks her, Do you think they should know about the baby? Marguita understands Lorenzo's silent language. She smiles and, moving next to Lorenzo, lowers her eyes in embarrassment.

"Actually," Marguita says, "I think this is a good time to be close to all of you, now that"—she pauses and looks at Lorenzo—"well, now that . . ." Lorenzo places his arm around Marguita's shoulders, pulling her nearer to him. Marguita looks down at the floor again as she adds, "Now that we are going to have a baby."

"A baby?" Carmela repeats in disbelief. She looks at her son, then at his young wife, Marguita, and seeing the sparkle in their eyes, the old lady's formal and stern manner changes to that of a little girl jumping rope in the fields of old Castille as she claps her hands while saying, "A baby! A baby!"

Puzzled by Carmela's behavior, Padrón asks, "What's happening?"

Carmela shouts at him, "They are going to have a baby and they are going to move here"—she points to the floor—"with us! Isn't that great?"

"What? *What?*" asks the old man again.

"A baby!" shouts his wife, beaming with happiness. "They are going to have a baby! *A baby!*"

"A baby?" says Padrón, still puzzled, until he looks at Lorenzo and at Marguita, embracing each other. "Oh . . ." The old man finally understands. "*A baby!*"

And Padrón, who for the last few years since the death of his oldest daughter has seldom said a word or reacted to anything, pats his son's shoulders as he jubilantly nods his head up and down.

"Well done, son," he says. "Well done. *Well done!*"

Lorenzo looks at Marguita and smiles ear to ear.

Never has he been praised by his father for anything he has done in his life. Never. Just as his father has never embraced him—or even patted his shoulders, as Padrón has just done. Lorenzo is so proud that his chest seems about to burst. Marguita can read that immense pride in his handsome dark eyes, which are glittering as he looks at her with such a beaming smile on his face that it makes her smile as well—her first true smile since she stepped into this house. Though she still feels very reluctant about this move, Marguita tells herself that maybe something good will come of all of this, when she realizes how elated Lorenzo is.

Deaf Asunción, who does not understand what is going on, asks loudly, in that chalky, distorted voice of hers, "What's happening, what's happening?"

Carmela faces her deaf daughter and slowly mouths to her: "A baby." Then she repeats it as she pantomimes cradling a child in her arms, until Asunción finally understands what the commotion is all about.

"A *baby!*" Asunción shouts, making it sound as if the word were the most wonderful word of all the words in the world, and then she smiles big: a huge, broad smile that shows every one of her large, immaculately white teeth.

They are all shouting and laughing and asking, "When is the baby due, when is the baby due?" when a grinning Padrón, who seems as if he has just awakened from a long, bad dream, turns to Lorenzo's brother.

"Fernando," the old man says, "go to the dining room, and there, in the bottom drawer of the serving buffet, way in the back, under the napkins, there are several bottles of sweet Spanish sherry. One of them should say VINTAGE 1898 on the label. Bring it here."

Seconds later, Fernando brings the old, dusty bottle into Lucinda's room. And when she sees it, Asunción rushes to the kitchen and returns almost immediately, carrying cordial glasses so they all can celebrate the good news, while Marguita keeps looking at Lorenzo, the same beaming smile still on her face, for she knows that she—they—have made the right decision.

Everybody is filled with exuberant happiness.

Everybody, that is, except Loló, who watches Lorenzo and Marguita embrace each other with more than a glint of envy in her dark, gypsy eyes.

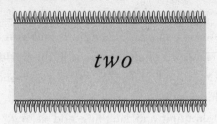

two

L oló has always been a puzzle.
    Not only to everyone who knows her—
including her whole family—but even to herself.

The second of three sisters born in rapid succession, Loló is and has always been completely different from the other two: Lucinda, older than Loló by two years, and Asunción, younger than Loló by just over fourteen months.

Lucinda was not only the oldest of Lorenzo's three sisters, but the most beautiful as well, the heart and soul of her family. Her two younger sisters, Loló and Asunción, take after their father, Padrón. Like him they are tall, horse-faced, and slender—to the point of being too thin—and, just like their father, they keep everything to themselves, seldom if ever saying a word. Not so Lucinda, who, taking after her mother, Carmela, was petite, vivacious, impish, and always as happy as a castanet—just like her mother; mother and daughter being twin souls in everything but in their musical tastes. Born and bred in Spain, Carmela loves Flamenco soul-singing, *cante Jondo,* no end, for it reminds her of the homeland she left behind years ago when she came to Cuba—the sadder the song, the better. Lucinda instead adored Cuban music, with its florid and sentimental Italianate melodies that seem to float gently, like lazy, cottony clouds, over a tempestuously rhythmic African background.

Music was Lucinda's life.

Like all girls from nice families during the first decades of the twentieth century in Cuba, Lucinda and her two sisters studied to play the piano. Loló soon dropped out, for she felt she could not compete with Lucinda, and went to business school instead. Not so Asunción, who, not born deaf, kept on with her piano studies and just like Lucinda, eventually completed her music education at the conservatory. But where Asunción's playing was, like herself, quiet, gentle, and shy—though equally as competent as Lucinda's—Lucinda's playing was confident, sparkling, and poised, even to the point of being bold.

Lucinda would sit at her piano—one of those black Victorian uprights filled with heavy carvings that used to adorn the living rooms of most Cuban middle-class homes at the time—and she would play for hours, filling the house with the glorious sounds she could get out of the instrument, and letting her boisterous music spill not only all over the large interior patio of her home, but even into the narrow and always shaded street fronting her house, bringing her special kind of sunlight into it.

Oh, was Lucinda good!

Just as she was the heart and soul of her family, she was the heart and soul of many a party. Barely twenty then, her long, black hair kept brilliantly glossy with violet-scented oil, her dark eyes sparkling with energy—eyes that were framed by the darkest eyelashes, the envy of a lot of her girlfriends—Lucinda, never shy, would sit at the piano—any piano, anywhere—and play and play for all the world to dance. Lilting Viennese waltzes would be followed by the latest American up tunes which would be followed by the latest Cuban *danzones*. These she could only play when none of the adults were around, for dancing to this kind of music was considered extremely risqué, which of course made it all the more desirable.

And then, how well did she accompany silent flickers!

Oh, was she good then!

Lorenzo, her brother—only ten at the time—was her official chaperone. He would walk by her side along the darkened streets of *La Habana Vieja* all the way from their home to the picture-show theater, where Lucinda worked, and then he would sit by himself in the large, dark room, watching the same flicker over and over again and listening to Lucinda play until the theater lights would come on.

Lucinda was at her best then. No question about it.

When the silver-screen chase was on, her hands would fly all over the piano, creating a thrilling and infectious excitement. When pirate and buccaneer ships were about to bombard and sink their courageous opponents, tempests would generate tempests. When the good cowboys shot at the evil ones, there are some who'd swear they actually heard gunshots coming out of the piano. And when the lovers were close to each other, oh, how delicate, how sweet Lucinda's hands could be: white doves barely touching the keys could not be as gentle as her hands were.

And yet, how passionate were the lovers' kisses when they said good-bye to each other, as their black and white ghosts floated over Lucinda's piano beneath them. And how sad their yearning for each other, when Lucinda played. And how glorious that final moment when, after having overcome insufferable pain and agony, the lovers tightly embraced each other and, as long sighs and loud sniffles could be heard from the women in the audience, the lovers sealed their immense love for each other for beyond eternity with an ardent and everlasting kiss! Oh, yes, Lucinda was at her best then.

But Lucinda is no more.

There came a cold, and then consumption, and then the rest of it.

And then, when the black-shrouded family came back to their house, a black shroud was placed on top of the piano, sealing it.

For pianos must also mourn, just like everyone else.

Exactly two years after her sister Lucinda died, while her father, Padrón, was out on one of those long morning walks of his, Asunción went to the piano, opened it, sat at it, and began to play it.

Carmela, her mother, rushed across the large patio, reached the music room, and froze at the doorway, looking at Asunción, sitting at the piano.

"For a moment I thought it was Lucinda," she said and burst into tears.

Asunción went to her mother and held her.

"Lucinda is dead, Mamá," Asunción said. "She is gone. But . . ." There was a short pause. *But I'm still here,* Asunción wanted to add. *I too have a life of my own.* That was what she wanted to tell her mother. That was what she needed to tell her mother. But that was not what she said. "But we have to go on with our lives," she said, as she embraced her mother.

Carmela nodded, still crying. "Just don't let your father hear you."

After two years, two long years of painful silence in the old house, a house where people didn't walk but tiptoed; where people didn't talk but whispered; where people didn't live but pretended to; after two long, long years of painful silence, magical sounds could again be heard in the old house, filling the rooms again with the glory of music.

But only in the morning when Padrón was not in the house.

During those two long years, Loló, already out of business school, had started to work, and had created a life of her own very few people knew about. But Asunción had none of that. She never did. Her only refuge had always been her piano and her music. True, Asunción never had either the criollo touch or the understanding of the wild Afro-Cuban rhythms that had made Lucinda the star of many a social event in their little world in *La Habana*.

But she did have "a soulful touch that makes the ivories cry," as Carmela used to say.

Asunción had developed that touch years ago, while Lucinda was still alive.

A young man had begun to visit the house, calling on Asunción: an ice-delivery man who had exchanged his canvas-roofed horse cart for a full-time position working as a salesman in a brand-new appliance store that had just opened on Galiano, Havana's busiest street. The young man had a sensitive soul who liked the quiet gentility of Asunción and her kind smile. But for reasons untold, this young man had not met the approval of Padrón—or so Carmela said—and Asunción, dutiful daughter that she was, broke off her relationship with the young man before there was any relationship at all to speak of.

No other man ever called again on Asunción. But she didn't care, for after the break-up, Asunción had begun to pour all her soul into her piano, playing a new kind of music that was as full of passion and virtuosity as Lucinda's had been. But in Asunción's playing the fast runs and the lightning-quick arpeggios reflected not sunshine— as Lucinda's playing did—but internal storms. At times Asunción would manage to break through those dark clouds and then the music revealed a quiet sky, Asunción's cloudless sky, a northern sky where the sun seldom gets to shine.

Just a few months after she had taken up piano playing again, Asunción developed a very bad cold that grew worse and worse.

The family feared that she, like Lucinda before her, might also die of consumption. But she managed to survive. Except that she became totally deaf in both ears. She could not hear any sounds whatsoever. Her family took her to doctor after doctor, but to no avail.

The old Victorian piano in the front room was closed once again. This time forever, for this time the black mourning shroud covered not only the piano but Asunción's heart as well.

And ever since then, Asunción—like her mother, Carmela, and her father, Padrón—has kept on wearing black. Ever since. Even at Lorenzo's wedding, a little over two months ago.

But not so Loló, she with the dark, gypsy eyes.

The second child, Loló never had Lucinda's beauty, nor Lucinda's ability to make friends, nor Lucinda's musical talent. Nor was she ever as smart as her younger sister, Asunción.

Or so Loló was told again and again.

Whenever people met Carmela and her girls for the first time, Carmela would always introduce her daughters by saying: "This is my oldest girl, Lucinda, the pretty one. And this is my youngest, Asunción, the smart one. And this one . . . this one is my middle girl, Loló." So Loló would never hear her mother say anything—not a word, good or bad—about her. Lucinda would soon be welcomed and loved by anyone who met her, and Asunción would soon find refuge in a book, as she always did. But where could Loló go? Certainly not to the piano, for no sooner would Loló start to practice than she would hear her mother—who, being in the kitchen at the other end of the house, could not see who was at the piano—shout, "That's not the way the music goes, Loló! Don't you know it yet? You're playing it all wrong!" And then Carmela would yell, calling for help, "Lucinda, Asunción! Go show Loló how to play that piece!"

Loló always got this "Why can't you be more like your sisters?" treatment, not only from her mother but from her father as well, for Lucinda, the firstborn, was the apple of her father's eye, and Asunción made the old man feel proud, for she excelled at her studies in school, and teachers were constantly praising her.

But they never praised Loló.

No one ever did.

Children listen to what their parents tell them, and believe them wholeheartedly. So little by little the young girl Loló began to believe that, yes, she was no good, no good at all. After all, she was not beautiful. And she was not smart. And she had no talent. And she couldn't make friends. Wasn't that what she was told day after day after day? And by her own parents? As those thoughts seeped into her head, the young girl Loló began creating a world of her own in which she could find refuge and be at peace with her shy self, even though that shy self of hers, unable to make friends, kept thinking that she was certainly untalented and unquestionably ugly.

It was not until after she entered business school that her life changed—just as her body matured from girlhood into womanhood.

True, Loló told herself then, she was not beautiful.

But that didn't stop her from seeing how the ardent eyes of some of the young men at school stared at her, burning through her, disturbing her, and making her wet between the legs. Still, the shy girl inside her held her body back from those young men. But not the eyes. Those dark, gypsy eyes of Loló's would blatantly return the look. And yet no sooner would one of those young men approach her than the shy girl inside Loló would take over and make her fly away from him.

A girl can only do this so often until all of a sudden she is known as a tease, and men stop looking at her, which is exactly what happened. It didn't take long for the young men at school to tell each other, "Loló? Why waste time on her? Don't you see what she is? She looks at you and looks at you, and then, nothing. She's time wasted. That's all she is. Time wasted." The young men at school would return her look once, maybe even twice, but soon after that they would stop returning her look altogether.

This only confirmed what Loló thought of herself: that indeed she must be as ugly as she had always been told she was. Didn't those men who'd look at her once or twice with eyes burning through her skin end up staying away from her? Totally ignoring her? Bypassing her as if she did not exist?

Still, her dark, gypsy eyes kept on being bold and daring.

As for talent, Loló felt she had none. She could not make herself type. Nor take shorthand. And certainly she was not smart enough. She could not keep books—simple arithmetic was a Chinese puzzle to her.

One of her teachers, an elderly lady with gray hair and an understanding look in her eyes, told her, "Loló, child, why don't you become a telephone switchboard operator?" At the time a lot of American companies were opening branches all over Cuba and telephone switchboard operators were heavily in demand.

"What do I have to do to be one?" the young girl asked.

"Just be polite when you answer the phone, and then make a simple connection. That is all," the lady answered. "I'm sure you will be great at that."

The lady was right.

It has been there, behind the safety of the switchboard, where she is totally unseen by the callers, that Loló has been able to bloom and excel.

Shy no more, there, behind the safety of the switchboard, Loló can laugh, and joke, and gossip—with the other operators, and even with most of the frequent callers who have learned to recognize her high-spirited voice. For there, behind the safety of the switchboard, Loló has acquired a different voice, a voice everybody likes, a voice everyone wants to befriend. And there, behind the safety of the switchboard, she has become the Loló she never was but always wanted to be, a very different Loló from the one everyone has ever known. A very different Loló even from the one she herself thinks she is. Because there, behind the safety of the switchboard, Loló can think of herself as friendly. And talented. And yes, at times, even beautiful.

But no sooner does Loló move away from behind the safety of the switchboard than she again becomes the shy, untalented, ugly girl she imagines herself to really be.

Hoping to make herself beautiful, Loló has tried everything.

Except for the few pesos she gives her mother every month, and claiming that her job demands that she be well dressed, she has spent every other penny she has ever made—every single one—on herself. The latest clothes, the latest hairstyles, the latest makeup. The "latest" in everything. Thinking that those clothes, and hair-dos, and makeup will somehow transform her and make her appear on the outside the way she feels inside when she hides there, behind the safety of the switchboard.

But though now she dresses in the latest clothes, wears the latest hairdo styles, and uses the latest makeup techniques, Loló still remains inside basically the same shy, even naive, girl she has always been.

If anything, those things have made matters worse. Because those clothes, hairstyles, and heavy makeup make people think—and especially men—that the Loló they see is the real Loló. And upon meeting that Loló—the one they see, the one who is always dazzlingly dressed and made up—they are soon either disappointed or else they feel they have been taken, once they encounter the other Loló—the real Loló, the one that really is, the one that feels shy, and untalented, and, yes, even ugly.

Those two women—the Loló people see and the real Loló—are two different people, as different from each other as night and day.

Except when Loló hides behind the safety of the switchboard—in which case she feels whole, complete.

And except when she looks at life through those dark, gypsy eyes of hers.

Those are the very same eyes that are looking at Marguita and Lorenzo as they embrace in Lucinda's empty room while everybody else who is looking at them is filled with exuberant happiness.

Everybody else but her.

For as she looks at them, Loló realizes how much these two people love each other. Just as she realizes how impossible it will be for her—a thirty-one-year-old old maid—to find a man who would look and smile at her the same way her brother looks and smiles at his pretty wife, Marguita, a blond, blue-eyed young girl with an oval face, a tiny nose, full, sensual lips, and a voluptuous well-rounded Cuban criollo figure who is the diametric opposite of who Loló is— or can ever be.

But a girl Loló would give anything to be like.

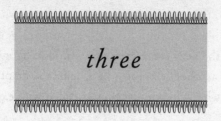

three

On the day before the last day of the month, the twenty-seventh of February, a Sunday—the only non-working day in the Cuba of 1938, for the workweek includes Saturdays—Marguita and Lorenzo move their meager belongings into Lorenzo's parents' old house, the one with the broken tiles, the dark, cavernous rooms with the patches of plaster fallen off the walls and the musty smell Marguita does not like.

Although this house is really large, it hasn't taken long for Marguita to learn her way around it, since its layout is so close to the layout of her own family house. All the rooms follow each other like cars in a train; all the bedrooms face the enclosed lateral patio; and they all are separated from it by a wall that runs the length of the patio and that consists primarily of tall, narrow shuttered doors that can be folded up like an accordion.

In the front of the house, facing the street, is the stately living room, which is the full width of the lot on which the house sits, followed by the music room. This is followed by Loló's room—the largest bedroom in the house—which is followed by the large single bathroom, which was originally a bedroom. This spacious room contains a water closet, a bidet, a footed white porcelain tub, a lavatory, and a tall and slender armoire to store towels and toiletries. Lucinda's former bedroom, now Marguita's and Lorenzo's, is on the other side of the bathroom. Next to this is Asunción's bedroom; followed by Carmela's and Padrón's bedroom; followed by the large dining room, which, like the kitchen that follows it, is also the full width of the lot. Behind the kitchen there is a sizable service yard, and, opposite it, is a large bedroom that has its own tiny bathroom in the corner. Originally meant to be used by the two or three live-in servants needed to maintain the house properly, this bedroom was shared by the two boys, Fernando and Lorenzo, until recently, when Lorenzo got married. Now, of course, only Fernando occupies it.

Following Marguita's instructions, the movers place the newlyweds' bedroom set—consisting of a chifforobe, a dressing table, a double bed with a thin, cotton-filled mattress lying on top of bedsprings that span the bed frame, and two night tables—in the room that used to be Lucinda's, next to the bathroom. The head of the bed is placed in the only place it can go, against the windowless party wall, looking at the opposite wall, the one made mostly of shuttered doors that separates the bedroom from the patio. These shuttered doors are the only source of light into the room, since none of the other three walls has a window. The chifforobe is placed on the wall separating the bathroom from the bedroom, while the dressing table with the large circular mirror is placed on the wall that separates their bedroom from Asunción's. The rest of their furniture—the bargain dining set made of a table, six dining chairs, and a serving buffet, which was the wedding present from Marguita's two older brothers, and two rocking chairs made of mahogany and cane—is placed in the large front living room.

How different this dark, musty room is from our pretty apartment, Marguita tells herself the moment the movers leave. As she looks carefully at the four walls of the bedroom that from now on is going to be the extent of her home, she is putting on a housedress, and sighs deeply, a sigh that seems to come from the bottom of her soul. That apartment is gone, the sigh seems to be telling her. Lorenzo reads her sigh properly, for he looks at her and sighs as well. But then he sees Marguita smile at him as she decisively begins to open boxes and organize their contents.

Within a couple of hours most of their other worldly possessions—articles of clothing, linens, shoes, hats, a couple of framed photographs—have found their way to where they belong. All except one last box, which Marguita finds in the living room, and which contains kitchen equipment. Marguita grabs it and starts to take it to the kitchen.

Since it has begun to rain, Marguita, who does not want to get wet, does what people who live in this kind of criollo-style house do when it is raining and they want to go from one end of the house to the other. Instead of walking the length of the patio—which is what is normally done when it is not raining—Marguita goes through all the rooms of the house. This is possible because to facilitate and increase cross ventilation in this style of house—something that is essential in hot and humid Cuba—there are no doors separating one room from the next, only tall and narrow plastered archways. These archways, perfectly aligned, are located at the corners of the room that are next to the patio wall—the one with the shuttered doors—and create a kind of an internal passageway that runs along that entire wall. This internal passageway is what everybody uses when it is raining. Which means that, with the exception of the bathroom, which is the only room in the house with a lockable door, the rest of the rooms in the house have no privacy whatsoever.

But privacy or no privacy, newlyweds must do as newlyweds must do.

Marguita and Lorenzo have waited several long nights to enjoy each other in bed. But the moon is full. And there comes a time when the inevitable can no longer be postponed. They have waited until they believe everybody has fallen asleep, and in the semidarkness of the hot night, lit exclusively by the moonlight coming through the open shuttered doors facing the patio, and barely covered by a thin cotton sheet, they begin to make love, trying to keep as quiet as possible so no one will hear them.

However, as most everyone knows, it is very difficult to keep totally quiet when one is having such a good time; and despite their best intentions, a soft moan manages to escape them here and there—just as the bedsprings beneath the mattress, though they are almost brand-new, manage to let a squeak escape here and there as well.

Marguita has closed her eyes in sublime ecstasy as Lorenzo, lying on top of her, enters her with the eagerness of a young bullock who has been penned for too long. The moment of truth comes, and, accompanied by one final loud squeak of the bed, Lorenzo collapses on top of her. Unaware of time passing by, Marguita seems suspended in heaven for those last moments of infinite pleasure, until she finally opens her eyes slightly—and is shocked by what she sees.

Standing in front of the open archway that leads into their room—the one by the bathroom—and lit by the intense pale-blue moonlight pouring into the patio, is the figure of a woman, who seems to be almost at the foot of their bed, staring intently at them. And as a startled Marguita stares back at her, that figure of a woman remains still. Afraid to move. Almost afraid to breathe.

Watching.

Just that. Silently watching.

With dark, piercing eyes.

It is only then, when she catches a glimpse of those dark, piercing eyes, that Marguita realizes who that woman is. Loló.

Marguita cannot believe what she is seeing.

She is deeply embarrassed and yet violently enraged at the same time, and two questions instantly flash through her mind. *How long has that woman been there?* Marguita asks herself. *How much of what Lorenzo and I were doing has that woman seen?*

Marguita keeps staring at that woman, and as she does, she finds in those insulting dark, gypsy eyes of Loló's fastened on hers the answers to those questions.

How long has that woman been there?

All the time, those eyes seem to say.

And how much of what Lorenzo and I were doing has that woman seen?

Everything, those eyes defiantly state.

As she finds those answers in Loló's affronting eyes, Marguita feels as if she has been profaned by them. Violated. Defiled.

Raped.

She shoves an exhausted Lorenzo out of her way, but by the time she manages to free herself the figure by the archway is gone.

She shakes Lorenzo violently. "Lorenzo, *Lorenzo!*"

"What's wrong, what's wrong?" a suddenly awakened Lorenzo whispers to Marguita, his voice urgent.

"Did you see her?" Marguita asks him, her voice shamelessly loud.

"Who?" Lorenzo asks, keeping his voice low.

"Loló," Marguita says, shaking and shaking her head in disbelief. How dare that woman, anyone, do a thing like that!

"Loló?" a bewildered Lorenzo repeats.

"Yes, Loló," an angered Marguita answers, fire already burning in her eyes. "Your sister, Loló. She was there"—Marguita points—"in that corner of the room, glaring at us as you and I made love." Marguita shakes her head. "I can*not* believe it," she says. "I just can't!" Naked as she is, an impulsive and raging Marguita is about to jump out of bed, go into Loló's bedroom, and ask that horrible, vicious woman what she thought she was doing in that archway, staring at them. But Lorenzo grabs her by the hand and stops her.

"Please, Marguita, please, let it go. Please," he says. Marguita faces him. "Get back in bed and try to get some sleep."

"But, Lorenzo—" Marguita starts to say.

"Please, Marguita. Loló is . . . well, she is . . . the way she is. Let's talk about it tomorrow. All right?" He looks at her. "I beg you. Please. Tomorrow is my turn to open the bookstore. I have to be there first, before anyone else. So, please, forget what happened. Get back in bed and let's get some sleep. Please?"

Marguita stares at Lorenzo for a while.

How can I ever forget what happened? she asks herself. Now I know that that woman saw everything Lorenzo and I were doing right from the very beginning. *Everything*. Her eyes told me so. And now I know that she was staring at me as I was doing what I was doing, taking Lorenzo fully in my mouth, doing to him what a lot of women like her, churchgoing spinsters, think is demeaning. Or even worse than demeaning. Dirty. What a lot of women like her think no decent woman, even if she is married, is ever supposed to do. To absolutely anyone. Not even to her very own husband. And now that woman probably thinks, like a lot of women like her, that I am just a bad woman, a cheap woman, a woman of the street, a whore, because only whores do what I did to Lorenzo. Take him in my mouth. But that woman is in the wrong! Just because I am a criollo woman and I enjoy what I do with my husband in the privacy of our own bed, just because of that I am not a bad woman. Nor am I cheap. Nor am I a whore. And I can*not* and I will *not* let that woman get away with what she's done! Who does she think she is?

Marguita looks again to where that woman was standing, and then again she begins to jump out of bed, when Lorenzo, again, grabs her by the hand and stops her.

"Please, Marguita. Please," he repeats, looking at his wife with tired, begging eyes. "Please, forget the whole thing and get back in bed. Please."

How can Marguita ever say no to this handsome husband of hers? Especially when his dark-brown eyes are looking at her in such a pleading way?

After sighing deeply, a very reluctant Marguita bites her lip and gets back in bed, lying as close to her husband as she can, covering herself protectively almost head to toe with the sheet, still enraged and yet trembling, almost in fear.

As Lorenzo falls asleep by her side, Marguita keeps on staring and staring at the archway where that woman was standing, seeing once and again those raping eyes looking at her with what . . . ?

Envy? Curiosity? Jealousy? Resentment?

An answer jumps into her mind.

Hate. That's it, she tells herself. That's exactly what I saw in those eyes.

Hate.

Intense, immeasurable hate.

Marguita shakes her head in total disbelief. Could that be, could that truly be, what I saw? *Hate?* Marguita asks herself, fastening her gaze to the place where that woman stood, as if she were able to find the answer to that terrifying question hiding somewhere in that corner of the room.

When the blueness of the moonlit night gives way to the ember-like fire of the early sun, Marguita's eyes are still open. And so they remain when that early fire gives way to the pink of dawn. And so they remain when that pink of dawn gives way to the pale straw yellow of an early tropical morning.

And still Marguita cannot understand, Why would any woman do a thing like that?

And what is worse, Why would that woman hate me the way she does?

And what is even worse, What have I done to her?

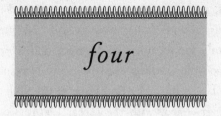

four

As soon as Marguita sees Lorenzo off to work early the next morning, she rushes back to their room, and there, desperately, as if she has gone mad, she puts on the first dress she can find, and just as she is, in her house shoes, not even made up, not even combed, she rushes out of that house and to a street corner a few blocks away, where she does not have to wait long at this time of morning for the streetcar that will take her all the way across town to her family's home in Luyanó. Once she finally gets there, as she rushes through the front door, which is never closed in the daytime, Marguita calls her mother again and again with great urgency in her voice, tears streaming down her cheeks.

"Mamá, Mamá . . . ! *Mamáááá!*"

Marguita has to shout to be heard, because right behind her the cacophonous noise of rattling streetcars, roaring buses, clattering delivery trucks, and sputtering cars nearly drowns out her voice. These deafening sounds come from a wide avenue, La Calzada, where Marguita's family home is located, and which is the main artery of Luyanó—the working-class barrio of Havana.

Regardless of how hard the times are in the Cuba of 1938—and they are very, *very* hard, with the Great Depression bringing the price of sugar to an all-time low, forcing all Cubans to tighten their belts, and then some—the traffic on the busy avenue remains absolutely maddening. As usual at this time of morning, when everybody is rushing to get to work, every driver is desperately trying to overtake the next one by maneuvering his vehicle as aggressively as possible—Cuban macho style—constantly honking, constantly attempting to pass each other, and constantly shouting as many foul insults as each driver knows—which are plenty. But Marguita, like everyone else who has lived in Luyanó for as long as she and her family have, is used to all this. Chaos, noise, foul insults, and the obnoxious smell of the car fumes that seem to hover perennially over La Calzada like a thick fog, are as much a part of the barrio as the bulls that every so often race in wild derangement from the train station at one end of a narrow, unpaved little street that crosses La Calzada—the Street of the Bulls—to the slaughterhouse at the other end.

As Marguita rushes through the front door, her mother, Dolores, who remains as handsome a woman at fifty-two as she has always been—even though she has begun to pull gray hairs out of her beautiful head of black hair far too often—is in the large dining room back of her criollo-style house. Wearing a homemade house-dress and flat slippers, Dolores is cutting a new dress for her youngest daughter, Perucha, who will turn ten in two and a half weeks. She finally hears Marguita's urgent call from the other end of the patio. Leaving everything just as it is—patterns, pins, scissors, yardsticks, and remnants of cheap patterned fabric spread all over the top of the huge dining-room table that all Cuban families have because of their large number of children—Dolores hurries across the patio, which is bathed in the early-morning light of a beaming tropical sun that is beginning to get hot.

"*Marguita!*"

This is all an astounded Dolores can say when she sees the disheveled condition her daughter is in. "What's wrong, my little love?" Dolores asks, deeply concerned, as she rushes to Marguita, who seems to be trembling out of control, as if she were running a high fever. The moment Dolores gets to her, she embraces her child tightly against her heart. "What's wrong, Marguita? Tell me, my love, what is it? Did you and Lorenzo have a bad fight?"

But Marguita says nothing. She cannot utter a word.

She just shakes and shakes her head, and then she bursts into tears again as she lets herself be embraced by her mother, who manages to walk her wobbly daughter across the patio and into the dining room in the back. There, Dolores places Marguita on a chair and goes to the kitchen, just to come back with a whole pot of coffee she was making, which she was planning to take to her husband at the butcher shop across La Calzada, as she does every morning.

"Here," Dolores says. "Have some of this. It'll make you feel better. Did you have any breakfast?" Marguita shakes her head. "Let me go get you—"

But Marguita won't let her finish.

Despite her embarrassment, Marguita opens her heart to her mother and tells her everything that happened—every little thing—confiding in Dolores the way she has done all her life, as tears of indignation and rage stream down her cheeks.

As Marguita talks and talks, revealing to her mother the most intimate details of her life as a married woman—details Dolores doesn't mind hearing, but was never expecting to know about—

Dolores stays silent, saying not a word. "Once the dam breaks, the water must gush out," says the Cuban proverb. But just because she says nothing, that doesn't mean Dolores is not listening attentively to what Marguita is telling her, trying to make sense of what Marguita is saying, and ultimately she begins to nod and nod in total agreement with her daughter.

Dolores knows very well how rigid and unbending the Continental Spanish code of life is. After all, she is the daughter of an ambitious, social-climbing Continental Spanish man who, through wheelings and dealings, became a wealthy landowner, and who disowned Dolores for disobeying his orders and eloping with a butcher—a man Dolores's father thought was way beneath Dolores's social class. As a result, Dolores's father never spoke to her again; he never let his other daughters, Dolores's own sisters, speak—or even write—to Dolores again; and he never allowed Dolores's name to be mentioned in his presence. Ever again. As far as Dolores's family was concerned, Dolores was dead and buried to them all. That's how rigid and unbending that code of life is—a code Dolores had dared to disobey.

And that same unwritten code states that there are things no woman—no *decent* woman, that is—can ever do in bed, not even to her own husband. Opening her legs to him at his demand and bearing his children, that much a decent woman can—and must—do, pleasure or no pleasure. That is her duty. But that is the extent of it. Anything else is dirty. Demeaning. Disgusting. Anything else is what whores—and only whores—do. That is what that code of life says. And pity the poor woman who dares to break that code. She is ostracized by all, shunned by friends, even by her closest friends. She is treated worse than a leper by everybody—*everybody*—including her very own family.

Dolores knows how easy it is to destroy the reputation of a woman in the world they live in. By calling her a bad woman. By calling her cheap. Even by calling her nothing at all, but just by raising the eyebrows significantly as the poor woman goes by, and merely dropping a few hints, making sure that sentences are left elliptically open-ended: "Of course you know what kind of a woman she is . . ." Dolores has seen it happen time after time. No proof is ever needed. All that is needed is getting a rumor started. And in most cases it is impudent women—just like the kind Loló seems to be—who start such rumors.

Dolores also knows that in circumstances like these the best thing to do is nothing at all, not to call undue attention to anything. That the best thing to do is just to sit back and wait—patiently—for the water to find its level.

Maybe nothing will come of this, Dolores tells herself, as she listens to Marguita's outpouring of emotions. And if something were to come of this, if that woman ever mentions a word about any of what she saw last night between Marguita and her husband, well, then, at that time we will take action. But until such time comes, *Do nothing*, Dolores keeps repeating to herself. *Just listen and be silent.* Which is exactly what she does, her face serene and calm on the outside even though inside she is, just like Marguita, seething with rage at the unfairness of it all. What right does anybody have to interfere between man and wife? Who is to say what is right or wrong when husband and wife get in bed? A churchgoing spinster? A eunuch of a priest? People who are not even married? How can they dare issue dictums about what they know nothing of? What do they really know? What do they think they know?

"I just wish I'd never have to lay eyes on that horrible and vicious woman again," Marguita tells her mother, her voice now more calm but still sounding both deeply outraged and deeply hurt. "But how can I, Mamá, when I am living in her very own home? Oh, Lord," an indignant Marguita prays, "please, grant me that one day I'll be able to avenge myself for what that woman is making me suffer! That is all I'm asking you. Please!"

Then, as tears of anger and frustration keep streaming down her cheeks, she adds, "Mamá, I cannot live a minute more in the same house as that woman. I just can't. I just can't face those people anymore. No, it's not them. It's not them at all. It's her. It's always been her. I tell you, Mamá. That woman is evil. I can tell. I saw it. It's there in her eyes. They've always looked at me with . . . I didn't know what. Contempt, I thought. Because I'm a poor girl who comes from Luyanó and I'm not as well educated as she is because I didn't go past grade school. Or because I'm not a career woman like her, and I don't work at some fancy office, and I don't make any money, and I have to make my own dresses from fabric remnants. Or because I don't know why, Mamá. That woman has always looked at me with eyes filled with something. I'd never been able to tell what it was. Until last night. But now I know. Those dark piercing eyes of hers were filled with hate. A hate so deep and so intense that it is frightening, Mamá, I tell you. *Frightening*. I don't ever want to face those evil eyes of hers. Ever again. I just can't. I'd rather live on the streets." She shakes her head. "What are Lorenzo and I going to do now?" she adds, almost in despair. "You know how long it took us to find that pretty little apartment of ours. I'm so sorry we gave it up! God knows how long it's going to take us to find another one!"

Dolores keeps hushing her daughter, "Don't you worry about anything, my little love. Between the two of us, we'll take care of it all."

Dolores's first idea is to offer Marguita and Lorenzo a room in her own house, but she knows that married people need a place of their own.

She also knows about an empty old house, not too far away from theirs, right on the Street of the Bulls, just around the corner from Hermenegildo's bodega, two doors down from it. This is a criollo-style two-story, two-family house, one family to a floor—and the bottom floor has been empty for a while. True, the house isn't new, and it isn't pretty, and it doesn't have a refrigerator or a gas stove, and it is facing the half-dilapidated wooden shacks where the mulatto women kept by Chinese men in the opium business live with their illegitimate children.

But it is cheap.

And it is available.

As she embraces her daughter and erases her tears, Dolores tells Marguita, "Wouldn't that house be great for the two of you?"

Marguita looks at her mother with incredulous eyes.

Could that be possible? Marguita thinks. A house of her own? Of her very own? And close to her own mother? Sometimes God does answer prayers. "But," Marguita says, "how could we manage it? We don't have the money. We've given all of this month's allowance to Lorenzo's mother, Carmela."

"Money?" says Dolores. "Let's see what we can do."

Dolores goes to her chiffonier and opens the second drawer from the top. She pulls out from the back of the drawer a handkerchief tied in a knot, and undoes the knot. Inside there is a bundle of money, several bills amounting to a fortune in 1938: thirty-four pesos! She gives them to Marguita.

"Oh, we can't accept that."

"I'm not giving it to you," Dolores says, "I'm giving it to the baby." She rubs Marguita's belly which is barely beginning to show. "Besides," Dolores goes on, "since when are you going to tell me what I can or cannot do? Here." She hands Marguita her own linen handkerchief, beautifully hand-embroidered by Dolores herself. "Blow. Hard. And get rid of those tears. Go wash your face and put on some makeup. We have work to do."

By the time Marguita gets out of the bathroom, Dolores has already gone across La Calzada, the broad avenue that separates her house from the butcher shop, and has fetched her husband, Maximiliano the butcher.

When he heard the story, Maximiliano instantly told his customers to come back some other time, hurriedly locked the heavy metal gates to the butcher shop, and, still wearing his blood-stained apron, rushed across La Calzada back to his home.

"What did that miserable bitch do to you?" he demands of Marguita when he sees her, the bull in him raging with fury, his huge, callused hands already clenched into fists.

"No time for that," says Dolores. "Let's see if Gudelio's house is still available. Here, take this." She hands her husband the bundle of money.

"Where did you get this?"

"Never you mind. I've been saving it."

"From the money I give to you?"

"Where else?"

Maximiliano turns to Marguita and winks an eye at her. "Well, now I know I've been giving your mother far too much money!" he says jokingly, and smiles as he gently pats the ample behind of his wife, Dolores, who is still as beautiful and as mischievous as ever, making Marguita smile at the two of them.

"Now," says Dolores as she removes Maximiliano's dirty apron, "Don't spend it all at one time. Try to bargain Gudelio down a few pesos."

"Woman!" replies Maximiliano laughing, "Are you going to tell me how to strike a bargain? *Me*? Tell me, who wears the pants in this family?"

This time it is Dolores's turn to smile. "You do, of course. You do. You always have. Now, let's get going."

"Oh, no," says Maximiliano. "Neither of you is coming with me."

"Oh, yes, we are," Dolores answers, "we definitely are. I certainly want to see the house my first grandchild is going to be born in. And, by the way, go wash your hands and comb that bristly hair of yours."

* * *

That evening, when Lorenzo gets back to his parents' house after work, he finds Marguita packing their things.

He doesn't have time to say a word.

He just looks at his wife, a question in his eyes—a question that Marguita answers by throwing more things into an old half-dilapidated straw suitcase which had been Dolores's and which is now Marguita's.

"We are moving," Marguita says. And then she tells an astounded Lorenzo about the great old house on the Street of the Bulls she has just rented—with the money her parents gave to her. "Well, not to me," she corrects herself, "but to the baby."

"But . . . what are we going to tell Mamá?" Lorenzo asks, concerned, as he begins to take the few clothes he has out of the armoire and hand them over to Marguita.

"The truth," Marguita replies, her loud voice sharp as a knife, as she closes one suitcase and opens the next. "That after what happened last night, there's no way I can live one more second next to that horrible"—she catches herself—"Lorenzo, I know she's your sister, but still she's a horrible and vicious woman and I will not live one more minute in the same house with her!"

Lorenzo says nothing. He just hands her his other suit, which Marguita takes off the wood hanger and begins to fold carefully.

It is then that Marguita glances at her husband and, all of a sudden, she remembers the look in Lorenzo's eyes when his father, Padrón, patted his shoulders the moment he found out about the baby. She had never seen Lorenzo look so proud—and yes, so handsome—as he did then. Remembering that, she realizes that she has been far too harsh on Lorenzo, for no reason at all. Whatever happened last night, it was not his fault. Nor his mother's.

She lowers her voice and in a much gentler tone she tells Lorenzo, "Or else, we can tell Carmela that"—she pauses, as if looking for the right words—"that this house is no good for the baby. That"—she looks around Lucinda's room—"that this house is too musty, and too dark, and too—" She doesn't finish her sentence. She turns to Lorenzo and faces him. "Lorenzo, just tell Carmela the real truth. That married people need to have a place of their own. I'm sure your mother will understand that. Wasn't that why she and your father came to Cuba? To find a place of their own?" Lorenzo looks at her and nods. "So, it's the same with us."

"But, what about the money?" Lorenzo asks, as he hands her his two other ties. "They still need it, you know that. And badly."

"The rent for that old house in Luyanó is a lot less than what we were paying for the apartment," Marguita says, taking her clothes out of the armoire. "So we can give your mother the difference in rent money plus the money you were already giving her while we lived in the apartment. Tell her that. It may not be much, but"—she faces Lorenzo—"Lorenzo, we have to do this. I cannot live in the same house next to that horrible, vicious woman one more minute, or I'll go crazy. I know, I know she's your sister, I keep telling myself, but . . . I couldn't sleep at all last night. Besides . . ." She gives him an embarrassed look. "I know I wouldn't be able to make love to you anymore, not with that woman living practically in the room next to ours. I'd be afraid she might do again what she did last night, and I couldn't bear living through that horrible humiliation ever again," Marguita says, her eyes beginning to tear at the painful memory.

"I know, my love. I know," he says as he goes to her and embraces her tightly. "I know that it can't have been easy on you, because it sure hasn't been easy on me, and I was born in this house!" He smiles at her. "You know how the old saying goes: '*No hay mal que por bien no venga*—Nothing's so bad that it doesn't bring some good.' Maybe that's why all this happened. For the good that's yet to come." He embraces her even more tightly. "Do you remember how much fun you and I used to have when we were *alone?*" he asks, emphasizing the word *alone* with a mischievous glint in his eye.

That glint makes Marguita smile. Her first smile. She nods.

"Well," Lorenzo says, his voice a whisper, "soon we're going to be alone again. Just you and I. Can you imagine what that's going to be like?"

Can I imagine *that?* Marguita asks herself.

Can I imagine cooking my own meals my own way? Or cleaning my own house my own way? Or listening to the kind of music I like, Cuban music, not Spanish music? Or doing as I want and not as I am told? Can *I* imagine that! She looks at Lorenzo. Or making love to my husband like I used to? With no need to keep quiet or hide under the sheets? With all the freedom and with all the enjoyment of letting go in total abandon, as he and I used to? Can I imagine *that!*

As she remembers what that was like, Marguita's eyes glitter with anticipated joy.

She smiles back at Lorenzo, who is so close to her. Yes, I can certainly imagine *that!* that wonderful smile of hers seems to be saying.

When Lorenzo sees the glitter in Marguita's eyes, and the smile on Marguita's face, he brings his wife even closer to him and attempts to kiss her. But he cannot manage to do it. Violently, he is pushed away by a very nervous Marguita, who looks over his shoulder in the direction of the archway where Loló stood last night.

In her mind Marguita can see that woman there again, exactly where she was and exactly as she was, lit by the moonlight in the semidarkness of the room—those piercing eyes of Loló's burning again through her. And as her mind remembers those horrible, vicious, insulting eyes, Marguita feels exactly as she felt last night. Violated. Defiled.

Raped.

Still unable to understand how a woman could have done as that woman did.

And why.

But thank God all that nightmare will soon be over, Marguita tells herself as she closes the suitcase and readies herself to leave this musty old house in Old Havana. Tonight they'll sleep at her parents' home in Luyanó, in what used to be her own bedroom. It will be a tight fit, what with her and Lorenzo sleeping in a twin bed, Marguita thinks. But it will be a lot better than spending another night in this house where that woman lives. And tomorrow evening, after her brothers come here, and with the help of Lorenzo they pick up whatever other possessions the newlyweds have and bring them to the newly rented house in Luyanó, tomorrow she and Lorenzo will be able to sleep peacefully where they belong, in a place of their very own—with the certainty that no one will be watching what she and her husband do in the privacy of their own home.

Because that's what the house in Luyanó will be to the two of them.

Home.

PART TWO

Refuge

five

Though considerably smaller, the two-family house the newlyweds are moving into—the one in Luyanó—is very similar to the house of Lorenzo's parents in Old Havana. Two bedrooms with a bathroom in between connect—train style—the living room at the front end of the house to the dining room and kitchen at the other end. However, in the Luyanó house, all the rooms are very, very small, unlike the house in Old Havana that boasts of many more rooms, all of them almost palatial in feeling. In both houses, all the rooms open, by means of shuttered doors, into a fully enclosed long, narrow patio, which in the Luyanó house is paved with cement.

"Where the children can safely play," said Dolores the moment she stepped in it, embarrassing Marguita no end.

The upper floor of the house in Luyanó is laid out exactly like the lower one, except that this upper floor has, instead of a patio, a balcony running the entire length of the house and overlooking the patio downstairs. This upper floor is occupied by another family, the Velascos, a married couple in their mid-thirties with two girls, aged seven and nine.

Because the lower floor of the house has almost no privacy whatsoever—for the people upstairs can look down into the patio and its adjoining rooms at all times—that floor has been left unoccupied for a long, long while until Marguita and Lorenzo rented it. When Dolores and Marguita first visited the house, earlier today, Dolores loved everything about it, as she had to. After all, what other choice was there? But she didn't like the almost total lack of privacy the house had. She said nothing to Marguita, of course; she didn't want to discourage her daughter, whose mind was still fresh with the painful memory of what "that woman"—as Marguita has begun to refer to Loló—had done to her. But Dolores thought that she'd better do something about it, for she knew how important privacy was to everybody. Especially to newlyweds. And—particularly—to Marguita, after what the poor girl has just lived through. So right then, as she stood in the middle of the patio of Marguita's new home, Dolores decided to have a friendly talk with Marguita's upstairs neighbor, Señora Velasco, and see what could be done to remedy the situation.

A short and pleasantly plump woman, Señora Velasco is a very good customer of Dolores's husband, Maximiliano the butcher. A couple of hours after the house lease was signed and sealed, right before noon, while Marguita is back at her in-laws', packing her things and getting ready to move, Dolores manages to arrive at the butcher shop exactly when Señora Velasco is there.

"Señora Velasco, what a pleasant surprise! Do you know that my daughter Marguita and her husband just rented the lower floor of *your* house this morning?" Dolores asks, gently underlining the word *your*.

Dolores knows with total certainty that Señora Velasco already knows about it.

News runs in the barrio faster than you can say "Cubanacán," the aboriginal name for Cuba. Especially since Dolores herself gave the news to Pilar, the fat woman with the glass eye who is her next-door neighbor and who is the prime source of gossip in all of Luyanó—if not all of Havana.

"Now that our families are going to be close neighbors, so to speak," Dolores says, "I was wondering if I might come and visit you to pay our respects, perhaps later on today?"

"To pay our respects" was a classic phrase Cubans used at the time on occasions such as this, for this was the neighborly thing to do.

"Why, sure," Señora Velasco answers, genuinely flattered.

Although Dolores has known the much younger woman facing her for a while, she has never been to Señora Velasco's house, and Señora Velasco is more than proud to welcome into her home the butcher's wife, Dolores, a woman the entire barrio loves and respects.

So, as Señora Velasco rushes back to her house to make sure it is in perfect order and impeccably clean—to meet the scrutiny of a visitor, as custom demands—Dolores rushes back to hers, where she had already told her old cook, Lucía, to prepare a large tray of *buñuelos*—delicious deep-fried Cuban pastries shaped like the number 8, made of sweet potatoes and squash and served with honey poured abundantly over them.

Later on that afternoon, wearing one of her better dresses—made by herself—and armed with a tray covered with a white linen kitchen towel, exquisitely embroidered by Dolores herself, Dolores goes to visit Señora Velasco. Since this is Dolores's first visit to the Velascos' home, and since the two women do not yet know each other well enough, this first visit is supposed to be limited to just a few minutes, and only to the living room of the home, for such demands the unwritten etiquette code of criollo manners.

After a few pleasantries are exchanged, Dolores hands the tray to Señora Velasco.

"I hope you don't mind that I brought you a little something," Dolores says.

"Oh, thank you so much," Señora Velasco replies, accepting the tray and delicately lifting one corner of the beautiful linen towel covering it. "*Oh!*" she exclaims with utter delight when she sees what is hidden under the beautifully embroidered linen towel. "*Buñuelos!*"

"They are Lucía's specialty, as I'm sure you know," Dolores says. "Even Pilar says they are the best *buñuelos* she's ever put in her mouth—and that woman knows about sweets," she adds, making Señora Velasco chuckle. Pilar's addiction to anything sweet is notorious—but not quite as notorious as her addiction to the spreading of gossip, at which Pilar is, by all accounts, unbeatable. "I just hope these *buñuelos* are as good as usual," Dolores goes on. "I've been so busy all day long today that I didn't even have a chance to taste them before I brought them to you."

"In that case, why don't we taste them together?" answers Señora Velasco, who cannot keep her eyes off the scrumptious-looking delicacies.

Dolores instantly responds politely, "Oh, no, no, no! You go and you enjoy the *buñuelos*. You and your girls. I brought them for you and your family."

"Oh, no, Dolores," Señora Velasco replies back. "Please, I insist."

"To tell you the truth, I'd love to, I honestly would," says a resigned Dolores, "but, you know *buñuelos*, they're so messy to eat, with all that honey. I'm afraid that I would probably spill some of it, as I'm known to do, and make a pretty mess out of this beautiful floor of yours." She points to Señora Velasco's living room floor. "How do you ever manage to have this floor so sparkling? The floors of my house never shine like this one of yours do, Señora Velasco. What is your secret?"

"Vinegar," Señora Velasco says, bursting with pride. "White wine vinegar! Just a few drops of vinegar in the water, and the results . . . well, you can actually see them," she adds, pointing to her shiny Cuban tile floor, which is almost a mirror.

Now much more at ease with Dolores, and still dying to try these famous *buñuelos* of Lucía's, Señora Velasco smiles at Dolores. "I tell you what," she says in a confiding, intimate tone of voice—the tone of a woman who is now addressing a close friend, not just a plain neighbor—"why don't we go to the dining room and try these *buñuelos?* I'll make us some coffee and—"

"Oh, no! Under no circumstances can I allow you to do anything like that!" Dolores says instantly. "I would never want you to go through all that trouble just for—"

"It will be no trouble, no trouble at all. Please, come. Follow me."

Since the house of Señora Velasco has no patio, Señora Velasco leads the way using the balcony that runs the length of the house. This is precisely what Dolores aimed to achieve with this visit, for she wanted to see how much of the lower floor—and of the lower floor *rooms*—could be seen from this balcony.

To her dismay, as she walks by, she realizes that from different places along the balcony she can see not only all of the patio but also into every room in the house, the newlyweds' bedroom included.

No good, no good, Dolores tells herself as she follows Señora Velasco. Something has to be done, but what?

Suddenly, her eyes focus on the railing at the edge of the balcony: a cast-iron railing held by thin, vertical square rods spaced 8 inches apart. An idea flashes through Dolores's head. "Oh, my," she says, taking her right hand to her head while holding tight to the railing with her left hand. "For a moment I got dizzy, when I looked down at the patio."

"Yes, that happens to a lot of people who come visit us," Señora

Velasco says. "I myself used to feel a little dizzy when we first moved here."

Dolores cannot walk. She remains standing, holding tight to the railing, which moves slightly back and forth as she holds on to it. "Is this railing safe?" she asks. "It feels a little loose to me, doesn't it to you? And look how far apart these rods are. I don't think that's safe. For your girls, I mean. I bet they can fit their heads in between, and then what?"

"I know," Señora Velasco says. "I often have asked myself the same question. But I don't know what to do about it."

"I don't think you could replace this railing, could you? The price would probably be a small fortune. If I were you, I'd talk to Gudelio, the owner, and maybe he will be able to do something about it."

"We—I mean, my husband—did talk to Gudelio, and Gudelio said that this railing had been approved by the building inspector, and that if we wanted to do something about it, then that would be all right, but that we would have to pay for it. My husband, as you can imagine, didn't think he—"

A sudden gust of air lifts Dolores's skirt and Dolores instantly lets go of the railing to hold her skirt down. "Am I glad there was not a man down there right now!" she says, interrupting Señora Velasco and chuckling as she points down at the patio. "If he had looked up while my skirt was flaring, well, you know," she says, her face red with embarrassment, "he probably would have seen, well . . . what only my husband has seen!"

This idea had never crossed Señora Velasco's mind.

Since she and her family moved in, almost a full year ago, the lower floor has been unoccupied. But, of course, now, after Marguita and her husband move in, there will always be a man living down there. And he might accidentally be looking up when a sudden gust of wind—

"I never thought of that," Señora Velasco says, now concerned.

After all, she tells herself, she does have two daughters. And then, of course, there is herself.

The following morning, while Marguita is busy organizing her things in her new house, Pancho the carpenter goes upstairs to the Velasco home and begins to install a tall wooden fence rigidly attached to the railing, the cost of which will be shared between the Velasco family, who will pay for one half, and Maximiliano and Dolores, who—unknown to Marguita—will pay for the other half. Once Pancho the carpenter completes his job, anybody who looks up from the patio will not be able to see anybody walking along the balcony upstairs. And anybody who is walking along the upstairs balcony will not be able to look down into the patio. Which is the way it should be, Dolores thinks, when two days later she comes to visit Marguita and sees the excellent job Pancho the carpenter has done.

Well, Dolores tells herself, privacy no longer being the issue, maybe now we all will be able to sleep in peace, she thinks, for she, Dolores herself, has not been able to sleep for the last couple of nights, trying and trying to understand how could it be that Loló— that any woman—would do as Loló did. And why.

Even last night, as Dolores tossed and turned in her bed, Maximiliano sleeping peacefully by her side, she kept thinking, How dare any woman do a thing like that! But then she told herself, I must calm down and keep myself under control. Bad enough there's already all that bad blood between Marguita and her sister-in-law. I must not stir any of that any further. I must not fuel Marguita's anger any more than I must not fuel my own. I must plant the seed of peace between the two of them, Dolores repeated to herself as she kept tossing and turning in her bed. Certainly, if I ever want to sleep peacefully again, it is imperative that I—that Marguita and I— learn to forgive that woman and forget all that happened. Especially Marguita. Dolores shook her head and smiled to herself as she brought into her mind the image of that stubborn mule of a daughter of hers, who seemed to be thinking of nothing but revenge. But revenge only generates more revenge, Dolores thought. She knew of Cuban criollo families hating and killing each other for generations, and over what? Over nothing. No. I cannot and I will not allow that to happen to my family, Dolores assured herself. Marguita is perhaps still too young, too immature, to understand what hate can do to a person's heart, to know how destructive it always is. She has to grow up and mature, and I must help her achieve that. That's what mothers are for. Only then will she be able to forget that woman, when she forgives her for what she did. Only then. And Marguita must learn that. For her own good. For her very own good.

Now, as Dolores stands in Marguita's patio, which is radiantly clean, Marguita is by her side, looking up, like her mother, at the handsome fence that Pancho the carpenter has built.

"Isn't that nice of the Velascos to build that tall fence?" Marguita says. "I didn't even realize that without that fence they could be looking down at us at all times. And that would have been *so* embarrassing! Can you imagine what it would have been like, Mamá?" Marguita asks.

Dolores does not say a word. She just nods and smiles in agreement as she looks at her daughter, standing by her side and also smiling—Marguita's light hair glittering gold against the brilliant turquoise rectangle of a sky that is framed by the tall, pale pink stuccoed walls of the patio of her safe haven.

Of her home.

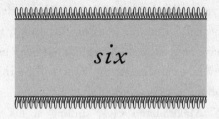

six

"They have no furniture," a sleepless Dolores whispers to her husband that same night.

"What do you mean, no furniture?" a sleepy Maximiliano answers.

They are lying in bed, side by side, close to each other, the way they always do. Even though their children are now grown up and out of the house—save for Perucha, their ten-year-old—they still love to talk to each other in whispers when they are in bed.

It must be the intimacy they like, for Perucha is sound asleep in her room. Dolores herself put her to bed.

"What you heard," Dolores goes on. "No furniture. Whatever few pieces of furniture they have was barely enough to fill their tiny apartment, and now this house they have just rented has two bedrooms and a separate living room and dining room."

"So? When you and I got married, we had even less."

"It's not only that," Dolores goes on. "It's that, well, the house does not even have an icebox, so Marguita has been using ours. And soon, before any of us realize it, the baby will be there with them. How are they going to manage then?"

"Didn't we?" Maximiliano says, smiling at his wife. "I never heard you complain."

Dolores sighs.

"I didn't have a mother to help me," she replies, her voice suddenly sad, for Dolores's mother died in childbirth only minutes after Dolores was born. "But Marguita does," Dolores promptly adds, letting that painful memory of her mother go by. "She has me. Besides, look at you. You've always had a profession, and you've always been the best there is at it. Even your own father, who is a master butcher, says so. You've always been your own man, so I never had to worry about anything. But Lorenzo . . . he is a good boy, but"—she pauses—"he doesn't make that much. Marguita told me. He only makes sixty-five pesos a month. And out of that he told his family he is going to give them ten pesos every month, to help them out. How far can those other fifty-five pesos go?"

There's a long silence.

Those few pesos did not go far, not even back in 1938.

"We don't have that much, I know," continues Dolores, always able to read her husband's mind. "But we still have more than they do. And if we could help them out . . . not them—I know the two of them can manage perfectly well without us. I'm thinking about the baby."

Maximiliano raises himself up, leans against the headboard of the bed, and looks at her.

They are almost in total darkness, since they are lighted only by the little bit of moonlight that filters in through the tall, shuttered doors to the patio.

"What do you have in mind?" Maximiliano asks. "I know you have something in mind. I can feel it."

"I went to Gonzalo's store this afternoon, right after coming back from Marguita's to look at the fence Pancho the carpenter built at the Velascos's balcony—and, by the way, Pancho did a great job. It's very well built and very private. Nobody will be able to look down into Marguita's patio anymore. So don't forget to thank him."

"I already paid him."

"Yes, but did you thank him?" she asks, though she knows very well what his answer will be.

Just as she expected, Maximiliano shakes his head.

"Well, then, thank him the next time you see him. Tell him he did a great job, because that is the truth. Don't you like it when people tell you you did a great job at something, even if you get paid for it?"

Maximiliano nods.

"Well, so does he. So thank him next time you see him. He really did a great job, I tell you. Go see it for yourself."

"All right, all right, I'll thank him, I'll thank him."

"Good," Dolores says, smiling to herself. Then she goes on. "In any event, Gonzalo showed me this beautiful, beautiful refrigerator he has that just came in from the United States. It's really small, but it *is* a real Frigidaire"—she pronounces it Cuban-style: "Free-hee-dye-reh"—"and he said he can let us have it 'on the cheap,' being that it would be a present from you to your first grandchild. I know that it is almost twice as much as an icebox—but since Marguita had a refrigerator in the little apartment she had to give up . . . besides, Gonzalo told me that in his opinion, '*That* is the future. Soon the icebox will be a thing of the past.' So . . . what do you think?"

Maximiliano looks at her firmly.

"So that's it," he says and then shakes his head. "You bought it, didn't you?"

"They haven't delivered it yet. But if you don't think it's a good idea, I'll—"

What can Maximiliano do but smile at this wife of his who can make him do anything she wants by just looking at him. "You know, Dolores," he interrupts her, "at times I wonder what it is you have that can control me at your total whim as if I were your puppet. It must have been something the nuns taught you, and well: how to manipulate people. How you know as much as you do will always puzzle me. But I tell you, one of these days I'm going to break out of my chains and shackles and run as far as I can away from you to get back my freedom."

"Go ahead, do it," Dolores says, covering herself with a thin cotton sheet and turning away from him. "Who's stopping you? But if you do, let me tell you that you would leave me no other choice but to chase after you." She smiles to herself. "After all, I did it before, I can do it again. Or don't you remember?"

"You wretched creature!" A now fully awakened Maximiliano leans over her and, grabbing her, turns her around and pulls her to him. "I do remember, don't think that I don't," he adds as he tightens his embrace around her.

The following afternoon, right after Lorenzo has gone back to his job at the bookstore after his noontime meal and siesta, Marguita is surprised by a large truck that pulls up in front of her house, and by two huge men who are at her front door, an immense crate by their side.

"Where do you want it, Señora?" one of them asks, politely.

Seconds later, Marguita is jumping up and down and screaming, laughing and crying at the same time.

Upon hearing all that shouting, Señora Velasco, who is upstairs, hurries to the balcony and stands on her tiptoes trying to look over the tall fence Pancho the carpenter so carefully built, which encloses the balcony running all along above Marguita's patio. Unable to see what is going on in Marguita's house, she immediately rushes downstairs to find out what is causing all this commotion. When Marguita opens her door, Señora Velasco is about to ask, "Is everything all right, Marguita?" But Marguita does not give her a chance. She grabs her upstairs neighbor by the arm and takes her across the length of the patio and into the dining room.

"Look, Señora Velasco. Look, look!" Marguita says, the words bursting out of her mouth like a shower of incredible happiness. "Look what my parents bought us! Look, look! Isn't it wonderful?"

Marguita's kitchen is a very small room, long and narrow, almost a closet. One of the side walls is totally taken up by the coal-burning stove and the coal storage bin next to it, while a *lavadero*—a washing sink—takes up all of the other wall, so there is no room at all for a refrigerator inside the kitchen. In fact, the kitchen has no counter space at all—and no wall cabinets. All the food has to be stored in the dining room, and it is there, in the dining room, that Marguita does all the food preparation. This she does sitting down at the elaborately carved dining table that is part of the elaborately carved dining room set that was the wedding present from Marguita's two brothers.

Painted black and badly crowding Marguita's small dining room, this dining room set was carved by a very famous man in the barrio right after he came out of jail and restarted his furniture-making business.

Fulgencio, as the cabinetmaker is called, had been sent to jail for stabbing to death both his adulterous wife and her lover with his carving knife. But he came out free, standing tall and proud, for with that act—as his lawyer vigorously and successfully stated during the trial—he had avenged himself and cleansed his honor the way a Cuban criollo man must, as demanded by the Cuban criollo code.

What people don't know, what people don't even suspect, is that since the night of the murder to this day, Fulgencio has not been able to sleep, the vision of the woman he loved beyond reason staring at him, begging him to spare her life, to give her another chance, to forgive her.

As he raised the knife in the air, he thought about doing just that: forgiving her, sparing her life, giving her—giving themselves—another chance. As he glared at the knife in his hand, he thought that perhaps he was as much to blame as she was for what had happened to them and to their marriage. But then, as he held the knife in the air, he remembered the sneering faces he had seen around him, the faces of men and women who knew of his wife's infidelity and who smiled at him derisively; the same sneering faces and derisive smiles he would have to face for the rest of his life if he didn't thrust his carving knife deep into his wife's heart. Not being able to face those faces, he did just as those faces demanded. He lowered his arm and carved the life out of his wife just as he had carved the life out of his wife's lover, tearing his wife's heart apart. It was only then that he realized what he had done, for it was only then that he saw himself for what he really was: a cowardly man who was unable to face the rest of his world and stand up to it. Disgusted with himself, he threw the carving knife on the floor and, totally covered in blood, knelt down and embraced tight to him the body of the woman he had adored, staring into her empty eyes and praying to make her come alive again with his embrace. But then he heard the sounds of people rushing to where they were, in response to her screams. The minute he heard them, he let her body fall to the floor, searched for his carving knife, found it, grabbed it, and then, holding it in his hand, he stood up. That was exactly how people found him, proudly erect on his feet, unashamed of himself, defiantly sneering at the body of the adulterous woman—"the whore," as he called her—lying lifeless at his feet by the side of her dead lover.

After the trial, Fulgencio gained a notoriety which certainly didn't hurt his business—that more than doubled—nor his success with women, who saw in him someone they admired, a "real" man, for he had done as a Cuban man must to safeguard and protect his honor, which is the very essence of a Cuban man's life.

And it is there, framed by Fulgencio's dining set in Marguita's already crowded dining room, that Señora Velasco sees proudly standing in a corner a really small but blaringly sparkling refrigerator—"A real Free-hee-dye-reh"—its naked and unornamented white shiny metal surfaces in sharp contrast to the elaborately carved black furniture that surrounds it.

Minutes later, the moment Señora Velasco leaves, Marguita, still in her maternity house dress and slippers, runs out of her house toward her mother's house, which is located just around the corner, on the other side of Hermenegildo's bodega.

"Mamá, Mamá! *Mamááááá!*" Marguita calls and calls as she enters her family's house, whose door is not locked. She sees Dolores in her bedroom, making her bed after the siesta. "Mamá!" she calls again. And as she rushes to Dolores and kisses her and embraces her, tears of joy stream fluent and uncontrollably out of her eyes.

Although on occasion Marguita and her mother have been known to disagree with each other—as any two people who dearly love each other at times disagree with each other—the relationship between the two of them has always been a really close one. Dolores has always had intimate, close relationships with all her children, true, but somehow, in Marguita's case, this relationship has always been different.

Special.

Marguita was but a toddler when Maximiliano had to leave their home in Batabanó, the little fisherman's village south of Havana where he and his family lived, to come to Havana, in order to start a new life after their Batabanó home had totally vanished, devoured by a raging sea during a vicious hurricane. For several long months Dolores and her children—four at the time—were left living with Maximiliano's parents, an old couple, who took care of them, clothing and feeding them, even though at times the old couple barely had enough for themselves.

During that difficult period of her life, when she found herself living with her in-laws, alone and away from her husband, Dolores often found refuge in her little girl, Marguita, who was barely five.

After all the heavy household chores were done early in the day—by Dolores, for she would not allow Maximiliano's old mother to sweep or mop or make the beds or wash or iron—and after the siesta, while her three older children were back at school after having had their noontime meal with them, Dolores would go on long walks with Marguita, ending often at the shore. There, mother and child would sit on the golden sand, which sparkled as if it had been sprinkled with tiny diamonds, and after looking at the placid, turquoise sea framed by gently swaying palm trees and glittering in the sun, and after smelling its invigorating aroma, mother and child would begin to play "Friends and Neighbors," the mother being "Señora Dolores," who had just come to visit her closest friend: her little girl, "Señora Marguita."

And though Señora Dolores knew perfectly well that Señora Marguita, the pretty young girl sitting opposite her, could not truly understand her, during those games Señora Dolores would tell Señora Marguita everything that was burdening her heart, talking to Señora Marguita as if the young girl were indeed her best friend—which in a way she was. It was Señora Marguita who shared Dolores's fears, and hopes, and dreams. It was also Señora Marguita who upon seeing her mother cry would also cry with her. And it was also Señora Marguita who, unknowingly, with her infectious laughter, would restore Señora Dolores's faith, helping the real Dolores face another day.

It should have been difficult for Dolores to learn to be a mother, for she never knew her own. Hated by her own father, a wealthy man who saw the baby girl as the reason why his beautiful wife had died, Dolores was sent at an early age to a boarding school in Havana, run by nuns. There she learned to do everything—from the most menial task to the most delicate of embroideries—and to do it all well and with a song in her heart. And yet, though she knew no mother, or maybe precisely because of that, she was not only a great mother to her children, but their closest friend as well, instilling in all of them a deeply felt love of family.

"You must always do whatever it takes to keep the family together, no matter what," Dolores constantly tells her children. She, who no longer has a family, after her wealthy father disowned her when she eloped with the penniless butcher Maximiliano, he with the blond hair, the insolent blue eyes, and the winning smile. "Don't you ever let anything come between any of you," she adds.

She, whose two older sisters have not spoken to her for time immemorial.

She, who is dead to her family.

Dead and buried.

At times Dolores asks herself if those talks by the sea during those "Friends and Neighbors" games made Marguita into the crybaby she is, for Marguita can start to cry at the drop of a hat.

Which is exactly what she is doing right now, in Dolores's bedroom, as Marguita embraces her mother.

"Do you like the refrigerator, *amorcito mío*?" Dolores says, as she tries to quiet her daughter, still sobbing out of control. "Hush, hush, my little love. What would your father say if he were to come in and find you crying like this? He would think you didn't like his present. After all, it was his idea. Have you seen him yet?"

Marguita shakes her head.

"Well, then, let's dry those pretty blue eyes of yours and go tell him you like what he got you, because you do like it, don't you?"

Marguita, still sniffling and still not able to say a word, just smiles and nods.

"Then, what are you waiting for? Go into the bathroom and wash your face while I change shoes. Then we can both go across the street and say hello to him. But I cannot go in these shoes," Dolores adds, pointing at her *chinelas*—fabric house shoes, Chinese style, with no heels. "Come on, hurry up, let's go see him together."

It doesn't take long for all the women of the entire barrio to rush into Marguita's house to see the new refrigerator. Not when there is someone like Dolores's next-door neighbor, Pilar, the evil gossip with the glass eye, who shouted—yes, *shouted*—the news out her window.

At the time, the few people in the barrio who could afford them had iceboxes in their homes, Dolores one of them. But no one in the entire barrio—absolutely no one—had an electric refrigerator. And Marguita's refrigerator is not just any refrigerator.

Oh, no. It is a *real* Free-hee-dye-reh.

"The best of the best!" as the catchy jingle on the radio keeps constantly telling everyone.

"It actually makes ice," Marguita explains to one astounded neighbor woman after the next, "so there is no longer a need to buy any more ice from Otero the iceman, nor to clean all that watery mess. And look," Marguita points out, "you can store fresh vegetables here. And eggs here. And even ice cream, can you believe that? You can store ice cream up here, in the freezer, and it will not melt. Isn't that great? Now you can have ice cream at any time of the day or night. Isn't that great?"

To which one astounded neighbor woman replies, "Isn't science wonderful?" while another one says, "Is this progress or what?" while still another one adds, "What will those Americans think of next?"

Are you happy now?" asks Maximiliano that very same night, the minute he gets in bed next to his wife. Dolores cuddles up close to him, for she loves to feel his warmth around her.

"I've always been happy ever since I met you," she says, her answer almost a purr.

"Don't change the subject," Maximiliano says, pulling away from her. "You know what I'm talking about."

"Yes, I'm happy. Marguita loves the refrigerator you gave her—excuse me, the Free-hee-dye-reh—and so do I," she says pulling herself close to him. "By the way," she adds, embracing him tight, "I told Marguita that the baby's crib is going to be my present."

Again pulling himself away from her, Maximiliano raises himself up and leans against the headboard.

"The crib? *Your* present?"

"Why, sure. Since the refrigerator was your present, well, I am entitled to give presents, too. And what better than a crib? So I told Marguita that that would be my present."

"And where are you going to get the money to pay for *your* present?"

"Oh, I have ways," Dolores says, her voice again a purr, her dark eyes full of mischief.

"Lord, woman! You are going to get us broke before that boy is born!"

"Who says the baby is going to be a boy? I already bought a pink blanket for her."

"So long as she's not as cunning and manipulative as you . . ."

"Oh, but she will be. If you think I can trick you into doing anything, just you wait till your baby granddaughter is here. After all," Dolores says, "I myself will teach her every trick I know. Every single one. So I'm warning you. Just you wait."

As usual, Maximiliano pretends to be exasperated by her, but he is such a bad actor, no one can ever believe him.

Suddenly a thought crosses his mind.

He smiles to himself as he looks at his wife of so many years, a not-that-well-hidden glint in those insolent pale-blue eyes of his. Then he pulls her close to him and grabs her tight in his arms as he says, chuckling, "Come to think of it, soon you're going to be a *grand*mother. Have you ever thought about *that*?"

Dolores smiles back at him. "Grandmothers are still one hundred percent women," she answers, her eyes as mischievous as ever. "Have *you* ever thought about that?" she adds, heavily emphasizing the *you*.

"No, I haven't. But I guess I'm going to find out real soon."

"Oh, you are?" an impish Dolores asks him, as she allows her husband of so many years—the grandfather-to-be—to surround her—the grandmother-to-be—with his arms, and they both tighten their embrace around each other.

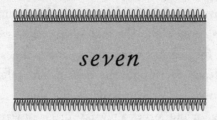

seven

In the sacred privacy of their new home, Marguita is waiting impatiently for Lorenzo.

She is not just impatient but fumingly so.

She is fuming not only because it is Saturday night and Lorenzo is late from work—something that has never happened before—but primarily because her evening meal, a meal on which she has worked for over three and a half hours, is now two hours cold, probably inedible, and she thinks she may have to throw it away and waste all of it! As if that food hadn't cost money. And plenty of it! Money they cannot afford to squander, things being as tight as they are.

To calm herself down, Marguita has swept and

swept the tile floors of her home again and again. But to no avail. Every movement of the broom has done nothing but fuel her anger. Now she is mopping the floors once again, even though they are already as shiny as mirrors. Every time she wrings the mop to squeeze the dirty water into the pail—dirty water which by now is perfectly clear, for she has done this so many times the floors are immaculately clean—every time she does it, she tells herself, Wait till I get my hands on Lorenzo. And as she thinks that, she wrings the mop once again and forces a few last drops of water to drip from it. But then she makes herself think of Lorenzo's sister, Loló, and of Loló's dark, gypsy eyes staring insolently at her in the middle of the night—and as she makes herself think of "that woman," as Marguita calls her sister-in-law, she tightens her hands around the mop and wrings it with passionate fury until she forces the very, very last drop of water to drip from it.

Even now, after six weeks have gone by since she and Lorenzo moved into this house, even now Marguita cannot and will not forgive—or forget—what that woman did to her. Just as she cannot and will not find satisfaction until she can avenge herself.

This is what her criollo heart keeps telling her she must do: *Avenge yourself*. This is what the criollo world in which she has lived all her life commands her to do: *Avenge yourself*. Affronts must be paid for—the criollo code demands it—for only then can the affronted person live honorably. This is the same code that forces a man to cleanse his soiled honor by killing not only his adulterous wife but her lover as well. Criollo men are not the only ones who have to live by this code. Criollo women must, too. It is the dishonored criollo woman inside Marguita who keeps reminding her of what Loló did. Just as it is the dishonored criollo woman inside Marguita who keeps clamoring not for justice, not for restitution, not for reparation, but for plain and simple revenge. How she is going to achieve it, Marguita still does not know. But she will avenge herself. Revenge she will get. Of that Marguita has no doubt whatsoever. Her time will come, the dishonored criollo woman inside Marguita keeps reminding herself. All she has to do is wait.

Dolores has tried and tried to divert Marguita's heart from these vengeful thoughts "which only corrode the soul," she tells her daughter. But she has not been able to succeed. Whenever she hears her mother tell her, "Marguita, my love, that woman is going to be one of your child's aunts. Her blood is already running through your child's veins. Forgive her, please. I beg you to forgive her," Marguita bites her lip and shakes her head.

"Mamá, please, I beg you, don't ask me to do that, because there's no way I can ever forgive that woman. You weren't there when it happened. You can't understand the horrible humiliation I went through when I saw that look of condescension in her eyes. Whether she's my child's aunt or not, how can I let her look at me again unless she apologizes to me—and on her knees—for what she did? And even so I don't think I could ever forgive her. So, please, Mamá, let me be."

Dolores is not the only one who has been asking Marguita to forgive Loló's affront.

Lorenzo himself has brought up the same subject several times, begging Marguita to forget all about Loló. "Marguita, don't you see that Loló is just the way she is? That she's always behaved in strange ways? Let me tell you, my love, no one in my family has ever been able to know what my sister Loló is really like."

Every time Marguita hears Lorenzo say that, she thinks, Well I do know what your sister Loló is really like! She may call herself a career woman, make a lot of money, and buy the most expensive clothes there are. But inside, she's nothing but a vicious and horrible woman, always thinking that she's better than anyone else, and always waiting to be served and bowed to by all. By her sister Asunción. By her own mother, Carmela. Even by Lorenzo. By all. But *this* time, the dishonored and outraged criollo woman inside Marguita keeps reminding her, *this* time that woman is dealing with *me*. And

I'll be damned if I serve her and bow to her like everyone in Lorenzo's family does, because I will not let myself be intimidated by her. She may be evil incarnate. But even if she is, I'll put that woman in her place, even if that's the last thing I ever do in my life.

That is what Marguita thinks every time she hears Lorenzo start to plead Loló's case.

And that is exactly what Marguita is thinking right now as she starts to mop the dining room floor once again.

Though her attention is fully focused on the mop, Marguita is able to hear the sound of a key turning the lock to their front door.

She raises her eyes and sees Lorenzo come in at the other end of the house.

Looking extremely contrite, his tail between his legs, his eyes downcast, Lorenzo slowly closes the front door behind him, though not without much difficulty. He turns, and putting a smile on his face, he begins to walk slowly toward Marguita, struggling as he does, his feet dragging one behind the other as he heavily plods the length of the house. He is still half drunk, but he hopes it doesn't show too much. Once he reaches the dining room he looks up, just to find Marguita who, mop in hand and wearing an apron over one of her better dresses, is biting her lip and staring at him with fiery eyes as she stands expectantly by the dining table, which is all set for dinner.

It has taken Lorenzo almost a full hour to get back home on the bus from the jai alai palace, where he and his buddies went on the spur of the moment to celebrate payday, the end of the month. His face red with shame, as Lorenzo places the key back in the right-hand pocket of his pants, he feels a wad of money inside. It is then he remembers he's won one hundred pesos by betting twenty pesos—almost a third of his monthly salary—on a guy his friend Berto, who three years ago was a jai alai champion himself, told him to bet on.

One hundred pesos! Enough to pay rent for four, almost five months!

It was only as he sat on the bus on the way back that he realized what he had done.

What if he had lost those twenty pesos? How would he have explained that to Marguita? They barely can cover expenses as it is, what with him giving ten pesos every month to his family and with them having to pay twenty-two pesos of rent for this old house month after month after month, when he only makes sixty-five pesos a month! But the rest of the guys kept taunting him, making fun of him, asking him again and again: "What are you, Lorenzo? A man? Or a mouse?" And of course he had to prove to them that he was not a mouse. So he went ahead and placed the bet. But right then, just a second after he had done it, he realized that by placing that bet he had indeed acted like a mouse, because he had done so for fear of being taunted by the rest of the guys.

Wasn't that stupid? he asked himself. Doing what I didn't think I should do because of fear? It was good he had won, he thought, as he stepped off the bus. And then he promised to himself that, taunting or no taunting, he will never again bet on anything. He just cannot take chances. Certainly not with the way things continue to be in Cuba, with hundreds of thousands of men out of work, a lot of them starving—many even homeless.

And definitely not with a child coming.

His still out-of-focus eyes see Marguita looking at him, and without saying a word, Lorenzo finds the wad in his pocket, pulls it out, opens his hand, and shows the money to her, as an explanation.

All of a sudden, Marguita seems puzzled by something.

She lets the mop fall noisily to the floor, brings her hands to her belly, and then she begins to laugh and cry at the same time.

"What's wrong, what's wrong?" Lorenzo asks, deeply concerned, as he rushes to her, the money still in his hand.

"It kicked," Marguita says. "The baby is—oh, here. Put your hand right here. Can you feel it? The baby's kicking!"

Not knowing what else to do with the wad of money in his hand,

Lorenzo puts it back in his pants pocket, then places both his hands on his wife's belly and waits for a while. He feels nothing. He is about to say something when suddenly he feels it.

His child. Alive! Alive and kicking! His very own child!

Lorenzo doesn't realize it, but he is crying, just like Marguita is, and, just like she is, he is laughing at the same time; both of them crying and laughing at the beauty of it all.

Minutes later, they sit at the beautifully set table—he at the head and she at his right side—and hold hands across the corner of the table for a moment. Then, they begin to enjoy their dried-out, almost inedible *pernil asado*—roasted loin of pork—in the privacy of their own home, a small, old, criollo-style house that to them seems like a miraculous palace.

After clearing the table, a smiling Marguita brings dessert—guava shells in a thick syrup served with cream cheese. Her anger at Lorenzo now totally vanished, she says, using a serious tone of voice Lorenzo has seldom heard before, "I guess *this* changes everything, doesn't it?"

Lorenzo looks at her, puzzled.

He is still a little high, from all that rum they had at the jai alai palace, and from winning all that money, and from having felt his baby kick.

"What do you mean?" he asks.

Marguita sits at the table, an earnest look on her face as she looks him in the eye. "I mean, I really didn't know, I really didn't *feel* that I was carrying a baby until just now. Up till minutes ago, it was all like a dream come true. But still that, a dream. Distant. But now . . . now I know that the baby is already here, with us," she says, gently caressing her belly. "And I think we have to sit down and plan our future." She pauses briefly, just to add, "And the baby's future."

"We're already sitting down," says Lorenzo, snickering, trying to lighten the subject.

He is too tired, and too sleepy, and besides, all of this talking about the future scares him a little.

"Lorenzo," Marguita says, keeping her eyes deeply fastened on Lorenzo's, "please, listen to me. Something happened this afternoon, a little after you went back to work. Something important."

Lorenzo looks intently back at her, saying nothing. Listening.

"I had just finished making the bed, after the siesta," Marguita continues, "when I heard a lot of shouting on the street. So I ran to the entrance door, opened it just a little bit so I could look out, and saw a crew of prisoners in their uniforms working on the sidewalk. They were being supervised by several armed guards, who were shouting orders at the prisoners. You know we've been having problems with the supply of water. Well, these prisoners were breaking the cement sidewalk with their picks so they could get to the water main and fix it, Pilar told me later on—you know how she is, how she always knows everything. They had taken off their shirts, tied them around their waists, and they were working so hard and under the hot afternoon sun that they were totally covered with sweat. Their arms, their shoulders, their chests were glistening with thick drops of sweat. And they smelled—Lord, I could smell them even from the front door! And the worst thing of it all was that I recognized two of them. Ignacio and Colberto. Lorenzo, I tell you, it was horrible. Those two boys are still teenagers. They grew up in this neighborhood. Just last year, before we got married, they worked as delivery boys for Hermenegildo. When I saw them, I remembered hearing that they had been caught stealing stuff from the bodega, apparently so they could buy marijuana, or something awful like that."

Marguita moves her chair closer to Lorenzo's and embracing her waist, she adds, her voice urgent, "Lorenzo, please, listen to me. I don't want our child to end up like one of those young men. I don't want our child ever having to work with a pick for a living, or to steal something and end up in jail. I will not let that happen. I want our child to get a good education. So he can be somebody. So he can get out of this neighborhood."

Marguita smiles at Lorenzo, who is still looking intently back at her, saying nothing. Still listening carefully.

"I thought I'd finally gotten out of this barrio when I married you and we moved to our little apartment in Belascoaín," Marguita continues. "But—well, things happened, and I'm back here, back in Luyanó again. And I'm happy, I am. Still, I don't want our child to grow up in a place like this. I don't want him to end up like Ignacio and Colberto, in prison, doing hard labor, picking at a concrete sidewalk in the middle of a hot afternoon. I want to take him—I want to take all of us—out of this barrio as soon as we can. So our child can get a good education. Maybe even go to a private school."

Lorenzo is still looking intently back at her, saying nothing. Still listening carefully.

"Lorenzo," Marguita adds, her voice now calm, assured, "we can't raise a family on sixty-five pesos a month. Oh, sure," she adds before Lorenzo can utter a word, "we probably can manage fine with this child. But what will happen when the next one comes? How are we going to manage then? And how are we ever going to be able to afford the kind of education I'm dreaming of for our children?"

She pauses as she looks inquiringly at Lorenzo, awaiting an answer.

Lorenzo smiles at her. "Marguita, my love, all of that's a long, long way into the—"

"No, it isn't," Marguita interjects abruptly. "We've been married barely half a year, and look at us. I'm already five months pregnant, going on the sixth! Before we realize it, this baby will be here, with us. And then, God willing, there will be others. And then—"

"And then God will provide," Lorenzo interrupts her, quoting the Bible.

"God provides for those who provide for themselves," Marguita replies instantly, quoting her mother—who is Marguita's Bible. She stands up. "Lorenzo, let me tell you something I know." She moves toward her husband, an engaging smile on her face. "You're just too bright to stay a clerk at a bookstore for the rest of your life."

The way she said "the rest of your life" sounded like an eternity to Lorenzo, who remains quietly sitting on his chair.

"You know a lot about business," Marguita goes on, moving closer to him. "You went to business school. You know how to type and take shorthand and keep books and all that. And that's great. But you can do much better than that. Lorenzo, you are very, very smart," she says standing behind Lorenzo, still in his chair, and leans against him, her arms embracing him from behind. "Almost as smart as you are good-looking," she adds, and kisses his unruly dark hair, with its sweet smell of hair tonic. Lorenzo leans back against her. He loves to feel her arms tighten about him. "Do you remember what you told me when we first started to go out together?" she asks.

"I've told you so many things, how could I remember what I—"

"I mean about your dream of being your own man. Of becoming a professional man. Even a certified professional accountant."

"Oh, that! That was just a—"

"What would it take?" Marguita interrupts him, pressing her head against his.

"Oh, I'd have to register at the university, and—but that's a lot of money. And—"

"Isn't the university free? I thought it was."

"Yes, it's free it is, but . . ."

Lorenzo pauses, thinking of the possibilities.

That dream is still there. He has been hiding it, he may have almost forgotten it. But that dream is still there. If only that were possible, he thinks. But . . .

He shakes his head.

"No," he says, "even free as the university is, we still wouldn't be able to manage it. There's all that traveling back and forth. And that costs money. And besides, there's a lot of things to be bought, you know," he says, "like paper and pencils and . . . and, yes, books. A lot of books and—"

"But, Lorenzo," Marguita says, "you work at a bookstore. So, with your discount, books should be cheap. And even if they aren't, we could buy used books. Or maybe the people at the store could let you borrow them, so we wouldn't have to pay for them. You know how careful you are with your books."

"That may be so," he says. "But still, how could I ever—I mean . . ." He stands up and looks at her. "Go to school again? At my age?"

She smiles at him. "What age? You're only twenty-three. Now if I had said that, it would have been different, because after all I'm a lot older than you."

"Yeah, sure! By two months!" He chuckles, and brushes his lips against hers.

"Yes, and that makes me the wiser," she says, caressing with the tips of her fingers his pencil-thin mustache. "Being older than you, as I am."

Lorenzo playfully pats her well-rounded behind. "You are not wiser," he says. "You're just crazier." He pulls her close to him. "How could *I* go to school? Don't you see I would have to go nights so I could hold on to my job?" He holds her tight to him. "Has it ever occurred to you that someone like me would prefer to spend his nights here, right here, next to someone like you, doing something much more pleasurable than going to night school?" he asks jokingly, and presses her more tightly against him.

"Hey, not so tight. Don't forget I'm a pregnant woman!"

"Yes, a pregnant woman who also happens to be a voluptuously delicious and mature *older* woman. Don't you know guys really go for older women? Especially if they are like you . . . crazy."

"I don't mind your calling me crazy," Marguita says, "provided you admit that I am also wise." She pauses and stares at him. "Am I?"

"Why, sure," he says. "After all," he adds, a glint in his eye, "you did marry *me!*"

"Well, then, that settles it," Marguita says decisively, pulling slightly away from his tight embrace.

Lorenzo gives her a puzzled look. She stops him from saying anything by touching his lips with the fingers of her left hand, her "good" hand, for she is left-handed, as she looks him deep in the eye and smiles broadly. "As a wise and mature older person, this is what I say: you go to night school. And that's that!"

"No way. How could we ever manage to—"

"Oh, we'll manage somehow," says Marguita, with not a single trace of doubt in her voice as she closes his arms tight around her. "You leave that to me." And with that she puts her hand in his pocket and gets out the wad of money he had placed there earlier.

"Hey," Lorenzo says, "that's *my* money!"

"Not anymore," Marguita says, as she hides it in her cleavage. "From now on," she adds, a mischievous smile on her face, the same kind of smile she has often seen illuminating the face of her mother, Dolores. "From now on this money is school money!"

Lorenzo embraces her even more tightly to him and avidly searches for her mouth as his hands begin to caress her. And as he does, and as he leads her into their bedroom, and as he begins to make love to his wife in the sacred privacy of their own home, Marguita's face is beaming with joy—the thought of "that woman," Loló, and of what "that woman" did totally gone from her mind. Erased.

At least for the time being.

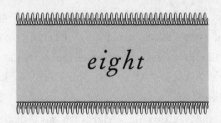

eight

The boy was born in a caul.

Estela, the midwife who seconds ago helped deliver the baby, looks at Marguita—still lying exhausted and out of breath on the delivery bed— and tells her how lucky she is.

"In all my years as a midwife I've never delivered a child in a caul before," she says, and then, after smiling broadly at Marguita, the gray-haired old nurse adds, "And you know what that means, don't you?" She doesn't wait for an answer: "That great things will happen to this child. Look at him," she goes on as she places the newborn boy on a stainless steel table. "Look how clean he is! Not even a single drop of blood on him!"

The boy recoils at the touch of the cold steel surface, and his tiny right hand grabs the edge of the table.

"Marguita," says Manuel, the doctor who has just delivered the baby, "look at your son! Look what he's doing!" The three of them, Marguita, the midwife, and the doctor, look at the baby boy, whose tiny right hand is grabbing hard to the edge of the stainless steel table where he has been placed. Doctor Manuel, smiling, turns to face Marguita, whose beaming eyes are fastened on her baby boy. "The survival instinct," Manuel the doctor adds, as the midwife measures and weighs the baby, and stamps his footprint on a medical chart.

Ever since Manuel the doctor built his own clinic, he has stopped delivering babies. But he has made an exception in this case because Marguita is the daughter of his best friend and closest buddy, Maximiliano the butcher. Manuel himself has delivered two babies for Maximiliano's wife, Dolores. First, Iris, a pretty little girl born with a blue heart who quickly returned to the same Heaven she had come from, and two years later, Perucha, a hefty, healthy girl who was the spitting image of her father, and weighed close to twelve pounds when she was born.

Equally as hefty today, ten years later, as she was at birth, Perucha is now with her parents in the front room of a private hospital suite Manuel keeps on the top floor of his clinic for the use of patients who are close friends or part of the family. Holding in her hands a gift-wrapped present for the new baby, she is on a small sofa flanked by her mother and father, and surrounded by a bunch of relatives who fidget endlessly as they sit on narrow folding chairs that were rushed in by the staff.

The Spanish parents of Lorenzo, the expectant father, are in that same front room as well. Lorenzo's mother, Carmela, dressed totally in black—as always—is silently rubbing the worn beads of her rosary while her husband, Padrón, also dressed in immaculate black, sits by her side, saying nothing and politely staring into the faraway distance.

Continental Spaniards are like that, criollo Cubans say. Always behaving as if they were carved out of stone.

And those criollo Cubans must be right, because Carmela and Padrón are behaving exactly as expected of them. And so is the group of Cubans, who are also behaving exactly as expected of them, that is, constantly talking, constantly moving around, constantly making jokes, and in this case, constantly making bets as to, "What will it be, a boy or a girl?"

It all started last night, the minute the call came from Lorenzo that Marguita's time had arrived. Marguita's mother, Dolores, who has a weak heart, ran to the clinic with her daughter, heart palpitations and all. She has been there since they arrived, but the long wait has not shown on her face yet. Hours ago Manuel the doctor told her, "Dolores, please, I beg you to go home. It may take a long while yet, and, believe me, I will call you as soon as the baby is born. You need to lie down and sleep." But that kind of behavior is inadmissible to a Cuban woman, particularly one who is a grandmother-to-be—and for the first time! So Dolores adamantly said, "No." She would stay up all night long and suffer with Marguita for as long as it took. And she has been doing just that. It was her husband, Maximiliano the butcher, who brought their hefty daughter, Perucha, a girl he dotes on, to the clinic when he came early this morning, and the rest of the family has been showing up, arriving in spurts.

Dolores sees Lorenzo's sisters arrive.

Asunción, the deaf one, is as usual dressed all in black, providing a strong contrast to her sister Loló, who is elegantly made up, her glossy black hair stunningly twisted behind her neck, and wearing a simple though obviously expensive tailored suit made of a beige silk faille, with matching shoes and purse.

Dolores welcomes them, greeting each of them equally with a sincere smile on her face.

But underneath it, she is asking to herself, What is Marguita going to say when she finds out that "that woman" is here? Those two, Marguita and Loló, have not seen each other since the night Marguita caught Loló staring at her as she and her husband were making love. Marguita doesn't even want to hear that name, Loló, mentioned in her presence.

Bringing a large tray, Celina, the wife of Manuel the doctor, comes in and passes around dark Cuban coffee to the fourteen or so people already crowding the room, all of whom are eagerly waiting for some news. As they sip the heavenly coffee, they all keep talking as softly as they can—for Cubans, which is loud enough—interrupting their talk just to resume the betting whenever a new relative arrives and asks the same question all over again. "What will it be, a boy or a girl?"

Each time she is asked, Dolores says, "I don't care, provided the baby is healthy." Each time he is asked, Maximiliano, who has brought with him a sealed box of the best cigars money can buy, answers, "A boy, of course." And so does Lorenzo, the father-to-be, who is nervously pulling at his hair. Perucha, the ten-year-old, wants a baby girl, she says, "to play with." Maximiliano's sons are not there yet; after all, somebody has to be at the butcher shop working. But they each made a ten-peso bet with Manuel the doctor that it would be a boy.

Manuel, still in his scrub suit, enters the room where everybody is waiting expectantly. "Where's the father?" he asks.

Lorenzo stands up, his legs shaking.

"Congratulations," Manuel says as he shakes hands with him. And then he adds, addressing his question to the women in the room, "Did any of you bring a pink blanket?"

"Oh, no! Don't tell me it's a girl!" blurts a disappointed Maximiliano just as his hefty daughter Perucha stands up and, beaming with happiness, hands Manuel the beautifully gift-wrapped box she's been holding in her hands. But Manuel will not accept it. He just grins, as he looks at Maximiliano and says, "Well, you can return it, because if that child is a girl, she has the biggest balls I've ever seen!"

Laughing loud belly laughs as he breaks the seal of the expensive cigar box in his hands, Maximiliano, bursting with pride, says, "I knew it, I knew it," and begins to pass thick Cuban cigars to everybody in the room, male and female alike, while Lorenzo, not knowing what else to do, just sits down, his knees still shaking. "The boy is twenty-one inches long and weighs eight pounds and seven ounces!" adds Manuel, addressing his words to the room at large, though nobody seems to be listening to him anymore.

"How's Marguita?" asks Dolores.

"Better than ever," answers Manuel. "Right now she's feeding the baby. We'll bring them up here in a little while. Now everybody listen," Manuel says, raising his voice. Then, pointing to the door leading to a small bedroom with a hospital bed and a crib, he adds, his voice a command, "I want only two people in that bedroom at any time, do you all hear me? Only two!"

But who can talk sense to a group of loud Cubans, some of whom are shouting loudly, laughing loudly, joking and jumping up and down while others are loudly crying and blowing their sniffling noses?

Even Lorenzo's father, Padrón the Spaniard, a man who seldom if ever utters a word, is so excited by the birth of his first grandchild, that even he stands up, goes over to Lorenzo his son, shakes his hand, and says, "Very well done. Very well done!"

Manuel, still standing by the door to the hospital suite, sees Maximiliano begin to light up his thick cigar. "Maximiliano," he shouts, "what do you think you're doing? No cigar smoking in here! This is a hospital! All men, out! *Out!*" Manuel points to the door by his side, and the men begin to exit.

As he goes by Manuel, Maximiliano hands his friend one of his thick cigars, pauses, and then gives a deep Cuban-style man-to-man embrace to his buddy who embraces him back. Maximiliano exits, as well as Manuel, who immediately comes back and tells the women in the room, "By the way, I forgot to tell you, that boy is going to be lucky all of his life. He was born in a caul." And with that he leaves.

Little Perucha turns to her mother.

"Mami, what is a caul?" she asks.

Dolores answers her. "When the stork came, she brought the baby wrapped very, very well, and that pretty wrapping is called a caul."

"Oh," says Perucha, holding the gift-wrapped box in her hands and showing it to her mother, "you mean, like a gift?"

Dolores smiles as she embraces the last child she would ever have.

"Yes, *amorcito mío*, my little love," she says. She is embracing this daughter and she is remembering another daughter she embraced in this very same room a long time ago, a baby girl who was born little and blue, with a broken heart.

"Like a gift."

With all the men now out of the front room of the suite, all the women look at each other for a few moments, not really knowing what to do next. And then suddenly they all begin to laugh and cry and cheer and yell, all of them at the same time, when they see that Marguita is being wheeled into the suite, her newborn in her arms.

Though the two nurses accompanying Marguita and her baby try as hard as they can to impose some kind of order in the room, there is no way this deafening roar can be tamed—not until Manuel the doctor himself comes in, at which point a hush falls heavily over the suite.

Under the supervision of Manuel, who stands like a guard by the door leading into the private bedroom, Marguita and her baby are taken inside and the door closed after them. Just to be reopened minutes later, when Marguita and her newborn are quietly at rest on the hospital bed.

As the nurses wheel the gurney away, Manuel steps outside the door.

"I want two and only two people in this room at one time," he says again, pointing to Marguita's bedroom. "Starting with the grandmothers. Dolores, and you, too, Carmela, please. Come in."

"May Perucha come in too, Manuel?" asks Dolores. "I promise she'll behave."

Manuel smiles at little Perucha and nods.

"Sure, go in, Perucha."

Perucha smiles from ear to ear, and carrying her wrapped gift in her hands, she steps with her mother into Marguita's room to meet her little nephew, the newborn baby.

Manuel turns to the rest of the women in the room. "I'm going to go fetch the men, so Lorenzo and the two grandfathers can get to meet the baby. I'll be back in a couple of minutes. Now, remember what I said: I want two of you and only two of you in that room at any time. And I mean it. No exceptions. Oh, and stay only for a couple of minutes. Marguita and the baby need some rest."

Following doctor's orders, soon it is time for Carmela, Perucha, and Dolores to leave Marguita's room, so the next pair of women can come in and meet mother and baby.

"Mamá, could you help me with this?" Marguita says as Perucha, Carmela, and Dolores are leaving the room.

"What do you need, my love?" Dolores asks, turning around and going to Marguita.

Marguita lowers her voice. "Mamá," she says, "I saw that 'that woman' was there, in the front room when they brought me in. Please, I beg you. Don't let 'that woman' come in. Please."

"Marguita," Dolores replies, keeping her voice low, almost a whisper, "that woman has a name. Her name is Loló and she's one of your child's aunts. I can't go out there and tell her not to come in. It's just not right. Can you not forgive her on a day like this? Please? Can't you do that? If not for you, or for your baby, for me? As a favor to me?"

Marguita sighs deeply.

"I'll never be able to forgive that woman, Mamá," Marguita tells her mother, her voice irate. "Never!" But then she looks at her baby son by her side and then back at her mother and adds, resignedly, "But I will let her come in. Only because of you. Only because you ask me. But I will *not* talk to her, you understand? I don't even want to say hello to that horrible and vicious woman!"

Dolores looks at her daughter and shakes her head. She knows how mulish Marguita can be. But Dolores is too wise not to know when to give in.

"All right," she tells her stubborn child, "just pretend you're asleep when she and her sister enter the room."

Moments later, when it is Asunción's and Loló's turn to enter the bedroom, Dolores, who has been standing at the door and serving as a guard, hushes them. "Marguita's asleep," she mouths to Asunción, knowing that she cannot hear her. Loló and Asunción begin to go back to their seats but Dolores stops them. "Oh, no, go in. Go in," she mouths to Asunción again as she gestures the two sisters to enter the bedroom. "Go in and look at the baby." Then she turns to Loló. "Just keep it quiet, Loló," she whispers. "As you can see," she says, looking at her pretty daughter, who does not have to feign that she is peacefully sleeping, "my poor girl . . . she's exhausted."

Asunción and Loló enter the room where Marguita is lying asleep next to her newborn son. Loló, who is standing behind Asunción, looks first at Marguita, who has an angelic smile on her face as she sleeps, and then at Marguita's child, who is lying quietly by his mother's side.

And as she looks at mother and child, Loló asks herself, Will I ever know what it is like to have a child of my own?

PART THREE

Eunuch

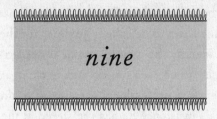

nine

Finally all alone—for visiting hours are mercifully over—Lorenzo and Marguita are looking at their newborn, who still does not have a middle name.

Before the baby was born, the two of them went through hundreds of names. But the time has come to make one last decision, for after spending almost an entire week in the hospital suite, tomorrow morning Marguita is going back home and the baby must be officially registered in the hospital records. He needs to have a full name so he can become a full person under the law. Months ago they decided that if the baby turned out to be a girl, they were going to call her Marga, like her mother—Marguita is just a diminutive—or if a boy, Lorenzo. So the Lorenzo part of the boy's name was settled long since, and the two of them have already been referring to their son by a shortened version of Lorenzo, calling him Renzo, or even by a diminutive, Renzito. Still, neither Marguita nor Lorenzo wants their son to be called "Junior," for they want the boy to have his own identity. So a middle name is needed to differentiate the child from his father, who has no middle name at all.

Lorenzo, a certified professional accountant in the making—now that at Marguita's insistence he has registered at the university and is to start night school in two weeks—has written down one boy's name after another, neatly compiling them in a long list that he has arranged in alphabetical order, and which, as Marguita gets ready to breast-feed the baby, he has started to read aloud, each name preceded by the boy's first name: Lorenzo.

This litany of Lorenzo this, Lorenzo that is putting both mother and father to sleep when Estela, the midwife and nurse who welcomed little Renzo into this world, comes into the room, a form in one hand, a pen in the other.

"Well," she says, "are we ready yet?"

Panic suddenly awakens the sleepy parents.

"Can you give us a few more minutes?" pleads Lorenzo, showing Estela the long list in his hand—several pages of neatly written names. "I'm not through reading all these names to Marguita and we still—"

Estela sighs.

She has gone through this many a time before. She knows she will have to go through it again with the next set of parents after Lorenzo and Marguita leave the hospital. Why is it that parents are always so unprepared? she asks herself as she looks at her watch.

"I'm off duty in twelve—no, eleven minutes. So I give you until then and not a minute more. This should have been completed a long time ago, the minute the baby was born. I don't know why it is that everybody waits until the very last minute! I'll leave this right here," she says, placing both the form and the pen on Marguita's night table by the bed. "Have it filled when I return. The doctor placed me in charge of this and by the time I get back on duty tomorrow afternoon you all will be gone, so this has to be done today. Please, I beg you. It's been a long day, and I would like to get home on time, all right?"

She leaves the room without waiting for an answer.

Lorenzo begins to read the rest of the names as fast as he can: Lorenzo this, Lorenzo that, Lorenzo the other, when the baby begins to regurgitate his food, for Marguita has become nervous all of a sudden, and as we all know, babies can instantly feel what their mothers are feeling—and vice versa. Noticing this, Lorenzo stops his litany, grabs the pen, and begins to write on the form.

Marguita looks at him, puzzled. "Lorenzo, what do you think you're doing?" she asks, standing the baby up close to her body, holding his head over her right shoulder with her right hand and patting his back with what she calls her good hand—her left hand—to burp him.

"Writing the baby's name down, as I was told to do," he says.

"Let me see what you're putting down," she demands, starting to stand up.

"I decided to call him by both our names. Lorenzo Marguita. We both made him, so it is only fitting that—"

"You haven't written that down, have you? I won't have my son bear a woman's name! Who ever heard of that? Where did you get that crazy idea?"

"Too late," he says, showing her the form. "I already wrote Lorenzo Ma—" Suddenly he stops talking, grabs the pen, and adds a few letters to the boy's name.

"Lorenzo," Marguita says, a clear warning in her tone of voice. "What are you—?"

"Here," Lorenzo says, showing her the form.

She reads it. "Oh," she says, after a while. And then she says the boy's name aloud.

"Lorenzo Manuel."

She pauses, as if savoring the name. "I like it, I really do. I love the way it sounds."

"I knew you would. Don't tell anybody, nobody needs to know why we named him as we did. But you and I will always know that the boy carries both our names. A little disguised, sure, but still both our names. My name and your name. Well, at least the first two letters of your name. So that will be our little secret." He looks at her. "Have I ever told you that I love your name?"

Marguita shakes her head. Miraculously, the baby has fallen asleep on her shoulder.

Lorenzo goes to her, leans over the rocking chair, and whispers, "Well, now you know." Then, delicately embracing both mother and child, he is sharing with Marguita one of those long, ardent kisses they both love, the kind they give each other only when alone in the privacy of their bedroom, when all of a sudden they hear someone behind them clearing her throat.

"Didn't Doctor Manuel tell you that you have to wait at least forty days before . . . you know what?" Estela the nurse says, chuckling.

All red in the face, Lorenzo pulls away from Marguita. Then, grabbing the form and the pen, Lorenzo hands them to the old nurse, who automatically places the pen in her breast pocket while looking perfunctorily at the form, until she reads the name.

"Oh, so you named the boy after the doctor!" she says, elated. "Good choice, good choice! He's going to be so happy when he finds out! He'll be a great godfather to your child, you'll see," she adds. "He's such a good man."

The filled form now in her hand, Estela quickly leaves the hospital room, not realizing that she has left behind a thoroughly disconcerted pair, Marguita and Lorenzo, who are staring at the door as if the nurse were still standing there, the two of them with a look of utter consternation on their faces. Never, not even once, did they think of Manuel the doctor—not even for the slightest second—as they were searching for their child's middle name.

Then, at the same time, at the very same time, the two of them, Marguita and Lorenzo, begin to laugh, very softly at first, then louder and louder, until the baby, awakened by their laughter, opens up his eyes. And though his parents know it is impossible for a baby so little to do anything like that, they'd swear they see the baby smile ear to ear, as if he, too, wanted to join in his parents' fun.

However, even if the boy's name—Lorenzo Manuel—does bring an immense amount of secret pleasure to both Marguita and Lorenzo whenever they say it aloud, the name does not seem to satisfy either of the boy's grandfathers. In the least.

In the very least.

When he hears about it, Marguita's father says, "But why not Lorenzo *Maximiliano?* That sounds like the name of an emperor, doesn't it?" the blond, blue-eyed butcher adds, recalling the name of the first and only emperor of Mexico after whom Maximiliano himself was named, just like his father, and just like his father's own father, an Austrian man who fell in love with Cuba the minute his light-blue eyes met the dark glittering eyes of a beautiful Cuban girl when he was on his way to Mexico.

And when he hears about it, Lorenzo's father, the Spaniard—a man who seldom utters a word—says, "But why didn't they call the boy Lorenzo *Padrón?* That sounds like the name of a king, doesn't it?"

When Lorenzo finds out what Maximiliano said, he tells Marguita, "Yeah, as if I were going to name my son after an emperor who lost his head!" and then he draws his index finger across his throat, making Marguita laugh no end. And then he adds, "As for

Papá, he knows damn well that no Spanish king has ever been named Padrón. So, why would he ever say a thing like that?" In any event, since the name Manuel does not exist at all in either family, both grandfathers keep asking their wives, "Now why did they name the boy after Manuel the doctor?" But whether the boy's grandfathers like it or not, the boy has officially been named and registered as Lorenzo Manuel, and Lorenzo Manuel he is going to be christened.

In Cuba, a christening is taken very, very seriously. Not because it is a religious ceremony, which of course it is, but rather because it is an occasion for a huge party.

And if there is one thing Cubans love to do, that is it: to party.

Like in a lot of old-fashioned fairy tales, people—relatives, friends, even distant acquaintances—come from all over the island to attend the christening, bearing with them gifts aplenty for the newborn: sheets, blankets, baby caps, and toys, most of them handmade, hand-embroidered, even hand-carved.

Now, parties of this scale need to be organized way in advance, so Cuban christenings normally take place several weeks, sometimes even months, after the baby is born.

This is a practice that Catholic priests utterly dislike, for they claim that should the child die unchristened, the child would then spend eternity in limbo, not in Heaven, as he would had he been properly christened before his death. Occasionally, an emergency christening is done when the child's life is in great danger, in which case he is christened unceremoniously, right at the hospital. But even then, should the child survive, a second "official" christening takes place, this being a joyous, almost orgiastic, celebration of life where people eat, drink, and dance all day long, even all night long—and then some.

For a christening, two things are needed: the baby, of course. And the godparents.

Getting the baby is relatively easy—and pleasurable for the most part—after all, nature does take care of that. But selecting the god-parents? Now, that is not an easy task in the very least. It is almost as difficult as selecting the child's name—or even more so, for being a godparent is not only a great honor but also a great responsibility in Cuban society.

"Officially," godparents are not supposed to do much.

Their job—again, according to the priests—is to make sure that the child is properly raised in the Catholic faith should the child's parents be unable to do so, for whatever the reason. In fact, during the official ceremony, in church, the prospective godparents must solemnly swear to do just that.

But "extra-officially," godparents are selected for political rea-sons.

That is, a man and a woman are chosen who would help take care of and provide for the child not only—God forbid!—should some-thing happen to the child's parents, but even while the child's par-ents are alive.

As in all political races, nominations are discreetly made by any member of the child's family, and then subjected to votes until the final candidates are selected and offered the honor. Refusals are considered extremely rude, so they rarely if ever occur. And when they do, people—entire families—have been known to stop talking to each other. Upon acceptance, the godparents take a lot of responsi-bilities upon their shoulders, the first one of which is to make all the necessary preparations for the church christening, which includes bearing all the costs not only for the christening itself but for the subsequent party as well.

During the short cab ride back home from the hospital, late the next morning, with the baby snugly cradled within her arms, Mar-guita faces her husband, sitting by her side. "Lorenzo," she says, "I've been thinking that perhaps my Cuban criollo father and your Spanish mother should be the child's godparents. What do you think of that?"

Though in the back of her mind Marguita feels that she cannot forgive, let alone forget, what that woman Loló did to her—still, for the last few days, while at the hospital with a little time on her hands, she has been pondering different ways of bringing Lorenzo's family and her own closer together. For the good of her child. One way, she thought, would be to select one godparent from one family and the other from the other family. Maybe then I might be able to achieve more understanding between the two families, she told herself, even though she knew how arduous a job that might turn out to be, for the two families are as different from each other as day and night. Hers is a head-to-toe Cuban criollo family whose ancestors fought bravely against the Spaniards; and Lorenzo's, their arch-enemy, a family of acerbic Spaniards, who despite living in Cuba for thirty-six years still take pride in speaking with a distinct Continental Spanish accent, lisping every one of their cs and zs—something criollo Cubans poke fun at.

At first, when Marguita made that proposal, Lorenzo liked the idea. But later on, when he gets back home after work, after he embraces her and kisses her, Lorenzo tells her, "Marguita, my love, I've been thinking that perhaps the other way around is better. I mean, my Spanish father and your Cuban mother may make a better godparent couple because, let's face it, Marguita, whether the boy's godfather is either your dad or mine, men don't know what to do about this kind of thing. And Mamá would not be any good at it, with her living so far away, all the way across town. While, on the other hand, your mother, Dolores, would make a wonderful god-mother—and you know it. And in addition, she lives just around the corner. Besides," Lorenzo adds, "knowing your father, I certainly doubt you'll ever persuade him to do anything like this. So . . ."

Lorenzo has already convinced Marguita, and the two of them are getting ready to offer the honor to the elected candidates when Celina and her husband, Manuel the doctor, appear at the door, beaming with excitement and bearing a load of presents, already taking for granted that at least he, if not the two of them, have been chosen for the job.

As he comes in, Manuel the doctor is grinning ear to ear. After all, hasn't the boy been named after him? He tells the happy and surprised parents, "In my entire life as a doctor, I've never had a child named after me! And when Estela the nurse came in for her shift, late this afternoon, and told me all about it . . . boy! That was such a great honor," Manuel the doctor says, adding with a chuckle, "and an even greater surprise! Celina and I don't know how to thank you."

Not knowing what to do, Lorenzo and Marguita just sit there, wide-eyed and pretending to smile, while Celina and Manuel the doctor keep talking and talking about "We'll do this, we'll do that."

Since Cubans take silence to mean consent, by the time the doctor and his wife are about to leave, it is already an accepted fact who the child's godparents are going to be. Who could have said no to Manuel the doctor? As Estela the nurse said, "He is such a nice man!" Besides, since he is married to Celina, who is Maximiliano's second cousin, Manuel the doctor is now considered to be part of the family. So, refusing him is unthinkable. It would have been a great offense. And it would have been an even greater offense to refuse his wife, Celina, who really *is* part of the family.

Right before they leave, a thrilled Celina embraces Marguita again and again.

"Marguita, Marguita," she says, "I'm so excited, *so* excited. Now, don't you worry about a thing. You just relax and fatten that baby while I take care of everything. Think of that as doctor's orders. Right, Manuel?" she turns and asks her husband, who, beaming with excitement, just keeps nodding and nodding as he replies, "Right!"

Moments later, now all alone in their home, Lorenzo looks at his still-astounded wife.

"Well," Lorenzo says, trying to make light of the whole thing, "we finally got our godparents!" He shrugs. "Now, what's next?"

Marguita looks at him and smiles.

"I don't know about you, but as for me . . . I'm just going to follow doctor's orders. You heard Celina. 'Just relax and fatten your baby,' that's what she said, and I'm going to do just that—and nothing else. Let her take care of everything as she wants to. After all, she's the wife of a doctor, so she should know what she's talking about, don't you think? I can think of much more pleasurable things to do," she adds as she looks at her husband with those sparkling pale-blue eyes of hers that Lorenzo loves so much.

"Oh, no, no, no! Don't you dare look at me like that," Lorenzo warns her. "Not until those damn forty days we are supposed to wait go by."

"Why, have you been counting?" Marguita asks, feigning innocence.

"Me?" Lorenzo replies, lowering his voice to a whisper as he gets intimately close to her. "No," he adds, maliciously, taking his wife's beautiful oval face in his hands and whispering to her. "Why, have you?"

"I sure have," Marguita replies almost immediately, as she embraces her handsome husband and sighs deeply. "I sure have!"

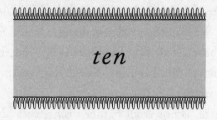

ten

Since she is going to be little Renzo's godmother, Celina, the wife of Manuel the doctor, is now in charge of all the arrangements for the christening. So she goes to the Little Church of the Perpetual Succor at the top of the hill, right on the Street of the Bulls, where the ceremony is to take place, and there she meets with the priest, Father Francisco. A short, thin, and wrinkled old man, Father Francisco is known, respected, and believed in by everybody in Luyanó, even though most people in the barrio seldom if ever bother to go to church. And this includes the whole of Maximiliano's family, all of whom are very religious, yes, but churchgoers? That, they are certainly not.

"Church?" Maximiliano often says, addressing his words not only to his children but to anyone else within earshot of the butcher shop. "There's my church," he adds, pointing at the limpid turquoise tropical sky that, framed by luscious palm trees, is visible from the butcher shop. "Who needs gold and diamonds and fancy vestments when you can have all of this for nothing?" And then he tells his audience. "Look at this beautiful world that surrounds us! What better church can there be?"

That, of course, is not at all Father Francisco's idea of a church.

To begin with, there is little gold in Father Francisco's church, and the little bit there is, is painted, if that much. Diamonds, there are none. And as for fancy vestments, Father Francisco's are faded and heavily darned. So when Father Francisco is asked by Celina to christen Maximiliano's first grandson, he is thrilled, for he sees it as a godsend, a divine opportunity to convert Maximiliano and his family, and make them realize how important going to church is—Father Francisco's church, that is.

Father Francisco knows how important Maximiliano is in the barrio. A tall, handsome man, with a ruddy face, piercing blue eyes, and golden hair cut bristlelike, military style, Maximiliano does cut an imposing figure in Luyanó. On top of that, he is considered a highly learned man—and a highly opinionated one—for he reads a lot. And as if that were not enough, he is also known as a poet, because he has written lyrics to many Cuban songs now considered classics. So a lot of people listen to him and follow his advice.

For years Father Francisco has been telling himself, Now, if only I could convince Maximiliano the butcher to come to my church, well, then, the whole barrio would follow suit, and then, God only knows what we all could achieve. Even through his tired eyes, the old priest can envision a school for the children to learn about God, a playground for the children to play safely, not on the streets, and even a new coat of paint for his little church, which really needs it.

And for years Father Francisco has been praying for an opportunity to make all these dreams a reality.

Who says prayers are not answered? Father Francisco tells himself moments after Celina leaves his church, when, after rushing to the altar he lights a candle as a way of thanking Our Lady of the Perpetual Succor for this immense favor that has been granted to him. And then, kneeling in front of her, he humbly prays.

"Please, Mother of God, illuminate me. Don't let me fail this time. Please."

Regardless of how Maximiliano feels about churches and priests, all of his children have been properly baptized. Dolores—who was schooled by nuns—has seen to that. Christened they all are, but not by Father Francisco, since most of Dolores's children were born in Batabanó, the little village south of Havana where Dolores and Maximiliano are from. However, it was Father Francisco who, years ago and at Dolores's urgent request, rushed to the hospital suite at Manuel's clinic. There, the old priest baptized Iris as Dolores delicately held the blue baby in her arms, moments before the pretty girl ascended to Heaven. Just as it was Father Francisco who christened Perucha, the hefty girl who is Dolores and Maximiliano's last child.

But in the first case, the christening took place at the hospital. And in the second case, though it was held at Father Francisco's church, the christening ceremony was not attended by Maximiliano, who was not feeling exceedingly well—or so Dolores told the old priest. But who was certainly feeling well enough to attend the party immediately following and dance until the wee hours, Father Francisco was careful to observe.

Maximiliano's refusal to set foot inside a church—any church of any organized religion—is known by all in the barrio, for Maximiliano enjoys making public his opinions on these matters as often as he can from the pulpit of his butcher shop.

"Churches were invented to extort money from the weak," he

says, "so that a few men, the so-called priests, who are good for nothing at all, can get away doing precisely nothing at all, while a bunch of *mojigatas*"—old maid prudes, as Maximiliano calls the few women who rush to church every morning at dawn—"keenly listen to them, oohhing and aahhing at every word they say, as if they were infallible gods, when they are nothing but men. But, as we all know," he adds, defiantly staring at his customers—most of whom are the same *mojigatas* that he has just referred to—"even the best men make mistakes." As they hear these words, to them so sacrilegious, the *mojigatas* immediately cross themselves. But that does not stop Maximiliano, who goes on with his tirade by adding, "It'll take a real miracle for a guy like *me* to set foot inside a church!"

As Father Francisco kneels in front of the Mother of God, he prays for that miracle.

And right then, apparently illuminated by Our Lady of the Perpetual Succor, an idea suddenly bursts into his head, an idea he instantly decides to pursue. When he stands up again and looks up at his Lady, the old man nods and smiles knowingly as he reverently winks an eye at her.

That same evening he goes to visit the happy new parents.

Marguita and Lorenzo are thrilled to welcome Father Francisco. Their living room is empty, except for two mahogany and cane rocking chairs. They offer one to the old priest and Marguita sits in the other one, holding her newborn, while Lorenzo rushes to the dining room at the other end of the house for a chair, brings it in, places it next to Marguita, and sits on it.

"What a happy occasion this is!" Father Francisco says, smiling broadly, his dark eyes glittering as they echo his words, which ring totally true. "If there is something I love to look at it is a young couple like you, deeply in love with each other, and already with a child.

And what a beautiful child this is! Do you mind if I look at him?" The old man stands up as Marguita opens up the blanket wrapping her child and proudly shows the priest her baby son. Father Francisco sits back in his rocking chair. "I understand you want to call him Lorenzo Manuel," he says. "A great choice, for Lorenzo means 'selected' and Manuel means 'the chosen one.' Those two great saints will be protecting him all his life."

It is only moments later, while tasting the dark Cuban coffee Marguita has just brought him, that the priest finally gets to the point of his visit and asks the question he has been meaning to ask all night long.

"How long have you two been married?"

"Oh, much less than a year," Marguita answers. "How long has it really been, Lorenzo?" she asks, turning to her husband.

"Let's see," Lorenzo says, as he counts with his fingers, "we were married December eleventh, and Renzito was born October third. Today is—Oh, today is the eleventh of October! Today we've been married exactly ten months."

"Well, then, happy ten-month anniversary," says the old priest, raising the tiny cup of coffee in his hands, as if making a toast. Then, as he is sipping the delicious-smelling infusion he adds, "I don't mean to sound . . . well, too inquisitive, but"—he pauses briefly—"how come I didn't get to marry you?"

"Oh," instantly replies Marguita, chuckling, "nobody married us. I mean," she adds, this time slightly embarrassed, "we just had a civil wedding. You know, the kind with a justice of the peace."

The old priest suddenly puts down the tiny white cup in his right hand on the tiny white saucer in his left, making a loud clinking noise that seems to reverberate all over the almost empty living room. "You mean to tell me that you two are not married by the church?" he asks with wide-open eyes—as if he didn't already know the answer.

Marguita looks at Lorenzo, who answers for them, shaking his head. "No."

"Oh," says the priest. That is all he says. And then he says nothing.

Nobody does, for what seems to be an enormous amount of time.

"Something wrong?" a concerned Marguita finally asks. "We just didn't have the money for . . . well, you know, a church wedding is expensive, and—"

Father Francisco shakes his head and smiles at them. "That's what everybody thinks, but it is not so. A church wedding requires nothing but two people in love and an old man like me, who acts as their witness in front of God. That is all. And, to tell you the truth, I'd prefer to baptize your son knowing that the union of the two of you was blessed and consecrated. Why don't you do it? Get married by the church, I mean. We could do it privately, in the sacristy, right before the christening. And for no fee. How's that for a bargain?"

"You mean to tell me," Marguita says after a while, "that we could have a church wedding after all?"

"Of course you can," the old man says. "And I'd be more than honored to be your witness."

Marguita looks at Lorenzo, and since Lorenzo has never been able to say no to whatever those beautiful blue eyes of his wife's ask him to do, he turns to Father Francisco. "You said we can do it right before little Renzo is baptized?" he asks. The old man smiles at Lorenzo and nods. "Well, then," Lorenzo continues, "we'll do it. Is there anything we need to bring? A ring, anything?"

"The only thing I need is a certificate that you have been baptized," Father Francisco says."

"How do we get that?" Lorenzo asks.

The old priest faces Lorenzo. "Just find out from your parents where you were baptized, then go there, and ask for a certificate of baptism. In your case, Marguita," the old man adds, facing Marguita, "since you were born in Batabanó, ask your mother where you were baptized, send them a note, and they'll be happy to send you a certificate by return mail. As simple as that."

Well, it was not as simple as that.

Marguita did get her certificate, and within a week of her asking for it. That is true. But Lorenzo . . .

"Mamá," an impatient Lorenzo tells his mother, Carmela, "first you tell me you don't remember where I was baptized, and now you tell me that you don't even know if I was ever baptized at all? How could anything like that have happened?"

Carmela shakes her head. "I don't know, Lorenzo. I just don't remember. It all happened such a long time ago. How can I remember?"

"You don't have any records at all?" asks an amazed and somewhat irritated Lorenzo.

Carmela again shakes her head.

"And Papá doesn't remember anything about it either?"

"No," Carmela says conclusively, "your father doesn't remember either. He wouldn't. None of us does."

But she did remember.

She just was not telling.

Lorenzo had been born during a very difficult time in Carmela's life. Her husband, Padrón, had abandoned her all of a sudden and disappeared, going nobody ever knew where, leaving behind a desperate Carmela who had to struggle with four young children plus the newborn Lorenzo. What time did Carmela have to get the boy baptized when all she could do was work her fingers to the bone, washing and ironing other people's laundry, just to put food on the table?

Padrón did come back, months later, offering no excuses, and Carmela asked no questions, for a woman with five children can afford no pride. That period of their lives was forgotten, perhaps even forgiven. Erased. As if those hard months—almost a full year— had never existed. It was better that way. What difference did it make what had really happened? The important thing was that Padrón had come back to Carmela and to his children, and that was that.

Except that Lorenzo never got baptized.

"I'm sorry, Father Francisco," a shocked and still angry Lorenzo tells the old priest the next day, "but it seems that in all probability I've never been baptized at all."

"Don't you worry, my son," a smiling Father Francisco replies. "Even if you weren't, we can still make a Christian out of you, the same way we can make a Christian out of your son—and on the same day, if you wish. Right before I get the two of you married," he adds, looking at Marguita, who is silently standing by her husband's side. "But, like your son," the old man goes on, addressing Lorenzo, "you'll need two godparents. Why don't you ask your parents-in-law if they would like the honor? I'm sure they won't say no. Certainly not to you, the father of their first grandson, will they?" Father Francisco chuckles to himself as he remembers that refusal to serve as a godparent is considered a very serious offense in Cuba.

And who happen to be Lorenzo's parents-in-law?

Dolores, for one, and the other, someone who has never set foot inside Father Francisco's church—or any other church, for that matter: Maximiliano the butcher.

How did Father Francisco know that all of this was going to happen exactly as it did?

There are some—a few—who would give you the same answer the priest would: "Faith, my son, faith." But Father Francisco knew perfectly well, just as the whole barrio knew—thanks to fat Pilar, she with the glass evil eye, who had been more than eager to spread the news—that Lorenzo and Marguita were "living in sin," for they had not been married by the church. In addition, Father Francisco must have bet—and heavily, in all probability—that either Marguita or Lorenzo would not be able to get hold of a baptismal certificate, something that happens frequently in Cuba, where records are not consistently kept by anyone.

In any event, once Maximiliano is asked for the honor, how can he say no?

Nonetheless, he does.

"Oh, no, Lorenzo," the butcher tells his son-in-law when Lorenzo asks him to be his godfather, "I'm too old for stuff like that. I'll leave that to younger folks. Being a godfather is a serious responsibility. Me, well, I'm afraid I'll have to pass on that. I'd be no good at it. I wouldn't even know what to do."

"But Father Francisco said that you don't have to do anything," replies Lorenzo. "All you have to do is to stand next to me and hold a candle in your hands as Father Francisco sprinkles water on my head. That is all."

There is a long, long pause.

Maximiliano looks at his wife, Dolores, who looks back at him, a glint in her eye as she says, after a while, "Of course he'll do it, Lorenzo. We both will. We both will be honored to be your godparents."

S ome people in the barrio call it the power of faith.
    Others call it a miracle.

But on the day his first grandson is to be christened, Maximiliano the butcher enters the sacristy of the Little Church of Our Lady of the Perpetual Succor. And there, inside the church, he stands by his wife, holding a candle in his hands—just as he was told to do—while his son-in-law is being christened. And there he stands, as his son-in-law marries his daughter for a second time, this time under the supervising eyes of a smiling God—and of a priest who never once stops beaming. And there he stands, by the side of his closest friend and buddy, Manuel the doctor, as his first grandson is being christened—all of these events taking place one right after the other right after the other.

And during all this time, Maximiliano the butcher, who is fuming inside, keeps asking himself, How did I ever get shoved into this? as he keeps staring with eyes now angry, now questioning, at Father Francisco, who, during the three successive ceremonies never once bothers to look back at him.

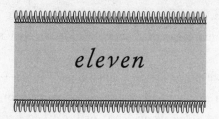

eleven

Everybody is there at little Renzo's christening party. That goes without saying.

Everybody.

The entire barrio shows up, not only to celebrate the christening of Maximiliano's first grandchild, but, in addition, to witness the almost incredible miracle that has taken place. Maximiliano—yes, Maximiliano the butcher, the man who claims that he does not believe in churches and that it would take a real miracle for a guy like him to set foot inside a church—that same man has given in, has set foot inside a church, and has even assisted the priest during the christening ceremony! And while some people in the barrio look at the blond butcher with a vaguely sneering smile, most people do not really care, for the child's godparents, Celina and her husband, Manuel the doctor—one of the few people in Cuba to have some money left—have pulled out all the stops. And this is *some* party!

And when Cubans say that, they mean it, for they sure know how to party.

Meant to take place inside Maximiliano's house—for it is much bigger than Lorenzo and Marguita's—the party soon starts spilling out to the broad sidewalk in front of it. When people passing by ask, "What is going on?" all they get for an answer is either an ice-cold bottle of beer, or a shot of rum—or both—if the person asking the question is a man; or, if it is a woman, a taste of a not-so-barely-spiked heavenly punch made of mangoes, coconuts, and guavas.

Celina's father, Rubén the singer, is there. And so are the two other men who form part of the Trío Los Rubenes. It doesn't take long for the three of them to pull out their guitars and maracas and begin to play and sing, while the people, inebriated by the beauty of it all, begin to dance with the total abandon of Cuban criollo men and women. Drums soon join in, and before anybody realizes it, the party has already gone past the sidewalk and into the street, where people of every color and every race and every creed under the sun begin to shake their bodies with intense fervor and sweat heavily until their bodies begin to glisten as they all celebrate the christening of little Renzo.

Even when one policeman comes, and then another, even they join in the party—though on the sly, of course. They simply go inside the house, where, in the privacy of the large patio, they say to no one in particular, "Now make sure you keep the party just on the sidewalk," as they toast to the health of the baby again and again before they start to leave, at which point some girl or another grabs them and starts to dance with them. And what's a man to do then? Especially if that man has one drop of Cuban blood inside him? Dance the policemen do, even as they leave the party with one or two ice-cold bottles of beer not-so-well hidden under the dark-blue shirts of their uniforms.

Though Celina has rented a lot of folding chairs, almost all of them remain folded and piled in a corner, since broad open spaces are urgently needed for more and more people to dance. Except for the few chairs occupied by the members of Lorenzo's family, all of whom are sitting the way you'd expect a family of Spaniards to sit— that is, as proper and as circumspect as if they truly were carved out of stone—in a corner of the entrance room to Maximiliano's house, a large room normally empty except for four large rocking chairs, now nowhere visible.

As always, Lorenzo's mother, his father, and his deaf sister are dressed head to toe in the black of the deepest mourning—what they've been wearing since Lorenzo's oldest sister died. But not so Lorenzo's other sister, Loló, who is expertly made up and expertly coiffed, and who is wearing an elegant and obviously made to order low-cut burgundy-red dress that shows a lot of cleavage and that has a tight, bias-cut skirt with wide godets at the hem.

Marguita has made an explicit point of being in any other room of the house but in the entrance room. Which? It doesn't really matter, provided she is as far away as possible from "that woman."

Bad enough Marguita had to invite her to the christening. And worse yet having to greet her and say hello to her. But how could she not do it? After all, Loló is one of the child's aunts. And besides, today is such a special day. The day of Lorenzo's christening, of her own church wedding, and of Renzito's christening. Marguita certainly does not want to spoil this great day for herself or for anyone else just because of Loló. She will not give the woman the pleasure. So if it meant inviting her, and greeting her, and saying hello to her, so be it. But still . . .

Even after she moved away from Lorenzo's family's house—which is also Loló's—and made a new home, and became a mother, even after all that, Marguita can still not face Loló. Every time Marguita looks at that woman all she can see are those piercing eyes of Loló's as she stood near the foot of Marguita's bed, watching Marguita and her husband Lorenzo while they were making love.

So, to avoid unnecessary problems and confrontations on such an important day as this, Marguita—whose desire to avenge herself on Loló has far from subsided—has made sure that she and her son, and her parents, and brothers, and sisters, and even her husband, Lorenzo, they all stay in one room, and Loló and the rest of Lorenzo's Spanish family in another, as far away from Marguita as Maximiliano's house will allow.

The christening party is really beginning to get going when Father Francisco and his acolyte, Father Alonso—a young priest who assisted Father Francisco during little Renzo's christening—come in.

After each of the two priests thankfully accepts one of those ice-cold bottles of beer that somebody hands out, which tastes, oh, so good! in the almost suffocating heat of a tropical midafternoon, they espy in a corner of the large entrance room Lorenzo's family, whom they met at the church, and whom they know to be Continental Spaniards, just as both priests are. With tremendous difficulty, the two priests manage to make their way through the boisterous crowd to where Lorenzo's family is sitting.

Once they get there, after they greet them, Father Alonso goes to a corner of the room, picks up a couple of the folding chairs piled there, brings them back to the group, unfolds them, offers one to the old priest, and takes the other one for himself as both priests sit by Lorenzo's family.

As they sit side by side, the two priests—who despite the stifling heat inside the house are still wearing their black cassocks, as priests do at all times in Cuba—could not be more different from each other. While Father Francisco is a short, thin, wrinkled old man who has lived in Cuba for innumerable years, his acolyte, Father Alonso, has just arrived in Cuba from Spain, and is a young and handsome specimen of a Northern Spaniard.

Barely out of the seminary, which he entered nine years back, right at the onset of puberty, Father Alonso has glossy dark hair, a deeply cleft chin, and an apparently perennial dark-blue five-o'clock shadow. A lot beefier than Father Francisco, and taller than the much older priest by a full head, Father Alonso has dark-blue eyes deeply set under black eyebrows that seem to want to run into one. But where Father Francisco's eyes are always jovial and mirthful, Father Alonso's eyes are always downcast and melancholic. Serious. Far too serious for such a young man. Since his dream was to do missionary work among the poor, the minute Father Alonso stepped off the boat, the bishop of Havana allocated him to the poorest parish of his see, Luyanó, where the young priest is learning the ropes, so to speak, under the patient guidance of old Father Francisco.

Suddenly, a mulatto young woman with magnificent dark eyes and an ample bosom that begs to burst out of the tightest bias-cut dress ever, starts to twist and jerk violently in the middle of the entrance room. "*Le bajó el santo, Le bajó el santo*"—"The saint has descended on her"—people suddenly begin to shout to each other as they hurriedly make room for the girl upon whom the saint has descended, so she can move and dance as freely as anyone must do when under the influence and possession of the saint.

Old Father Francisco, although born and educated in Spain, has spent his entire life as a priest in Cuba—where Catholic beliefs and primitive African rituals often blend into one—and he has seen this happen many a time. He looks at the girl who is whirling apparently without control in the hands of some powerful and mysterious force, and then, facing Lorenzo's family, says, "Isn't it wonderful what the power of faith can do? Look at that girl. She truly believes that she is in the hands of a saint who is controlling her body."

He turns and faces his young assistant who is looking at the girl, aghast. "The Greeks used to do the same thing, you know, Father Alonso. They, of course, didn't call it a saint but a muse. And just as we do, when we celebrate Mass and ask God to descend upon us so He can illuminate our lives, the Greeks prayed for the muse to descend right before they'd begin to perform a play, or a rite, or any religious ceremony. For unless the muse descended, such a ceremony was bound to fail, they thought." Father Francisco pauses briefly as he looks admiringly at the dancing girl. "And the Greeks were probably right, because, look at that girl," he adds, addressing his words to no one in particular. "Look how magical and beautiful her movements are."

For a long while the eyes of everybody in the room are fastened on the young girl, who keeps wildly contorting her body as she follows the tempestuous rhythms of the African drums apparently coming from everywhere.

The eyes of everybody, that is, except the dark, gypsy eyes of Loló, cryptic and mystifying, which are fastened on the young priest's.

And the puzzled eyes of the young priest, candid and clear, which, now facing Loló, seem to be unable to evade her piercing glance.

A few moments after the girl collapses, totally exhausted from her turbulent dancing, Maximiliano comes in, a thick cigar in his hand, and, unfolding a chair, sits close to the priests, by Lorenzo's family.

"May I offer you one of these Macanudo cigars, Father Francisco?" Maximiliano asks jovially. "I think you deserve it. After what you've gone through today, I mean. You must be *so* tired. All of that sprinkling and sprinkling!" He looks the old priest right in the eye as he adds, "The things a man must do to earn a living!"

Catching the not-so-well-disguised sarcastic tone in Maximiliano's cutting words, Father Alonso is ready to stand up and answer the butcher, but Father Francisco stops him with a gesture.

"But he's absolutely right, Father Alonso," the old priest tells his young acolyte as he smiles broadly at Maximiliano—an honest and winning smile that reaches for the very bottom of Maximiliano's heart, but that fails to soothe the savage beast already raging inside the butcher.

"You know, Father Francisco," Maximiliano goes on, his broad smile not quite able to mask the sharpness in his voice, by now verging on anger. "I was just told by Lorenzo that it was *your* idea that my wife and I become his godparents. Is that so?"

The old priest silently nods in agreement, mischievously smiling to himself, because the idea of making Maximiliano come to his church was indeed his—perhaps with a little help from Our Lady of the Perpetual Succor.

"So it is true, then!" a more-than-irate Maximiliano says. "It was *you* who put that stupid idea into Lorenzo's head. Which means that if I finally went inside a church—I mean, if you got *me* to go inside a church. *Me!* Who do not, have not, and will never *ever* believe in churches and certainly not in *your kind of church*"—the now raging butcher adds, heavily underlining the entire phrase—"if you got *me* to go inside a church, it was because of your . . . let's just call it 'priestly conniving,' for lack of a better term. Isn't that so, Father?" Maximiliano the butcher adds, staring now openly and defiantly at the old priest.

"Well, son," Father Francisco says unflinchingly, grinning ear to ear as he adds, "as you yourself said . . . the things a man must do to earn a living!"

Caught by surprise by the old priest's clever retort, something he wasn't expecting in the least, Maximiliano—always a good loser—is instantly disarmed and begins to laugh heartily, loud belly laughs that are soon joined by Father Francisco himself.

But these belly laughs seem to baffle the young priest, Father Alonso, who, unable to understand the reason for them, looks around the room—only to find Loló's dark, gypsy eyes still intently staring at him.

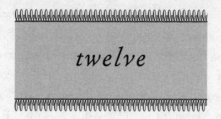

twelve

Though the thoughts of Loló, and of what Loló did to her, and of avenging herself, have never managed to leave Marguita, right now those thoughts have receded to the back of her mind, for Marguita has to face far more urgent and far more serious problems. She has just discovered that either she is unable to produce enough milk for her baby, or else little Renzo is too much of a glutton, and she cannot keep up with him. Desperately, she has tried every homemade remedy she was told about so she could produce more milk—and then some.

"The problem is that you have to eat for two," Dolores's neighbor Pilar—she with the glass evil eye—told Marguita. "I did, and now look at my daughter," Pilar added, pointing to her hefty teenage girl. "Look how big and strong she is!" So Marguita looked at Pilar's daughter and began eating for two. "The problem is that you don't drink enough milk," her upstairs neighbor, Señora Velasco, told Marguita. "Milk is good for you. And for your baby." And Marguita, who never liked the taste of milk, began mixing it with chocolate and having one milkshake after another. "The problem is this," someone else would say, "or the problem is that," somebody else would say. And Marguita would try this and that. But to no avail. She was gaining weight, and at a fast rate. But not her baby. And she didn't know why.

"Whatever the reason, the child is not getting sufficient nutrients," says Manuel the doctor, who is talking to a concerned Marguita in his office at his clinic. "That's why he hasn't been gaining as much weight as he should. But you have nothing to worry about," he adds. "There's nothing like mother's milk for a child, so I don't want you to stop breast-feeding him. At least not yet. But, for the time being, let's supplement the child's breast-feedings with a formula. Take a can of sweetened condensed milk and mix it half and half with boiled water, equal amounts of each," the doctor says. "Let the water boil at least five minutes. Then wait until it cools, and mix it with the milk. After that you can store it in—do you have an icebox?"

"Papá bought us a refrigerator," Marguita replies. "A Free-hee-dye-reh."

"Good," the doctor continues. "Then you can store the formula there. It should last you for a day or so. You go ahead and keep breast-feeding the baby as you've been doing, but after each feeding give the boy . . . let's start out with four ounces. If you see he takes all of it, increase it by an ounce. But never give him more than eight ounces at a feeding, all right?"

Marguita nods and is about to go.

"Oh, Marguita," Manuel adds, "don't forget to warm it before you give it to the child. Place the bottle with the formula in hot water until it feels warm. You can test it by placing the bottle against your cheek. If it feels nice and warm to you, then it will feel nice and warm to the baby. And Marguita," Manuel tells her, in a reassuring voice, "you're doing a great job, so don't be so nervous. Babies can feel that. That may be the reason you're not producing enough milk. So just calm down and everything will be all right."

Holding her child tight to her, Marguita stands on a narrow pedestrian island located in the center of the busy Calzada—as the broad avenue in front of Manuel's clinic is called—waiting for the streetcar that goes from Manuel's clinic back to her house.

How easy it is for Manuel the doctor to say do not be nervous, Marguita is thinking as she waits, cars honking both ways as they speed past her. What with Lorenzo going to night school and leaving me alone with the baby all night after I've been alone with the baby all day. And then, trying to make those measly sixty-five pesos of Lorenzo's last an entire month. Not even sixty-five pesos but only fifty-five, after he gives ten pesos a month to his family.

And now, to top it all off, this! My not being able to produce enough milk for my child. And my having to spend some of the precious little money we have to buy the milk I myself should be producing for my baby.

No wonder I'm a nervous mess, she tells herself as she sighs.

She knows she has money stowed away, but she doesn't want to think about that. So far she hasn't touched their nest egg, the one hundred pesos Lorenzo won betting at the jai alai palace.

That money is sacred. Not to be used, period.

Not even for emergencies.

The morning after she took the money from Lorenzo, Marguita went to her father's butcher shop and asked him to exchange the thick wad of twenty five-peso bills for just one one-hundred-peso bill, which Maximiliano did, asking no questions. Marguita took the single bill back home, folded it neatly, placed it inside a handkerchief her mother had given her—embroidered by Dolores herself—tied a knot around it, and hid it carefully in the back of the second drawer from the top of her chiffonier.

As far as Marguita is concerned, that single *hojita de lechuga*—"little lettuce leaf"—which is what Cubans call one-hundred-peso bills because of their green color—no longer exists. It has been banked. The back of the second drawer of her chiffonier is Marguita's bank.

She told Lorenzo that the money was to be used to pay for his expenses while he goes to night school at the university to become a certified public accountant. But she actually earmarked that money for her dream, a dream so intimate and so secret that she hasn't shared it with anyone—not even with Lorenzo.

And that dream is for her and Lorenzo to have a house of their own.

Fully paid for, that is.

A house they can truly call theirs.

She hasn't told this to Lorenzo because he is working and studying so hard, and he is under so much pressure, that she does not want to add to it. But when Lorenzo came home that night, months ago, with those one hundred pesos in his pocket, Marguita saw that money as the foundation of their house. She doesn't care how long it takes or how hard she and Lorenzo will have to work for it. But a house of their own they will have. Of that she has no doubt. In the least. So, if Lorenzo's fifty-five pesos a month is what she has to work with, so fifty-five pesos will have to do. No, fifty, because she is planning to save five pesos a month. For the house.

She gets on the streetcar and finds a seat all the way in the back.

How she is going to manage to save those five pesos, she has no idea. Not yet. But she will save those five pesos, no matter what, no matter how. She knows it doesn't sound like much, but five pesos a month is sixty pesos a year and . . . how much are houses? she asks herself as the old, clanking streetcar tries to make its way through the heavy morning traffic of Luyanó.

Marguita knows very little about banks, interest, or mortgages. She is totally naive if not ignorant about money matters.

And so is most everyone else in the Cuba of 1938.

Nine years after the Big Crash on Wall Street—which made the market price of sugar sink to its lowest ever, causing Cuban banks to collapse like a house of cards, and bringing the country to the very verge of bankruptcy—Cuba remains impoverished beyond belief. Little if anything is available, and whatever little there is has to be bought in cash, and paid in cash. From eggs and the occasional chicken—a rare delicacy in cattle-raising Cuba—to refrigerators and rent. And even sweetened condensed milk, which has to be imported from the United States, and which is very expensive.

"*No se fía hoy, sino mañana,*" reads the sign hanging on the wall of Maximiliano's butcher shop. "No credit today, credit tomorrow."

Paying in cash is Maximiliano's way. And Padrón's way.

And that is the way of their children.

The streetcar gets to the corner of Hermenegildo's bodega, and there Marguita gets off. Then, before she heads back home, Marguita decides to stop over at her mother's, say hello to her, and check on her, for Dolores has not been feeling very well lately.

Bad hearts run in Dolores's family.

Both her older sisters died of bad hearts soon after Dolores's father shot himself because he had lost everything he had betting on a fancy cock with large colorful plumes and sharp talons but with the cowardly heart of a chicken. And Dolores's baby girl, Iris, died also of a bad heart barely six weeks after she was born. Losing that child broke Dolores's heart. Literally. It was then that she began having palpitations for the first time. Hard as she tried, Dolores was not able to erase from her mind the sight of her baby girl, little and blue, suckling at her breast.

Dolores has never told anybody, but she feels guilty about losing her pretty baby girl Iris. She knows the little girl inherited the heart problem from her, since Maximiliano's parents are close to ninety and still as strong as horses. But she often tells herself that nothing would have happened if she had not made herself miserable during the time she was in Batabanó, away from her husband, living on charity with her in-laws, after she and Maximiliano lost everything they had in that horrible hurricane of 1926 that took more than twenty thousand lives in Cuba alone. She never told anybody how sad and depressed she felt back then. But she did share her feelings with her little daughter, Marguita, as the two of them, mother and child, sat on the golden sand by the sea and played "Friends and Neighbors." Dolores found great consolation in Marguita, too, when her baby daughter Iris died.

Lately, Dolores's weak heart has started to bother her again. She has been having chest pains and her breathing has become ever more difficult. This has happened before, but never like this, with this intensity and to this extent. Manuel the doctor told her to rest in bed, using several pillows. But since her breathing becomes more agitated and difficult in bed, for the last week Dolores has been sleeping nights sitting on one of the four rocking chairs in the entrance room of her house.

That first night a week ago, when Dolores began experiencing heart palpitations and a tightening in her chest, Maximiliano sat by her side in another one of the rocking chairs in their living room until Dolores, seeing how he was beginning to nod and fall asleep and had even started to snore, awoke him by gently tapping his arm.

"Don't be silly, go to bed," Dolores told him. "You have to go back to work early tomorrow morning, so you have to rest, while I have nothing to do all day tomorrow. Besides, I'm perfectly all right where I am. I'll join you in bed as soon as I feel better. So go to bed, go. Go!"

Maximiliano did go to bed that night—at Dolores's insistence—but Dolores preferred to stay all night in her rocking chair where she could sleep with some ease.

The next morning, Maximiliano stopped by Marguita's house and asked Marguita if she could keep Dolores company for a while, that he had an errand to do before he came back home for the noontime meal. Moments later, after rushing through her household chores, Marguita showed up at Dolores's house, bringing the baby with her, and laden with a ton of diapers and a few toys.

"What are you doing here at this time of day?" a surprised Dolores asked her. Then, seeing the hesitation in her daughter's eyes, she added, "Did your father put you up to this?" She didn't need to ask the question for she well knew the answer. "That man! If you listen to him, you'd think I'm on my deathbed."

Though she was holding the baby in her arms, Marguita instantly crossed herself. "Mamá, don't you ever say anything like that!"

Dolores laughed. "Why not? It's the truth, isn't it? We all have to die. Here, give me the boy." Marguita handed Lorenzo Manuel to Dolores, who placed him gently against her heart. Dolores smelled the boy's hair—as wavy as hers but as golden as Maximiliano's and Marguita's. "His hair smells so good," she said, inhaling deeply, her eyes closed, hoping to make the moment last forever as she thought of her other children, now grown-up men and women except for Perucha, still at home, and for Iris, her lost baby girl. "I have always loved the smell of Florida Water cologne," she added, tightening her arms around the boy.

The boy seemed to sense he was safe in her arms and lay placidly there, his large blue eyes open, staring at his grandmother, who suddenly began to breathe with some difficulty. Marguita, who was sitting by her side, instantly stood up.

"Mamá, are you all right?" she asked, her voice urgent. "Should I get you some water?"

Dolores shook her head and offered the baby back to Marguita, who took him in her arms. Marguita's eyes were glued to her mother. After what to Marguita seemed like an interminable period of time, Dolores, then much more calm, faced her daughter, who was still standing by her side.

"Marguita, if something should happen to me . . . ," she began. Marguita immediately tried to say something, but Dolores would not let her. "Please, sit down and let me finish," she added decisively, as she raised her hand. Obediently, Marguita sat on her rocking chair. Dolores continued. "You don't have to worry about your father. Or about Perucha. He and I have talked about this many a time and we've made plans. My love, don't look at me with such sad eyes. I'm not planning to die for a long while, but if I do I'm not afraid of death. I've lived a great life, and I've loved every minute of it. Even when those blessed nuns made me clean the toilets at school. Even then."

This made Marguita laugh loudly, breaking the tension.

Dolores smiled at her.

"All I want you to do is to make sure that our family stays close together. That your brothers and sisters keep loving each other as much as they have. And should any discord ever occur among any of you, I want you, my little love, to intercede and make peace among them. That's all I want you to do. You know I lost my family. I don't want my children to lose theirs, for whatever the reason. Will you promise me you'll do that for me?" Dolores said in that kind, gentle voice of hers. "Will you?" she repeated.

"Of course, Mamá," Marguita finally managed to say through her tears.

"Well, then, hand me the baby and go wash your face. Your father is due any minute for his noontime meal and look at you! You've always been such a crybaby! When are you going to grow up? Tell me, what do you think your father would say if he came in and found you looking like that? He'll probably scream at me, thinking that I was chastising you for something. You know how he has always taken your side, ever since you were born—because you are blond and blue-eyed, I guess. The only one of my children who took after him. No wonder he thinks you are the sun and the moon! So please, run and do as I tell you before he comes in and finds you like this."

Moments later, when Marguita came back into the living room, she found her father there. Maximiliano had gone to La Plaza de Mercaderes, the large market in the center of Old Havana, and there he had bargained hard, the way he always did, and had bought several large cushions with which he was now carefully padding Dolores's old cane rocker. He had also bought a little cane stool, padded as well, which he placed in front of Dolores so she could raise her feet and be more comfortable.

That is exactly how Marguita finds Dolores as she comes into her mother's house from Manuel the doctor: sitting in her rocking chair, half asleep, her feet on the little stool, a sheet folded in half covering her, a book on her lap. Marguita enters quietly and listens to Dolores's breathing, which seems to be no longer agitated, as it was days ago, but calm and gentle. This makes Marguita smile at her mother.

Dolores opens her eyes and sees Marguita standing in front of her, looking at her with loving eyes as she holds little Renzo in her arms.

"Isn't that something? I was dreaming about the baby, and I open my eyes and what do I see?" she says. "You and the baby. At first I thought the two of you were part of my dream. And maybe you still are. It must have been the smell of the baby's talcum powder that woke me up. Doesn't he smell great? I think a woman can smell a baby miles away. Certainly if she has ever been a mother. What did Manuel the doctor say?"

Marguita goes to her mother, kisses her gently on the cheek—as all of Dolores's children do, even her grown-up sons, when they greet her—and then she sighs as she sits by her side. "He says I'm too tense and nervous and that is why I cannot—"

"You? Tense and nervous? What about?"

"Oh, Mamá. I don't know. About so many things. I get afraid sometimes. That I don't feed Renzito correctly. Or that he's going to drown when I give him a bath. Or catch a bad cold. Or that the water is too hot. Or not hot enough. I don't know, I just worry. I know it doesn't make any sense, but I just do. And Doctor Manuel thinks this is why I don't produce enough milk for him. Or I worry that my milk is making Renzito sick. Maybe that's why he vomits most of it and has not been gaining as much weight as he should."

"Well, Señora Marguita," Dolores says, addressing her daughter the way she used to years ago when she and Marguita played their favorite game, "if you don't mind my asking you a very intimate question?"

Hearing her mother call her "Señora Marguita" makes Marguita smile. Almost a child again, Marguita addresses her mother formally, calling her "Señora Dolores," and joining in the game.

"Well, Señora Dolores," Marguita says, "as you know, among us, best friends and neighbors, no question can ever be too intimate."

"Have you told any of this to your husband, Señora Marguita?"

Marguita shakes her head. "No, I don't want him to feel more pressure than what he already—"

"But that's precisely what husbands are for, Señora Marguita," Dolores interrupts. "To share everything with. The good things and the not-so-good things. The more you share with your husband, Señora Marguita," Dolores adds, her voice gentle, her tone serious and yet kind, "the less tense and nervous you will be. And the less tense and nervous you are, the less tense and nervous your son will be. If I may ask, Señora Marguita, when was the last time you and your husband . . . well . . . you know."

It takes a few seconds for Marguita to understand what her mother has just asked her, and when she does, all a shocked Marguita can say is "Mamá!" after which there follows a short, embarrassing pause.

"I see, Señora Marguita," an immutable Dolores replies, barely able to hide a smile. "So then, it has been a long, long time, hasn't it?"

Marguita says nothing. She just nods. Then, evading her mother's eyes, she stares at the shiny Cuban tile floor and says, "Manuel the doctor told us we could have none of that for forty days before the baby was born and then for forty days after. So . . ." Marguita shrugs and pauses.

"Well, Señora Marguita, tell me," Dolores says, leaning forward and gently grabbing her daughter's face in her hands, "have you been counting?" Marguita tries to turn her face away to evade her mother's eyes, but Dolores will not let her.

"Have you?" Dolores insists.

"Lorenzo has. Yesterday he told me we still have two more days to go!" Marguita says, and sighs, her face as red as the inside of a watermelon.

"Well, Señora Marguita," Dolores tells her daughter, "I always follow the doctor's instructions to the letter, you know that. But in a situation like this, it seems to me that one or two days more or less won't make much of a difference. So, why don't you let me keep the boy here overnight, Señora Marguita"—Marguita is about to say something, but Dolores stops her. "Having him here will make me feel better and besides, you know that I'll take care of him as if he were my own son. So why don't you go prepare a good meal for your husband tonight and then, tomorrow, why don't you come visit me again? That way you can pick up the child and, Señora Marguita, may I tell you something?"

Marguita looks at Dolores, puzzled.

"Tomorrow, when we visit again, I don't think you'll be tense or nervous," Dolores says, a glint in her eyes.

Marguita begins to laugh, and so does her mother. "Are you sure you won't mind, Mamá? I mean, Señora Dolores? Having the baby here when you—"

"Not at all, my child—I mean, Señora Marguita. Not in the least. After all," Dolores says, "what are friends and neighbors for?"

When Señora Marguita comes to visit Señora Dolores to pick up her child early the next morning, she does not have to say a single word, for her beaming face says it all. And that same afternoon, though Señora Marguita prepares the formula following the careful instructions given to her by Manuel the doctor, she uses little of it.

Realizing that after all she may not have to buy as much of the expensive sweetened condensed milk as she thought, for she has been able to produce a little more milk the last couple of days, Marguita looks at her child, now asleep in his crib with a smile on his face. Then, with the same glint in her eyes that she's seen in her mother's eyes many a time, she tells herself, Well, Mamá's way has certainly been a nice way to save a little money.

Quietly, so as not to awaken little Renzo, Marguita goes to her bedroom, opens the right leaf of her chifforobe, and there, in the bottom drawer, nicely cradled among neatly folded bedsheets—heavily starched and crisply ironed by Marguita herself—she finds a ceramic piggy bank she keeps secretly hidden. She grabs it, takes a few coins out of her dress pocket—the few coins she had allocated for the sweetened condensed milk—and inserts them one at a time through the thin slit atop the piggy bank.

"*Para la casa*," she whispers aloud to herself as she does it. "For the house."

Marguita hasn't told Lorenzo the many little things she has been doing without in order to save a penny here, a penny there.

Like not having the woman who once a week goes to Dolores's house to wash and iron Dolores's laundry come to Marguita's house to wash and iron Marguita's. No, Marguita is doing that herself—and singing as she does it. Or like taking the streetcar to visit Lorenzo's parents in *La Habana Vieja* only once a month instead of every other week, as she used to, so Lorenzo's family can see how Renzito is growing up. But only during weekdays—when she knows for certain that "that woman" Loló is not there. Or even like not going to Xiomara, the barrio beautician, to get her hair cut.

Of all the things Marguita has been doing without, this has been the most difficult one to live with, for Marguita has never been able to stand long hair, and certainly not during this fall of 1938, with the heat wave Cuba has been going through, the worst in many a year. She'd been letting her hair grow for several weeks, when Lorenzo finally noticed it. She asked him, "Don't you like it?"

Surprised by Marguita's question, Lorenzo replied, "Why, yes, I do. I like it a whole lot. Especially when we're in bed, making love. I love the way it feels. But I thought you told me you didn't like to wear your hair that long. Don't you find it too hot?"

"Oh, no. Not in the very least." She smiled at him, a fiery spark in her pale-blue eyes. "And now that I know how much you like it, I like it even more," she added.

So she's kept her hair long and pocketed the money.

All of this may not sound like much, but still, it has enabled Marguita to save a penny here, a penny there—the way her mother, Dolores, taught her. And by doing that, Marguita has been managing to save if not quite the five pesos a month she meant to store away, then pretty much close to it. Every single penny of it aimed at her dream.

"For the house."

Marguita places her secret piggy bank back where she hides it, closes the chifforobe door, and heads for the kitchen, where she has been working on a white bean soup. Made with very inexpensive ingredients, its bland taste can easily be altered by adding different spices—but the soup requires almost constant stirring so it will not stick to the pot and burn.

It is there at the stove that Lorenzo finds her when he gets home for his noontime meal. He rushes to Marguita, stands behind her, and, embracing her from the back, kisses her golden hair, which smells of water of violets.

Still stirring her soup, Marguita leans against him, enjoying the warmth of his arms around her. "What's new?" she asks Lorenzo in a soft voice—as she does every day—for she doesn't want to wake up little Renzo, who is peacefully sleeping in his crib in the next room after his now plentiful midday feeding.

Marguita has a very inquisitive mind, which she inherited from both her parents, but since she and Lorenzo cannot afford a radio, or the buying of daily newspapers—to save a few more pennies—Lorenzo is her only provider of news. Well, Lorenzo *and* her good friend Pilar, who keeps the whole barrio informed about local news as it happens—sometimes even *before* it happens.

"Not much, except that this time I definitely think that the owner of the bookstore, Collazo, has totally gone out of his mind," Lorenzo answers Marguita as he goes to the *lavadero* and starts to wash his hands.

Though her focus is still primarily on stirring her thickening soup, Marguita faces him.

"Why, what did he do this time?" she asks. "He didn't fire you, did he?" she adds, half mockingly.

"Oh, no, no. He'd never do that. You know that he likes me, he really does," Lorenzo says as he dries his hands on a small kitchen towel by the sink. "The moment I'm through with school he's going to place me in charge of the accounting department. He told me that himself and I know that he means it. No, what I'm talking about is that building project of his, you know, that social club he's been talking about for a while, the one he wants to build right on Guanabo Beach for the use of his employees."

"El Club Cultural?" Marguita says, pronouncing the words Cuban style: "El Kloob Kool-too-*ral,*" with the accent on the last syllable.

"The same. Well, we had a meeting this morning. All the employees were there, and he told us he had decided to go ahead with it. So Berto, the champion—you know who he is, don't you, that tall, good-looking guy who was a jai alai champion?"

"The one who took you to the jai alai palace?" she asks. "The one who induced you to bet a fortune against your better judgment? The one who—"

"Yes, that one, that one," a chuckling Lorenzo concedes.

He knows only too well how Marguita feels about what he did that night, and how enraged she was when he came home drunk out of his mind. Though she surely didn't mind hiding in some secret place totally unknown to him the one hundred pesos he won then, following Berto's advice.

"Well," Lorenzo goes on, "Berto asked Collazo, point-blank, 'Do you mean to tell us that this club of yours, that it will be free for us to use?' And Collazo nodded. 'Yes, absolutely free,' the old man said. 'A place just to hang out, no work or nothing?' Berto kept asking. 'Sure,' Collazo said, addressing all of us, 'just a place so you guys can relax, go swimming, and have some fun.' Then someone else, I think it was Carlos, one of the mail clerks, asked Collazo why he was doing this, and Collazo said, 'Because I think of us as family, and because happy employees do a better job, and if we all do a better job we end up earning more money for the company . . . and thus for *me!*' And we all laughed when he said that, including him, for he really meant it—you know how much of a tightwad he's supposed to be. And he knows it. But I don't think he's as stingy as they say he is, because he then showed us a drawing the architect had done of the building, and Marguita, let me tell you, it looks great!"

Lorenzo picks up several plates and glasses and starts to set the table, as he continues.

"It's going to be a three-stories-high building housing locker rooms, a bar, and a dining room on the ground floor; several bedrooms plus a huge game room on the second floor; and a private suite in the form of a tower for the use of Collazo and his family on the third floor. They already started pouring the foundation, and the architect said it should be ready come this summer. Isn't that something?"

"It sounds like that building must cost a lot of money," Marguita says, as she ladles the already thickened white bean soup in two bowls and starts to take them to the dining room. "So the bookstore must be doing really well, don't you think?"

"I know it is," Lorenzo says, nodding his head, for he has been keeping the books for the bookstore. He stirs the soup. "Hey, this smells heavenly!"

Flattered by the sincere compliment, Marguita, a broad smile on her face, sits opposite Lorenzo at the dining room table, which is covered with a gingham-weave cotton tablecloth. Then she looks at him. "And yet, knowing how well the bookstore is doing, you still didn't ask Collazo for a raise, did you?" Marguita asks, knowing the answer.

Ever since Marguita convinced Lorenzo to go to night school so he can get a better job, and get his family out of Luyanó, the poorest—and the roughest—barrio in all Havana, so they can secure a better future for them and their family, ever since, Marguita has been encouraging Lorenzo to ask for a raise. Ever since.

Lorenzo looks at her and shakes his head.

"I meant to, Marguita. I really did. But after Collazo told us about the building, and about all the money he must be putting into it, how could I ask him for a raise? But I did get sort of a raise, come to think of it," Lorenzo adds.

Marguita looks at him puzzled. "What do you mean?"

"Collazo cut the workweek. Starting next month we won't have to work Saturday afternoons, just mornings. So that's sort of a raise, isn't it? The same money for less time, isn't it? And then, come summer, maybe even before that, we'll all be able to go to Guanabo Beach and have a good time. All of us! The club is for the use not only of employees but of their families as well, so all of us can go there. We, your parents, your brothers and sisters, your whole family. And mine, too. All of us. And all for nothing. Can you believe it? I can't wait. They say Guanabo Beach is incredibly beautiful."

Marguita smiles at him.

Yes, she thinks, all that sounds really wonderful. Still, none of that helps us buy a house. Or pay for a better education for little Renzo. Or make life a little easier for us. She sighs. A raise would be better, she tells herself as she tastes the thick white bean soup which is particularly good today—a lot better than yesterday's, or even the day before yesterday's.

Oh, yes! she tells herself once again. A raise would be a lot better.

thirteen

The Sunday following the completion of El Club
Cultural, the last week in June, a private ceremony is planned to inaugurate the handsome building properly.

This is meant to be a religious ceremony, almost
a christening, attended by priests and acolytes; and,
like all christenings, this ceremony is to be followed
by a party, of course. Which means that all the
employees of the Athena Bookstore, where Lorenzo
works, and their families and friends are invited to
go to Guanabo Beach and take a first look at this
building they all have heard so much about—a building that is truly a present from the owner of the
bookstore, Collazo, to those who work with him.

Lorenzo's boss is not really the miser most everybody thinks he is—though he does look the part. A big old man with big hairy ears, a big hairy nose, thick lips, and huge hands, Collazo is a hardworking Spaniard who loves books beyond belief and who saves every penny beyond comprehension, for despite the money his company makes, he wears the same tired old suit year in, year out, "until it finally falls off his body"—his employees jokingly say.

He came to Cuba in 1895, at the outset of what eventually would become the Spanish American War, to fight criollo Cubans, but after the war was finally settled in 1898, Collazo decided to stay on the island and start his own business. He bought an old, battered, two-wheeled peddler's cart with a white canvas top, and early every morning, after he loaded it to the hilt with books of every kind, he pushed it along the narrow cobblestone streets of Old Havana peddling his books, which he rented out for just a few pennies a day. But pennies a day began to add up really fast, and by the time Lorenzo started to work for him, back in 1935, Collazo was already the owner of the largest bookstore in Havana, was opening a second store on Galiano, the busiest street in all Havana, and was dreaming of becoming a publisher as well.

It was about that time that Collazo had a brilliant idea. In order to attract better men—and women—to his business, Collazo asked himself, why not organize a literary club where people who love books can get together informally and get to know each other? Of course, what Collazo really wanted was to discover talented people who could write, edit, and bring to fruition the books he was already envisioning in his mind. Within a month he found and leased a space in the very center of Havana, right on El Paseo del Prado, the wide avenue filled with ancient trees that connects the Cuban Presidential Palace and the Capitol with the magnificent Havana Bay. There "El Club Cultural," as the literary club was called, was established.

Founded in the month of February, El Club Cultural was a great hit. Everybody who was anybody in the world of ideas and books, from newspapermen to politicians, joined it and spent a lot of time there, doing nothing but arguing, as Cubans are bound to do, about anything—literature and politics being the most ardently attacked and defended topics—while at the same time they played dominoes and smoked cigars, every so often having a shot of rum on the side. Officially, drinking was not allowed within the club. But what Cuban has ever obeyed "official" rules? Great friendships were started there, and quite a few were terminated even before they were started, just to be restarted again at the next-door tavern over a shot of rum followed by an ice-cold beer chaser. Literary talent could be found there in droves—but the real kind of talent: the talent of ideas, not just the talent of empty words. In fact, the moment somebody would begin to drop abstruse and recondite polysyllabic words to show off, that very same moment the members of the club would start to poke fun at the word-dropper, who had to adapt to the literary standards of the club—or else. In matters of Literature—the word was always spoken as if it were spelled with a capital L—the members of El Club Cultural admired being clear, direct, succinct, and to the point. Their motto being: "Metaphors are the weapons of cowards." In all other matters—politics and women, that is—the norms were exactly the opposite: the longer at it, the better.

But then came summer, the summer of 1938. And what a summer that was!

Havana's summers are normally sizzling hot to begin with. This one was a killer. No one wanted to be in the center of the city where no breezes seemed to flow—so Collazo's club was literally abandoned. Deserted.

What to do? Collazo asked himself, for he himself was one of many who could not stand the tropical heat of a Cuban summer—and least of all, this one.

It was then that someone mentioned a magical word to the old man.

And that magical word was: *Guanabo*.

Located east of Havana and framed by mountains, Guanabo—a beach with a beautiful Cuban-Indian name—was a large cove a couple of miles long where the sand had not been trod on for centuries, and where the virgin sea was still crystal clear.

The moment he saw it, Collazo fell in love with the place. He immediately decided to build an extension of his literary club right there, at the very edge of the sea, for he was sure that there, in Guanabo, not only would people be able to argue politics and literature, but they would be able to do it half naked, as they went in and out of a placid sea that welcomed with its coolness the overheated bodies of all the members of the literary club as well as those of Collazo's employees, their buddies, and friends.

Collazo was right. No sooner were the footings dug in the sand, on the first working day of the new year, 1939, than requests for membership began to overflow his office. Collazo was in paradise. He knew that something good was bound to come of the interchange of ideas that would take place among all these men and women—the best Cuba had to offer. And that he, Collazo, would have something to do with it. He thought that what El Club Cultural stood for would be his legacy to Cuba, a land that had welcomed him, a soldier with no fortune, and had adopted him with open arms.

Maximiliano the butcher was in his own right a founding member of El Club Cultural. Because of the excellent lyrics he had written to many Cuban songs, Maximiliano was personally invited to join the club by Collazo himself—who at the time had no idea that Maximiliano's daughter, Marguita, was married to Lorenzo, who worked as a bookkeeping clerk in Collazo's main bookstore in Old Havana. It was also Collazo himself who invited Maximiliano to the grand opening of El Club Cultural in Guanabo. When Collazo told the butcher about his forthcoming plans for the official opening of the building, Maximiliano suggested to the old peddler, "Why don't you invite

Father Francisco to perform the ceremony? After all," Maximiliano added, "that crafty old priest is not only good company, but he's also excellent at that business of sprinkling water."

Despite their many differences—or maybe because of them—Maximiliano and Father Francisco started a feuding friendship the day of little Renzo's christening, after Father Francisco had conned Maximiliano into entering the old priest's church, something the aging butcher had said he would never do. Those two—Maximiliano and Father Francisco—who seldom talked to each other prior to little Renzo's christening, are now seen frequently in each other's company, arguing about this or that, in an everlasting debate where each of them sticks adamantly to his side of whatever they are arguing about; the two of them thoroughly enjoying these heated debates, as if they were fencing partners. And like fencing partners, no sooner has the match ended than they start to laugh at the whole thing, even though each of them claims he has won the debate.

Intrigued by Maximiliano's words, Collazo decided to meet this notorious Father Francisco, and since the two men are Spaniards, what better way than to ask the Father to join him at El Baturro, one of the most authentic Spanish restaurants in Havana?

There, after eating a succulent noontime meal of Serrano ham and spicy chorizos abundantly accompanied by pitcher after pitcher of an excellent red Rioja wine, the old priest grinned ear to ear as he admitted to the former book peddler, "Why, yes, Señor Collazo. Just as your friend Maximiliano the butcher says, I'm indeed excellent at that business of 'sprinkling water.' And I'll be more than happy to officiate at the opening ceremony of El Club Cultural in Guanabo."

A couple of months later the building was almost finished and the sprinkling ceremony was already scheduled to take place, when an unannounced hurricane appearing out of nowhere badly hit Guanabo Beach, and the sand in front of El Club Cultural, swallowed by the raging sea, receded to almost nothing.

Collazo went to the site with the architect, took a good look around the building, shook his head, and almost wept. He saw his dream collapsing in front of him. He knew that sooner or later there would be another hurricane. And that this next one would probably raze his building to the ground. It was not the money he had spent on the building that he minded—though it was sizable—but the disruption of his dream.

It was then that the architect proposed something that sounded almost unbelievable to Collazo's ears. A graduate of the Havana University School of Architecture, the young man had done advanced structural studies in the United States, and while he was there he had seen old Victorian houses being moved from one place to another by simply being lifted and slid over.

"Maybe we could do the same thing to our building," the young architect said as he stood by Collazo's side. "Since you own plenty of land, we may be able to lift El Club Cultural, slide it back, and set it on new foundations that would be set higher and farther away from the edge of the sea at high tide. Then we may even build a protective berm around it, to act as a barrier against future hurricanes."

"But . . . do you really think that this three-story building can be moved?" an anxious Collazo asked the architect.

"I think it may be possible," answered the young man. "Given that the building was built in the American style, with thin clapboards over a fairly rigid wood structure, it's very light in weight, so . . . I don't know, but we might be able to slide it back, say, a hundred and fifty feet from the edge of the sea at high tide."

Collazo looked the young man in the eye. "Do you really think it can be done?"

"I'd have to bring experts from the United States. But, yes, I think it can be done."

Collazo and the architect were standing on the few scarce feet that separated the building from the edge of the sea, and as they were looking at the building and talking, a wave came in, lapping on the sand really close to where they were standing, threatening to wet their feet.

The architect quickly moved out of the way to avoid it. But not Collazo. Lost in his thoughts, he just stood there, looking at his building as the sea caressed his feet.

"We'll do it!" he said.

Then, realizing his feet were wet, he added jokingly, as he pointed to his shoes and the cuffs of his old suit, which were drenched, "We'll just have to, won't we?"

Everybody thought Collazo was crazy. Nothing like this had ever been attempted in all Cuba. Newspapermen began asking questions as experts came from the United States, looked at the site, shook their heads, took measurements, shook their heads again, had meeting after meeting, remeasured everything one last time, and finally said, "We might be able to do it. But we cannot guarantee it."

"What are our chances?" Collazo asked.

"We'd say fifty-fifty."

That was all Collazo needed to hear.

A new foundation was poured, a high berm was erected on both sides of the building, the structure was raised using several hundred hydraulic jacks strategically placed, the plumbing lines were disconnected, and the day finally came for the building to be moved.

Every newspaper in Cuba had sent reporters and photographers to document either the successful move of the building or its total collapse.

As Cubans were betting heavily—the odds favored total collapse by a huge margin of 17 to 1—several heavy trucks were already where they were supposed to be, aligned and ready to pull the building.

Collazo stood quietly watching the whole operation, until the young architect came over to him.

"We're ready," he said.

Collazo looked at him and smiled.

"All right, then, what are we waiting for?" Moving to the man driving the first truck, Collazo said, "Go!"

The man turned on and revved the engine of his powerful truck, and the man next to him did the same thing, and so did the man next to him, and the next, and the next, and suddenly, the building took a first lurching step that made all the onlookers immediately run for cover. All except Collazo, who stood next to his young architect, a broad smile on his face as he saw the building move first one tiny inch and then the next and then the next.

That was the photograph that appeared on the front page of every Cuban newspaper the next morning: the photo of a big old man, with big hairy ears, a big hairy nose, thick lips, and huge hands who, wearing the same tired old suit he always wore, looked with the sparkling, almost defiant eyes of a young man at a dream coming true.

Bets were eventually settled—but not without a few fistfights here and there.

And the sprinkling ceremony was rescheduled for the last Sunday of the following month, when the building, now in its new location, protected by berms and proudly looking over the ocean it had dared to master, would be finally completed.

The eagerly awaited Sunday finally arrives.

Right after celebrating the early-morning Mass in their little church atop the hill in Luyanó, Father Francisco and his young acolyte, Father Alonso, are at the corner of La Calzada and the Street of the Bulls waiting for the bus to Guanabo Beach.

Painted navy blue inside and out, with golden letters reading GUANABO on the outside, and with tightly packed cane seats inside, this bus departs from Old Havana, where Collazo's bookstore is located, and makes several stops before it reaches its last stop within Havana itself, the barrio of Luyanó. From there the bus heads for Guanabo Beach. This final leg of the trip takes over an hour and a half, for the connecting road between the two places, though occasionally paved, is basically still a dirt road, with deep ruts and barely wide enough for a bus. It is so narrow that when two buses going in opposite directions meet on the road, one of them has to pull to one side to let the other one go by. And then the two buses have to go by so close to each other—and so slowly— that people in one bus can shake hands with people in the other as the buses pass each other.

Carrying with them a large and obviously heavy bag holding all the paraphernalia needed for the blessing ceremony—incense burners, vestments, and the like—as the two priests wait for the bus they blot and blot their sweaty brows with thin cotton handkerchiefs, for both Father Francisco and Father Alonso are wearing old black cassocks, heavily darned but immaculately clean. Like in most Latin American countries, as well as in Spain and Italy, heat or no heat, Cuban priests keep their cassocks on all day long. These black, long-skirted garments are worn on top of their regular clothes— pants and shirt.

There is something about a cassock that seems to remove the man out of the priest—much as a nun's habit removes the woman out of the nun. Therefore the priest becomes in the eyes of most people almost like a eunuch, a man devoid of sexuality; something that priests claim helps them in their mission of caring for all, men and women alike.

Also waiting for the bus and standing next to the two perspiring priests is Maximiliano the butcher, who is dressed impeccably in white, as usual, and who is, as usual, cool as a cucumber. Right by his side, and wearing a light cotton summer dress, made by herself of calico-print fabric remnants, is his wife, Dolores. While cradling in her right arm her baby grandson, little Renzo—just ten months old—Dolores is grabbing with her free hand the hand of her pretty ten-year-old daughter, Perucha. The young girl is exceedingly happy, not only because she is going to the beach—something she has never done before—but primarily because she is wearing a brand-new dress, also made by Dolores, that exactly matches her mother's. The baby's parents, Marguita and Lorenzo, are right behind them, in Hermenegildo's bodega, buying just-out-of-the-oven guava pastries and loaves of Cuban sourdough bread to take on this, their first excursion ever to Guanabo Beach.

Despite how excited Lorenzo was originally about this building and about going to Guanabo Beach, it took a lot of cajoling on Marguita's part to persuade him to come on this trip. Since Lorenzo is now going to the university five nights a week, Sundays are the only days he has some free time to catch up with his studies. And even though he no longer has to work on Saturday afternoons—for Collazo kept his word—when Lorenzo comes home Saturdays after working all morning, he is so exhausted from the busy week that he simply collapses on a bed and passes out. Besides, final exams are just around the corner, so Lorenzo, who felt that he was getting behind in his schoolwork, was very reluctant to come.

But reluctant or not, Marguita had already made up her mind.

And when Marguita—"the mule"—makes up her mind . . .

"Why don't you take your books along with you?" Marguita suggested, using her most mellifluous voice. "You can read in Guanabo as well as you can read here. And as for homework, I'm sure you can use a spare table in the dining room after everybody's had lunch, don't you think?"

Lorenzo looked at Marguita and shook his head. "You don't understand, Marguita," he said, pointing to the books and papers spread all over their dining room table. "Soon the school year will be over and I still have a lot of work to do. Look at this. I have these books to read, and a lot of papers to write, and—"

"But you've been getting straight *A*s. So I'm sure that—"

"That's how I've been getting straight *A*s, Marguita, by studying hard. Wasn't this your idea? That I go to night school?"

This was not going the way Marguita wanted, so she decided to try a different tack.

"But Lorenzo, think of little Renzo. Think how much fun he's going to have at the beach." Still Lorenzo kept shaking his head. "It'll be good for you," Marguita insisted. "You need some time to rest. And so do I," Marguita added. "We all need it," she said, holding her baby next to her. "The three of us, I mean." Seeing Lorenzo still shaking his head, Marguita bit her lip. She was running out of arguments and about to lose her equanimity and explode when one last thought entered her brain.

"All right, you win," she said, as if ready to give up. "We'll stay. But I tell you, Lorenzo, it will be a shame not to go. I mean, with all that beautiful sand, and all that wonderful sky, and all that glorious sun . . . can you imagine the great photographs you could take at the beach?"

The minute he heard that magical word, *photographs*, Lorenzo's ears pricked up.

For little Renzo's christening, Lorenzo's family, all of them chipping in together, gave Lorenzo a genuine Kodak camera.

"So we can have photographs of the baby," Lorenzo's mother said.

Obviously smuggled from the United States—for it was dirt cheap—this camera was one of Kodak's more complete models. It came with a flash attachment including a package of disposable bulbs and already loaded with a roll of black-and-white film, the only kind available then. Carefully following the Spanish version of the multilingual instructions included with it, Lorenzo shot the entire roll of film during Renzito's christening party.

A week and a half later Lorenzo went to the studio where the photos had been developed and printed to pick them up. Tiny as they were—not quite two by three inches, with serrated edges—the photographs were nonetheless wonderful. In one of them, a beaming Carmela, entirely dressed in black as always, her glossy white hair tied up in her usual bun, was seen standing up, holding in her wrinkled old hands her first grandson, little Renzo, a tiny baby wrapped in a long white lace christening gown and peacefully sleeping, while behind them Padrón, totally bald and like Carmela also dressed entirely in black, stood looking down with admiring eyes at the baby in Carmela's arms.

That photo did it.

It was a beautiful composition in almost pure black and white, yes—but in addition it had soul. The people in the photograph had been captured alive in a moment of great intimacy. Love permeated the photograph so completely that everybody who looked at it had no choice but to smile.

When Lorenzo went to pick up the photographs, the man who ran the studio told Lorenzo that he would let him have a free enlargement of that photo if Lorenzo would give him permission to make one for himself, so he could place it in the display window outside his studio.

When he heard that, Lorenzo was more than thrilled.

He instantly gave the go-ahead to the man, and a week later, when he went back to the studio to pick up his own copy, there it was, his photograph, in the studio's display window, beautifully framed.

Needless to say, from that moment on, Lorenzo was hooked on photography.

So when he heard Marguita say "photographs," and he thought of all of that beautiful sand, and all of that wonderful sky, and all of that glorious sun that Marguita had so dreamily referred to . . . no wonder his ears pricked up.

Looking at him from the corner of her eye, Marguita, smiling to herself, pretended she had not noticed anything. "Well," she said, sighing dramatically, "I guess we'll go to Guanabo some other time."

But of course, she knew better.

After what seems to be the longest wait ever, the Guanabo bus finally arrives.

It is over twenty minutes late, and the driver, annoyed by the almost incredible heat, and by the clattering people inside, and by the unbelievable bumper-to-bumper traffic, and by God knows what else, is fuming.

"Let's go, let's go," the driver keeps repeating and repeating as Father Francisco and Father Alonso get on. Behind them, as he helps Dolores into the bus, Maximiliano shouts to Marguita and Lorenzo, "Hurry up, people. The bus is leaving!"

Impatient cars behind the stationary bus begin to honk louder and louder as Marguita, dressed in a homemade pale-green cotton dress with a matching kerchief on her head, rushes to the bus, while Lorenzo, still at the counter of the bodega, is vainly looking in his back pocket for a wallet he does not seem to be able to find.

"Tell Hermenegildo we'll pay him later on, when we come back," Maximiliano shouts to Lorenzo. "Hurry up, Lorenzo. Come on! We got to go!"

Lorenzo rushes to the bus that has already started to move, and though he is carrying a huge paper bag in his right hand, he jumps on, hanging on for his life with his left hand to a handle by the door. Just then, the driver suddenly changes gear, jostling everybody as he violently maneuvers the bus around a sharp corner.

Inside the bus, people already sitting down stand up so they can begin to greet enthusiastically the new arrivals: the men with deeply felt man-to-man hugs; the women with lots of kisses which are only aimed at each other's cheeks but which are not carried through, for no woman wants to smudge her friend's makeup—and least of all her very own. Everybody seems to be so excited about this trip that the noise level inside the bus rivals if not outdoes the traffic noises outside.

Father Francisco and his young assistant, Father Alonso, walk to the end of the bus, where they see several scattered empty seats. A man stands up, letting Father Francisco take the window seat next to him, while Father Alonso finds an aisle seat two rows behind the old priest. Since he is the acolyte, Father Alonso is the one carrying the heavy bag that holds what is needed for the ceremony. He stands up to place it in the luggage rack above, made of thick jute strings tightly interwoven, and as he does, he has a strange sensation, as if someone were looking intently at him.

Still with the bag in his hands, he turns and glances around the bus.

There, in a rear corner, he sees a slender woman dressed all in black who is looking out the window with sad, distant eyes. He recognizes her, for he met her during little Renzo's christening party: Lorenzo's deaf sister, Asunción.

Sitting next to Asunción, on the aisle seat, is another slender woman. But this one is dressed in a white, gauzy, almost transparent dress, and has a glowing face beautifully framed by the glossiest black hair ever, tied in a tight bun at the back of her neck: Asunción's sister, Loló.

And yet, though he recognizes her, and though he knows she is there, Father Alonso almost fails to see her. For all he can really see are those dark, gypsy eyes of hers, mysterious and penetrating as ever, which are fastened on his, peering at him searchingly.

Surprised by those searing eyes that seem to burn through his skin, Father Alonso's heavy bag slips from his hands just as the bus makes one more sharp turn—but he is able to catch it before it falls to the floor, or on somebody's head.

People around the young Spanish priest instantly shout, "Hey, Father, watch it! That stuff looks like it weighs a ton!"

Hearing this, Father Francisco turns to his young assistant.

"Be careful, Father Alonso," the old priest says, "these sudden Cuban turns can be mighty dangerous and you may fall easily. Hold on tight to something."

Father Alonso manages to place the bag in the luggage rack, sits quietly, and though he still feels those mystifying eyes of Loló's behind him, he does not look back.

Instead, he takes out his rosary, and, closing his eyes, begins to pray, clasping his rosary so tightly that his knuckles turn white.

But no matter how tightly he clasps his rosary, he cannot control the blood rushing through his body, nor the feeling of that thing that hangs between his legs that, though hiding behind an emasculating black cassock aimed at making a eunuch out of a man, all of a sudden seems to be standing at attention.

fourteen

On the crowded and overheated bus lurching along the narrow dirt road that leads to Guanabo Beach, Father Alonso closes his eyes and prays and prays as hard as he can, trying to ignore what his body is telling him. But to no avail. No matter how hard he prays, his body will not respond to his prayers any more than his mind will not forget those dark, gypsy eyes of Loló's.

But then Father Alonso realizes that those dark, gypsy eyes of hers remind him of another set of dark, gypsy eyes. And then his mind travels back to a time long before he had become a priest and had chosen "Alonso" as his ordained name; a disquieting time when he began to feel the pains of puberty and he discovered, to his dismay, that his heart's desires were centered not on girls but on boys.

No, not on boys, but on a single boy. A schoolmate of his, his very own age.

Felipe Montalvo.

Wasn't that the reason he entered the service of the church? Because of what he thought was his unnatural attraction to Felipe?

A not too tall, not too handsome boy, with a broken nose, broad shoulders, and a broader smile framed by dimples, Felipe excelled in sports, and was one of the very few boys in the private Catholic school the two boys attended befriending the young man who would eventually become Father Alonso—at the time a teenage boy, deeply troubled by his inner life, who avoided facing it by immersing himself in his studies.

Why he and Felipe took to each other, Father Alonso cannot explain, even to this very day.

It just happened, Father Alonso recalls.

It all started when he began tutoring his classmate Felipe as an act of charity—or so he told himself—in algebra and geometry, subjects that were required for graduation, but subjects that Felipe had failed twice.

Felipe did manage to pass those subjects, and with excellent grades, and in the process, he and Felipe became intimate friends, spending a great deal of time together. So much so that before he knew it, he, who had never liked sports before, began to practice and enjoy them, although he was not particularly good at any of them—except for swimming, which he and Felipe really loved and at which the two of them excelled. This made both their parents extremely happy, for they could see how each boy was affecting the other, and for the better.

It wasn't unusual to see him and his friend Felipe laughing at the top of their lungs as they jumped on their bicycles at the end of the school day, race as fast as they could to a secret place of their own—

a very large pond, almost a lake, hidden halfway between their town and the next one—and once there, quickly strip off their clothes, dive fearlessly into the dark, almost black waters, and swim vigorously and at top speed to a large rock ledge directly opposite them.

It happened during one of those swimming sessions, while they were sitting naked on the large rock ledge that defiantly protruded over what the two boys called *nuestro lago secreto*—"our secret lake."

He caught himself staring at Felipe with questioning eyes for a long, long time, seeing Felipe as he had never seen him before. His eyes first noticed the thick black hair that almost overnight had sprouted in Felipe's armpits. Then, those astonished eyes of his slowly slid down Felipe's naked body, noticing, as if for the first time, his friend's broad shoulders, muscular arms, and powerful chest, until he ended up staring at the thick black mane of hair that encircled Felipe's manly organ, which proclaimed to the world that Felipe was no longer a boy but a true man—handsome, beautifully developed, and beautifully endowed by Nature.

No sooner had his eyes focused on Felipe's engorged sex than he felt that thing that up till then had just hung flaccidly between his legs get instantly stiff and hard—as thick and as engorged with pulsating life as Felipe's. It was then that he raised his puzzled and astounded eyes to Felipe's face, only to catch Felipe's puzzled and astounded eyes staring back at him. And he thought that he saw the question rushing through his own mind mirrored in Felipe's dark, almost black eyes. Cryptic, mystical eyes that seemed to belong in the face of a Gypsy man.

That was all.

Nothing else ever happened between the two of them.

But right after that day, claiming an infinite number of reasons, he and Felipe stopped seeing each other altogether. He went back to his studies, Felipe to his sports.

It wasn't long after that that he announced his decision to join the church and become a priest.

The day after he and Felipe caught themselves staring at each other—a look that had been laden with hidden urges and with scorching desire burning deeply within their eyes—troubled beyond comprehension, he went to his mentor and confessor, Father Cristóbal, and told him about what had happened between him and another boy, not mentioning Felipe by name.

Father Cristóbal tried to make light of the whole thing.

"Things like that happen to a lot of boys your age," the priest told the young boy kneeling in front of him, "so you do not have to worry about it. Nevertheless, to avoid any further problems, the best way is to keep from exposing yourself to temptation, as you well know. So from now on, keep away as much as possible from that other boy. In fact," Father Cristóbal went on, "it's best that you and that other boy do not see each other again for the time being. And pray, my son, for God to illuminate you and to guide you." Father Cristóbal paused for a second, just to add, "As I will pray for you."

What he never knew—what Father Cristóbal never told him—was that earlier that very same day "that other boy," his friend Felipe, troubled—like him—beyond comprehension, had come to confession, had told the old priest the identical story, and had received the identical advice from Father Cristóbal.

Weeks later, after going to his trusted mentor and telling him about his decision to join the church, he looked into the kind eyes of Father Cristóbal.

"Are you sure of your call?" Father Cristóbal asked the person kneeling in front of him, who was no longer a boy but now a young man.

Keeping his eyes downcast, he nodded. "Yes, Father, I am."

"My son," Father Cristóbal said, "the church is a mission, not an escape. It is not a place for a man to hide, either. No matter how much he would like to, a man can never, ever evade life. He would only fool himself if he tried that. A man must face life with a lot of courage and bend it to his will. Only then can a man call himself a man, for only then can a man call himself free. And only then can a man offer his soul to the service of God. Only then. When he is free. Free to look at all the options in front of him, free to weigh them carefully, and free to choose. Wisely. Never in fear, but with manly courage. Do you understand what I am trying to say?" the old priest asked, his voice earnest. "Have you studied your options and have you chosen properly, out of courage, and not out of fear? *Have* you, my son? Have you?"

"Yes, Father, I have," he answered decisively, without the least hesitation. "And no, Father, I'm not evading anything. Nor am I hiding from anything. I've felt the call of God. I have. It's right here, in my heart," he said, his voice overflowing with sincerity as he touched his chest. Then he looked his mentor in the eye. "I've prayed and prayed, asking God to guide me and illuminate my path, as you told me I should do. And God himself has been kind enough to answer my prayers."

"Well, then, my son," said Father Cristóbal, as he made the sign of the cross above the head of the young man kneeling in front of him, "may the will of God be done."

I thought the will of God had been done, thinks Father Alonso as he sits in the Guanabo bus and rubs and rubs the tired beads of his old rosary.

But was I mistaken back then? the young priest asks himself as he keeps on praying and praying, trying to erase from his mind those dark, gypsy eyes of Loló's, which were as laden with desire as those other dark, gypsy eyes of Felipe's had been.

Was I mistaken about Felipe? Father Alonso asks himself again. And about me? And about my call?

He shakes his head in utter confusion.

Was I mistaken, then . . . about everything?

PART FOUR

Unicorn

fifteen

Guanabo Beach is what everybody has been told and much more.

And so is El Club Cultural.

The moment people disembark the bus, after they stretch themselves for a second or so and inhale the pure ocean air of the almost virgin beach, they rush inside the brand-new building going Ooohhh! and Aaahhh! Money was certainly no object. Señor Collazo the book peddler may be a miser in his personal life, that's for sure, "but he certainly knows how to spend his money," people tell each other as they run up and down the stairs looking at the generous dining room below, at the huge game room above, and at the spacious locker rooms on either side of the wide entrance hall.

The ladies' locker room has individual showers and individual dressing cubicles, each with sliding sand-colored drapes, so a woman can change into her bathing suit in total privacy, as ladies' modesty requires. Men's locker rooms are not like that, of course, since criollo men are not meant to be modest about anything. Men have no individual changing areas, just a bunch of lockers with long narrow benches in between; and no individual showers, but a communal room with a dozen showerheads evenly spaced along three walls. People love the building, praising now this, now that. But what makes everybody go absolutely crazy is when they find out that the showers have both cold *and* hot water! "Now, *that* is the epitome of luxury," people tell each other.

Within minutes the lockers are all taken, all of them stuffed with everything from straw hats and suntan oil to parasols and diapers. But much as they all would like to, people have not yet changed into their bathing suits.

No. Not until after the religious ceremony is over.

Since everybody wants to cool down and swim in the turquoise sea—so they can then try the new cold and hot showers—they all begin to look with eager eyes at the two priests, Maximiliano first.

"Well, Father Francisco," he says as he holds open the door to the second-floor bedroom which has been assigned for the priests' private use, "let's hurry up and get on with the sprinkling bit."

Father Francisco pretends to ignore him and instead addresses his young acolyte.

"Father Alonso," the old priest says as he begins to rummage through his things, "I seem to have misplaced my sermon. Do you happen to—"

"Sermon?" an astounded Maximiliano says, interrupting Father Francisco before he can finish his sentence. "Nobody told me anything about a sermon. I thought all you were going to do was to sprinkle a little water and say a few Latin words and that was that."

"But my son," says a very serious Father Francisco, "Señor Collazo is paying us so handsomely to bless his building that we figured the least we could do was to let him have a little sermon. I don't want him to think we're cheating him out of his money, which as you know, is what a lot of badly intentioned people think we clerics do all the time." He sighs. "I wonder what I did with that sermon. After I worked so hard to trim it down and keep it as short as I could."

He faces Maximiliano. "You know what Voltaire used to say," he goes on, looking intently at the butcher. "He wrote a letter to some lady friend of his and in a postscript he added, 'I'm sorry this letter is so long, but I didn't have time to make it shorter.'" The old priest sighs again. "Well, I guess it's the same with me. If I don't find that sermon, I'll just have to improvise it, and then it'll probably be a lot longer than it should be. But, what can I do? I hope I didn't leave it behind."

"I'm surprised you should be quoting someone like Voltaire," Maximiliano says, still at the door. "Wasn't he a heretic who hated your kind of a church?"

"But he did write well, my son, very well indeed," the old priest answers. "Truth is truth. And in matters of truth I would quote not only a heretic like Voltaire but anybody, even you, Maximiliano. I'd even quote some of your own lyrics if that would make me a better priest."

Maximiliano shakes his head in silent exasperation. Then he leaves the room, quietly closing the door after him.

"Father Francisco," Father Alonso says as he spreads the contents of his bag on top of one of the beds in the room, "I don't remember seeing you writing a sermon for this—"

"I didn't?" Father Francisco interrupts. "I thought I did." He pauses, mischief in his old eyes. "Well, maybe I didn't," he adds, smiling at the young priest. "I must be getting old. That's probably what it is. Getting old. Maybe even too old."

Father Alonso hands Father Francisco the first of the several vestments needed for the ceremony and as he does, Father Francisco looks at his acolyte, noticing something different in the eyes of the young man; eyes that usually are limpid and clear, but that now seem furtive. Even evasive. Father Francisco asks himself, Why? And then he remembers seeing that woman Loló, on the bus; catching her staring at Father Alonso; and catching him staring back at her. And he remembers Father Alonso telling the old priest in confession how disconcerted he had been when Loló first set her eyes on him during little Renzo's christening party at Maximiliano's house. Is this what's disquieting my boy? the old man asks himself. His duty both as a priest and as the young man's mentor compels him to find out.

"You know, Father Alonso," he says, apparently continuing along his previous line of thought about getting old, "I never dreamed I'd be as old as I am. But let me share a secret with you. I'm really glad I am." He smiles knowingly at his acolyte. "Somehow the desires of the flesh are much less powerful when one reaches my age."

Upon hearing this, Father Alonso almost drops the thin white cotton garment he is holding in his hands.

"Desires of the flesh, Father?" he asks, his voice shaken. "*You?*"

"Oh, yes, my son," the old priest answers as he spreads open his arms to allow Father Alonso to help him get dressed. "One is only human, you know. God made me a man. And the man in me occasionally looks at the world with desirous eyes. And at women, too, I'm not ashamed to confess. The sex drive is a very powerful tool God has given all of us. But the priest in me has been able to transform that drive into my calling. And I think—I know—it has made me into a better priest. But it wasn't that easy, you know," the old priest adds, looking squarely at Father Alonso. "Several times I asked myself if I had made a mistake, choosing this life. After all, one can be working for God just as well whether one is a married man or a priest."

The young priest evades Father Francisco's inquisitive look as he begins to button the back of the semitransparent chasuble the old priest is now wearing atop his black cassock.

The old priest continues.

"One time I was really close to calling it quits. It can get mighty lonely being a priest, my son, mighty lonely. I was torn by my desires pulling me one way and my mission calling me the other way. All the vows I took when I was a young man like you were crumbling about me. For days I couldn't sleep. Until one night, in total despair, I knelt by the side of my bed and I repeated aloud all those vows I had taken. It was like"—the old priest pauses as if searching for the the right word and faces Father Alonso who is now looking intently at the old man—"like a confirmation. That's what it was like. Words I had barely meant when I was made into a priest all of a sudden acquired a different meaning, a full meaning." He smiles at Father Alonso. "That night, my son, I truly became a priest. That night I was ordained not by a bishop who is but a man, but by God himself. I felt his grace invading my soul. That night, my mission won. And it has been winning since then."

The old man chuckles. "Of course, that doesn't mean I cannot still see the beauty that hides in women's eyes. Yes, don't look so astounded. Even at my age, I do. But ever since that night I see that beauty as the work of God. And every time I see it, I thank God for it. As I thank him for giving me a helping hand when I needed it the most. If that ever happens to you, my son, do not ever hesitate to come to me and—"

An impatient knocking is heard at the door.

"Oh, Father Alonso," the old priest says, interrupting himself, "we better get going. These Cubans, they cannot wait to take their clothes off and go swimming!" He faces the door. "We'll be right out!" he shouts and then, turning, hurriedly gathers his things, readying himself to leave the room.

"But, what about your sermon, Father? Are you going to—" the young priest begins to ask as he lights the myrrh incense inside the silver thurible.

"It seems to me I've already talked enough for one day, don't you think, Father Alonso? I barely have any voice left. So, let's just go, do our sprinkling business, and bless this beautiful world we live in. There, my son," he adds, pointing to the door, "you lead the way."

The religious blessing of El Club Cultural is quite a beautiful ceremony in its austere simplicity. Men and women in lines follow the two priests as they slowly parade from one room of the building to the next, saying one Latin word after another as they do their sprinkling business.

When they climb the stairs to to the second floor, as they turn a corner, for a brief moment the eyes of Father Alonso lock on the eyes of Loló.

Seeing the beauty that hides inside those dark, gypsy eyes of hers—which remind him so much of Felipe's equally dark and equally gypsylike eyes—Father Alonso smiles at her, an open smile filled with admiration.

But this smile totally surprises and disarms Loló, who cannot tell what that smile means.

True, Loló has seen many a manly smile aimed at her. But those have always been intensely suggestive smiles accompanied by leering looks; smiles and looks that answered Loló's piercing way of looking. Still, Loló's drilling eyes have never been answered by the kind of gentle smile Father Alonso is giving her. Honest. Sincere. Devoid of the devouring intensity with which other men have always looked back at her.

This other smile of the young priest's is so different, Loló thinks.

Then, almost unaware that she is doing it, as she sees Father Alonso smile at her, Loló returns the young priest's smile with a smile of her own: a small smile that is barely perceptible. But a small smile that is, nonetheless, as gentle, as honest, and as sincere as Father Alonso's.

And as Loló smiles back at the young priest, she sees the kind, gentle eyes of Father Alonso brighten up and sparkle.

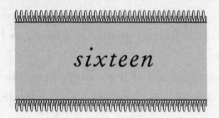

sixteen

The moment Father Francisco and his young acolyte do their final bit of sprinkling with holy water, and El Club Cultural is thus considered officially blessed by the hand of God, all the men, women, and children cross themselves, as they have been instructed to do. And then, after a barely concealed collective sigh of relief, they all run precipitously into the locker rooms, just to reappear, seconds later, dressed for a swim.

Barely covering their hairy chests with tight tank tops attached by buttons and belts to tighter bathing trunks that fully reveal their male anatomy in rigorous detail, the men, both young and old, after making sure that the women are looking at them, rush across the wide expanse of golden sand in front of El Club Cultural and jump fearlessly into the cool waters of El Mar del Norte—the North Sea—as Cubans call the little bit of water that separates the island of Cuba from the North American continent.

After they have let the men display themselves, the women, more modest and much less aggressive, wearing one-piece bathing suits with mid-thigh skirts, their heads covered with rubber bathing caps, daintily cross the beach and enter the ocean waters one step at a time. But not before they cross themselves—just in case they should drown, God forbid! in the shallow waters. And not before they sprinkle themselves with a few drops of the ocean water so their fragile bodies will not go into sudden spasms, as they have been forewarned by their elders can happen when bodies heated under the steamy tropical sun are suddenly exposed to the ocean's cool waters.

Why this should happen only to women and not to men is a mystery that the Cuban criollo lore has yet to explain.

Sure, at first there are a few young men who tease the girls and threaten to splash cold water on them; and sure, there are a few girls who scream, "Don't you dare!" as they all giggle and laugh. But soon after, men, women, and children have scattered all over the limpid sea, creating here and there groups of people, of whom only the heads are visible, for their bodies hide beneath the surface of the water, enjoying its precious coolness under the ardent tropical sun. Elderly matrons partly immersed in the water but remaining close to the sandy beach talk to other elderly matrons, thoroughly enjoying their perennial gossip as they pretend to care for the young children around them, while the shrill voice of a mother is occasionally heard shouting, "Juanito, don't go too far!" or seconds later, "Juanito, leave your sister alone!"

Meanwhile, as the young men and women gravitate toward each other—as young men and women everywhere are bound to do—and begin to play games or hold a conversation, the ever-present and ever-cautious chaperones, sitting on the sand and protected from the hot sun by huge straw hats or large beach umbrellas, keep their vigilant, eagle-sharp eyes on them.

Back in their second-floor room, Father Alonso is helping Father Francisco out of his garments, and as he does, he looks through the window at the distant ocean that seems to be so cool and so inviting. Father Francisco turns and catches his young acolyte looking out the window.

"Do you know how to swim, Father Alonso?" the old priest asks.

Father Alonso realizes that he has been caught looking with wistful eyes at the alluring sea. He blushes.

"I do. Back home, when I was a kid, we all did. Even after I entered the seminary, sometimes it would get so hot during the summers, a couple of us boys used to go to a nearby lake, take off our cassocks, and swim in our underwear. At times even naked—if nobody was watching. I used to love that," he adds, remembering how he and Felipe used to go swimming; remembering how he stole glances at Felipe that day as the two of them, naked, stepped out of the lake; remembering how beautiful and tempting the unruly mane of black hair encircling Felipe's manhood was; remembering how many times he was awakened from his sleep by the uncontrollable and violent spurting of his own body as he dreamed of Felipe, and of what he and Felipe were doing to each other.

"Well, then, why don't you go for a swim now?" Father Francisco asks, awakening Father Alonso from his reverie.

"Oh, no, Father Francisco," a disconcerted Father Alonso responds. "I couldn't do that. Not here, I don't think."

"Why not? Cuban waters are heavenly," the old priest says. "They are warm, but never too warm, nor ever too cool. Just that. Heavenly. I myself would love to go for a swim, but at my age, I'm afraid I'd catch a cold. But you . . . you're a young man. And swimming is such a great exercise, so why don't you go ahead and—"

"But Father Francisco, I'm a priest. It wouldn't look good for a priest to—"

"Nonsense! Priests are men, and men need to exercise to keep their bodies in shape. You know the Latin saying: *Mens sana in corpore sano*. Healthy minds inside healthy bodies. So to keep that mind of yours healthy, you must keep your body healthy. God wants it that way. So go for a swim. It's no sin to enjoy life, Father Alonso. After all, happiness is a way of praying. It's a way of giving thanks. I'm sure our Lord himself was a very happy man. Just as I am sure he went swimming with his apostles, just for the fun of it. He was a man too, don't you ever forget that. He loved life. Like we all do."

"But, but—" Father Alonso begins to say and stops.

Then, after a short pause, he adds, "You really think I can do it? I didn't bring anything—"

"Look, my son, take your cassock off, leave it hanging here, and go out using those back stairs," Father Francisco says, pointing to the exit stairs back of the club. "In your shirt and pants, nobody will even realize you were the young priest who came with me. And even if they did, they won't care. Then go for a nice walk along the beach. This beach seems to be very long and mostly deserted—at least that's what it looked like from the bus as we drove in. Believe me, I'm sure you'll find a suitable place where you can take your pants off and get in the ocean in your underwear. It'll be fun, I tell you. By the time you get back here, your underwear will be totally dried by the Cuban sun, I guarantee it, and nobody will know a thing. So go, have fun. You've been working so hard, you deserve it. Tell you what, if you wait for me, I'll go with you. I love to walk barefoot on the sand, right by the edge of the water, and get my feet wet. If you do that, your feet won't get too hot or burn. Maybe I'll even get in the water," the old priest adds as he sighs. "What do you say?"

Moments later, two barefoot men—one old, the other one much, much younger—exit El Club Cultural by the back stairs and begin walking along the sandy beach right at the edge of the water, letting their naked feet be caressed every so often by the coolness of the gentle ebb and flow of the sea lapping at them.

After a little while they each roll their dark pants up to about midcalf, so the pants will not get wet. Then, realizing that the beach is indeed mostly deserted and that the few people there, enjoying the inviting cool waters, are not paying any attention whatsoever to either of them, as they turn a bend, the younger of the two of them takes off first his shirt and then his undershirt, revealing the very pale, tight, muscular torso of a young man who is barely three, four years past being a teenager.

It doesn't take long before the older man, beginning to get tired from all that walking and walking under the scorching Cuban sun, finds a cool place away from the beach shaded by palm trees, right where the sand gives way to soft, mossy vegetation, and there he sits down, leaning against a couple of boulders. "I'll rest here a while, maybe even take a little nap," Father Francisco tells his young acolyte. "You go swim. Enjoy yourself. Then come pick me up, so we can go back together. Oh, and if you decide to take a little nap, which I highly recommend," the old man says, pointing to the canopies of the trees above him, "find a shady place like this. Just make sure you don't lie down under coconut trees like those over there. Believe me, you sure don't want a coconut to fall on your head!" Father Francisco adds, chuckling.

"Don't worry, Father," Father Alonso replies. "I'll make sure I follow your advice. Don't I always?" he adds as he places his shirt and undershirt in a bundle next to the old priest.

Then, after looking all about him and realizing that the two of them are totally alone on this segment of the beach, the young man takes off his black trousers, lets them fall on the sand right by Father Francisco, who is already beginning to snore, and in his baggy, pleated cotton boxer shorts, the young priest, now almost a child again, rushes to the ocean, where he dives into the water, praying in his happiness as he enjoys the heavenly beauty of it all.

seventeen

Marguita is on the sand, playing with her little boy, Renzito.

Claiming that she has gained a lot of weight while trying to produce enough milk for her child—something that didn't work, for Renzito has been exclusively on a formula for the last few months—she elected not to go into the water, for she didn't want people to see her in that condition, not until after she has shed those twenty-odd pounds she has gained since little Renzo was born. "It's one thing to have a well-rounded figure," she told herself. "Another, to be plump—if not chubby. Or worse." So she is still wearing the same pale-green dress and the same pale-green kerchief over her golden hair she was wearing when the two priests blessed El Club Cultural, while little Renzo, just a day past ten months old, is lying on a soft blanket Marguita brought for that purpose.

Lorenzo is not far from them.

Camera in hand, he is walking around his family, looking at the two of them—Marguita and little Renzo playing with each other—through the viewfinder of his little Kodak.

"Let the boy alone," he says. "Let me see what he does."

Marguita moves out of the way and stands behind Lorenzo who is aiming the camera at his son. The baby, who is naked beneath a pale green cotton tunic, lifts his arms and looks hesitantly at his parents. A sudden gust of breeze makes some sand fly into the baby's face and he begins to cry.

Marguita begins to rush to him.

"Don't," Lorenzo tells her, "let me shoot him first."

But Marguita will never listen to anyone while her baby is crying. Lorenzo is barely able to snap a photograph of the boy seconds before Marguita reaches her son.

"Oh, *amorcito mío,* don't cry, don't cry," she says, her musical voice almost a song. "Let's play. Here, let's play." She begins to clap her hands. "Clap and clap and clap we go," she sings, a childish singsong she herself has made up that usually quiets her pretty baby with the long blond curly hair.

But not this time.

This time, despite the clapping and clapping of Marguita's hands, little Renzo is still crying. "Look, my little love, look. Look," Marguita says as she kneels by the side of the blanket, grabs a little bit of sand in her two hands and shows it to her son as she lets some of it fall through her sieving fingers. "Look. Look!"

"Marguita, Marguita. Don't move! Just look up. At me!"

Marguita lifts her eyes and smiles broadly at her husband who all of a sudden snaps a photograph of her just as another gust of wind goes by.

"Oh, Lorenzo, why didn't you tell me you were going to photograph me? I'm not even combed. You probably wasted it."

"No, I didn't. I've never seen you look so happy as now, right now." He kneels by her side and whispers, "If it weren't because of all these people around us, I'd kiss you right here, right now. This is how I'm planning to remember you for the rest of my life. You're just incandescent today."

"Oh," she says, mockingly, "I thought I was always incandescent! Isn't that what you yourself—"

She cannot finish her sentence.

Lorenzo has leaned against her and whether people around them are looking or not, he has grabbed her by surprise and kissed her passionately, a kiss that is broken by the faint sound of something that sounds like applause, for little Renzo, on his blanket, is looking at them and beaming ear to ear as his playful little hands clap against each other.

His joyous clapping make his parents laugh.

And when he hears his parents laugh, little Renzo laughs loudly with them as well.

As she goes into the ladies' locker room to put on her bathing suit, Loló is still thinking about Father Alonso's smile, a smile she cannot eradicate from her mind. She is so disconcerted by it that as she begins to take her clothes off, she forgets to slide across her cubicle the curtain that provides and ensures privacy. It is only moments later, when she hears a little girl giggle and say, "Look, Mami, that woman has hair in her peepee!" that she suddenly realizes that though she is still wearing her high-heeled shoes, she is now standing stark naked in the very middle of the ladies' locker room.

As all the other women in the room look at her with censuring eyes, the little girl's mother abruptly pulls the girl out of the way as she utters to Loló, "You should be ashamed of yourself!"

Loló immediately rushes back to her cubicle and slides the curtain across just to remember that she left her bathing suit inside her locker. That was why I was crossing the locker room, to go to my locker to get my bathing suit, she tells herself. Well, they've seen me naked once, they can see me naked again. So, naked as she is, she steps out of her cubicle, crosses the room under the accusing eyes of the rest of the women inside, and goes to her locker, where she finds her bathing suit. She takes her shoes off and begins to get into her bathing suit, and as she does, she pauses, again remembering the beautiful smile Father Alonso had given her.

"Isn't there an empty cubicle where you can change?" an irate woman barks at her. "There are children around here. Little boys and girls. They don't need to see a grown-up woman like you walking around naked!"

Loló ignores her. She continues to change where she is, standing by her locker, as women dart around her, getting into their private cubicles and forcefully closing their curtains as a sign of resentment.

Loló's sister, Asunción, rushes into the locker room and goes to Loló.

"Loló, please," she implores in that chalky voice of hers. Loló looks at Asunción and raises and lowers her hand several times, making the sign everybody in the family makes to Asunción when she is speaking too loud. But Asunción will pay no attention to Loló's gesturing. She grabs her sister and begins to take her into an empty cubicle.

"Some lady came to get me. Please, Loló, go change inside a cubicle. I'll bring you whatever you need. So—"

Loló brusquely separates herself from her sister and looks at the women glaring at her. Then turns to her sister, mouthing her words so Asunción the deaf, who reads lips, can understand them. "It's none of those women's business to—"

"Loló, please," Asunción interrupts her. "Let's not make a big deal out of—"

"No, let's not," an angry Loló says as she places the last strap of the top of her bathing suit in place and exits the locker room in a huff, slamming the door and leaving her embarrassed sister behind, who silently bends down, picks up Loló's shoes, and places them inside Loló's locker.

Who the hell do those women think they are, Loló is telling herself as she begins to walk along the wide hallway that separates the men's locker room from the women's. Are those women so ashamed of themselves that they cannot stand to see a woman naked? For God's sake, I didn't even mean to do it. It was all because of that damn young priest. I wish he had not smiled at me the way he did. I was just so upset by—

Her thoughts change course when, in the distance, she sees Marguita coming in from outside, carrying her baby in her arms.

I don't want to see Marguita, she tells herself. Then shakes her head. No, the truth is I don't want Marguita to see *me,* she corrects herself as she turns around and exits El Club Cultural through the back door.

She still doesn't know what made her go into Marguita's and Lorenzo's bedroom that night over a year ago, when she stood at the foot of their bed and looked at them as they made love in the moonlight. She had looked at her brother and his wife in a detached way, as if she were not there, as if she were in a different room altogether, a scientist just looking at them, her subjects of observation.

It all seemed so simple, she told herself then as she watched.

She had heard a lot about the act of love. But she was not sure she could trust what she had heard.

She has yet to see a man naked. Even that night, she saw neither Lorenzo nor Marguita fully naked as they made love, for most of the time both of them were hidden beneath a cotton sheet and lit only by the pale-blue light of the moon. She just saw shadows moving, that was all. And heard those shadows moaning. It had been that moaning that awakened her as she slept in the room next door. And then she could not go back to sleep.

She kept telling herself not to get up from her bed, not to go to their room, not to look.

But she found herself doing it nonetheless—standing near the foot of their bed as if paralyzed, unable to do anything but observe. And then she remembers Marguita's eyes looking at her, eyes that went from shock to horror to embarrassment to rage to hate. It was only then that she, Loló, realized what she had done and, shocked at herself for having done it, left the room in a hurry, rushed back to hers, and threw herself onto her bed. Only to lie awake all night long.

The next day, Marguita and Lorenzo moved out of the house.

Loló didn't blame them.

If she had been Marguita, she would have done the same thing. She knows she was at fault. But on the other hand, she also knows she couldn't control herself. Like there are so many times she has not been able to control herself.

What is wrong with me? she often asks herself. Why do I have these urges? Why can't I be like the rest of the women? Like Asunción, for instance. Does she have these urges? Has she ever? Did my sister Lucinda have them? Or am I the only one in my family to feel these desires? Desires to be free. To do as I want—whether people like it or not.

She has never experienced the act of love. She has no idea what it will be like. Seeing a man naked in front of her. Having him caress and play with her body, as if her body were his. And his, hers. Opening up to him. Feeling the hardness of him inside her. And as she thinks that, and as her body begins to tremble with desire, she tries and tries to shake those thoughts from her mind. After all, she tells herself, she is Loló, ugly Loló, mare-faced Loló, thirty-one-year-old Loló, Loló the spinster. Loló the virgin. And like all virgins, she is afraid of the unicorn of man. And yet there is nothing more she desires than exposing herself to it.

Either to tame it.

Or to die from it.

She has been so submerged in her thoughts that she has not realized that she has been walking aimlessly along the beach, getting away from those women, and from that locker room, and from El Club Cultural.

Now she wishes she had not come. But Lorenzo had been insistent. And at the time it all seemed extremely exciting: to come and see this handsome building that is so close to the sea it seems as if the sea and the sand and the building were each a part of each other.

But now . . . now she does not think it was such a good idea after all.

Her thoughts travel back to Lorenzo, her little brother Lorenzo, who is as good as they come. She knows that ever since that night over a year ago he has been trying to make peace between Marguita and her.

Loló sighs. She has nothing against Marguita.

Well, yes, perhaps a little bit of envy. Marguita seems to be so happy, so contented. Fulfilled. Precisely what she, Loló, is not. She wishes Marguita would forgive her, but she hasn't had the time to talk to her, privately, woman to woman, and apologize for what she did. She would love to do that, but she doesn't think Marguita will ever let her. Ever since that night, whenever they see each other, Marguita has been curtly polite to her—and extremely so, almost to the point of being rude, but not quite—treating her as if she, Loló, were not even a stranger, and certainly not a part of the family. Marguita does nod to her in silent greeting when she sees her. But that is about all she does. Loló has tried to talk to her sister-in-law, but since that night Marguita's eyes have looked at her with a coldness that she, Loló, has not been able to melt.

Loló looks about her.

She has been walking and walking and as she looks back she can only see, far away, a hint of the tower atop El Club Cultural. She turns around and faces the sea.

The beach does look inviting. Peaceful. There are only a handful of people in this area. Couples mostly. Smiling women and men wanting to be left alone, she feels they are telling her as she glances at them.

Obediently, she goes on walking, leaving the couples behind.

But as she does, she wishes she could be one of those smiling women next to one of those smiling men. And no sooner does she think that than she remembers Father Alonso's smile.

A thoroughly disarming smile. Gentle. Kind. Loving.

That was it. His smile had been loving. It had made her feel good. About herself. And about the rest of the world.

The memory of that wonderful smile of his that illuminated his face makes her smile as well. And though she is not aware of it, her smile transforms her face, making her gentle. Kind. Loving.

Even beautiful.

For that wonderful smile of his that illuminated his face seems to be now illuminating hers as well.

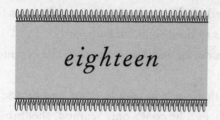

eighteen

Fresh from a short swim in the ocean and from a long shower, where he enjoyed the luxury of the hot water available on command in El Club Cultural, Maximiliano the butcher leaves the locker room. He is, as always, impeccably dressed in white, and, as always, smelling of Florida Water, the lemon-scented eau de cologne he loves. Carrying in his right hand an electric fan, the kind that swivels, he makes his way into the huge kitchen of El Club Cultural, and once inside, he begins to prepare himself for the task at hand, for he has been given the honor of cooking the banquet meal for all the guests at the opening ceremony of El Club Cultural.

In Cuba, where macho men love to strut by smoking huge, thick cigars as visual metaphors for the sizes of their sexual members, cooking is an art form reserved exclusively for women, even in the best restaurants. And yet, as unbelievable as it may seem, cooking is something Maximiliano the butcher dares to do.

And he dares to do it well. Magnificently.

However, before he gets into a kitchen, two conditions have to be rigorously met.

The first is that since he is a butcher and he and his family eat meat day in, day out, he cooks only seafood, shellfish being his great specialty. And the second is that he, being a man's man, cooks *only* for men; each of them being a close personal buddy of his—buddies who range from politicians to embezzlers, professions that in Cuba can easily be found in one and the same person—each of those buddies having, like him, a large, passionate appetite for everything important in a man's life: cayman hunting, deep-sea fishing, great sex, and, of course, great food.

This means that the menus he devises are aimed at satisfying the most demanding and at the same time the least delicate palates in the world. Maximiliano's cooking is certainly not for the weak. It reflects him: a corpulent man of Germanic ancestry with pale-blue eyes, bristly golden hair, and colossal strength, as tall and as handsome as the man he was named after, the first and last emperor of Mexico, shot to death by the Mexican populace after introducing Viennese waltzes to mariachi bands.

However, for this occasion—and for this occasion *only*—Maximiliano the butcher was maneuvered into cooking for the large group of guests comprising both women and men, all of whom were invited to attend the blessing ceremony of El Club Cultural. This was accomplished with the help of Maximiliano's closest friend and buddy, Manuel the doctor, who forced Maximiliano's hand, so to speak.

Whenever Manuel and Maximiliano and the rest of the gang go hunting or fishing, it is always Maximiliano who cooks for them. The guys do not know what makes the food Maximiliano prepares so unbelievably good. Is it that they are exceedingly hungry when they eat it? Or is it the excitement of eating what they themselves have just caught? They don't really know. What they do know is that the food prepared by Maximiliano is just this side of heaven. The minute all of those men get back to their homes and are questioned—no, not questioned but interrogated—by their wives, they just go on and on about what a great meal Maximiliano the butcher fixed.

Maximiliano the butcher? the women ask in total disbelief.

Maximiliano the butcher! the men answer.

Well, it didn't take long for the handsome butcher who was already famous as a poet and as a songwriter to become equally famous for his cooking—cooking women had never, ever tasted. What was there about his cooking that made it so special? the women asked themselves.

Well, we all know how insistent and determined women can be. When they want to know something . . .

It all started with Manuel's wife, Celina, who is also Maximiliano's distant cousin.

When Manuel told her about the big shindig that was being planned to celebrate the opening of El Club Cultural, of which Manuel was one of the members of the organizing committee, Celina immediately suggested, "Why don't you guys invite Maximiliano to cook for all of us at the club's blessing? After all, isn't he the best cook you know? You yourself have often said so. Or were you just exaggerating?"

Manuel looked at her. "He is the best. No question about it. But he'll never do it. Cook for women, I mean," he answered, thinking that was that.

But though he had been married to Celina for several years, he sure didn't know his wife who, being a Cuban woman, did not know the meaning of the word *no*. What do Cuban women do on occasions such as this? Exactly what Celina did. She insisted and insisted until an exasperated Manuel finally said, "You want him to cook, why don't you ask him yourself?"

That was all Celina needed to hear. "I got your approval, then, to ask him?"

"You got my approval," Manuel replied. "But I'm warning you, he'll never do it. I know."

"Do you wanna bet?" Celina asked, peering deeply into her husband's elongated, black, almost Oriental eyes.

Manuel's eyes became more slitlike than ever as he answered, "Sure. Whatever you say. But you'll never win."

"Will you pay for the dinner if I get him to say yes?"

"Yes, I will. I'll be delighted to pay for it." He smiled at Celina. "And if I win, which I know I will, what do *I* get?" he asked.

Celina looked at him, mischief in her eyes. "We'll talk about that when it happens," she answered. Then, ignoring Manuel's warning, Celina went straight not to Maximiliano but to Maximiliano's wife, Dolores.

Now, Dolores could never say no to Manuel. It was Manuel the doctor who delivered her two babies born in Luyanó, and it was he who told Dolores the painful truth about her baby girl Iris, who had been born with a blue heart. When Manuel spoke to her about Iris's condition, he did it with great care, even extreme care, his voice breaking at times, but he had not hidden anything from her, and Dolores admired that. It was because of what Manuel told her that she called Father Francisco and the baby girl was able to be christened barely moments before she went back to the Heaven she had come from. Her baby was gone, and that had broken Dolores's heart. But Dolores had found great relief in knowing that her little girl had been baptized before she departed and that she was now an angel partaking in the glory of God.

The same way Dolores could never say no to Manuel—nor to Manuel's wife—Maximiliano could never say no to Dolores. As far as he knows, Dolores is and will always be that girl who stole his heart with a single glance, even though to this day she says it was he who was staring at her. His love for her is and will always be the intense love a criollo man feels for his wife.

So when Dolores asked him to cook for this event, Maximiliano asked no questions. He just called Manuel and said, "I hear you're footing the bill for this banquet, so I hope you got a thick wallet because I'm going to splurge."

"Go ahead. Splurge," a surprised Manuel said on the telephone. Then, after he hung up, he turned to his wife. "How did you ever manage it?" he asked.

Celina looked innocently at Manuel. "I have ways," she said.

"Obviously. But—" Manuel started to say.

"Don't ask," Celina interrupted. "A woman never, *ever* reveals her secrets," she said, smiling coyly at him, "and certainly not to her husband!" Then, this time smiling to herself, she added, "Soon we'll see if my cousin Maximiliano is really as good a cook as you men say he is."

Totally unaware that the women are eagerly waiting to try his food so they can rate him as a chef, Maximiliano enters the kitchen, places the fan on a counter, and immediately goes over the several huge bags filled with softshell crabs, which he plans to cook and serve at the banquet, to ensure that they are fresh.

They are.

He then carefully inspects the huge crate of avocados that was just delivered to the club, telling himself that the Lord only knows how somebody found them, and how much Manuel the doctor must have paid for them—when food of any kind is so scarce all over Cuba, because of the Depression. After he finds the avocados satisfactory, he steps onto the patio to make sure the table has been properly set.

The two-story-high patio, lined with whitewashed walls, is roofed for the occasion with white canvas stretched from one end of the space to the other, shading the patio from the brilliant tropical sun. Underneath this translucent canopy is a huge U-shaped table made up of many smaller rectangular tables put together one against the other, covered with white linen tablecloths draping down to the floor, their fronts decorated with garlands of interwoven palm leaves. Followed by the five waiters assigned for this service—personally selected by Maximiliano—the butcher walks slowly around the table, counting and carefully inspecting the fifty-three place settings, which are neatly defined by starched white-linen napkins folded in the shape of pleated fans and inserted inside footed glasses.

Happy with the way his instructions have been carried out to the letter, Maximiliano goes back into the kitchen. There, he removes first his jacket, then his shirt, hangs them on a hook, puts on a white bib apron, plugs the fan in, turns it on, aims it at himself, washes his hands thoroughly, and then shoos everybody out of his realm.

No one, but no one, will ever know his cooking secrets. Absolutely no one.

Once he finds himself all alone in the kitchen, Maximiliano takes off the bib apron, his pants, and his undershirt, and wearing nothing but his baggy white-cotton drawers and the white shoes he always wears with white socks, begins to check the crabs one by one, making sure that they are male and alive. After all the female and the dead male crabs have been discarded and the rice properly measured, he sets everything next to several huge flat-lidded pots filled with the chicken stock he prepared earlier, to which he adds a lot of saffron filaments that turn the broth a pale yellow. He goes out the door leading from the kitchen into the service yard looking for two cases of beer he placed there this morning, the moment he arrived in El Club Cultural, to warm up in the hot sun. He brings the wooden cases filled with beer bottles into the kitchen, and places them on top of the tin-covered wood table he has been working on, making a loud clank. Using a metal bottle opener screwed to the side of the worktable, he proceeds to open one bottle after another of that warm, yeasty-smelling beer, pouring the contents into two huge deep pots until they are half full. Then he grabs the crabs one at a time, carefully, from behind, to avoid being pinched by them, and delicately places them into the beer-laden pots.

This is his cooking secret: Getting the crabs drunk before he cooks them.

Maximiliano knows without any doubt that, like all shellfish and like a lot of men, crabs simply love sun-warmed beer. That it makes them happy. So, when they die, he tells himself, they die happy. And if one dies happy, one goes straight to heaven. So that's why they taste of heaven when you eat them. That is his theory. And he knows he is right, for so he has been told. Besides, the proof of the pudding is in the eating. And when plate after plate of his cooking gets back to the kitchen licked clean, as they do every single time he cooks, well, isn't that proof enough?

Once all the crabs are swimming in the warm beer and getting drunk, he goes to the kitchen door and calls Teodosio, the head-waiter.

Maximiliano knows that after he throws the measured rice into the hot chicken-saffron stock, and after he stirs it once, covers it, and lowers the heat under it to almost nothing, the meal will be ready in exactly twenty minutes. Just as he knows that food must be served exactly when it reaches "its point," as he always says. Not a minute before, not a minute after. So, when the headwaiter enters the kitchen, Maximiliano tells him, "Teodosio, please, go tell the men—I mean, all the people—that the meal will be ready whenever they want. All I need is twenty minutes. So find Manuel the doctor and ask him at exactly what time the meal should be served. Once the time is set, it is set. And I mean it. I want everybody sitting and salivating at the table right then and there, when the food is *at its point,* and not a second later. Is that clear?"

Maximiliano does not raise his voice. He doesn't have to. His intentions have been made clear. Quite clear.

"As clear as water," Teodosio says and runs to the bar, where the men are playing *cubilete*—a poker game played with dice—to let them know that Maximiliano wants to set the serving time for the meal, and that once it is set, he wants everybody at the table on time. Not a second later.

"Or else I think he might get angry," he adds cautiously, knowing very well that nobody ever wants to see Maximiliano the butcher angry. Besides, the men are beginning to get hungry.

"He said he only needs twenty minutes?" one man asks. Teodosio nods. "Well then, twenty minutes it is," the man adds, looking at his watch." Let's say at one o'clock."

Teodosio is about to go back to the kitchen and tell Maximiliano when another man says, "Hold it, shouldn't somebody go up and check with the two priests first? Find out what time they'd like to eat? After all, they're the stars for today's show. I'm sure Collazo expects them to bless our meal as well, doesn't he?"

Alberto, one of the assistant waiters, goes upstairs.

And when he knocks again and again at the door, getting no answer; and when he opens it—for the door was unlocked—and he sees nobody, Alberto rushes back to the bar downstairs.

"The room is empty," he tells the men, most of whom are already half drunk.

"Empty?" they say.

"There's no one there, that's what I mean," Alberto says. "I saw two cassocks hanging in the closet, and two pairs of shoes by the sides of the beds. But there is no one there. I looked all over the club for them, but I haven't seen either of them. Nobody has."

"Well," a man says, "we'd better go find them, or else we won't eat. And I'm getting hungry. Where do you think they are?"

"Probably getting drunk somewhere they can't be seen, if I know priests," another man says, making the rest of them laugh and nod as they start out in different directions.

nineteen

Father Alonso has not noticed the passage of time.

How can he?

Never has he experienced anything like this, he thinks as he immerses himself in Cuban waters. The ocean is so warm and so inviting. And so easy to swim in. Back in Spain, the lake he and Felipe used to go to was cold and saltless. But ocean water, with its high salt content, makes it so much easier for him to stay afloat.

After swimming vigorously for a long while, enjoying the powerful thrust of his muscles until they got sore—muscles he had almost forgotten he had as he keeps them always hidden under his black cassock—he is now floating on the ocean water totally at the mercy of the sea, letting the currents beneath the calm surface of the ocean carry him to wherever they want, keeping his eyes closed as his face is bathed by the beaming tropical sun. Didn't Father Francisco say that happiness was a way of praying? Well, Father Alonso tells himself as he drifts, cradled by the warm, womblike waters, what better prayer than this, the simple enjoyment of God's gifts?

He has seen a lot of poverty among the people in his parish—Father Francisco's parish, that is. But he has yet to see in their faces the unhappiness he has always associated with being poor.

Now, as he floats in the Cuban ocean, he begins to understand why.

Cuban people don't need much, he tells himself, for they already have so much to be thankful for. Food is always plentiful, sometimes just for the grabbing: mangoes, bananas, papayas, you name it, succulent tropical fruits growing everywhere. Even here, the beach is lined with coconut trees, the coconuts lying on the sand just waiting to be picked up. And then, the people, no matter how poor, are so handsome, with that beautiful honey-colored skin of theirs. And healthy, for the most part, for their health care, like their education, is totally provided by the state, with a little help from the church. And then there's that stunning Cuban music. At times so violent, at times so soothing. But always so exciting. And always so filled with inner joy. The same kind of inner joy he is experiencing as he floats.

"Thanks, Lord," he says aloud, "for all the gifts you have bestowed upon us. Please, Lord, make the rest of the world realize this. The sooner they do, the sooner they'll be at peace with themselves. Please."

Suddenly, a wave breaks over him, waking him up.

He smiles to himself. He had almost fallen asleep as he floated. He stands up and gets out of the water, not sure where he is, his thin cotton boxer shorts, thoroughly wet, tightly clinging to him.

He looks around and sees no one. This area of the beach seems to be totally deserted. His sore muscles feel good, though tired. He is about to start walking against the direction of the current, back to where he left Father Francisco peacefully napping under the palm trees. But first he finds a shady place right where the sand gives way to soft, mossy vegetation, behind a sand dune that shields him from the beach and from the ocean and from anyone who might come that way, and there he takes off his shorts and wrings them a couple of times so they will dry quicker.

Then, lured by the soothing song of the palm trees gently swaying above him, almost a lullaby, and by the peaceful world that surrounds him, the young priest places his shorts on the soft, mossy soil and lies down by them in the shade, cradling his head in his hands. And as he does, he remembers the dark, gypsy eyes of Loló— eyes that look so much like Felipe's—staring deeply into his while he hears in his mind Father Francisco's words. "Of course, I still see the beauty that hides in women's eyes. Yes, even at my age, I do. But . . . I see that beauty as the work of God. And every time I see it I thank God for it."

Then, remembering the kind, gentle smile that he had given to Loló in the clubhouse as the words of Father Francisco echoed in his ears; and the kind, gentle smile he had received in return from her, Father Alonso, just like Father Francisco, also thanks God for the beauty that hides in women's eyes that allows him to erase from his mind the beauty that hides in men's eyes as he lets himself fall asleep to the magical, alluring song of the surf.

Footprints have been guiding Loló. Footprints on the beach. Following them, she has walked and walked, away from it all—from the women scorning her, and from the men leering at her, even from her own sister—leaving behind everything and immersing herself in this feeling she has today, a feeling of glorious freedom—a feeling that increases the farther away she gets from it all.

She is still walking when suddenly she finds herself feeling thankful.

She doesn't know what has motivated it. She just lets herself go with the joyous feeling, treasuring it. Cherishing it.

It must be the beach, she thinks. Or the sun. Or the sea. Whatever it is, she feels exhilarated. Content.

Satisfied with herself.

She goes by couples looking into each other's eyes, but she pays no attention to them. She notices a set of footprints on the sand: small, delicate footprints—the footprints of a woman—interwoven with much larger ones—the footprints of a man—and curious, almost like a child playing a game, she begins to follow them, the footprints leading to an area concealed behind dunes. As she approaches, she hears behind those dunes a soft and controlled yet intense moaning, the same kind of soft, controlled, and intense moaning that had drawn her down the hallway of her house the night she caught Lorenzo and Marguita making love.

That night she wanted to see what lovemaking was like. That was the reason she did what she did then. But she remembers that afterward she felt so embarrassed by what she had done that she does not want to relive the experience ever again. And even though she still has those urges to find out what lovemaking is like, she decides not to disturb the intimacy of that couple softly moaning behind the sand dunes. Turning away she goes back to the beach, where she again begins to walk until she finds another set of footprints—small, delicate ones again interwoven with much larger ones—also leading beyond the sand dunes, and she smiles to herself when she sees them.

There is no longer envy in her smile. This is a different kind of smile. A gentle, kind smile. Loving. The same kind of smile the young priest gave her, liberating her, she thinks. Those thoughts make her realize what is making her feel as she does.

That smile of his.

And those glittering eyes of his.

She finds yet another set of footprints veering away from the beach. But these are different. These are both large, masculine prints. Curious, she follows them, and before she realizes it she runs into an old man lying down in the shade, peacefully sleeping. She turns away quickly, so as not to awaken him, when she thinks she has seen that man before. She turns again to look at him, and it takes her a while to see in that skinny old man in his shirt, suspenders, and pants rolled up to midcalf, the same priest who christened little Renzo a while back and who just blessed El Club Cultural. The same old priest who came with the young one. She turns to go, when she sees another set of footprints, a single set this time: large footprints set far apart from each other and deeply pressed into the sand—the footprints of a man who was running. She follows them, but the rushing footprints lead only to the edge of the water, and there they disappear, erased by the lapping waves.

She sighs and keeps on walking, all by herself, enjoying the sun on her face and on her body, until she runs into one more set of footprints. Broad, manly footprints, evenly spaced. Again, curious, she follows them, careful not to disturb them. These footprints lead from the edge of the water to beyond the sand dunes. She reaches the end of the footprints and sees them disappear where the ground, covered with budding vegetation, becomes soft and cool, no longer sand. Unable to follow the footprints any farther, she turns around to go back to the beach.

This area seems so quiet, so empty, she thinks as she scans it.

So peaceful.

It is then that she hears a soft, distant murmur, like the rhythmic breathing of a person fast asleep. She follows those gentle sounds and before she realizes it she runs into a young man who is lying sound asleep next to his underwear.

And even though he is totally naked, this time it doesn't take her long to know who this young man is.

Many times before Loló has wished she could control her urges, those urges of hers that seem to push her and push her. But this time . . . this time she is thankful she has those urges. Urges that compel her to stay there and study the body of the naked young man in front of her. She looks at him in total innocence—she a child, he a child—until she feels the need to be like him.

Free. Liberated. Naked.

Delicately she takes her bathing suit off, letting it fall silently to the ground. Then she kneels in front of this godlike young man who with his kind, gentle smile has brought such contentment into her life. She focuses first on his face, that seems to be angelic, admiring his dark eyebrows, and the dark-blue shadow framing his face, and the deeply carved cleft in the middle of his chin. Then she focuses on his tight young body, admiring his arms, his hairy armpits, his thick neck, his muscular torso, his feet, his legs, his thighs, the unruly mound of black curly hair encircling his manhood, a virile member that is stiff, hard, and engorged as the young man soundly sleeps.

She feels the need, the urge, to share her feelings with him. To awaken him to her. To enter the same kind of world she saw Marguita and Lorenzo enter, and inhabit the same kind of heaven she saw Marguita and Lorenzo inhabit. She feels the need, the urge, to experience the kind of ecstasy she saw Marguita experience, and to make the young man lying at her feet experience it all as well. She feels the need, the urge, to become—if only for a brief moment—a woman, a true woman, the same kind of woman Marguita was that night. A woman totally at ease with herself.

And with the world.

She unpins her hair, letting it loose so it hangs in soft curls past her shoulders, leans over the naked man in front of her and delicately begins to kiss his body: the deeply carved cleft in his chin first, then his neck, his broad chest, his nipples, his legs, his thighs, caressing his body with her long black hair as she tenderly kisses then licks his virile member until it finally explodes into her mouth, causing the naked young body beneath her to stir and to awake.

Feeling an almost unbelievable ecstasy, the ecstasy of his own body bursting out of him, and as an answer to this paradisical joy, the young man opens his eyes. And though he is still clouded by the immense pleasure, and though the torrid tropical sun momentarily blinds him, his gaze meets the dark, gypsy eyes of Loló, who is kneeling on the soft and mossy soil in front of him.

He looks at this bewitching vision in front of him—the same vision he was having in his dreams—and smiles at this vision with a kind, gentle smile that is answered by another smile, equally as kind and gentle as his.

It is only then that he realizes whom those eyes really belong to.

And that the owner of those eyes is naked. Just as he is.

And that this is no vision.

Startled, he starts to pull himself up on his elbows away from her, but her body meets his in a tight embrace as her mouth searches for his with the same intensity with which he finds himself responding to hers.

Then, after his lips taste and savor those vibrant lips of hers, his mouth begin to trace the contours of her body—he a child, she a child—kissing her neck, her shoulders, her breasts, her nipples, her legs, her thighs, wounding and scratching her skin with the rough stubble on his face as his hands and his mouth explore her body until both mouth and hands find the darkness between her legs, which open up to him.

So this is what it's like to be a man, the young priest tells himself, his eyes closed.

So this is what it's like to be a woman, Loló thinks, as she begins to experience the almost incredible warmth of his igniting her.

But soon her thoughts disappear, melting into nothingness as she closes her eyes and enters a world that is totally and absolutely free—free of time and free of space; free of everything—when she feels him urging himself into her. This time it is she who awakens to this vision in front of her. Opening her eyes, she guides the young man away from her, makes him lie on the ground, and then, keeping her gaze steady on his, she straddles him and lets herself be entered by him—she in total control of his every movement—closely watching his face as it slowly changes from one moment of ecstasy to the next, pain intricately interwoven with pleasure, until those moments begin to rush closer and closer together and until she feels herself burst with indescribable waves of pleasure upon pleasure as she feels him burst anew inside of her.

They are holding on to each other and she collapses on top of him, their bodies lying on the soft, mossy soil. But he struggles with her until this time it is he who is on top of her, and this time it is he who forces her body to open to his call, this time it is he who enters her anew, his youthful body knowing no limits, while she embraces him tight to her, her vision blurred by the tropical sun piercing through the crests of palm trees and giant ferns as he bursts again inside of her and then, exhausted, this time it is he who collapses on top of her.

Still inside her world of visions and dreams, extending her arms and caressing him all over, she feels his back, taut and yet loose, until her hands finally end up fondling his mane of hair, wet with sweat, dark, glossy hair that gloriously smells of ocean water and of unbridled sex. She begins to kiss his hair when a distant voice is heard calling, "Father Alonso, Father Alonso!"

No sooner does the young man hear that than he stands up, grabs his shorts from the sandy soil, and as he begins to put them on he begins to run, rushing toward the voice he has just heard.

"I'm here, Father Francisco, I'm here," the young man shouts as he crosses the wide expanse of sand.

He sees Father Francisco coming toward him.

The young man runs even faster toward his mentor. "I fell asleep," he says, upon reaching the old priest. "I hope it's not too—"

He sees two men, who are members of El Club Cultural, walking with the old priest.

"Let's rush back to El Club," one of them tells the young man. "I'm starving, aren't you?" he asks the young priest. "Maximiliano the butcher, who is our cook today, told us that he needs twenty minutes before any food is set on the table. So the sooner we get back there, the sooner we eat. Come on, *Father*," he says, when he notices that the young man is wearing nothing but his underpants, "I'll race you back to El Club."

Father Francisco hands the young man his pants, shirt, and undershirt, which he had left lying close to where the old priest had fallen asleep.

The young man hurriedly puts them on and, without looking back, starts to race toward El Club Cultural.

But then, remembering who he is, the young man—now Father Alonso—slows down, and keeping his eyes downcast, walks slowly by the side of Father Francisco, the old priest, who smiles at the young priest as he walks by his side.

"Did you have a good swim?" Father Francisco asks.

The young priest does not look at him.

He just nods several times, his downcast eyes melancholic and serious.

Far too serious for such a young man.

Half an hour later, showered and dressed in his black cassock, which seems to emasculate him and make a eunuch out of him, the young priest stands in the second-floor room, close to his mentor, helping the old man get ready for the final benediction of the day.

On the floor below, in the women's locker room, a quiet and modest Loló is inside a dressing cubicle, stripping herself of her bathing suit, covered with grains of sand. Unnoticed by any of the men who had come to retrieve the young priest, she had let them all go way ahead of her, and she arrived at El Club Cultural barely moments ago. She slowly passes her hands all over her body, and notices in the long, narrow dressing-room mirror the blotches of red left on her white skin by the rough stubble of the young man who made her into a woman.

She wishes she could shout it out. "I am a woman now. Finally. I am a woman."

But she feels that becoming a woman is something so intimate and so deliriously pleasurable that she cannot share this with anyone, let alone the world.

She closes her eyes and she finds herself back where she was only moments ago. In his arms, her body covered by his. Her body embracing his. Her body welcoming him inside. Her body pushing violently against his. She doesn't know how she will be able to survive the next few moments, when, during the banquet, her eyes will meet his again; she now a woman, he now a priest. Will he smile at her? Will his smile be the same kind of smile he had given her before? Will she be able to smile back at him? Will her smile be the same? And then she asks herself, How could this happen? And then, Did this really happen?

In the floor above her, the young priest buttons the cassock of the older man, and, unaware that he is doing it, sighs—a long, deeply felt sigh that seems to come from the bottom of his heart.

The older man turns to him. "Me, too," the old priest says.

The young priest looks at his mentor, feeling totally disconcerted.

"I feel just like you feel," the old man adds. "Wishing I too could have stayed lying on the mossy ground by the beach, shaded by the crests of palm trees and inebriated by the breezes. For a moment, I stopped being a priest. For a moment I stopped thinking about poor children who need to know about God and have enough food to eat and a safe place to play and live, and about a church that needs another coat of paint, and I felt just like any other man, enjoying the great gifts the good Lord has made available to all of us." The old priest sighs, a long, deep sigh that seems to come from deep within his soul, as he adds, "Sometimes, my son, it is a great thing to stop being a priest, if only for a moment, and get back to being just a man." Then he smiles at his acolyte. "I'm sure the good Lord himself felt as you and I do this very moment. After all, he was a man. Just like you and me."

Father Alonso says nothing. He just closes his eyes for a second, as if in total agreement. But a second is long enough to transport him back to where he was minutes ago, his lips tasting the lips of a woman, savoring the body of a woman. His hands discovering the body of a woman. His body becoming one with the body of a woman.

Yes, he too is a man, he thinks.

Finally he can say that. Finally and completely. Unquestionably so.

All those doubts he ever had about himself, all that thinking about his feeling unnatural desires for Felipe, gone out of his mind. Exorcised. Totally.

By the scent of a woman.

He goes to the door, opens it, and, followed by Father Francisco, he begins to lead the way downstairs. To the dining room. Where the food "at its point," as lovingly prepared by Maximiliano the butcher, is waiting to be blessed. Where the people will be found seated around the large U-shaped table covered with immaculate linen tablecloths and adorned with palm fronds. Where he will be able to peer again into those bewitching, dark, gypsy eyes of hers.

He places his two hands together, as in a prayer, and he is able to smell the intense aroma of her body still lingering on the tips of his fingers. He bows his head, to bring his nostrils closer to the tips of his fingers, inhales deeply the precious scent on his hands, and, keeping his eyes downcast and melancholic, as he knows he must, he begins to walk down the stairs—the tip of his fingers touching his nose as he immerses himself in the smell of her body, which is now part of his.

He knows that eventually he will ask God's forgiveness for what he has just done: breaking his vows, vows he made of his own free will to God himself.

But he will have to do that later.

Not now.

For as he walks down the stairs, the smell of a woman on his hands encircling him, inebriating him, Father Alonso feels his manhood—that has been hiding under the cassock he wears to make a eunuch out of him—rise up and stiffen.

The man under the cassock a eunuch no more.

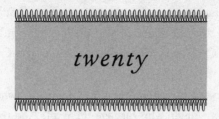

twenty

When, earlier this morning, Dolores, who was in charge of seating arrangements for the banquet, asked her daughter where she and Lorenzo would like to sit, the only thing Marguita asked for was to be seated far away from "that woman," Loló. "Bad enough I have to share the same bus with her," Marguita told her mother, trying to keep her voice calm and low.

Dolores didn't like what she heard.

Taking Marguita aside, she spoke to her daughter in that sweet voice of hers, soothing and yet firm. "Marguita, *amorcito mío*, this has gone on far too long. You're now a mother. And so am I. But that woman, that *poor* woman," Dolores added, underlining the word poor, "that *poor* woman is not a mother, and she may never get to be one. So have some compassion for her. Forgive her. Let those rancorous thoughts fly out of your mind, my little love. Trust in your own mother. Don't do it for her. Don't do it for me. Do it for yourself. The moment you forgive her you'll feel so much better, I know. One always does, when one lets go of all those resentments."

Marguita looked at her mother, a woman disowned by her own family, and yet a woman who forgave them all. And then she thought of "that woman," Loló. It's true what Mamá says, she told herself. That woman is not a mother. And probably she'll never be one. Isn't she already way over thirty? And with no one calling on her? What chances does "that woman," that *poor* woman, have of ever enjoying what I have? A baby and a husband to love her, to call her incandescent—as Lorenzo just called me?

Marguita sighed, for in her heart she knew that her mother was right.

Marguita has always thought of herself as forgiving, so forgive she may. But she has also always thought of herself as having the memory of an elephant, who supposedly never forgets. So, will Marguita ever forget what "that" woman did to her? No, she will not. But forgive . . . ? Maybe.

"All right, Mamá, I'll think about forgiving her," she said. "I promise you. But still, don't seat me close to her. I beg you, please."

Marguita had seriously been thinking about forgiving "that woman" when she heard about what had happened in the ladies' locker room. This only infuriated her. Leave it to "that woman" to parade around naked, Marguita told herself. She probably thinks that she's better than anyone else and that she can do as she pleases. What kind of a woman does she think she is? Marguita asked herself. If only one day I could put her in her place, she wishes. Would *I* like to teach "that woman" a lesson! And as she thought all this, the idea of ever forgiving "that woman" vanished totally out of her soul, for in Marguita's heart "that woman" deserved no forgiving.

D olores and Teodosio, the headwaiter, worked out all the seating arrangements and by now all the guests are at their places, waiting for Teodosio and the rest of the waiters to bring out the food.

The two priests, plus Collazo and some of the elders—including Maximiliano and Dolores—occupy the center of the huge U-shaped table. On one side of the U, several of Collazo's employees and their wives are seated side by side, including Marguita and Lorenzo. On the opposite side of the U, more employees, friends, and their relatives are seated, including Loló, who is sitting next to her sister Asunción. But because the inner area of the large U has been left empty to facilitate the serving of the food, and because all people are thus sitting on the outside of the U, though Marguita is as far as possible from "that woman," as she requested, she still can see her every time she raises her eyes, for "that woman" is sitting right across from her—though with plenty of air space in between.

The food is brought from the kitchen on large silver serving trays that are covered, and is then placed on a serving table located at the very center of the open U, but close to the head of the table, where the two priests sit. Father Francisco stands up, followed by Father Alonso, who stays a little behind and to the side of the old priest. The covers are removed, and as the delicious, mouth-watering smell of the meal inundates the large patio, which is pleasantly shaded by the translucent canopy above, Father Francisco sprinkles the food with holy water, which Father Alonso carries in a silver container. Then, after the old priest blesses the food and after all the guests lower their heads and thank the good Lord for what they are about to eat, the waiters begin to serve the food, which the ravenous people quickly devour.

As people begin to ask for seconds—and even thirds—Collazo stands up, a glass of red Rioja wine in his hand—his third. Or maybe even his fourth. "Ladies and gentlemen," Collazo says, his tongue a little slow, his speech a little blurred, "I want to make a toast to my dear friend Maximiliano the butcher, who's not only a poet of a butcher and a poet with words, but who's also a poet with food. Those of you who ever doubted it, well," he adds, pointing toward the table, "here's the proof! All you have to do is look at all these empty plates!"

A loud round of applause answers Collazo's remarks. Upon hearing it, Maximiliano instantly stands up and with a gesture begs the guests to be silent. "Ladies and gentlemen," he says. "It is not I we should be toasting, but two other people. First, my dear friend Manuel the doctor, who, as you all know, is paying for this incredible amount of food, which we more than welcome because in times like the ones we're going through, when most of us have trouble placing food on our tables, here we are, enjoying this stupendous banquet. And we owe it all to him."

Upon hearing this, everybody applauds enthusiastically again.

"And, last but not least," Maximiliano quickly adds, interrupting the applause, "to our great friend and mentor, Collazo, a man who not only loves books"—he pauses significantly—"almost as much as he loves his red wine," he adds, lowering his voice jovially and making everybody laugh, "but who is a brave and courageous man, in whose vocabulary the word *fear* does not exist. It is he whom we have to toast and toast for having built this wonderful building right on the sand, a building that will outlast all of us, for it is a building that has learned to tame the ebb and flow of the sea."

Everybody drinks and laughs and applauds and has more to eat, leaving no room for dessert, which is going to be served much later in any event, for that is the custom.

As people begin answering one toast with another and then another, and as more and more wine is shared by all, the young man inhabiting Father Alonso, who like everyone else has been seriously partaking of the wine, finally dares to look across the table: a clandestine glance that hopes to find, and at the same time hopes not to find, those dark, gypsy eyes he is avidly searching for. But his eyes do not fail to meet those mystifying eyes of hers he so much fears and loves, for those dark, gypsy eyes have also been searching for his all banquet long, darting at him clandestine looks that hoped to find, and at the same time hoped not to find, those glittering eyes of his she so much loves and fears.

It is then that Marguita raises her eyes and, not really meaning to, accidentally catches "that woman" looking intently at someone at the head of the table.

Curious, Marguita turns her face and catches Father Alonso at first looking back at "that woman," and then facing away from her, as if avoiding her eyes.

Marguita shakes her head in total disbelief.

This is unbelievable, Marguita tells herself. "That woman" has reached the utter limit of degradation, Marguita thinks. She looks at her again so as to confirm what she just saw: Loló making eyes at that poor, innocent Spanish priest. A shocked Marguita shakes her head again when she again catches "that woman" looking at the young priest and smiling.

There's no mistaking that look, Marguita tells herself, remembering how she and Lorenzo used to steal looks at each other.

But then she is even more shocked when she catches the young priest smiling back at "that woman."

A magnificent dessert of guava shells in heavy, sticky syrup is soon followed by a second one of grated coconut with cream cheese; both of them instantly followed by dark-as-ink Cuban coffee that smells heavenly and is served with a ton of sugar. Once this is done, the meal is officially over, and the women elegantly withdraw from the men, who stay at the table, smoking cigars, sipping Spanish brandy, and arguing about literature and politics—all of which brightens the heart of the old book peddler Collazo, whose dream was this. After a long while, Father Francisco looks at his watch and nods to his acolyte. The two priests then excuse themselves and go back up to their second-floor room to gather their things and get ready for the trip back to Havana.

Father Alonso, still a little inebriated from all that wine and all those after-dinner drinks, looks at his old mentor and, after debating what to do, his tongue still a little blurred, says, "Father, may I ask you a question?"

The old priest smiles back at his young assistant. "Sure, son, anything you like."

Father Alonso clears his throat several times and then, stuttering once or twice, says, "It has to do with . . . well, with what you said earlier this morning. Remember? About the beauty that hides in women's eyes?"

Father Francisco nods.

"Oh, yes," he says, "a gift. A great gift from the good Lord."

"Well, Father," the young priest hesitantly begins to ask, but does not seem to be able to carry on his question.

"Yes, my son?" Father Francisco says. "Don't be shy. You may ask me anything you like. That's what I'm here for. That's the job the bishop has entrusted to me. To guide you in your first steps in this difficult life of service to God that you and I have chosen."

There's a short pause. Then, a blushing Father Alonso faces away from Father Francisco as he asks, "Father, have you . . . have you ever been with a woman?"

"What do you mean?" the old priests replies. "Have I known a woman sexually? Is that what you mean?"

The young priest, his face as red as a yam, nods.

"Yes, I have known a woman," Father Francisco says. "It all happened a long time ago. When I was about your age, I guess. Before I became a priest, let it be known."

"And . . . even so . . . ," the young priest begins.

The older priest does not let him finish. "Yes, my son," he answers, "and even so, even after I had known a woman, I chose this life of ours. Even so." He chuckles. "Tell me, how old are you now?"

"Twenty-two. Well, almost twenty-two. I'll be twenty-two in two months. Next October."

"And you entered the seminary at what age?"

"I was just thirteen when I . . . when I felt my vocation."

"I gather that you have not . . . known a woman, then," Father Francisco says, and sees the young priest become even redder in the face. "That's all right, my son. It's no sin to be a virgin," the old priest says as he turns to the young man by his side. "I don't know what is best, to have known or not to have known a woman before one becomes a priest. I truly don't know. Many men enter the priesthood far too young, before they have experienced life. How can they give proper counsel about things they don't know about, about things they haven't experienced? I've often asked myself that very same question, and I always end up giving myself the same answer: God will find the way. God will help those inexperienced young priests like you and teach them how to guide the needy. If he can move mountains and raise the dead, can he not guide an innocent man such as you and make a great shepherd out of him? Trust in God, my son. Let him guide you, as I know he will. Always follow his call, and do as your heart tells you, for God speaks directly to you through the heart. Listen to your heart.

Always listen carefully to what your heart is telling you, for the heart is never wrong."

He pauses briefly. "Does that answer your question?" he asks.

This is followed by a long silence.

"Yes, Father," the young priest finally says, as he looks at the old man and smiles at him a shy, gentle smile.

"Is there anything else you would like to ask me?"

The young priest shakes his head.

"Well, then," the old priest says, "let's get our things ready. It's getting late and I don't want to be late for the bus. Bad enough we were late for lunch. Well, not quite late. But almost. Almost. Thank God for those men who came to get us and woke us up just in time, don't you agree?"

"Yes, Father," the young priest says after a while.

"Just in time."

The trip back to Havana is very, very quiet.

Those who are not tired are either full or sunburned or all of the above. And all of them are sleepy. So sleepy that by the time the bus leaves Guanabo behind, as the sun sets behind their backs, painting the limpid tropical sky with luminous hues of red, orange, and purple, most people inside the bus are already sound asleep, some of them even snoring.

Except for Father Alonso who, holding tight to his rosary, will not close his eyes.

Or Loló, who looks steadily ahead of her, past everything, as if in a trance.

Or Marguita, who, quietly holding her baby in her arms and letting her husband lean against her and sleep, keeps looking first at "that woman," then at the young priest.

But seeing that neither one of them is stealing looks at the other, she tells herself that she must have been imagining things. It must have been the wine, she thinks. That was what it was. The wine. I shouldn't have tasted it. Not in my condition.

Then she smiles at herself.

Maybe that is why Lorenzo found me so incandescent today, she thinks.

And then she blushes. For even though she has not told her husband, or anyone else for that matter—not until she knows for sure—she believes she may be with child again.

PART FIVE

Second Moon

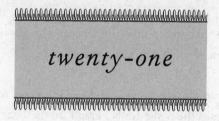

twenty-one

Once the two sisters get back to their home in Old Havana, Asunción rushes to her parents and tells them in that chalky voice of hers what a great time they all had, how beautiful El Club Cultural is, what great food they ate, and how wonderful the whole Sunday excursion turned out to be. Loló, on the other hand, claiming to be exhausted, lets herself collapse on her bed. And exhausted she is— by thoughts that have been galloping and hammering inside her head.

None of this was meant to happen, Loló tells herself as she falls on her bed.

None of this was meant to happen, she keeps telling herself hours later, as she lies sleepless in the middle of the night, looking up at the heavily carved plaster ceiling that seems to be hovering oppressively over her.

Or was it? she asks herself one more time as she shakes her head.

Was it meant to happen? And to happen the way that it did?

She is elated that she is now the woman she always thought she could be, the one she felt she was entitled to be.

But why him? Of all people, why him?

She is afraid to close her eyes, and yet she loves to do it, for the moment she closes them she finds herself on the beach, lying on the soft, mossy soil and surrounded by dancing palm trees, the rhythmic sound of the alluring surf distantly singing as her body and his body, deeply entwined, are pulsating together as one. The thought is too much for her to bear, there, where she is, alone in her bed. For she wants him there. In her room. With her. In that same bed. By her side.

But who is he? she asks herself. Who is this man who made me a woman?

She knows little about him. Not even his real name, only the name he chose when he became a priest. He is young, she tells herself. A lot younger than I am. But still, young as he is, he is nonetheless a full man. Just as he is a full priest, that much I know— for he is able to celebrate Mass and hear confession.

This last thought enters her brain like a bullet rushing through it.

That's it. Confession! I have to go to him, confess everything to him. Ask for his advice. For his help. For his guidance. For his blessing. But then she shakes her head again. No, I don't want any of that. Why should I try to fool myself? What I want, what I really want, what I really need, is to hear him speak to me, she tells herself, knowing that she has seldom, if ever, heard his voice. Realizing that, she shakes her head one more time. How could I have done what I did? she asks herself.

Then, when she is unable to answer it, that painful question is followed by myriad others, equally as trying to her. What will he be thinking of me? That I am a whore? A despicable woman who sleeps with the first man she sees? That I have done this many times before? That I like to seduce young men? Or . . . and then, though she tries not to ask it, she asks herself one more question, one final question that torments her all night long.

Or . . . is he thinking of me . . . at all?

Back in his cell of a room in the basement of the little church of Our Lady of the Perpetual Succor in Luyanó, the young priest is asking himself those very same questions.

None of this was meant to happen, he keeps telling himself as he lies sleepless in total darkness on the narrow cot he calls a bed.

Or was it? he asks himself one more time as he shakes his head.

Was it meant to happen? And to happen the way that it did?

He is elated that he has known a woman, so much so that he has not washed his hands, to keep her smell lingering on the tips of his fingers for as long as he can manage.

Like her, he is afraid to close his eyes, and yet he loves to do it, for the moment he closes them he finds himself on the beach, lying on the soft, mossy soil and surrounded by dancing palm trees, the rhythmic sound of the alluring surf distantly singing as his body and her body, deeply entwined, are pulsating together as one. The thought is too much for him to bear, there, where he is, alone in his bed. For he wants her there. Not him, Felipe. *Her.* Loló. In his room. With him. In his bed. By his side. Finally he can close his eyes and fantasize about a woman, not about a man, even though he knows it is wrong for him, a full priest, to do either. He, who broke his vow of celibacy. He, who is a celibate no longer, thanks to her.

But who is she? he asks himself. Who is this woman who has so deeply transformed my life? And maybe even irrevocably so?

He knows little about her. So little! Barely her name, Loló, a name he has begun to worship. Just as he has begun worshipping her, who to him represents WOMAN with capital letters. I know I'm young, he tells himself. A lot younger than she is. But none of that matters to me. I just wish I had met her before I met Felipe; before all that confusion and turmoil Felipe stirred in my heart; before I decided to become a priest, which is what I am and what I will be for the rest of my life, because I am fully ordained. Fully able to celebrate Mass. And fully able to hear confession.

This last thought enters his brain like a bullet rushing through it.

That's it. Confession! I have to go to Father Francisco and confess everything to him. Maybe that will help me. Maybe.

But then he shakes his head again. No, I don't want any of that. Why should I try to fool myself? What I want, what I really want, what I really need, is to hear her speak to me, he tells himself, knowing that he has seldom, if ever, heard her voice.

Realizing that, he shakes his head one more time. He has tried to kneel by the side of his bed and has tried to recite his vows. But he has not been able to do it. He has not been able to promise the Lord what he knows he cannot achieve. He might be able to lie to himself. He might even be able to lie to Father Francisco, perhaps. But he cannot lie to God. No. Not to God.

He is just elated that he did as he did. That his body did as it did. That he proved to himself that he was as much a man as any other man on earth.

And yet, how could I, a priest, have done what I did? he asks himself.

Then, when he is unable to answer it, that painful question is followed by myriad others, equally trying to him. What will she be thinking of me? That I am a horrible man? A despicable priest who sleeps with the first woman he sees? That I have done this many times before? Or . . . and then, though he tries not to ask it, he asks himself one more question, one final question that torments him all night long.

Or . . . is she thinking of me . . . at all?

Those painful questions need to be answered.

The following morning, right after he has finished helping Father Francisco celebrate the early-morning Mass—the first Mass of the day—Father Alonso goes to the sacristy. There, he takes off his white acolyte robe and after kissing his sacred stole, a symbol of his priesthood, he places it across his shoulders. Then, holding his breviary in his hands, he reenters the church and crosses the narrow main nave to go the confessional located at the other end. As he crosses in front of the altar, he genuflects before God, as he knows he must do. But as he kneels, his reddened tired eyes—the eyes of someone who has not been able to sleep all night long—carefully avoid looking at the altar. Just as he has avoided looking at Father Francisco during the Mass. Just as he has avoided looking at the few people, all of them women, who are there at this time of morning watching him go to the confessional. Just as he has avoided looking at himself in the mirror, even as he shaved.

He sits in the booth, turns on the light indicating that he is available to hear confession, and, though he and the person who comes to him to confess his sins are securely masked from each other, he can still make out those dark, gypsy eyes of Loló's through the cane divider that separates her from him as she kneels in front of him—her scent invading his soul. Then he hears her whisper, her voice a painful melody ringing deeply inside his heart.

"I couldn't sleep last night. I just couldn't. At all."

That is all she can manage to say.

To which all he can answer is, "Neither could I, neither could I," his voice, like hers, also quivering with despair.

When Loló got up early this morning, much earlier than usual, she surprised her mother, Carmela, who was already in the kitchen boiling the water and the milk to make coffee. Upon seeing her eyes, red and tired from lack of sleep, Carmela, concerned, asked her daughter, "Child, are you feeling all right? You look tired. Did you get enough sleep? What are you doing up at this time of day? It's still—"

Loló smiled at her mother.

"I'm all right, Mamá. It's just that today's the birthday of Gloria, one of the girls in the office, and we all are going to surprise her before she gets to work."

Then, after realizing how easy it is to tell a lie, she ran out of the house as fast as she could to make it to the early-morning Mass in Luyanó. She had decided not to wait for the streetcar. She just couldn't. She didn't have the time to spare. She hailed a cab. "How much to Luyanó?" she asked. When the man answered, she sighed in relief as she clutched her purse against her. She had just enough money to go and come back. "Hurry up, please," she said and climbed inside the cab. As the cab drove her to Luyanó—a long half hour away by cab, even at that early time of day—she kept telling herself: I must do it. Talk to him. Find out how he feels. She was desperate to know what he thought of her. All night long she had planned this visit. She had rehearsed in her mind every word she was going to say, and every step she was going to follow afterward.

Now, upon hearing his tremulous voice, she is happy she came to the church in Luyanó, happy she risked being seen here where she does not belong, and happy to talk, not to the young priest, but to the young man who made her a woman.

For now she knows.

His voice confirmed what her heart has been telling her. What her heart had wished for all night long. That he has been thinking of her as much as she has been thinking of him.

"What are we going to do now?" he asks.

"I don't know. I can't even think straight anymore," she says, looking at her watch, knowing that she's in a rush; that she doesn't want to be seen; that she has to get to work. "We must meet and talk," she adds, her voice urgent. "But not here. Not here."

"Where?"

"Do you know where the Hotel Inglaterra is, in Old Havana?"

The young priest shakes his head. Then, realizing she cannot see him for he is in the dark, he replies. "No."

"The Hotel Nacional?" she then asks, her voice taut to the point of breaking.

This time the young priest nods. "Yes." He had been there to a dinner given to honor the bishop, not long after he had arrived in Cuba.

"I get off work at three in the afternoon. I can meet you there in the lobby of the hotel, at ten after three. Then we can go somewhere else."

"Somewhere else?" he asks.

"Yes, where we can be alone. So we can talk."

"But where?"

"I don't know where. There are places. I know. I've been told. I'll find out. I have to go now. I'm already late for work. I don't want to be seen here, near you. I don't belong here in Luyanó, in this—"

"But when should we meet?" the young priest interrupts her.

"When?" she pauses briefly, slightly disconcerted. "Today, of course," she replies, her voice beginning to show the strain she has been living through.

"I can't. Not today. Mondays are mission days. I have to go to—"

"Then, when?" she asks—demands—impatiently.

"Tomorrow," he says. "Tomorrow."

"Tomorrow, then," she replies, and begins to get up when she interrupts herself. She kneels in front of him again. "Oh, if you have a suit, please wear it. It will be less conspicuous. I think you'll be able to change in the men's room in the hotel. It's in the basement. Just go down the stairs. You can't miss it. I don't think it would be wise for us to be seen together while you're dressed as a . . . well, you know. In your cassock." She is about to stand up and go when she hears him address her.

"Do you want to confess anything?"

"No," she says defiantly.

Then, after a short pause, it is she who asks him, "Do you?"

The young priest closes his eyes.

Does he?

He knows he has broken his vows to God. He knows that he last lost God's grace. And yet . . . he feels as if he has been reborn. For now he feels secure of his own manliness. Of his being the man he once thought perhaps that he was not.

He opens his eyes.

"No," he says.

That is all he can say. "No."

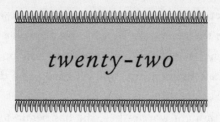

twenty-two

Not wanting to be seen in that area of Luyanó by anyone—least of all by Marguita—after Loló leaves the little Church of Our Lady of the Perpetual Succor, she carefully avoids walking on the Street of the Bulls, where Lorenzo and Marguita live, and scurries along a narrow side street until she reaches La Calzada Avenue. There she hails a cab to take her back to where she came from, Old Havana.

As the cab rushes through the streets of Havana—which are, at this time of morning, extremely busy—Loló doesn't let the constant honking of horns and the constant four-letter words drivers shout at each other as they get to each intersection bother her.

She hears none of that.

Her mind, occupied with other thoughts, will not let her hear any of it. She feels jittery. Nervous, yet excited at the same time.

No, not excited, but exhilarated.

For now, after she has spoken to him and seen how responsive he is to her and, at the same time, how inexperienced he really is—even more so than she is—she realizes that from now on whatever else happens with their relationship, she will have to be the one managing it.

Though the thought worries her, she has begun to accept it as a challenge, and she is the kind of woman who will never back away from a challenge. She does not know what will become of the two of them in the future. At this moment she does not want to think about what's to come in the faraway future. She just wants to think about what to do next.

What's the next step we must take? she asks herself.

By the time she gets to her job, she is already more than an hour late.

She runs through the elegant lobby of the twelve-story building owned by the Cuban Telephone Company, a branch of the Bell Telephone Company run by Cuban men trained in Miami, and stands impatiently waiting for the elevator.

After a short while, tired of waiting, she rushes up the stairs, five flights up.

When she finally gets to her place, behind the safety of her switchboard, she is out of breath, her face flushed.

"Well, are we late today or what?" says Zafiro, the tall mulatto girl with straightened hair and thick red lips who sits next to Loló. And then she lowers her voice. "You owe me, and big. The Owl"— as the telephone operators call their superintendent, Señora Francisca Olivar y Argüelles, for she wears large, thick, round glasses—"was looking for you. I told her you'd gone to the bathroom. When she came back, half an hour later, and asked for you again, I told her I thought I'd seen you go back to the bathroom again. That you were, well, you know . . . that it was one of your bad days. Then she just dropped by here again, less than five minutes ago. So . . . now you know what to say when you see her." She looks around. "What happened? Did you finally get to sleep with a man last night?" she adds, chuckling, for she knows—just as every girl on the floor knows—that in spite of whatever kind of a woman Loló seems to be because of her way of dressing and because of her way of looking at men, in spite of all that, she is still a virgin. "And with little hope of ever *not* being one," the girls tell each other behind Loló's back.

"Don't I wish," Loló answers Zafiro's question, trying to make a joke out of a painful truth, though as she replies to her friend she cannot make herself chuckle, like Zafiro does. Had I not wished for him to be naked, in my bed, by my side last night? Loló thinks.

Suddenly her board lights up.

"*Teléfonos*," Loló says, answering the call.

After Loló makes the connection requested by the calling party, she faces Zafiro.

"Lorenzo, my brother, invited my sister and me to go to Guanabo Beach yesterday. And we did. We spent the whole day there, under the sun. It was wonderful. You have to go there. But tell me . . . look at me, Zafiro, and tell me, did I get too much sun? Isn't my face all red? I may have overdone it," she adds. "I certainly don't want to peel. Not now." She pauses for a second, thinking of the young priest and of what he would say if he saw her all red and peeling. "I mean," she goes on, "I hate it when people peel, don't you?"

"Sugar," Zafiro answers with a smirk, "look at me. People of my color do not ever peel, so I wouldn't know what you're talking about." She begins to laugh loudly.

"Ladies!" a stern voice is heard behind their backs. Upon hearing it, Zafiro instantly straightens up. "More decorum," the voice is heard again, this time a little closer. "This is, after all, a place of business!" Loló feels a slight tap on her back. She turns.

"Good morning, Señora Olivar," she says.

"Are you all right?" a concerned Señora Olivar asks Loló. "Zafiro told me that you . . . I mean, that today's one of your blessed days, and that you—"

"It wasn't that," Loló interjects, interrupting the older lady with the gray hair who is looking at her with kind eyes hiding behind thick eyeglasses. "It's my stomach. I've been feeling a little dizzy. It must have been something I ate yesterday. I'm just not—"

"Well, Loló," the old lady says, "you know you can go home anytime if you don't feel good." She takes a quick glance at Zafiro. "I won't say this to all the girls around here, but"—she faces Loló again—"*you* are such a good employee, always on time, always conducting yourself properly, with such decorum that, well, if you need to, you may take a couple of days off, anytime you're not feeling well. And I mean it. I will not hold it against you. I know how good you are and that you won't lie to me." She glances at Zafiro again. "I wish I could say the same about everyone else in this room," she adds, and sighs, just as Zafiro's and Loló's boards light up.

"*Teléfonos*," each of the girls says as "the Owl" moves away from them.

Moments later, during their midmorning break, the two girls go outside the building for a sip of coffee and to stretch their legs.

Loló faces her friend. "Zafiro," she asks, her voice slightly hesitant, "when you and your boyfriend Celestino started going out . . ." She pauses. "That place that you and he used to go to, you know, to sleep together, I mean . . . well, you know, that *posada* you told me about. Isn't that the one that's just across from the Hotel Nacional, right on . . . what's the name of that side street? You know the one?"

"Aha!" Zafiro replies, looking at her friend and blowing at the steaming cup of coffee in her hand, a paper cup so little it is almost invisible. "So you *did* meet a man at the beach and now you want to—"

"That's not it," Loló replies immediately. "I thought I saw the Owl and a man come out of the Hotel Nacional and I watched them until they turned the corner. And then they disappeared."

"Was it the really the Owl?" an astonished Zafiro inquires. "At her age?"

"I couldn't swear to it. But it did look a lot like her. You know, the way she moves, the way she carries herself? And how she always wears those elegant suits of hers? Well, the woman I saw did. I was just passing by the hotel and—"

"Did you see them go up the narrow street right behind the hotel? You know, the narrow lane, the one that follows the length of the gardens?"

"No, I don't think so," a hesitant Loló answers.

"Well, then, whoever they were, they didn't go to the posada I know," says Zafiro. "They may have gone to another one, but I think there's only one in that area. The one Celestino and I used to go to before we got married was on that narrow lane, right behind the gardens. No one could ever miss it, because of the red lights over the doors." She sighs. "I wish you were sure it was the Owl. Wow, would I like to know! All of that 'decorum this, decorum that,' of hers, and she ends up going with a guy into a room to spread her legs wide for him, like any other woman on earth! Wouldn't it be great if that woman was the Owl? Maybe one of us should go back there and see if it is true. Wouldn't it be great if we could catch her?"

"Oh, no," Loló says, "let her be. If she is having an affair, well, so be it. Maybe that is exactly what she needs."

"Maybe?" replies Zafiro, almost spilling the coffee in her tiny paper cup. "Sugar, that is *exactly* what that woman needs: a good jump in the sack! Don't we all?"

I think that's exactly what you need," says Father Francisco when he sees the tired, red eyes of Father Alonso. "A lot of sleep. So stay in bed. You probably had too much sun yesterday. Too much of this Cuban sun makes you tired, I know. It exhausts you. It used to happen to me. But by now, after thirty-two years of life in Cuba, I'm used to this climate. But, you, my son—"

Father Alonso interrupts him.

"No, Father. Today is mission day. I cannot let you go alone. I'm feeling perfectly all right." He pauses. "Well, maybe I'm not," he adds. But he doesn't let the old priest say a word. "But I know I'll feel a lot better once I find myself doing my mission. After all, Father, that's why I became a priest. Please, I beg you. Don't make me stay here. Please. Let me go to where I belong."

How can Father Francisco say no to such an honest plea?

Half an hour later, the two priests are walking around an area where the poorest of the poor—the jobless and the homeless—have made their own.

In the United States such an area was called a Hooverville. Or a shantytown.

In Cuba it was called "*Llega Y Pón*," which means, "Come and Claim."

Located next to Luyanó, this area occupies the side of a large hill. There a small city has been built, using what wealthier and luckier people have discarded.

With cardboard, mud, leftover broken bricks, even old clothes stretched over wires, the homeless have managed to erect shelters to keep themselves from the rain—which in Cuba falls steadily six months every year—and from the torrid sun—which in Cuba shines every day. This has been done haphazardly. Upon arrival, every newcomer claims a piece of land as his or her territory, and there his meager belongings are scattered. Entire families live there, along narrow, ill-defined, muddy aisles—for one cannot call them alleys, let alone streets.

If ever there was a picture of poverty, this is it, thinks Father Alonso as he and Father Francisco make their way through it.

And yet, how beautiful these people are, Father Alonso tells himself. And, despite all the apparent haphazardness of the construction, how well organized it all seems. Showers and toilets have been erected by the people themselves, with the help of government and church, in different areas all over the large expanse of land. And recently, the church and the inhabitants were busy building a large structure they were planning to use as a nursery school. But how can anyone teach anything to children with empty stomachs? So this school area has been transformed into a large kitchen and dining area where food is made available to anybody, not only children, who comes to its door.

It is there that Father Alonso sits, on the floor in a corner, surrounded by children of all ages who are sitting on the floor just as he is—and even by some of their parents who, standing in the back, watch silently as the young priest begins to teach them all the Lord's Prayer.

Breaking it up into short, simple sentences, each one easy to memorize, Father Alonso repeats one sentence several times and then asks his students to repeat it after him. Though compulsory public education is provided for all school-age children in nearby schools, religion is not part of the official curriculum. So religion must be taught, the church elders decided. But how does one explain the love of God to people who have no homes? To people who live almost like animals in places not that much better than pigpens? To people who have not enough food to eat?

" 'Our Father who art in Heaven,' " Father Alonso says. And then he hears the children in front of him, sitting on the floor just as he is, repeat it.

" 'Our Father who art in Heaven,' " they say.

As they say it, Father Alonso looks at each of them: beautiful, angelic children, the most fortunate of them wearing rags, the rest naked, their bellies extended, filled with parasites, for though health care is provided free of charge by the government, the people there are too afraid to seek it. Or even too ignorant to know what to do about it.

Thinking that he must help bring proper health care to these people, just as he is bringing the word of God to them, Father Alonso loses his concentration, a concentration he regains when he hears his angelic congregation repeat one more time, " 'Our Father who art in Heaven.' " So much work needs to be done, he tells himself as he looks at his children dreamily, praying for a great future for each of them, as he says, " 'Hallowed be Thy name.' "

"Hallowed?" asks a child sitting in front, awakening Father Alonso.

"That means blessed," he explains.

"Blessed?" asks another child, still unable to understand.

"That means beloved of God," Father Alonso explains. "God loves all of us."

"All of us?" a child in the back asks. "The good ones and the bad ones, too?"

"Yes, he does. He loves all of us. We all are his children, so he loves all of us. The good ones and the bad ones alike," Father Alonso says. "God knows everything. He knows that sometimes things happen, and some people may do bad things, even if they don't mean to. Like taking someone else's ice cream, or candy. Or like disobeying your parents. God doesn't like people to do bad things. So even though he still loves you with all his heart when you do something bad, he may get a little angry at you, just like your mami does when she calls you and you don't come to her. But when that happens, all you have to do is tell the truth to God, and then he, who's always loved you, is no longer angry with you, and he smiles at you again."

"But if God knows everything, why do you have to tell him the truth?" asks an older boy, almost a teenager, who has been standing in the back. "Doesn't he know it already?"

Father Alonso raises his eyes, looks at the boy, and smiles at him, a kind, gentle smile filled with love. "God does that because he knows that when a person tells a lie, the heart of that person will ache and ache until that person tells the truth. Who wants to live with an aching heart? God wants that person to feel good. And for that person to feel good, all that person has to do is go to him, tell the truth to him and ask for his forgiveness. And God is always so good, *so good* that if you mean what you say, he always forgives you."

"Always?"

"Always."

"No matter what?" the same older boy asks.

"No matter what," Father Alonso replies.

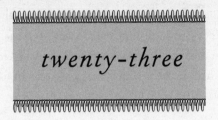

twenty-three

"Congratulations," says Doctor Manuel the following afternoon, when an excited Marguita, carrying her baby in her arms, is admitted to his office. "You were right. The tests just came back and it seems that you and Lorenzo are going to be parents for a second time! Have you thought about the child's name?"

A red-in-the-face Marguita smiles hesitantly at Doctor Manuel.

"Lorenzo does not know a thing about it yet. I haven't told him. I mean, I didn't want to tell him anything until I was sure. I myself didn't think it could happen so quickly. After all it's been only, what, just over ten months since Renzito Manuel was born."

"Healthy parents make healthy children," Doctor Manuel answers. "Nature has its own way of doing things. Perhaps if you had kept at breast-feeding the boy . . . that generally stops ovulation from occurring. But once you stopped producing milk altogether, we had no other choice but to put your baby on a steady formula. And now, just you look at him! No wonder this kid drained you!" he says, as he smiles at the handsome, blond, blue-eyed boy he himself delivered not so long ago, his godchild, named after him.

Then he raises his eyes to Marguita.

"Now the question is, what are we going to do about you, Marguita? You've gained quite a few pounds this last year. We have to be a little more careful this time, we want to make sure that both you and the new baby stay healthy and in good shape during the next few months. Here, I've prepared a special diet for you," he says and hands her a typewritten piece of paper. "I don't want you to gain too much weight during this pregnancy, so stick to this diet, and I mean religiously, you understand? And then come see me at the end of the first trimester." He looks at his calendar. "That will be the first week of November. All right?"

Marguita begins to leave the office when she turns. "Doctor Manuel," she says, addressing the godfather of her child formally as she was taught to do since she was a little girl, "you won't tell anybody, will you? I mean, you won't tell Lorenzo, or Papá, or—"

"Marguita," Doctor Manuel answers, "whatever happens in a doctor's office is strictly between the patient and the doctor and it is no one else's business. I know you want to run and tell your husband and that old bull of a dad of yours about the new baby, so don't worry, I will not say a word to them or to anyone else. Not even to my wife. Doctors are bound to absolute secrecy. Like a priest. So go home and be sure I won't say a word." Marguita smiles at him. "And stick to that diet," he adds as he guides her to the door. "I want to hear no excuses when you come back, you hear?"

***

When Father Alonso arrives at the magnificent lobby of the Hotel Nacional, he finds himself disoriented at first.

Striking a curious image, that of a young priest in an old black cassock seemingly at a loss in the middle of this palace made of onyx, crystal, and gold, his eyes immediately find the broad marble staircase covered with a rich, dark-red plush carpeting that leads to the upper mezzanine, but it takes him a while to find the lesser stairway, also made of marble but uncarpeted, that goes to the basement, a discreet bronze plaque above it reading:

BARBERSHOP. CONCIERGE. REST ROOMS.

Designed by the famous American architects McKim, Mead, and White, the Hotel Nacional is a monumental structure, standing tall, almost like a lighthouse, facing the Atlantic Ocean and located not far from the American embassy in the fanciest part of town, *El Vedado*—a word that means "forbidden," for at one time that area was the hunting grounds of royalty and nobility when Cuba was still a colony of Spain.

Father Alonso descends the stairs and enters the men's rest room.

There, to his surprise, he finds a large chamber where several men have obviously been smoking—and heavily—for the smell of their cigars is still patently discernible, and then, as he goes through an open doorway into the men's room, he finds a man, the custodian of the rest room, elegantly dressed in the hotel uniform of brown and gold, and standing by the washbasins. The young priest wasn't expecting this. Beneath his cassock he is wearing a suit—a black suit, the only one he owns—and has with him a small bag into which he is planning to place the cassock after taking it off. But he doesn't want to do any of this in front of the man. Or in front of any other man, for that matter. He wants nobody to know what he is about to do. Not knowing what else to do, he exits the washroom.

He looks around, hoping to find a place where he can take off his cassock.

The process is simple. All he has to do is undo a few buttons at the top, free his arms, and then the cassock, of its own weight, will fall to the floor. He sees, in the corner of the smoking lounge, a small bronze plaque reading: TELEPHONES. He goes there, and as he turns a corner he sees an area where several telephone booths, made of mahogany and bronze, are located. The space is totally empty. He walks back into the smoking lounge, makes sure that it is still empty, and there he undoes the top buttons of his cassock.

Then, keeping the top part of the cassock closed with his right hand, he steps back into the area of the telephone booths, and there he frees his arms and lets the cassock fall to the floor. He hurriedly steps out of it, grabs it, folds it, and is placing it inside his bag when he hears the sound of footsteps coming down the stairs. He quickly runs into a telephone booth, and, holding his breath, pretends to be on the telephone until he hears the steps go into the washroom. He steps back into the lounge, the cassock now in its bag, and straightens his pants the best he can as he starts to climb up the stairs.

Right before entering the main lobby again, he looks at himself in a mirror by the top of the basement stairs. And as he does, he finds in the mirror, standing behind him, those dark, gypsy eyes looking at him admiringly.

As he turns around, she moves close to him.

He says nothing. His heart is beating so fast that he can say nothing. He just looks at her, as if searching her face for a sign.

He gets it when he sees her smile at him, though this time it is a questioning smile, to which he responds with a questioning smile of his own.

Without saying a word, she grabs his arm and leads him away from the palatial room and back into the streets, which are filled with people rushing every which way. There, still in silence, they move swiftly past the hotel gardens until she finds a small, narrow lane.

She knows the way.

Yesterday afternoon, after she left work, she came to the hotel and circled the area around the hotel until she found the place she had heard so much about, the famous posada where Zafiro and Celestino, her boyfriend, used to go to enjoy their afternoons together. She sees the doors, some of which have their red lights on, indicating that the room is empty and available.

She also knows what to do next.

Just as she knows exactly what to expect.

Pretending to be curious about this kind of things, yesterday she had asked Zafiro for details, and Zafiro had given them to her—as well as a few pesos, for after paying taxi fares to and from Luyanó. Loló had been left with no money at all. "To buy a present for a cousin of mine who's getting married," Loló told Zafiro as she borrowed the money, and lied. Lying was coming easier to her. "I'll pay you back as soon as we get paid."

Zafiro nodded. She knew she wouldn't have long to wait, for they'd get paid in three more days, the last day of the month.

"Wait here," Loló tells him, her voice a whisper.

These are the first words that have been spoken so far between the two of them.

Then she adds, "I'll go in first and close the door behind me. Then, when I open it again, come in."

She leaves him alone and with a gesture asks him to keep silent.

She goes to one of the red-lit doors, opens it and enters. Once inside, she goes to the other door on the opposite side of the room, which she has been told leads into a hallway, and stands behind it. Just as Zafiro told her, in a few seconds she hears a light rap at the door followed by the raspy voice of an apparently older woman. "Three pesos for the day. One peso for three hours."

She gets one peso from her purse and places it inside a small drawer that is located on the surface of a tiny, pivoting panel that is part of the door leading to the hallway. She moves away from it so as not to be seen as she unlocks the tiny panel with the drawer and swivels it around its pivot.

The person on the other side collects the money from the drawer and then says, "You have until six thirty-five. If you want to stay longer, just place another peso in the drawer later on."

Then, after the little drawer swivels back to its original position again, the drawer now empty, as Loló locks the tiny door, she hears the person behind the door step away. Loló has not seen that person, that person has not seen her.

Loló goes back to the front door, and opens it partway.

Within a few seconds he steps in. She locks the door behind him.

Though the room is really tall, it is not too wide. But it is still wide enough to hold an immense bed against one wall, surrounded by mirrors, and a tiny bathroom to one side, its door ajar. Above the entrance door, a large transom with colored glass admits the light of the midafternoon sun, creating prisms of rainbows inside the room that are multiplied by the mirror located above the bed.

But he fails to see any of those rainbows.

And so does she.

They embrace each other, and she searches tentatively for his lips, just as he searches tentatively for hers.

And then the room with the myriad rainbows slowly dissolves around them.

W hat causes things to happen is difficult to tell. But somehow on that Tuesday afternoon, the room with the myriad rainbows is not the only thing that dissolves around Father Alonso and Loló.

Can she pinpoint when and why it happened? Can he?

Back in her room, she asks herself, Was it the lies I told my mother, my boss, my friends? Everybody? Even my own self? Or was it the embarrassment of having to meet him in a hidden place as if he and I were criminals? Or was it his face, a face filled with doubts, with fear, even with terror—the same doubts and fear and terror my own face was filled with when I looked at myself in the tiny mirror in the tiny bathroom in the posada room?

Back in his room, he asks himself, Was it the lies I told Father Francisco so I could leave the church in midafternoon? Or was it the embarrassment of changing clothes in some hidden place as if I were a criminal? Or was it my trying to fool myself, pretending that I desired her as I once desired Felipe, as my heart still desires Felipe? Or was it the faces of those children yesterday? The faces of children who need me? Whose eyes remind me of my mission? Of all the promises I made to myself—and to God—to die leaving the world a better place than the one I found when God created me and gave me my call? Or was it that I was not honest when I heard my call?

And then he asks himself one more question.

Did I even hear my call?

A shattering question that triggers many others.

Or did I just think I did? To escape? To hide? To evade life?

He remembers the advice of Father Cristóbal, his mentor back at the private boys' school he and Felipe attended. "My son, the church is a mission, not an escape. It is not a place for a man to hide, either. No matter how much he would like to, a man can never, ever evade life. He would only fool himself if he tried that. A man must face life with a lot of courage and bend it to his will. Only then can a man call himself a man, for only then can a man call himself free. And only then can a man offer his soul to the service of God. Only then. When he is free. Free to look at all the options in front of him, free to weigh them carefully, and free to choose. Wisely. Never in fear, but with manly courage. Do you understand what I am trying to say?"

That is what old Father Cristóbal said a man must do before he offers himself to the service of God, Father Alonso tells himself.

But is that what I did?

Have I been courageous enough to face life? To choose my own way? Or have I been cowardly in choosing this way of mine, to ignore the turmoil still harbored in my soul, so I can hide my head in the sand and pretend that all is well with me, that nothing has ever been wrong with me?

When I offered my soul to the service of God, did I offer it of my own free will, because I wanted to? Or did I just do it out of fear? Fear of these feelings I have for another man? Fear of not being considered enough of a man? Fear of being different from all the other men? Fear of what other people may think about me? Fear of being found out? Was that why I have been feeling so proud of myself from the moment I finally knew a woman? Father Alonso asks himself in disbelief.

When I did with her as I did . . . was that it?

Did I do it out of *fear*?

Not being able to answer his questions as he lies on his cot, Father Alonso shakes his head—just as Loló shakes hers as she lies on her bed.

Neither one of them knows what truly happened. What caused it.

But one thing is certain.

This time, after they took possession of each other, this time they both discovered—and at the very same time—that they were no longer the same people they were two days ago.

Two days ago, they were like children exploring each other. Two days ago, they felt totally at ease with each other, and totally at peace with themselves. Two days ago, they shared their innocence with each other. Two days ago, their lovemaking was impulsive, instinctive, spontaneous. Free. Chaste. Even pure.

But this time . . .

This time none of that existed. No, not any longer.

This time they were neither children exploring each other nor at ease with each other, nor at peace with themselves. This time they did not share their innocence with each other. Nor was their love-making this time impulsive, instinctive, spontaneous. Free. Chaste.

And certainly this time their lovemaking was no longer pure.

All that was gone.

And even though nothing was said as they said good-bye to each other, this time they both knew that they would never see each other again.

For this time they both knew that they had eaten of the forbidden fruit.

And the eyes of them both were opened, and they knew that they were naked.

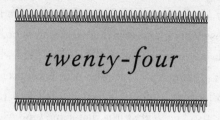

twenty-four

That night, in the loneliness of his tiny room, the young priest kneels at the foot of his cot, and recites aloud his vows: of obedience, of poverty, and of chastity, saying the words with a reverence that is new to him, for he means every word; every word comes not from his lips but from the bottom of his heart.

From the deepest part of his soul.

As he kneels in front of God, the young priest remembers that the first time he said these words, less than two years ago, when he was ordained in Spain, he had meant them. Or at least he thought he did. But at the time he did not know what those words really meant, what those vows really entailed.

Up till then, those words were just that: words. Words that had not been tested. Words he didn't know then were only symbols for actions.

But now, tonight, as he throws himself on the floor and lies prostrate in front of God, the young priest feels that God is listening to every one of those words, and that it is God who is ordaining him this time. Not a bishop. Not the Church. But God. God who has forgiven him. God who is guiding him. God who with his supreme will and wisdom decided to let him, a young priest, be led into temptation. But the young priest also knows that it is that same God who gave him the strength and the grace to survive it. Just as it is that same God who is now clearly showing him the way.

All night long he pondered the same questions over and over again, until he came to the only conclusion he found to be true: I did receive the call from God, he told himself. That call was honest and will always dwell deep, within my heart. Everything else means nothing to me. Those other questions, those other doubts, have finally been eradicated from my mind.

He knows he has been tested.

Just as he knows he has survived the test.

For now he knows that he is as much of a man as any other man, regardless of how he feels toward Felipe or toward Loló, because none of that has anything to do with real manliness, the kind of manliness he knows he carries deep inside of him. And now he knows that the man inside of him is a courageous one who is looking neither to hide nor to escape but, instead, a man who dreams of a better world and who is taking steps to make that world a reality.

With how much more compassion and love will I look at people who come to me for confession from this night on! Father Alonso tells himself. How much better a shepherd will I be from now on! Because God has shown me what it is to be human, what it is to be a man. And because God has also shown me that man can overcome all those human weaknesses and frailties inside of him and become like a god when his actions are guided by his dreams.

And by the truth.

"Oh, Lord, thank you," the young priest prays aloud right before falling asleep, "thank you for revealing yourself to me as human and as godlike as you are!"

That night, the slender woman with the dark, gypsy eyes also falls asleep, also thanking God for what he has done for her: letting her be a woman, a full woman. For removing from her eyes that look of envy with which she now knows she used to look at other women. And that look of awe and of curiosity and of desire with which she now knows she used to look at men.

Now she knows what that look of hers meant.

And now she knows why men looked back at her as they did.

But now she also knows she is past all that. For now she knows what she wants: a man who will look at her with the same kind, gentle eyes with which the young priest looked at her two days ago, when they both were innocent. A man who will smile at her with the same kind, gentle smile with which the young priest smiled at her two days ago. And a man who will induce her to look back at him with the loving eyes she has seen Marguita and Lorenzo look at each other, when they think no one is looking.

She closes her eyes, and as she falls asleep she is transported into a new world where she can finally live free of rancor and free of resentments and free of fear.

Free. At last.

As Loló, she with the dark, gypsy eyes, and Father Alonso, the young priest, find within themselves a peace they had lost, Marguita, lying next to Lorenzo, her husband, cannot make herself fall asleep.

And neither can Lorenzo, lying next to his wife.

Earlier in the evening, when Lorenzo came back home from the bookstore for a quick bite to eat before he ran to night school, Marguita welcomed him with the great news Doctor Manuel had given her.

Whatever reaction Marguita was expecting, that she did not get. No, not at all.

When told the news, Lorenzo did embrace her. But it was a different kind of an embrace from the one he had given her when she told him she was carrying their first child. That time Lorenzo had yelled with joy after he embraced and kissed her again and again. This time, his embrace was short, and it was followed by nothing but a long, awkward silence. Lorenzo did not say a thing. He just let go of her and shook his head. Then, after a while, he faced his wife, who was gazing at him with a trace of apprehension in her eyes. He sat in a chair and, emptying his pockets of silver, he placed all he had in them—a few coins, as well as his wallet, holding just two one-peso bills—on the dining table.

"Look at this," he said pointing to what was on the table. "This is all I have left until the end of the month. As it is, we barely have enough to cover our expenses from month to month. And that is with only one child. How are we going to manage when we have two? I don't see how we can do it unless I get another job at night and quit school."

"No, that you'll never do!" Marguita said forcefully. "I won't let you quit school. Not now. Not until you complete your studies. Not until then."

"Then what do you want me to do, Marguita? Give up the money I give to my parents? You know I can't do that. They barely have enough to put food on the table."

"Maybe if your brother Fernando could give them a little more money. Or your sister Loló."

"Fernando, maybe. But Loló . . . she'll never do that," Lorenzo replied.

"Of course she won't and do you know why? Because you keep on doing it and because she takes advantage of your being such a good son, that's why."

"So what do you want me to do, Marguita? Stop helping my family?"

"No," Marguita said. "Of course not."

"Then what?"

"Then . . . God will provide," said Marguita, who was already on the verge of tears.

"God provides for those who provide for themselves," Lorenzo replied instantly, quoting Marguita quoting her mother. "Isn't that what you always tell me?" Then he added as he stood up, "It's not only the money, Marguita. It's the time. And the worries. I still have at least two more years to go at school. You know I have to spend whatever free time I have studying. Tell me, how will I be able to study with two kids crying at the same time? I don't want to see them lack anything. Or you. Or me. I don't want to see them suffer. I don't want to see any of us suffer. Or go hungry. Or . . . It's not that I don't ever want to have another child. I do, Marguita, my love, you know I do. But now? Now? Now may not be the right time for another child."

"But, Lorenzo," Marguita said, "it is now when God is sending the baby to us. We cannot tell him when and—"

"Marguita," Lorenzo interrupted, "have you told anybody about . . . about this?"

Marguita shook her head.

"No," she said. "The only person that knows about this other than you is Manuel the doctor."

There was a long pause.

"Marguita, please listen to me," a reasoning Lorenzo began to say. "Manuel is now family. He's the baby's godfather. I think . . . I think that maybe we should go talk to him. Let him advise us. See if there are other options. Ask him if he might be able to help us out somehow."

"Lorenzo, what are you talking about?" uttered Marguita. "Help us out? What do you mean, help us out? What other options are there, Lorenzo?" a nervous Marguita begins to ask. "You don't really mean what I think you do, do you? That I should go to Doctor Manuel and ask him to help us get rid of this baby? Of *our* baby? Lorenzo, how can you even propose a thing like that? Do you want us to murder our own child?"

"No, I don't want us to do that. I'm just considering whether there is any way you could put a stop to this pregnancy."

"It's the same thing, Lorenzo. How can I stop it without killing my child?"

"No one has been born yet, Marguita. There is no child. There is not even a trace of a child, yet. It's invisible. Microscopic. Nobody can see it. Not even Manuel can."

"I cannot believe I am hearing you say this to me," Marguita said, and rushed into the bedroom where she threw herself on the bed weeping.

After a while, Lorenzo came to the bedroom and sat down next to her.

"Marguita," he said, caressing her blond hair, "you know I love you beyond limits. So, if a second child is what God is sending us, well, then, a second child we will have. We'll just have to hold back all our other dreams"—he stops her before she can say a word—"I don't mean give them up altogether. Just hold back. For a little while. So if it takes a couple more years to finish school, so be it. We'll manage somehow."

When she heard this, Marguita remembered she herself said those very same words, "we'll manage somehow," the day Lorenzo got home late after winning one hundred pesos at the jai alai palace. "School money" she called those one hundred pesos then. Money she meant never to use, not even for an emergency. Money she meant to become the foundation of a home of their own. Money meant to be sacred. But money that is already gone. The handkerchief knot had to be undone a long time ago, and the single one-hundred-peso bill exchanged. Food had to be placed on the table. The refrigerator's electric bill had to be paid. Even condensed milk had to be bought for her baby. And now . . . what are they going to do when the new baby arrives? How will they be able to manage?

"Marguita, please, don't cry," said Lorenzo. "You know I don't like to see you crying like that."

He embraced her tightly to him; she embraced him tightly to her.

But as they did, they both asked themselves the same question: *Am I doing the right thing?*

Lorenzo ate his dinner in silence and ran to school.

While there he did nothing but go over his accounts, figuring out where he could save, and how much.

The only possibility he saw were his travel expenses, which were high, what with his going to school at night. He might have to give up transportation altogether and walk to class, he thought. But then he would never be able to make it to school on time. Or if he did, he would be dead tired after all that walking. Which meant that he would not be able to pay attention. Which meant that he would be missing a lot. Which meant that his grades would suffer, maybe even to the point of failing. Which meant that he would not be able to graduate. Which meant that he would never get a chance to improve his position at the bookstore. Which meant staying as he was, a bookstore clerk, for the rest of his life. With little or no prospect of ever getting a better position.

Not seeing a clear future in front of him, he rubbed his eyes and shook his head.

While Lorenzo was at school, Marguita sat at the dining room table and began going over her accounts, figuring out where she could save, and how much. But hard as she tried she could not save but a couple of pennies a day.

Perhaps if I were to wash and iron other people's laundry, she told herself. She knew Lorenzo's mother Carmela had done it—the old lady herself had told Marguita. If Carmela was able to do it . . . well, so would she. A woman will do anything, anything to feed her children. But then, Carmela's kids were grown up and in school when she did all that, Marguita told herself. How would I be able to manage laundering and ironing with two kids by my side, both of them babies? And then she remembered that she had not produced enough milk even to feed her first baby. So, on top of all the other expenses, they would have to buy the milk to feed this second baby, as well.

Not seeing a clear future in front of her, she rubbed her eyes and shook her head.

By the time Lorenzo came back from school, Marguita was already in bed.

Lorenzo took off his clothes in silence and lay next to his wife—he facing away from her, pretending to sleep; she facing away from him, also pretending to sleep.

Both of them knowing that neither one of them was asleep.

Both of them asking themselves the very same question they have been asking themselves all night long as he sat silently in school and as she silently did the dishes and put little Renzo to bed.

Am I doing the right thing? Am I doing the right thing?

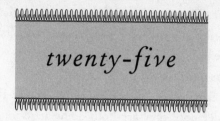

twenty-five

When Loló gets to work the following morning, and sits behind the safety of her switchboard, Zafiro looks at her and shakes her head in awe.

"What's happened to you, sugar?" she asks. "You look like a brand-new person."

"What do you mean?" Loló asks.

"I don't know. I can't pinpoint what it is that's different about you. Let me see, you don't have a new hairdo. That dress of yours I've seen before. It must be the . . . the what? Tell me, sugar, what did you eat last night? Whatever you ate, I want to eat it, too, because, Loló, you just look radiant today." Suddenly Zafiro smiles a mischievous smile aimed at Loló. "I know! You finally slept with a guy last night!"

Upon hearing this, Loló starts to giggle, which causes Zafiro to laugh. Except that when Zafiro laughs, it seems as if the whole world is doing it. The whole world, that is, except Señora Francisca Olivar y Argüelles, "the Owl," who rushes to where Zafiro and Loló are and clears her throat several times.

"Ladies, please, please. More decorum."

But hearing that word, "decorum," only makes the two friends laugh even louder until they are both doing it so loudly that everyone nearby laughs as well.

Everyone else but Señora Francisca Olivar y Argüelles who, irate, finally manages to say, "What's so funny?"

Zafiro, who has been laughing to the point of tears, says, her slurred words almost incomprehensible, "It's just that I asked Loló if . . . if the reason she looks so good today was . . . if last night she had . . . finally . . . slept with a guy!"

Her uproarious laughter stops abruptly when she sees the Owl's sharp eyes aimed at her, giving her a piercing, daggerlike look.

The old lady, whose look is as stern and serious as can be, asks Zafiro after a while: "Well . . . ?" She pauses. Then her face sketches a smile as she adds, a twinkle in her eyes, "Did she . . . ?"

And then it is the old lady who begins a contagious laugh that makes everyone else on the floor laugh as well, though they keep looking incredulously at the Owl, as if asking themselves: "The Owl . . . laugh?"

Loló herself cannot explain it.

But when she looked at herself in the mirror earlier today as she readied herself to come to work, she did notice something new about herself. Gone were the wrinkles around her eyes, and around the edges of her mouth. There was a softness about her she had never seen before.

Her own mother, Carmela, when she served breakfast to Loló, noticed it.

Using an old Spanish expression, she smiled at her daughter and said, "Loló, *niña, hoy tienes el bonito subido.* Loló, child, today your beauty is up."

It must be true, Loló told herself after the Owl went back to supervise another area of the immense floor. Today my beauty must be up. She smiles to herself. It must be because I slept all night long, just like an angel, she tells herself. Who would have imagined that? Me, sleeping like an angel?

Her board lights up.

"*Teléfonos,*" she says.

And gets to work.

A s Loló is busy making connections, Father Alonso sits inside the tall, semigothic confessional in his little church that is in such a bad need of a coat of paint, and turns on the light, indicating that he is available to hear confessions.

He too woke up today feeling like a brand-new man. A whole man, he tells himself. Sure of himself. Sure of his mission. Sure that he is taking the right steps and that he is going in the right direction. A man like Father Francisco, who has known a woman, yes. But a man, also like Father Francisco, who has finally been ordained by the good Lord himself, and who can now transform that very powerful tool God has given all of us, the sex drive, into his calling. He smiles to himself. Knowing Loló was a wonderful experience. Even a transcendent experience, for his life is different now. Thanks to her, it has totally changed. And for the better. He realizes that for years he had hidden a desire to know a woman, and that God himself had given him that desire. But now that he has finally satisfied his . . . his what? His curiosity? Now he is free to pursue his dream. Now he can actually set all that aside and become the priest he has wanted to be, ever since he felt the Lord's call stir within his heart.

He thanks the good Lord again for his help and guidance as he welcomes the first person who kneels in front of him in the safety of the confessional—a woman, he can tell, because of her scent. But this scent of hers no longer stirs his blood. Rather it makes him more at ease with himself.

The woman says, "*Ave María, purísima.* Hail Mary, the purest," the standard words people used at the time when approaching confession.

And he answers as expected, "*Sin pecado concebida.* Conceived without sin."

The moment he says it, he realizes that now he can fully understand what those words mean. For the lovemaking he experienced the first time with Loló was that kind: innocent in the simplest meaning of the word.

That is, free of guilt. Free of sin.

Just that, innocent.

He makes the sign of the cross and hears his first confession of the day.

L orenzo, at work, seems, on the other hand, utterly nervous, insecure. Since they are near the end of the month, he is closing the books, which usually takes a couple of days.

But never has he made so many mistakes.

I must take hold of myself, he tells himself. I must calm down and think about what I am doing. But he shakes his head. His thoughts are in Luyanó, with his wife. With his pregnant wife. He sighs deeply.

Collazo, who is passing by, asks him, "Are you all right, son?"

Collazo calls all his employees sons or daughters, which in a way they are. The old man may be a miser in his personal life, but if so, he is a miser who loves and cares for his family, the people who work not for him but with him—because Collazo puts as many hours on the job as anyone else in his store, if not more.

Lorenzo smiles at the old man.

"I didn't sleep very well last night," he admits.

"Oh, well," the old man replies, "that's what having a baby can do to you. Keep you awake all night long. Or so I've been told," he says, "because as you know, I don't have a child of my own. I mean, one that I know of," he adds, chuckling. He pats Lorenzo on the shoulder. "Go have some coffee. It'll wake you up. There's nothing like Cuban coffee to perk you up. Have it on me, tell Luciano to put it on my account." And with that, he leaves.

Lorenzo stands up and starts to go downstairs, to the street, to get some coffee from Luciano, the coffee vendor. But halfway down the stairs he asks himself, What was I going to get? He shakes his head. Unable to remember what it was he was about to do, he goes back up to his desk. It is only when he sits down that he slaps his forehead. Coffee! That's what I was going to get!

But by then it's too late. He decides to stay where he is. He looks down at his accounting ledger and begins to add columns of numbers.

Just to realize that every time he adds a column the total is a different amount.

As she is fixing the noontime meal, Marguita is debating what to do. Should she go to her mother? Consult her?

Marguita doesn't want to burden Dolores with any of her problems. Besides, what problems are these I am talking about? she asks herself. Didn't Lorenzo agree with me to have our baby, no matter what? Whatever else was said last night was said and forgotten. Erased. So then why should I keep asking myself over and over if we are doing the right thing? We are, aren't we?

Dolores has not been feeling well again, and again she has been sleeping nights in her rocking chair in the living room of her house. That is why Marguita does not want to go visit her. Because she is afraid that if she does, she will open up and tell everything to her mother.

There's no hiding anything from Dolores, Marguita knows, for Dolores can see through her daughter as if Marguita were transparent.

Besides, it wouldn't be fair to tell Mamá about any of what happened last night between Lorenzo and me, Marguita tells herself. It would upset her. Make her more sick. And if there is one thing Marguita never wants to see, it is her mother sick.

She hasn't told this to Dolores—she hasn't told this to anyone, not even Lorenzo—but every time Marguita leaves her mother's house, after she sees with what strenuous difficulty Dolores breathes, she goes home and cries. She cannot stop doing it. She sees her mother ail and instantly she becomes again the crybaby— *merenguito rechupete*—that she has been all her life.

Marguita cannot conceive of life without her mother. Dolores has always been not only the greatest mother there is, Marguita thinks, but the greatest friend there is. As well as the greatest neighbor. Marguita loved those days spent on the seashore in Batabanó when she was a toddler. She doesn't remember much about those days, except one time, which she can remember clearly.

That day, after playing "Friends and Neighbors" for a while, she and her mother were building a sand castle when Marguita turned her eyes to her mother and saw tears running down Dolores's cheeks.

"Why are you crying, Mami?" Marguita asked.

"Oh, it's nothing, Señora Marguita," Dolores hurriedly answered, hastily erasing her tears. "It was just this sand," she said, pointing to the golden sand on the beach. "Some of this pretty sand must have blown away and gotten in my eyes, and when that happens, it always makes me cry. Has that ever happened to you, Señora Marguita?" Dolores asked her pretty five-year-old.

The little girl nodded.

"You have to be very careful when you are playing with sand, Señora Marguita," Dolores added, grabbing a little bit of sand in her hands. "Sometimes it just escapes your fingers, like this," she said, spreading her fingers and making a sieve. "And when that happens, and if the wind blows it your way, well, sometimes some of those tiny, tiny grains get in your eyes and make you cry. You cannot see them, because they are so tiny. But nonetheless, if they get in your eyes . . . well, you know. They make you cry. So remember that, Señora Marguita. Sometimes you cannot really see the things that make you cry. So, if you find yourself crying, and you don't really know why, well, maybe it's because you just got some tiny little grain of sand in your eyes."

As Marguita begins to prepare the daily formula for little Renzo, she asks herself, Where else can I go to for help, for guidance? If not Mamá, who? Doctor Manuel . . . ?

It is then she hears the distant midday bells of the little Church of Our Lady of the Perpetual Succor calling for the midday prayer, the Angelus. As she hears those bells, she thinks of Father Francisco. But then she discards the thought.

Why bother the old priest? she asks herself. Why go to confession when there is nothing I am ashamed of? When there is nothing I'd have to confess?

The time to bathe her son is nearing.

She puts Renzito on the patio, inside his walker where he is safe, and then goes to the kitchen where she begins to boil the water for his bath.

During this entire summer, the summer of 1939, the city of Havana is having serious problems with water supply and Luyanó, being the poorest barrio in all Havana, does not have running water at all times. The barrio gets water for two hours in the morning, and for two hours in the evening. That is all. Mornings, everybody rushes to use the bathroom before the water is cut off. Then water has to be stored—in the bathtub, in pots, in pans, in what-have-you—for that water has to last the rest of the day until early evening when water service is restored again for a short time.

So, to bathe Renzito—something Marguita likes to do outside on the patio right at noon, when the sun is at its highest and the patio as warm as it can be—Marguita has to fill Renzito's bathtub, which is not really a bathtub but a pale-blue enameled metal pan standing on chrome legs that is a present from Celina, the wife of Doctor Manuel.

Using a metal pail, Marguita brings cold water from the bathtub, where she collected it earlier today, and pours it into Renzito's bathing tub until it is a little over half full. Then she goes to the kitchen. There she keeps a huge metal soup pot that has two metal handles and which earlier in the day she half-filled with water. She places it on top of the coal-burning stove and heats it until the water boils. Then, using hand towels wrapped around those two handles, she grabs the boiling pot of water, which weighs a ton, and takes it to the patio. She then mixes it with the cold water already in the tub until she feels that the temperature is perfect for her son.

It is only then that she bathes little Renzo.

Marguita loves doing this. As far as she is concerned, Renzito is still very much like a doll to her: a living, blond, blue-eyed doll of a boy she loves to bathe and feed and sing to, and then put to sleep. She is at her happiest when she is with her child. How could any mother not be? she asks herself. Her son is not *like* an extension of her; he *is* an extension of her. She would gladly give her life for his at any time, no question asked, no hesitation possible.

Today, as she begins to bathe her handsome boy, her thoughts travel to that other child, the one growing inside her, the one who is invisible. The one no one can see, not even Manuel the doctor. And then she wonders, What if Doctor Manuel were mistaken? What if

I were not with child? As she asks herself those questions, she sighs as she tells herself, We would not have any problems then, would we?

And then she hears herself saying, "I must have sand in my eyes." When she finds herself crying.

For she knows that neither she nor Doctor Manuel are mistaken.

When Lorenzo gets home for his noontime meal, he opens the door and finds Marguita waiting for him.

He doesn't have to say a word.

He just looks at her, a question in his eyes—a question that Marguita answers by rushing to him and throwing herself in his arms.

"I've been thinking," she says. "About last night." She pauses. "Perhaps you were right. Perhaps this is not the right time for another baby. Perhaps . . . perhaps Doctor Manuel might be able to help us."

He embraces her tight to him.

"Let's not rush into this," he says. "We still have time. Let's give it some thought."

"No, Lorenzo," she replies. "I can't go on living like I have since last night. Not being able to sleep. Not being able to . . . to do anything. I've been going crazy. I find myself doing something and I forget what it is I'm supposed to be doing. I'm afraid I might hurt little Renzo, do something wrong. Feed him the wrong food. I don't know. I just can't go on like this, Lorenzo. I think you and I should decide what to do and then go ahead and do it. Whatever it is we decide, I don't want anybody ever to know about it. I just don't want anybody ever to know."

"Calm down, my love. Calm down," he says. "We'll go to Manuel and see what he has to say. Maybe . . . I don't know. Maybe the laboratory made a mistake." He sees Marguita shake her head. "Maybe there are other solutions. I don't know. Let's wait. Let's just wait, all right? A couple of days. A week. Until next month. Let's sit down and go through budgets and figures. Marguita, we just can't make this kind of decision on the spur of the moment. We have to think it over." He looks at her. "One way or another whatever we decide is going to affect us for the rest of our lives. So let's give it plenty of thought." He sighs. "And Marguita, whatever we decide, it will be our decision and our decision only. Yours and mine together. We must both agree, and wholeheartedly, that we are doing the right thing, no matter what that decision is. All right?"

Marguita nods and leaves his arms to go into the kitchen.

Moments later, as their food is being slowly reheated, Marguita begins to feed little Renzo. Sitting at the table in a tall baby's chair that cost a bundle of hard-earned and hard-saved money, the baby has by now graduated to a different kind of food: thick purées of pumpkin and malanga—an inexpensive Cuban potato-like root—that are lovingly boiled and prepared by Marguita herself, and that the baby eats with great pleasure, clapping his hands as he does. Following this, Marguita gives the baby a serving of milk, still made with expensive, sweetened condensed milk, imported from the United States, for Renzito is still on a formula. Then, after she cradles her baby to sleep in her arms, softly singing to him in that beautiful voice of hers, little Renzo is put in his crib, facing up, as Doctor Manuel taught Marguita to do, covered with a light cotton blanket, but leaving his tiny feet out, so it won't get too hot beneath the blanket during the steamy Cuban afternoon.

It is only then Marguita and Lorenzo sit at the table.

But neither he nor she can eat a thing.

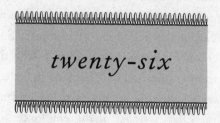

twenty-six

Loló does not understand—or maybe she just does not want to understand—what is happening to her.

This month is the longest she has ever lived through in her entire life. How long is it going to last? she keeps asking herself, as she waits and waits for something to happen.

But something does not happen.

Not being able to control herself anymore, as soon as she hears the three o'clock chimes, while the other girls are waiting for the elevator to go down, Loló rushes upstairs, two flights up, to see if she can still catch Señora Díaz in her office.

An older woman originally trained as a nurse,

Señora Díaz was hired by the telephone company four years back to provide first-aid assistance to the company's employees, but it soon became evident that she had an uncanny ability to deal with female employees who went to her not only for first-aid help but for advice as well. So, at the beginning of last year, Señora Díaz was promoted to personnel manager in charge of the division dealing with switchboard operators, all of whom are female, becoming the first and only woman to hold such a position within the company. Still called Nurse Díaz by most of the employees—something the old lady encourages, for she feels it inspires confidence and trust—Señora Díaz is highly respected and admired by all, and a lot of the women working at the company keep going to her, not only for first-aid assistance when it's needed, but for personal and professional advice as well. Though she is now an executive of the company, Señora Díaz has made it clear that she keeps her door open to all.

And that is just how Loló finds it.

She knocks on it gently and steps into the room right as the gray-haired woman is cleaning up her desktop and readying herself to leave.

"Señora Díaz," she says, "do you mind if I ask you a couple of questions?"

"Could this wait until tomorrow morning?" Señora Díaz asks, not looking at Loló as she keeps putting folders into an old file cabinet by the side of her desk. But when she turns and catches Loló looking at her, she sees something in those dark, gypsy eyes of Loló's that make the graying older woman stop what she is doing. Still holding several folders in her hands, she leans against the desk. "Are you all right?" She pauses. "One of those bad headaches of yours again?"

Loló shakes her head from side to side.

During the last few months, Loló had been complaining of horrible migraine headaches. But those had disappeared totally. She hasn't had one ever since—when? Loló asked herself days ago. Ever since that wonderful day in Guanabo, weeks ago, when I became a woman.

"Well?" says the older woman.

Loló looks up at the nurse. "What does it mean," she says haltingly, "if one's, well, you know . . . woman's thing . . . if it's late?

"Period?" the older woman says.

Loló nods. "Is that really bad?" she adds. "As bad as—"

"Why do you ask? Are you late?"

"Oh, no, no, no. It's not me." Loló blushes until she becomes the color of embers. "It's . . . it's one of the girls. Not me. Not me."

Señora Díaz looks at Loló and shakes her head. She is in constant wonder at how little the young women—and even the not-so-young women like Loló—who work right there in the telephone company really know about their own bodies. For years she has tried to create a course offering sex education for those very same women, most of whom are still virgins—what Cuban women of the period are supposed to be until the moment they marry. These girls, the old lady knows, know little, if anything, about that important part of their lives: sex. And what they know is generally grossly distorted. But the powers that be, upstairs on the executive floor, all of whom—but her—are married *men*, keep avoiding the issue, telling her, "Señora Díaz, why don't you just let Nature follow its course?" Every time she hears that, an infuriated Señora Díaz replies, "Well, in my opinion, there are times when perhaps we should show Nature what course to take!" But of course that kind of thinking is anathema in the Cuban society of the time. Words like "contraception" and "abortion" are never to be mentioned. They just do not exist. They cannot even be found in the Spanish dictionaries.

"Being late could mean a lot of different things," Señora Díaz says as she answers Loló's question. "There are many reasons why menstrual delays can happen. A sudden loss of weight, for example. Or too much stress. Or too much pressure. Or . . . well, many, many reasons."

Then, after a short pause she asks, "Loló, this girlfriend of yours . . . she is not married, is she?"

Loló shakes her head.

"I see," says the older lady. "But she has been sexually active, right?"

There is a long pause.

"Not much," Loló finally answers.

"Not much?" Señora Díaz asks, raising her eyebrows. "Loló, she either has or she hasn't. Which?"

"Maybe once or twice. That's what she told me."

"Once is all it takes, Loló."

Another long pause.

"So . . . You think . . ."

"Loló, I don't think anything. Like I told you, a late period can mean a lot of things. Or it may mean nothing at all. How regular is she?"

"Very regular. Every twenty-eight days, on the dot. That's what she told me."

"And how late is she?"

"Over two weeks."

Señora Díaz shakes her head very slowly from side to side and lets out a deep sigh.

"Loló," she says, "your girlfriend may be pregnant. And the best thing to do is to find out for sure if she is or not, before we do anything else. You understand that, don't you?"

Loló nods silently.

"All I need is a sample of her urine to find out." The old lady goes to a large filing cabinet at the opposite end of the room and opens the bottom drawer. Then, after finding what she has been looking for, she turns and faces Loló. "Here, take this sealed container with you. Ask your friend to break the seal right before she fills it up, just to this line. And Loló, tell her that whatever the result is, this is absolutely confidential between you, her, and me. No one else will find out about it. No one else in this entire company. Tell her that she has my word on that. Then, once we have the results and we know for sure, we will decide what to do next."

She hands the container to Loló, whose hand is badly shaking as she grabs it. Noticing this, Señora Díaz takes Loló's hand in hers and adds, "And, Loló, tell your friend not to worry. Everything's going to be all right, believe me, Loló. I know. Everything's going to be all right."

She lets Loló's hand go and looks at Loló with a confident smile on her face.

Loló evades Señora Díaz's knowing eyes as she takes the container and places it inside her purse—her hand still trembling. "How long will it take?"

"One day. If you can get hold of your friend right now and get me the sample, by tomorrow afternoon I should have the results. Do you think you can still find her?"

Loló nods.

"She's waiting for me. Downstairs. In the lobby."

"Run down and see if you can get her to provide me with a sample right now. I'll wait here for as long as I have to. Then I'll send it into the laboratory, and by tomorrow we should have the results of the test. And Loló," the older woman repeats, "tell her this is strictly between her and us. Think of this room as the office of a nurse, and the office of a nurse is sacred, like that of a priest. What goes on here, between these walls, is just our business and no one else's at all. Do you understand?" Loló nods. "Tell her that and, Loló, please, don't look so nervous when you talk to her. I don't want her to panic. There's no reason to panic. There never is. So take it easy."

Loló smiles at the old lady and then rushes to the elevator.

Moments later she is back, a filled container in her hands.

T he next afternoon, at the end of the workday, after nervously waiting all day long for this moment, a moment she fears, Loló finally takes a deep breath and, forcing herself to smile, she pretends to walk nonchalantly into Señora Díaz's office, though her knees are badly shaking.

When she sees Loló come in, the nice gray-haired old lady, who was sitting behind her desk expecting her, greets her with a smile, and with a gesture of her hand invites Loló to have a seat.

Loló shakes her head.

She just stands there facing Señora Díaz, rigid, frozen, as if she were in a courtroom awaiting a verdict; as if the older lady in the elegant business suit were both jury and judge, totally aware that the rest of her life pivots on what this nice old lady with the gray hair will tell her.

Either the simple "No" Loló hopes for.

Or the fateful "Yes" she dreads.

Noticing how pale and frightened Loló is, Señora Díaz stands up, goes to the door, which Loló left ajar, and quietly closes it.

Then, without saying a word, she goes back to her desk, where she sits, opens a drawer, takes out a plain white, business-size envelope, a corner of which has been ripped open, and pulls a single sheet of paper out of it.

Loló does not move, does not even blink, as Señora Díaz reads her the results of the test.

Then Señora Díaz stands up, and, from behind her desk, she hands Loló the sheet of paper, so Loló herself can read it.

Loló looks at it for the longest time, the plus sign on the paper appearing to be, in Loló's eyes, not a positive sign at all, but rather a negative cross: a horrible, terrible, negative cross that stares her in the face.

It takes Loló a long while before she notices that Señora Díaz's hand is still extended toward her, and before she realizes that the older lady, still standing behind her desk, is waiting to get the sheet of paper back. Loló, embarrassed, not daring to look at Señora Díaz, barely nods once as she silently hands the sheet of paper back to the older lady.

When she has the sheet of paper in her hands, Señora Díaz waves it gently in front of Loló. "This test is ninety-seven percent accurate when the result is positive, so we are pretty sure the girl whose test this is is pregnant," she says. Then, making her voice as gentle as she can, she adds, "Loló, honey, this girl here . . . this girl is you, isn't it?"

Loló, still standing up, still frozen, still rigid, nods.

"Loló," the older lady says, "why don't you sit down?"

But Loló shakes her head. She doesn't want to sit down. She feels that if she were to sit down, she would never be able to drag herself out of that chair.

There is a long, long pause finally broken by Señora Díaz who, in a kind voice, asks, "Loló, have you said anything yet to the child's father?"

Loló looks at the older lady and like a scared child who is afraid to utter a word, she just shakes her head.

"Is he a married man?" the older lady asks gently, her voice ever so soft as she addresses the child she sees in front of her, the child Loló has become.

Loló again shakes her head.

The older lady smiles. "Well, then," she begins to say, "if he isn't, things may turn out for the best after all. I'm sure the moment you tell him about his child, he'll—"

But Loló starts to shake her head and shake her head so violently from side to side that Señora Díaz, seeing the gigantic stress that Loló is under, interrupts herself.

"All right, Loló, all right. I won't insist. If you want to tell him, that will be all right. And if you never want to tell him, that will also be all right. All I am suggesting is for you to think about it. After all, Loló, whoever that man is, he *is* the child's father. Whatever happened between the two of you, he has the right to know. You may not think so now, but he may want to know about his child. A lot of things can change when he finds out about his child, Loló. I've seen it happen before. Trust me, Loló. Go tell him and you'll see. You'll see how everything will turn out for the best. I know, child, I know. Everything always does."

Loló looks at her with puzzled eyes, weighing what Señora Díaz has just said.

Then, after a short while, she shakes her head again.

Still standing behind her desk with the sheet of paper with the test results in her hand, Señora Díaz sighs softly, almost to herself, and shakes her head gently. "All right, all right," she says. Then, sitting down on her desk chair, she places the sheet of paper on the top of her desk and her hands folded over it, as if clasping it, and, looking up at Loló, she begins to speak slowly, deliberately, the way a teacher does when she wants to make sure she is being clearly understood.

"To begin with," she says, her voice sounding decisive, official, "let me assure you, Loló, that nobody in this building knows about this, unless you've told them. Let me repeat this, Loló. Nobody. Except you and me. Not even the people who ran the test. As you saw, your name does not appear anywhere on these test results. Only mine does. A lot of girls walk into this office daily, so there's no way this"—she points to the paper—"can be traced to any one of them in particular. And certainly not to you."

Then her voice becomes gentle, kind, no longer the official voice of a teacher, but the voice of a mother, the voice of a friend.

"Loló," she adds, "listen to me. This is very important, very important. Whatever happens, whatever other decisions you make, people won't know about any of this unless you tell them. But listen, and listen to me well. No one will ever need to know. Absolutely no one. To begin with, you won't show for a long while, so we have plenty of time to think and to do what's best for you and for the child." She pauses, then asks, "Have you been having any morning sickness?"

Loló shakes her head.

"Good. But even if you were to have it, there are many other reasons why people get sick, so nobody will associate that with your being pregnant. In fact, here," she says, getting a bottle of pills she had on top of her desk and handing it to Loló, "I got this for you. Take it. Notice that I changed the label outside so it doesn't say that it is for morning sickness but for migraine headaches, like the ones you used to have. A lot of people feel nausea when they have migraines, so it's perfectly natural to take these. Loló, whatever happens, you must take good care of yourself, do you understand me?"

Loló takes the bottle in her hands and nods.

"All right," Señora Díaz says, her voice again official but still kind, the voice of a caring teacher, a voice that not once had shown the slightest sign of judgment, not once. "Now, let me tell you some of the options we have, some of the things that we can do." She raises her eyes and smiles gently at Loló.

"As all you girls know, I belong to a society that can help women in cases like yours. All the help is anonymous. They will never know who you are, you will never know who they are. But we have funds to send you somewhere away from Havana. We'll select where later on, but this will be someone's home where you can be taken care of properly and have your child. Nobody needs to know about this, and I mean it"—she underlines it—"*nobody*, not even anyone in your family. You can tell them that because of your excellent performance here at work you are being promoted and that you are being sent somewhere for a short period of time. I still don't know exactly where—I'll have to think about that. But you don't have to worry, because the promotion will be real. And well deserved, I may add. For the last few months my colleagues and I have been observing how good you are at your work, how much you seem to enjoy it, and how extremely well you relate to the other girls in your section. And last week, during our monthly executive meeting upstairs, your name was one of the very few that came up for a promotion. So, once you get it and you are transferred, you'll be able to work there until your child is born."

She looks at Loló, waiting for some reaction, but seeing none, she proceeds.

"Then, and believe me, Loló, I know this is hard. But I would advise you to decide as soon as possible to give the baby up for adoption. If you decide to do it within the next few weeks while you're still in Havana, by the time the baby's born he or she will have a home and a family."

Señora Díaz pauses for a second, while she looks into Loló's face, which is normally white but which has become so extremely pale it is almost ghostly.

"Loló," the older lady stresses again in that kind, gentle way of hers, "I know this is hard, honey, very hard. But think. There are many people out there who are not as lucky as you are because they can't have any children, and those people are dying to adopt one. They will care for your baby, and they will love your baby more than you think possible, because they want that baby so badly. Many of them will pay for all your expenses and even give you some small stipend. You won't have to live on public welfare, nor will your name appear on anything, except on the adoption papers, which you'll have to sign. Loló, child, please, look at me," the old lady says.

Loló raises her dark, gypsy eyes that have been looking down at the glossy terrazzo floor and looks at Señora Díaz, whose gray eyes have great kindness and love emanating from them.

"Loló," the older lady says, "if you decide to do this, nobody, but *nobody,* will ever know about this except you. And I mean it. Not even the people running the place where we'll send you. Before you go, we'll give you a ring to wear. A simple gold band. That by itself will stop a lot of people from asking many embarrassing questions. You'll be surprised what that simple gold band can do," she adds.

Loló looks at Señora Díaz and says nothing.

This month is one of those months that happen only every so often that have two full moons. Because the moon was full on August 1, tonight, on the thirtieth day of August, a second full moon is lighting the night sky, casting an intense pale-blue light on Loló's bed.

But by the time of this second moon, as Loló lies in bed, tossing and turning, unable to sleep, she already knows what she didn't want to know, what she can no longer deny. What she now definitely knows to be incredibly true: that she is carrying inside of her the child of a man who is much younger than herself, a young man with glossy dark hair, a deeply carved cleft chin, and an apparently perennial dark-blue five-o'clock shadow on his face. The child of a young man with deeply set dark-blue eyes who has barely said a word to her. The child of a young man who wears a cassock and who has consecrated his life to God. The child of a young man who took the name of "Alonso" when he was ordained.

But the child of a young man whose real name she does not even know.

PART SIX

Abortion

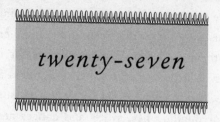

twenty-seven

In the total darkness of her room, as she lies in bed next to her husband with her eyes wide open, Marguita feels the magical light of a pale-blue moon bathing her, but she fails to see any trace of it. And yet, somehow, she knows the light is there somewhere. She feels it—the intangible, invisible light pressing on her as it envelops her with its coldness. But though she turns her head and looks all around her she cannot manage to see any of that magical pale-blue light she is feeling.

She hears rustling, rushing sounds above her.

She raises her head.

There, way above her head, she sees something she has never seen before: a strange silver glittering, a sparkling source of light that seems to change its shape constantly, transforming itself all the time.

She squints her eyes hard, trying to focus them on the glittering silver disk above her, until she is able to see emanating from it a diadem of pale-blue rays of light that seem to be shimmering as they filter and dance through the rushing, rustling water that surrounds and covers her. Marguita realizes her weightless body is being tossed around within a whirling sea; a turbulent, surging sea that, covering and surrounding her, swirls and dances around her, now with wild abandon, now with tumultuous motions.

She tries to open her mouth to say something, to scream, to ask for help. But she cannot do it. *Asesina,* she hears a voice from above filtering through the swirling waters devouring her. *Asesina.*

Murderer.

She tries to move toward the voice, toward the glittering silver disk, but her body won't respond to her commands; her body now a thing of its own, no longer hers. She raises her eyes and sees, above the glittering, rushing water, her own mother pointing her index finger down at her.

Asesina, she hears the same voice again.

Murderer.

It is her mother's voice. Mamá, where are you, Mamá? she wishes she could say. But words fail to come out of her mouth.

Hard as she tries, her body does not—will not—respond to her wishes. Marguita commands and commands her body to move, to rush to the voice above her, to break through the surface of the swirling waters above her again and again and again until she sees an arm stretch past her toward the glittering disk. Her right arm. She knows it is her right arm, but she does not feel it belongs to her anymore. She sees the right arm that used to be hers stretch past her, the right hand that used to be hers desperately reaching up for the glittering silver disk above her. She opens her mouth again, to say something, to scream. But she cannot do it. She feels herself getting farther and farther away from the glittering silver disk, as the reaching arm that used to be hers gets farther and farther away from her as well.

Desperately, frantically, she commands herself to scream. Demands it. Again and again, until she feels her mouth finally starting to open up. But no words come out of it. She looks up again, at the right hand that used to be hers, a small distant hand now miles away from her. She commands her body one more time, and this time her body manages to obey. Marguita feels a scream beginning to burst out of her open mouth, just as the right hand that used to be hers pierces through the surface of the wildly rushing waters that envelop her, condemning her to drown.

And then, all of a sudden, she is floating above a rough sea.

A miracle, she thinks.

She looks up at the glittering silver disk above her and sees that the sparkling light she felt before is coming from the beautiful face of a kind, gentle lady, her *virgencita,* her Little Virgin, the one Marguita prays to, who, dressed in a golden robe, is floating on a silver moon, an incandescent halo of blinding light surrounding her face as she smiles at Marguita from above. Marguita smiles back at the gentle lady as she begins to ascend toward her, Marguita's eyes beaming with an internal peace and joy she has not felt ever before as she stares at the beautiful face of the lady. And then suddenly Marguita's smile freezes on her lips, when she sees the eyes on the face of the lady become the accusing eyes of her own mother who, staring piercingly deep into Marguita's eyes, seem to be saying:

Asesina.

Asesina.

Asesina.

Murderer.

* * *

Loló shakes her head again and again and tosses and turns around in her bed, unable to fall asleep. And then she remembers Señora Díaz's words. "After all, Loló, whoever that man is, he *is* the child's father. Whatever happened between the two of you, he has the right to know. You may not think so now, but he may want to know about his child. A lot of things can change when he finds out about his child, Loló. I've seen it happen before. Trust me, Loló. Go tell him and you'll see. You'll see how everything will turn out for the best. I know, child, I know. Everything always does."

Yes, Loló tells herself. He has the right to know. She sighs. But after we did as we did, and the way we did it . . . wouldn't he think that this child is not his? That it may be someone else's? Why would he believe me? In his eyes I am probably nothing more than a common woman, a bad woman, *una cualquiera,* she tells herself, using the expression Cubans use to refer to whores.

She feels a migraine headache coming. She rushes to the bathroom where her pills are. She takes one. Then another.

If only it were this simple to—

Her thoughts simply stop.

Oh, Lord, she tells herself when she realizes what she has just thought. Forgive me, forgive me. She looks at herself in the small mirror above the medicine cabinet in the immense bathroom. How could I have thought what I did? How could I have wished what I just wished on my child? When having a child is the one thing I have always wanted, more than anything else in the world?

Back in her room, Loló falls on her bed—but still cannot manage to fall asleep.

Options, Loló thinks. What options do I really have? What options are there? What options can there really be for me?

Everything seems to be so unreal to her. As if she were part of a *novela,* one of those Spanish soap operas the Cuban radio stations love to play at all hours of the day and night; the kind her mother

Carmela loves to listen to religiously as she mops the worn marble floors of her old house, or makes the beds, or cooks.

What would have happened, she thinks, if when I arrived from work I had told my parents, "Papá, Mamá. I'm going to have a baby."

She imagines the look on her parents' faces. She can see it so clearly. At first they would not have believed her, that much she knows. Things like this do not happen, cannot happen to anyone in their family, to their daughter, to her. Maybe her parents would have thought that she was joking. But in Cuba a girl does not joke about this kind of thing. Then, enraged, Padrón, her old father, his face red, his voice shaking, his hands already made into fists, would have asked, "Who did this to you?" demanding to know the name of the culprit, the name of the man who has taken advantage of her, so he could be forced to make amends—or else he will be stabbed to death by someone in her family, for that's what a Latin family must do to cleanse its honor once it has been stained. As if she had not consented to it of her own free will. As if she had nothing to do with it. Because Loló knows that no one in her family would accept any explanation for what she has done other than rape; because things like this never happen—can never ever happen—to a nice girl like the girl she is—was—unless she is forced. Violated.

Loló has to smile at herself.

It all sounds so melodramatic. As if she were not thinking the words at all but as if she were listening to them on a radio *novela*. She sighs. It is only melodramatic when it happens to someone else, she thinks. But when it happens to you . . .

She imagines her radio station heroine proudly standing up to her parents and adamantly refusing to name the father of her child. "Dead first," she hears the heroine proudly say, "*Primero muerta.*" Why should she give the boy's name away? the radio heroine asks her parents. It was not the boy's fault, the heroine says.

No, it was not his fault, Loló repeats in her own mind, echoing the heroine of the radio soap opera she has been listening to inside her head. Just as it was not my fault either, Loló adds. It was nobody's fault.

And if it was somebody's fault, it certainly was not the baby's.

When she found out that her pregnancy test had proved positive and that she was, without a shadow of a doubt, pregnant, the first thought that crossed her mind as she stood in front of Señora Díaz was, How easy everything would be if only I could get rid of this baby inside of me!

Then, before she left Señora Díaz's office, Loló turned to her and, though she was deeply embarrassed by what she was planning to say, did manage to ask the old lady, "Señora Díaz, do you think that I . . . I mean, is there some way I could . . . you know, get rid of the baby?"

"You mean an abortion?" the old lady asked, her voice gentle, kind.

When she heard that word, *abortion*, Loló felt as if a cold electrical current had just run through her body. She never thought anything like what she was going through could ever happen to her. To other women, yes. But to her?

"Is that what you mean?" the old lady continued.

Loló simply lowered her eyes as a way of nodding.

"I can't offer you any help with abortions," the old lady said, matter-of-fact. "To begin with, they are illegal. No doctor would ever perform one. Well, some of them do, but only at the request of relatives or very close friends. And if they do perform them, they have to do it in hiding, like criminals. Doctors who are caught performing abortions instantly lose their licenses and may even end up in jail. And, Loló, unless they are performed by a professional in perfectly sterile and antiseptic surroundings, abortions can be very, *very* dangerous. Deathly so. So, please, I beg you, don't try anything like that. For your own sake, child, for your own sake."

Loló understood and nodded.

She hated the very word. *Abortion*. And yet, that had been the first thought that had crossed her mind as she stood in front of Señora Díaz yesterday and found out the truth about herself.

And about her baby.

But now she asks herself, How could I ever have considered getting rid of my own child? How could I ever have thought about punishing, *murdering*, my own child, for something I myself did? If anything, I should be the one to be punished because it was I who, without thinking of any of the consequences, did as I did. Why punish my baby when it was I who acted, never thinking—never even remotely suspecting—that something like this could ever happen to me?

Or did I?

Wasn't this exactly what I dreamed of? Every time I looked at that young man in the cassock, did I not hear myself silently repeat the expression I've heard many of my girlfriends whisper to each other whenever they see a young man they like: "What a father for my children!" How many times have I heard myself saying that? she asked herself. Whenever I looked at him, was her answer. That many times.

Well, Loló smiles to herself, hasn't my wish come true?

The morning light encircles her.

She sighs, stands up, and goes into the bathroom.

As she enters the bathroom, Loló remembers that whenever any of her girlfriends would look at a young man and say those words, they all would look at each other and giggle. She certainly does not feel like giggling today. But I don't feel like crying either, she says to herself. How could I? The mere thought that I am carrying a child makes me happy. Elated. And yet sad and terrified at the same time.

All because of a piece of paper she does not have.

Why would a marriage certificate, a mere piece of paper with both my name and his name on it—a name I still do not know—make such a big difference? Loló asks herself.

She bends down and opens the faucet of the tub, noticing that the ring finger in her left hand does not have a gold band on it. A simple gold band worn on the left hand that would make everything different. Legitimate. All right. A simple gold band that would make her parents jump with joy at the news of her carrying a child, instead of crying in despair and wishing she were dead.

"You'll be surprised what a simple gold band can do," she says aloud to herself, quoting what Señora Díaz said to her. And then she sighs again.

That visit with Señora Díaz seems to Loló to be so far away, so distant, as if it happened to someone else, someone she'd read about ages ago. But no, it didn't happen to someone else I've read about, but to me, she reminds herself. And it didn't happen ages ago but yesterday afternoon, not even a day ago. Señora Díaz was so kind, she recalls, as she tests the temperature of the water to get it just right.

Then, after taking off her robe, which she hangs on the hook behind the door, and her underwear, which she places in the clothes hamper next to the armoire, she gets into the bathtub.

Funny, she thinks, Señora Díaz never once mentioned yesterday afternoon that I could keep my child. She embraces her naked belly already inside the warm tub water. Isn't that another option? I don't want to have to give my child away. His child. Our child, she thinks. Letting the warm water embrace her, her eyes look up at the white plaster ceiling as if searching for a sign. But failing to see it, she prays fervently, the words repeating and repeating in her mind over and over again, Oh, God, please, please, help me, please. I don't know what to do, I don't know what to do, I don't know what to do. She closes her eyes. If only all of this were just a nightmare, a horrible nightmare, she tells herself. If, when I open my eyes again, none of this had ever happened. If only I could set the clock back in time and I had not gone to Renzito's christening, then—

It is right then that she thinks of her brother, Lorenzo. And of the man who is the godfather of Lorenzo's child.

Manuel. The doctor.

She opens her eyes in horror.

Oh, no, no, Loló says to herself, I don't want to think about that. I don't want to have to go to him. I don't want Lorenzo to force me to go to Doctor Manuel. I don't want to have to ask Doctor Manuel to kill my baby.

Desperately, she looks up again at the ceiling.

Oh, God, please, please, she prays and prays with ardent fervor, help me, help me, she keeps saying over and over, her words filled with fright and despair. I don't want to lose my baby, she says, I don't want to lose my baby, I don't want to lose my baby. And as she does that she embraces her belly with great tenderness.

It is only then she begins to cry.

Loló hasn't cried once—no, not even once—since she found out the truth. She did not cry while Nurse Díaz talked to her yesterday afternoon; she did not cry as she walked back home; she did not cry when upon reaching her home she found herself all alone, having no one to turn to. No. She did not cry then.

But now, as she lies in the bathtub, the warm water embracing her, she begins to cry. Weep. Sob.

Not for her. No. Not for her.

But for her baby.

She stands up with great difficulty and, with water dripping from her naked body, she falls on her knees, right there, inside the half-filled bathtub, her bare knees on the hard enameled base of the tub.

Please, Lord, forgive me, Loló prays. Not for having known him. Not for carrying his child, she cries.

But for wishing my child were dead!

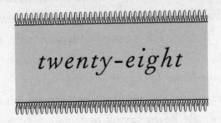

twenty-eight

After helping Father Francisco celebrate the early-morning Mass, Father Alonso goes to the sacristy, and, as he does every day, he takes off his white acolyte robe, places across his shoulders the sacred stole, and, holding his breviary in his hands, he reenters the church and crosses the narrow main nave to go to the confessional located at the other end.

As he crosses in front of the altar, he genuflects before God, as he knows he must do. But this time, as he kneels, his eyes glitter with a limitless internal joy when he looks at the altar, the way his eyes have been glittering now for days, weeks. Ever since the moment he opened up his heart to God and confessed everything he had done to one of his representatives on earth, Father Francisco.

The morning after he spent an afternoon with Loló in the posada room, Father Alonso told his mentor that he needed to meet with him, that he needed to have his mentor hear his confession. They met later on in the day in Father Francisco's own room, a cell of a room not that different from Father Alonso's. There, Father Alonso threw himself on his knees in front of the old man and, keeping his eyes down, told Father Francisco about the trial God had put him through and how God himself had helped him survive it.

The old priest listened quietly to Father Alonso, saying not a word to the man who, kneeling in front of him, was so earnestly opening his heart to God. Afterward, when Father Alonso raised his eyes and looked at his old mentor, he saw forgiveness in his eyes, for though they were closed, they were also filled with tears. "Please, Father, forgive me for what I have done. For breaking the vows I made to God." And the old man made the sign of the cross above him and said, "Go in peace, my son. Your sins are forgiven."

In his confession, Father Alonso did say, "Please, Father, forgive me for what I have done. For breaking the vows I made to God."

But in his confession Father Alonso never asked God to forgive him for having known a woman. How could he, when he feels no guilt in having done as he did? When actually he is proud he was able to do it? When by having done as he did he feels he finally became a true man?

Father Alonso sits in the confessional and turns on the light indicating that he is available to hear confession. Though he and the person who kneels in front of him for confession are securely masked from each other, he thinks he can still make out those dark, gypsy eyes of Loló's through the cane divider that separates them—her intimate scent as pervasive today as it was back then. He hears her whisper the same musical kind of whisper he heard so many weeks ago.

But today she is only a woman confessing her sins.

And he only a priest.

Moments later, the church now completely empty, a distressed young man dressed in a black cassock leaves the security of his confessional, rushes to the altar, and throws himself prostrate at the feet of God.

He has no one else to turn to but God.

What he has just learned he can tell no one—absolutely no one. He is bound by the secret of confession.

But now he knows he has fathered a child. A child of his own.

As Father Alonso lies before God, he sees in front of him the children at his mission, children with eyes full of longing, children he will no longer be able to work with, children he will no longer be able to teach, to help, to see them grow up and mature and become men and women of goodwill. And he sees his mission, his work, his life, his dreams, the dreams he has been holding and cherishing for such a long time, ever since he felt the call of God enter his heart, he sees those dreams, his everything, collapse in front of him. For he knows he must do as he must, as an honorable man must.

Oh, God, he prays. Now that I feel I have truly found my mission. Now that I am so secure in myself. Now that I know I can truly be the shepherd I vowed I would be. Is this, God, your way of punishing me? Father Alonso asks the tall, slender figure of an emaciated Christ nailed to a cross that hangs above the altar. For my feeling so proud of having known a woman? For not feeling guilty about what she and I did? For feeling so immensely relieved that I was not that other kind of a man I thought I was? A man with unnatural desires for another man? For not having asked you to forgive me for what she and I did? Is this, God, your way of punishing me? he asks again and again as he lies prostrate on the floor at the foot of the altar, his hands clenched into fists.

Making an immense effort, Father Alonso lifts himself on his elbows, and looking up, peers intently into the eyes of that Christ hanging above him, desperately searching in those eyes for an answer.

But those eyes, which seem to be lost in a faraway distance, provide him with none.

Father Alonso breaks down, crying.

Sobbing.

"Oh, Lord," Father Alonso says aloud, opening his hands and showing his palms to that Christ hanging above him as he offers the same prayer Jesus offered at the Mount of Olives: "If Thou be willing, remove this cup from me: nevertheless, not my will, but Thy will be done!"

That is all Father Alonso can say.

"But Thy will be done! Thy will be done!"

Lorenzo gets home for his noontime meal and when he opens the door, he finds a teary-eyed Marguita waiting for him. He just looks at her, a question in his eyes—a question that Marguita answers by rushing to him and throwing herself in his arms.

"What's wrong?" he asks, deeply concerned.

"I can't go on like this," she says. "I almost killed Renzito today."

When Lorenzo hears this melodramatic statement, he has no choice but to smile at Marguita. He's been married to her long enough to know her tendency to dramatize even the most insignificant event. "What happened?" he asks.

"It's true, I almost killed him. I was getting ready to give him his bath, and I had already put the cold water in his tub, so I placed him in his walker while I went to the kitchen to get the pot of boiling water, like I always do. I don't know what I was thinking about, but as I was bringing the boiling pot to the patio, the boy ran into me with his walker, making me trip, and some of the boiling water spilled on his walker. Thank God nothing fell on him. I would have killed myself if I had burned my son. Oh, Lorenzo, I just can't go on like this. We have to decide and then we have to go to Doctor Manuel and get the whole thing done with. It's driving me crazy, this waiting and waiting. For what? I see no other way out. Right now your going to school is more important than anything else. We are young, aren't we? We can have other children. I'll just have to—" She bursts out crying.

"Hush, Marguita. Hush," he says, leading her back into the dining room. "We'll go see Manuel and see what he has to say."

D o you know what you are asking me to do?" Manuel the doctor tells Marguita and Lorenzo that same afternoon.

They are in his office, the two of them sitting quietly, listening to Manuel, who keeps shaking his head as he speaks.

"I know it is done. I know a lot of people do it. But Lorenzo," he adds, "I may lose my license, my practice, my clinic, if word of this gets out."

Lorenzo sighs as he keeps his eyes looking down to the floor.

"But that's not the point," the doctor goes on. "The point is that there's a life right now inside Marguita. Invisible, yes. But a life nonetheless that is struggling against so many odds, trying to grow up and mature. A life begging to come forth. I am a doctor, Marguita," he tells her. "When I became a doctor I swore first and above everything to do no harm." Manuel sees how tense and apprehensive Marguita and Lorenzo seem to be at what he has just told them. On the other hand, he also knows how difficult it must have been for them to come to see him and ask him for his help. "I know that I am Renzito's godfather, and that I am bound to help you as much as I can. So what you ask me to do, I will do."

Upon hearing this, Marguita sighs.

Lorenzo grabs her hands tight in his.

"All I am asking you to do is to think it over." Lorenzo is about to say something, Manuel stops him. "To think it over *again*." He faces Marguita. "We still have time. The procedure is simple provided it's done within the first trimester, so we still have plenty of time. So, please, give yourselves"—he looks at his calendar—"two more weeks. If by then your decision remains the same, well, then, we'll take care of it. Right here, in this office. It won't take long and you'll be able to walk back home the same day," he tells Marguita. He smiles at them. "I know, I know you've thought about this a whole lot already. So, if you want to, we'll get it done right away. I just think that a lot of things can happen in a couple of weeks, and—"

Marguita begins to cry.

"What is it, Marguita?"

She shakes her head. "I just don't know . . . I just don't know if I can go on like this for two more weeks, Doctor Manuel," she says, her words difficult to understand. "I almost killed Renzito the other day when I almost spilled boiling water on him. At times I don't even know what I'm doing. This thing is consuming me. I think about nothing else." She raises her eyes to the wise doctor looking at her. "I just want to get it done." She pauses. Then adds, "I just don't want you to think ill of us. It's just that—"

"Oh, no, Marguita," the doctor interrupts. "How can I think ill of any of you? I just want to help, that's what we doctors are for. I just need to make sure you know what you're doing. You're not the only couple who is going through all of this at this moment. Many couples are. Things are very difficult out there, many couples don't have enough to put food on the table as it is, and many of those couples are already burdened with children they did not want, and tell me, what's going to happen to those unwanted children? Will they be abused, hurt? By their own parents?"

Manuel notices Marguita looking questioningly at him.

"Don't look at me with those eyes, Marguita. It's true. You'd be surprised by what I have seen. Right here, in my own clinic: children who have been badly hurt by their parents, children who arrive here with broken arms, broken legs. Every time I see one of them, I tell myself that I swore not to do any harm—like all of us doctors—and yet, I ask myself, what is worse? Putting a stop to a pregnancy, or letting those unwanted children come into a world where they experience nothing but suffering from the day they are born? I don't know, I just don't know what's the right thing to do. That's why I must rely on your judgment. And that's why I was begging you for a little time. Not for your sakes, but for mine. But, now, after what you told me, that you almost hurt little Renzo, my own godchild . . ."

He shakes his head. Looks at his calendar. "Can the two of you come next Monday? That's the day Estela is here to help me. Her I can trust completely. I know she won't say a word about this to anybody, and neither will I. Be assured of that. So . . ." He checks his calendar. "Next Monday?"

Lorenzo and Marguita look at each other.

Then Lorenzo grabs Marguita's hands and nods.

"I'll see you next Monday, then," the doctor says, as he stands up and leads his concerned patients to the door.

"Oh, I almost forgot that Saturday is Renzito's birthday," he says upon reaching the door. "So I'll see you then. And remember, smile. For little Renzo's sake. Smile. Everything will be all right."

Father Alonso enters Father Francisco's cell of a room that same night.

The room is lit only by a twenty-five-watt bare lightbulb hanging from the high ceiling, casting the large shadows of both priests on the whitewashed plaster walls, naked save for a plain wooden crucifix on the wall behind the old priest's cot.

"Yes, my son?" the old priest asks.

Father Alonso kneels in front of him and begins to cry.

Father Francisco lifts the young man. "What is it, my son?" he asks, deeply concerned as he embraces him. Never has he seen Father Alonso like this. Never.

Father Alonso shakes his head, pulls himself away from Father Francisco's embrace, and again kneels in front of him.

"Father," the young man says. "Consider this an official request from me." He takes a deep breath, so he will not break down again. "Please, inform His Excellency the bishop that I wish to get a dispensation from my vows."

Father Francisco looks with kind eyes at his young acolyte. "On what grounds?"

Father Alonso wasn't expecting this question. He says nothing.

"You know you'll remain a priest for the rest of your days," the old man continues. "Even when you receive full dispensation from the pope, you will nonetheless remain a priest. Until the day of your death." He sees Father Alonso nod. "But before we submit your request to the church, we must know on what grounds."

Father Alonso looks his old mentor in the eye.

"On the grounds that I'm not fit to be a priest. That I'm not fit to be called a disciple of Christ. That I'm not fit for this garment I wear, nor for what it represents. On the grounds that I am a sinner."

"Sinners are we all," the old priest says. "I the first."

He smiles at his young protegé. "Nobody's perfect, my son. Nobody can expect perfection from anyone else. I don't. The pope himself doesn't. He's as imperfect as you and I are—so long as he's a man. He recognizes our human faults, our human frailty. Just as Christ did. And yet, Christ, who was also man, can forgive us all. So, if he can, who are we not to forgive?"

"Yes, Father," the young priest says, "I know that. I know that I can be forgiven for what I have done. But when a man steals something, even though Christ can forgive him, he must still make full reparation for his offense as part of his absolution. Isn't that the teaching of our church?"

Seeing the old priest nod, Father Alonso continues, "Well, Father. I feel as if I have stolen something. And I'm bound by God to make full reparation for my offense, just like any of those people who come to me for confession. So those are my grounds, Father. You may tell His Excellency the Bishop that I am requesting dispensation on the grounds that I must make reparation for my sins. Once that is achieved, once I have fully atoned for my sins, then . . . with God's permission, I will return, and perhaps then I'll get to be the priest I always wanted to be, the one I feel is inside of me. May God welcome me then and grant me that great honor. But until then, Father, I must do as sinners must. I must make full reparation for my sins."

"What reparation is this you must do?" Father Francisco asks.

"My lips are sealed."

"By confession?"

"My lips are sealed."

That is all Father Alonso can tell his old mentor: "My lips are sealed."

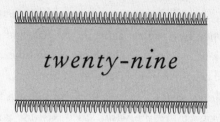

twenty-nine

"If the mountain doesn't go to Mohammed . . . ," Dolores begins to say as she enters Marguita's house, when all of a sudden she sees Marguita burst into tears.

"What is it, my child?" Dolores asks, rushing to her daughter and embracing her tight. "What's wrong?" Marguita just presses herself against her mother. "You and Lorenzo had a fight? Is that it?"

Marguita gets hold of herself. Then she tells her mother, her voice shaky, "How did you know?"

"Oh, my little love, is there anything about you I don't know?" Dolores says as she again embraces her pretty daughter next to her heart.

Marguita lets her mother embrace her—but her

eyes are lost in the far distance as her mother begins to caress her hair. Never has she lied to her mother. Never. Never has she held anything back from her mother. Never. And yet . . . now . . .

"Now listen, child," Dolores continues. "How many times have I told you that when two people fight, let the wiser of the two give in first? Hey, look at me and tell me. How many times?"

Marguita looks at her mother and sketches a smile.

"Well," Dolores says, "between you and me, we both know that of the two of you you're the wiser, so next time you see Lorenzo come in, just go to him, tell him he was absolutely right, and let him win. Men need to feel they have won arguments, child. It makes them feel strong. Manly. What they do, what they say, may not make any sense to you or to me but that's the way men are. I should know, after I've been married to that bull of your father for how long? Oh, well, for a long, long time." She pauses and smiles to herself. "Your father and I, we've had our fair share of fights, so trust me, my little love, I know what I'm talking about! So, go along with Lorenzo, tell him he was right, even if you and I know that he wasn't in the least. Make up, and then"—she smiles mischievously at her daughter—"and then jump in bed and make me another grandchild!"

Startled by her mother's words, which seem to hit right on target, Marguita embraces her waist and then, laden with guilt, not daring to face her mother and trying to control herself so she will not burst into tears, she turns and evades Dolores's eyes, which are now no longer mischievous but deadly serious. For Dolores, utterly dumbfounded by Marguita's reaction, is able to do nothing but to stare at her daughter as she wonders, What is really going on?

Zafiro looks at Loló when Loló gets to work after the noontime meal, and shakes her head in awe.

"What have you done, sugar?" she asks. "The Owl just came by and asked me about you. She told me she had something to tell you. I asked her what it was, and she said it was none of my business, so I'm just—"

"Oh, Loló," Señora Olivar's voice is heard behind them. She sounds excited, almost to the point of being exhilarated. With a gesture, she asks Loló to follow her. They go outside the switchboard area and into the side corridor, where things are more quiet. "I have great news for you," the old lady tells Loló. "We just received word from the home office and guess what?" Loló stares at the old lady. "Tell me, how would you like to go for a long vacation to Miami, all expenses paid?"

"Me?" Loló asks.

"Well, it's not really a vacation. You see, Loló, the home office has selected a few girls. You are the only one from our group here in Havana, I've been told. Apparently they are introducing a new switchboard, or something like that, I don't know the whole story, Señora Díaz is the one who knows. But in any event, they want girls who already know a little English to go to the United States and learn this new technique and then come back here and demonstrate it for all of us. So, when Señora Díaz asked me if I knew of a 'good girl,'" the old lady says looking sideways at Zafiro, "why, of course I recommended you. So there you are. I believe that your training in Miami will begin in a couple of months or so. From now until then you'll be sent to an English school to improve your language skills and then . . . oh, Loló, imagine that! Miami!"

"But, but . . ." Loló begins to say. "But why won't you go, Señora Olivar? You are much more qualified than—"

"Oh, no, I couldn't. I am a supervisor. My job demands I stay here, taking care of all my girls. Oh, no, I couldn't go. It wouldn't be proper of me. A woman has to have some decorum. Oh, no, I couldn't go. That's why I recommended you. So, what do you say? Is this a great thing or what?" She pauses. "Of course, I know you'll have to consult your parents. But Loló, this is such a great opportunity, don't even think about it! Just go ahead and do it. Oh, sure, you'll have to work, and you'll be away from all of us for a while, I know that, but . . . oh, Loló, I am so happy for you! Think about it . . . Miami! And then you may even be sent to New York! Aren't you the lucky one!"

Loló smiles at her.

"Thank you, Señora Olivar," she manages to say.

"Oh, I forgot the best part," Señora Olivar adds. She lowers her voice as she pulls Loló aside. "You'll get a nice raise starting the moment you say yes. Ten pesos a month for now, twenty once you come back! Isn't that nice? So go home now, if you wish. Go, talk to your parents, and then tomorrow morning come back and tell me what you have decided. All right?"

A disconcerted Loló goes back to her place behind the switch-board and as she gathers her purse, which she had placed where she always does at the foot of her chair, she tells Zafiro what the Owl just told her. Then, still disconcerted, she leaves the room. She is so deep in thought that she does not even realize she has not said good-bye to Zafiro, who looks at Loló and then turns to the girl sitting to her other side.

"Some people have all the luck in the world," Zafiro says, just as her board lights up.

Instead of going home, Loló slowly walks up the two flights that separate her from Señora Díaz. When she enters her office, Señora Díaz, sitting behind her desk, welcomes her with a smile.

"Did Señora Olivar talk to you?" she asks. Loló nods. "Well," the old lady says, "have you made up your mind yet?"

Loló looks at her. "Does Señora Olivar know about . . . about me?" she asks, hesitantly.

"Of course not," a hurt Señora Díaz adamantly replies, her voice sharp. "No one knows."

"But then . . . I don't understand . . . is this job for real?"

The old lady answers, her voice now gentle, kind, again the voice of a friend, the voice of a loving teacher. "Of course it is. Loló. In a company this large, there is always something new brewing. How else can a company such as ours improve? I make it my business to find about new programs, and I also make it my business to suit people to those programs. That's one of my jobs here. After all, that's what a personnel manager is supposed to do, to match personalities to jobs. So I—as well as a lot of other people—we all thought you'd be perfect for this job. And Señora Olivar was the first to agree. This isn't going to be an easy thing, Loló, this new job. You'll have to study and work at it, and hard. But I'm sure that by the time you come back, you'll be an excellent teacher. I have no doubts about that. So you'll be able to train the rest of the girls, and train them well."

Loló is still looking at the older lady, still not saying a word. Then, hesitantly, she asks, "Does anybody else know about . . . me?"

"Of course not, Loló," Señora Díaz replies. "I've told you already. No one but the two of us knows about you. I mean, not unless you told somebody. Did you?"

Loló nods.

"Him?"

Loló nods again.

"And what did he say?"

What can Loló answer to that? Can she tell Señora Díaz the truth? That when she told him, he just said all he could say: "Go in peace, your sins are forgiven!"

"Nothing," Loló answers. "He said nothing."

"I see," says the older lady.

There follows a long pause.

"Well," Señora Díaz adds after a while, "what have you decided to do, then?"

"I'll take the job," Loló says.

"And about the baby? Have you decided?"

Loló brings her hands to her belly, caressing it as she were already caressing the child. "Do you think I might be able to . . . to keep my baby?"

"Do you mean you want to keep and raise your child? As a single mother?"

"You don't think it's such a good idea, do you?"

"It's not what I think, but what you think," Señora Díaz answers. "But, Loló, this is Cuba we live in, remember that. I won't say think of your own life. Or think of what people will say about you. Or think about how happy they'll be pointing their accusing finger at you. No, I don't want you to think of any of that. Instead, Loló, I want you to think of your child. Tell me, Loló, what do you think your child's life will be like in school, when all the other kids ask him who his father is? Do you want your little boy to resent you all his life because he's illegitimate? Because he doesn't have a father? And what if you have a girl? Do you want her to suffer all her life because her mother was a bad woman, *una cualquiera*, as the other girls and even teachers in school will tell her you were? In this backward world of ours, innocents do pay for their parents' mistakes. I don't like it, and I will fight it till the day I die, but that's the way this world of ours is until somebody does something about it."

She stands up. "So, I beg you, Loló, before you make your decision, think first and above everything else about your child. We'll do whatever it is you decide. The decision is yours and yours only to make. But I recommend that you give up your child for adoption once you are in Miami, for your child's own sake. And then I hope you'll come back here and join me in my fight against ignorance and hatred. Loló, you're not the only woman in the world who's made the mistake of trusting a man who didn't deserve it. Other women have done just as you did. Other women have had to give their children away."

She moves from behind the desk and comes closer to Loló.

"Loló, look at me. Child, I know exactly what's going through your mind, I know exactly what you're thinking because, Loló, I'm one of those other women. I also had to give up my child. My son now has a family of adoptive parents who adore him and whom he can respect. I'm going to fight whoever I have to until the day comes when a woman doesn't have to do that ever again. But until then, I beg you, Loló, think of your child. Think of your child first and foremost. And if you do, I'm sure you'll decide to give him up for adoption. Just like I did."

This blatant confession surprises Loló. She had no idea.

She looks at the older lady with the gray hair and the kind, gentle eyes and sees in her a quality she had not noticed before. The older lady smiles at Loló.

"Loló," she says, "I want you to know that you are totally innocent, as innocent as your child. Do you understand what that means?"

Loló looks at her and smiles back.

"Then, run to Señora Olivar, and tell her you'll take the job."

Loló is about to leave. She turns and faces the older lady with the gray hair.

"Thank you, Señora Díaz."

"Elmira, Loló. That's my name."

"Thanks, Elmira."

That night, after she gives her family the news and a bottle of vintage wine is uncorked in honor of Loló's good fortune, Loló falls into her bed but cannot manage to fall asleep.

She knows there is a life inside her. And she knows she will protect that life above all.

She also knows that he, the child's father, is entitled to know about her decision.

She does not want his permission. She knows she does not

need it, Señora Díaz herself told her. But nonetheless, she thinks he must know.

Monday morning, during confession, I will tell him, she thinks.

And then she remembers that tomorrow, Saturday, is Renzito's birthday. And that she is expected to be in Luyanó with the rest of the family, to celebrate. And that probably so will he.

She sighs. She does not want to see him. It is bad enough to talk to him when their eyes cannot meet through the cane divider of the confessional. But seeing him there, in the flesh. How can she talk to him? How can she tell him what she is planning to do? What she thinks he must know? I wish I didn't have to go to that party, she tells herself.

She falls asleep, only to awaken in the middle of the night.

Her gaze is still fastened to the white plaster ceiling when the first rays of the sun begin to inundate her room, making it seem as if she were in a world of fire.

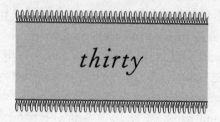

thirty

If people thought that Renzito's christening was a party to end all parties, let them think again, for today is Renzito's first birthday, and this time *both* Maximiliano the grandfather and Manuel the godfather have joined forces to throw a party that will go down in history.

Just from looking at what is being served, one would never guess that people all over Cuba are still scrambling for food—for the Great Depression is still heavily weighing down the price of sugar, and when the price of sugar is down, Cubans starve.

They do—but not at this party.

Where Maximiliano and Manuel managed to get the food nobody knows, but the large dining room table is covered with a linen tablecloth embroidered by Dolores for this occasion and on top of it there are platters filled with thick slices of roast pork—served with black beans and rice, of course—and with langostinos and shrimp fried in a butter and garlic sauce that is divine, and with chicken slowly roasted under banana leaves, and with avocado slices in a tart vinaigrette, and with fried bananas of both kinds, the ripe ones and the green ones, and with guava *pastelitos*—pastries—and with mangoes, and *mamoncillos,* and coconuts, and papayas, and . . . with you name it. The works. And then there's that great punch that "brightens the darkest night," as the ladies say. And that great rum that "puts hair on your chest," as the men add. And to top it off, all of that great music!

Maximiliano has invited some of his buddies, the guys he writes songs with, all of whom are there, harmonizing the party with their singing and playing. There are even a clown and a magician—both of them hired by Manuel to entertain the children. But who of the adults is going to pay any attention to either of them when all that music is filling not only the patio of Marguita's house, but every room, and is already beginning to spill into the street?

The door to Marguita's house is kept open to anyone in the barrio, Spaniards, criollos, black and white alike, for they all are clients and friends of Maximiliano the butcher, all of whom love the butcher and all of whom want to join him and partake in this celebration. Even the mulatto women across the street, the ones who are the *queridas*—the mistresses—of the Chinese men in the opium business, even they and their children have joined this party, for this entire block of the Street of the Bulls—that narrow little side street that is not even paved—this entire block seems to be quivering and dancing all the way from La Calzada Avenue and Hermenegildo's bodega at one end of the block to the little Church of Our Lady of the Perpetual Succor at the other end.

Presents cover not only Renzito's crib but they have spilled over into the adjoining room and now cover the whole of Marguita's and

Lorenzo's large bed—for presents are displayed for everyone to see, as is the custom. Most of them are toys: a large top that whistles as it twirls, a music box that sings Cuban songs, even a baseball glove that comes with a baseball and a complete baseball uniform.

And then the dancing begins.

And when the dancing begins . . . watch out!

At first, the patio is just trembling with excitement.

But soon that excitement begins to become delirious, as men and women start to sweat to the drunken beat, and start to pour all their sexuality into their movements, making their bodies pulse and vibrate as they dance, barely brushing each other, teasing each other in such a way that the entire patio is no longer just trembling but is now sizzling with anticipation.

What a party! What a party!

Even Lorenzo's parents, Padrón and Carmela, who are quietly sitting in the front living room—a room with two large cane armchairs nobody ever uses—seem to be having a good time. And why shouldn't they? After all, this is a dual celebration for them. Not only has Renzito reached a full year and is a healthy and smiling boy, but Loló has also told them about her success in her chosen career and about her promotion. "Aren't we the lucky ones," they keep telling each other.

Asunción is helping Marguita as best she can, making sure there are clean towels in the bathroom, that the platters are filled the moment they are emptied, and that there are plenty of napkins on the table. She can hear none of the music and none of the noises in the house, both of which are deafening. But she can see the excitement that surrounds her, an excitement that is quite contagious, for even she, deaf Asunción, is feeling it somewhere inside her and she, who seldom smiles, is now smiling from ear to ear as she goes around making herself busy.

Only Loló does not yet seem to have caught any of this excitement.

She is in Renzito's room, where she has been for a long, long while, doing nothing but looking at the crib.

She raises her head and sees Father Alonso.

Following Father Francisco, Father Alonso just entered Renzito's room and now the two priests are standing, like Loló, by Renzito's crib, apparently looking admiringly at the presents on Renzito's bed. But only Father Francisco is, for Father Alonso cannot keep his eyes—that are far too serious for such a young man—away from Loló.

At first, Loló was reluctant to come to this party. She thought that both priests would be invited to come and she did not want to run into them. But she is one of the boy's aunts, and it would not have looked good for her not to come. Besides, she told herself, sooner or later he and I are bound to see each other again, and then what?

Whatever happened between the two of us happened and there is nothing either of us can do to change it, Loló reflected. It was what it was. "A cloud passing over the horizon," as Cubans would say. Whatever we both did that first time brought an exhilarated joy to me, even to him, she thought. But then all that joy was gone that second time around. When we held each other and kissed in the secrecy of the posada room, I realized that his world and mine are different, that we do not belong together; that it is best to keep what happened between us a secret—a secret that will bring joy to me every time I think about it, she told herself then.

She still thinks the same now, even after what she's gone through, even after what she knows she will still have to go through.

On the other hand, Father Alonso has been eager to come to this party. To see her. To talk to her. To let her know of his decision to leave the priest's life behind and become a man just like any other man: a man able to marry. Ever since he made his decision about getting a dispensation from his vows, that thought has invaded his soul.

To marry her.

What else can he, an honorable man, do? How else can he atone for his sin?

At first he thought that whatever had happened between the two of them had happened and that there was nothing either of them could do to change it. It brought great joy to him. Knowing a woman. But all that joy was gone the second time around. When they held each other and kissed in the secrecy of the posada room, he thought that her world and his were different, that they did not belong together; that it would be best to keep what happened between them a secret—a secret that would bring joy to him every time he thought about it.

But now he no longer thinks the same. Now he thinks—he knows—that he and she will be able to recapture what they once had, even now, even after what he's gone through, even after what he knows he will still have to go through. He has total and absolute faith that it will happen. The good Lord will make it happen. Wasn't that what he prayed for? For God's will to be done? And everything that has happened, hasn't it all been his will?

Upon entering Renzito's room and seeing Loló, Father Francisco greets her with a polite nod, and then Marguita, who was walking behind them, ignoring Loló—as she always does since that fateful night, by now almost two years old—says, "Come this way, Father. Renzito's had so many presents that we had to put a lot of them in our room. Follow me, please. This way."

She leads Father Francisco away while Father Alonso stays behind in Renzito's room. Father Alonso grabs the music box on the bed, opens it, and as the angelic music fills the room with a sentimental Cuban love song, in a low whisper he addresses Loló.

"I have asked for my dispensation," he says, his voice filled with tender emotion.

When she hears this, Loló stares at him, her dark, gypsy eyes asking a question.

His eyes focused on the music box in his hands, he goes on. "It will take a while. Only the pope himself can grant it. But as soon as I have it, then . . . then we'll be able to get married."

Loló turns to him. "You would do that for me?" she asks him directly, no longer worried about who may be looking at them, who may be hearing them.

He looks at her, puzzled, as if her question made no sense to him. No sense at all. "Of course I would," he answers decisively. "Of course. For you. And for the baby," he adds, smiling at her.

Deeply touched by the words of Father Alonso, Loló, against her will, begins to cry. Not wanting anyone to see her, she rushes out of the room and into the bathroom, which incredibly is empty and available. She closes the door behind her and leans heavily against it.

Outside the bathroom door, the deafening noise of the party can be heard, laughter and gaiety everywhere. But laughter and gaiety that cannot manage to mask the sobbing on the other side of the door. Because Loló knows, even if Father Alonso doesn't, that this match was not made in heaven. That no matter how hard they try to make it work, she and this man do *not* belong together. She knows that without a doubt. She's known that ever since the afternoon in the posada room, where they found they had nothing to say to each other. Neither "Thanks," nor "I'm sorry."

Nothing.

And yet, here he is, that man, willing to set aside his entire life for her.

He said he would do it for me, Loló tells herself. But that is not so. He is not doing for me, but for the baby. She embraces her waist. Yes, of that I am totally certain. Because had it not been for the baby, would he have ever considered going to the pope and asking for his dispensation so he could marry me?

She shakes her head, answering herself with that gesture. And then she has to smile.

When she realizes that had it not been for the baby, she would not have even remotely considered his marriage proposal.

Despite the busyness of everything that's been going on during the birthday party, Dolores has found the time to look at Marguita, her mother's eyes seeing something that perhaps no one else can.

Marguita looks tired. Even sad.

Amid the commotion going on, and the noises and the gaiety and laughter surrounding all, Marguita seems to be in a different world altogether. A world of her own. And so does Lorenzo, Dolores notices.

She shakes her head and wonders what is going on.

But then she smiles to herself. A lover's quarrel, no doubt. A cloud passing over the horizon, she tells herself. A little sand in the eye.

Maximiliano the butcher, dressed in white pants, white shoes, and wearing an elegant white linen guayabera—a pleated Cuban folk shirt—comes to get her. Grabbing Dolores by the waist, he takes her to the patio, and embracing her tight to him, they begin to dance a *danzón,* an old Cuban dance which is the most sensual and at the same time the most elegant of them all.

The two of them dance and you can see just by looking at them that those two belong together. That he is as deeply in love with her now, after so many years since they first danced together, as she is in love with him, that man with an emperor's name who has given her wonderful children. Oh, yes, you can tell, just by looking at them. The way Maximiliano's eyes keep constantly looking at Dolores, avidly searching for hers; the way Dolores's eyes keep constantly evading Maximiliano's whenever she feels them on her—and yet, the way she returns the look when she thinks nobody is looking. Oh, yes, those two are in love—and madly so.

Still. After these many years. You can tell.

S omeone knocks at the bathroom door.

"Occupied?" that someone asks.

Upon hearing this, Loló, still inside the bathroom, her eyes now dry, puts on her best smile and opens the door—only to find Marguita there, little Renzo in her arms.

Swiftly, keeping out of Marguita's way, avoiding Marguita's eyes and not saying a word, Loló lets Marguita and her child into the bathroom as she exits almost furtively, hoping that her eyes, still red, have not betrayed her.

Then, determinedly, she starts for little Renzo's room, hoping to find Father Alonso there.

She has had time to think and she now knows what to say to him.

Her decision has been made: she will take the job, go to Miami, and give the child away. That's what she told Nurse Díaz yesterday. And that's exactly what she will do. Just as she had decided to do yesterday.

It's best for me. And for him. And certainly it's best for the baby, Loló told herself yesterday.

Just as she tells herself now.

It is best. For all of us.

She has told her family all they needed to know, and all they will ever get to know: that she got a promotion. That she will go to Miami for a few months. That she even got a raise. She even told Carmela that since she doesn't need the extra money she will give her mother those extra ten pesos she will be making each month, making Carmela beam with happiness. She has even given Señora

Díaz the authorization to begin placing the child. She just asked that the future parents of her baby be of Cuban descent living in Miami, for she wanted her child to be able to speak Spanish. That was all she asked for. Señora Díaz said that she thought that would be possible, and that she would get on it right away.

On her way back to Renzito's room, Loló steps out onto the patio and catches Maximiliano and Dolores dancing really close to each other, surrounded by their friends and neighbors, all of whom are looking at them with admiring eyes. She looks at the dancing couple and her eyes, like everybody's, also gleam with admiration. She has never seen her own parents dance. She wonders, if they did, would they dance as close together as Dolores and Maximiliano are right now? She remembers the time Padrón left. Those were hard times, she thinks. For Mamá. For all of us. Not knowing where Papá was, not knowing if he would ever come back. Were my parents ever as deeply in love with each other as Maximiliano and Dolores are? For there can be no doubt about what the butcher and his wife feel for each other. None whatsoever.

This brings a bittersweet smile to her face.

If only I were as deeply in love with the father of my child, she tells herself and sighs. How much I'd like to deceive myself, she thinks. But then she shakes her head. No. I won't lie to myself. And no, I won't let him lie to himself, either. He belongs where he is. In that world of his. Taking him away from that world of his would destroy him. And I won't allow that.

Her mind made up, a resolute Loló goes inside the house, searching until she finds Father Alonso, still by the crib, his eyes lost in the far distance. She goes to the crib, grabs the colorful top, and spins it in her hand as she looks at the young priest, whose deep-blue eyes seem to be so sad.

"I'm touched by what you just told me, Father Alonso," she says, addressing not the man but the priest in him. "But I don't think any of that will be necessary." She stops him from saying a word. "You see . . . everything that happened was . . . it was just a false alarm."

Father Alonso stares at her with incredulous eyes.

"I was late and, well, you know what that means, don't you? I thought I was, well, with child. But it all turned out to be a false alarm. I was going to tell you Monday morning, during confession. But I'm happy we got to talk tonight. So you see there's no need for you to do anything. Certainly not for me."

Father Alonso does not know what to say.

But she tells him what she knows he is thinking: "It's better we both keep our memories just as they are. Let's pretend we were two innocent children playing games on the sand. And we were, weren't we?"

Her sister Asunción rushes into the room. "Loló," she says, "hurry up, hurry up! They're going to break the piñata."

Loló follows Asunción out of the room, leaving behind a disconcerted young man, who looks at the music box still in his hands, which has ceased playing its song. The young priest winds the key beneath the box, making it sing again, a romantic Cuban love song. He listens to it for a few seconds and then closes its lid, stopping the music. He places the music box inside Renzito's crib and sighs. Then, pretending he lost something under Renzito's crib, he kneels down, and as he does he says a quick prayer.

"Thanks, Lord," he utters to himself, "for giving me another chance to be the shepherd I vowed to you I would be. For teaching me the sorrows and agonies of what it is to be a man. For letting me know how much of a frail man I still am. For making me a better man. And, with your guidance, a better teacher. And a better priest."

"Father Alonso, have you lost something?" he hears Father Francisco ask as the old priest reenters the room.

"I thought I had," the young priest replies, standing up. "But I hadn't."

He smiles at Father Francisco, a small, tentative smile tinged with sadness, but—still—a smile.

His first smile in days.

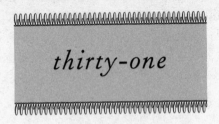

thirty-one

Lost in thought, Marguita is in her tiny kitchen, her mother next to her. It is way past midnight and the birthday party behind them has dwindled to barely a whisper. Only the very select few still remain in the house: intimate friends and family. For a long, long while both women have been standing side by side doing dishes in a routine way, not saying a word to each other. Dolores leaning over the *lavadero,* washing one dish after the next; Marguita drying them.

Dolores hands Marguita one last just-washed dish.

Still in a world of her own, Marguita takes it

and starts to dry it mechanically, almost as if a third person were doing it.

Dolores looks at her daughter and wonders what is really going on inside her child's head. Having "that woman," Loló, in her own house, is this the reason why Marguita is so troubled? Is this the reason why Marguita's eyes have been evading mine? Dolores asks herself. Did Marguita and Lorenzo have a fight over Loló? Is that what this is all about? Dolores shakes her head. Well, she tells herself, if that is what is troubling Marguita, then the time has come once and for all to put a stop to this nonsense.

"Marguita, child, tell me," Dolores says, breaking the long silence with her gentle voice, which she keeps soft and low, "what do I have to do to have you go and make your peace with Loló?"

Her words awaken Marguita from her reverie, bringing her back to reality.

"Do I have to get down on my knees?" Dolores adds, smiling at her daughter, who gently shakes her head as she smiles back at her mother, wishing she could tell Dolores everything that is troubling her—but not daring to. For it is not the thought of Loló that has been bothering Marguita. No, not in the least. But that other thought, the thought of what she and Lorenzo have decided to do with their unborn child, the child she is secretly carrying, the child most people—including Dolores, her own mother—will never know about, the child who will cease to exist in just a few hours.

And yet, a child both Marguita and Lorenzo have already learned to love.

And deeply.

Misunderstanding the smile in Marguita's eyes, Dolores continues in that kind voice of hers. "Then, Marguita, go, talk to Loló, and forgive her. Don't you know that forgiving makes you a better person?" Dolores pauses and smiles at Marguita. "Don't you want to be a better person than you already are?" she adds.

Marguita tries to avert her eyes from her mother's—but Dolores will not allow it.

"Marguita," Dolores continues, her voice firm, though soothing at the same time, "this hate of yours has gone on too long, far too long. You must stop it, my little love, for hate corrodes the soul little by little until there is no soul left. I know. I saw it happen. My own father hated me all his life because he blamed me for the death of the woman he loved beyond reason, his wife, my mother, who died in his arms when I was born. So I had to grow up not only without a mother but also without a father because of that irrational hate of his. Tell me, my little love, what would have happened to me if I had not forgiven him, and from the heart? What kind of a woman would I have turned into? What kind of a wife, what kind of a mother would I have been?"

Marguita tries to turn her gaze from her mother's once again. But once again Dolores will not let her. With great tenderness, she grabs her daughter's face in both her hands and gently, ever so gently, she turns it toward her, making Marguita look at her.

"My love, hate is many times born out of fear, don't you know that?"

Puzzled by Dolores's words, Marguita tilts her head slightly to one side—as if she were a child carefully listening to what her mother is saying.

"It is," Dolores continues. "You may fear someone for whatever the reason. Sometimes people fear someone only because that person looks or acts different from them. And little by little that fear grows and grows until it becomes hate. But I didn't raise a child of mine to be afraid of anybody. So tell me, my little love, are you afraid of Loló? Is that it? Is that what's causing all of this hatred that has already begun to corrode your heart? My love, what could that woman have done to you that you can be so afraid of her?"

I? Afraid of that woman? Marguita asks herself. The thought deeply disturbs her and makes her forget, if only for a moment, that other thought that has been weighing heavily on her soul. That will be the day! Marguita tells herself. Why should I ever be afraid of that woman? Because she has a better education than I have? Because she works and makes money? Because she can afford clothes I cannot buy, not on Lorenzo's salary? She violently shakes her head and faces her mother.

"I am not afraid of that woman, Mamá," Marguita replies decisively, her voice sharp.

Her mother gives her a long, inquisitive look.

"Well, maybe I was, a long time ago," Marguita adds, "when she saw me doing with Lorenzo what she saw. But if I ever was afraid of that woman, I'm not any longer. Because now I know that what Lorenzo and I do in bed is our business, whether she—or people like her—approve of it or not. And, honestly, Mamá, I don't care any longer what that woman may or may not think of me."

"Then, my love, prove it to me—and to yourself. Go make peace with her. Forget what she did and forgive her. And do it from the heart, like I did. Go ahead, do it now, today, on the day of your child's first birthday. If not as a favor to me, or even as favor to you, my little love, then do it as a favor to Renzito, your baby."

Dolores looks at Marguita, that stubborn daughter of hers who is as mulish as they come. "I beg you, child," she says—"I mean, *Señora Marguita*," she quickly corrects herself, gently stressing the words as she smiles one of those famous mischievous smiles of hers at Marguita.

When she hears her mother call her "Señora Marguita," Marguita, whose eyes have been downcast, raises them and looks at Dolores.

Oh, how much would she like to open up her heart to her mother, the best "Friend and Neighbor" anyone in the world could ask for, and tell her everything.

Everything!

But she and Lorenzo have agreed to keep everything secret

between the two of them and no one else in the world will ever know anything about it—no one else but Manuel the doctor and his assistant, Estela the nurse.

Marguita is still looking at her mother when suddenly, for the first time in her life, Marguita no longer sees in front of her the woman she has known all her life but a very different one: a frail, tiny woman much smaller and much older than the one she remembers. Dolores's black and curly hair is beginning to go gray, even white in places; her mouth has tiny wrinkles surrounding it; and her face has an imploring look to it that Marguita does not remember ever seeing there before.

Marguita feels a sudden tenderness toward this woman, a new kind of tenderness she has never felt before. She feels she would like to embrace this woman, and hug her tight, and tell her with this hug how much she loves this older woman, so beautiful and yet so new to her.

Marguita has never thought of either Maximiliano or Dolores as old before.

But now that she is looking closely at this woman in front of her, this woman who has just smiled at her, this woman who has just called her "Señora Marguita," she sees in her mother a new kind of beauty she hasn't seen before, and Marguita loves her for it.

Still, the affronted heart of the dishonored criollo woman Dolores's words have awakened inside of Marguita begins to clamor again for what it has always clamored for: revenge. Always revenge. Never forgiveness.

Avenge yourself. This is what the dishonored woman tells Marguita she must do.

Avenge yourself.

But then Marguita looks again at this older woman in front of her, this mother of hers who now seems to be so frail and so tiny. And as she does, she remembers seeing her reclining in an old rocking chair, surrounded by cushions that her husband had lovingly placed around her, breathing with great difficulty, and telling her, "Marguita, if something should happen to me . . . all I want you to do is to make sure that our family stays close together. That your brothers and sisters keep loving each other as much as they have. And should any discord ever occur among any of you, I want you, my little love, to intercede and make peace among them. That's all I want you to do. You know I lost my family. I don't want my children to lose theirs, for whatever the reason. Will you promise me you'll do that for me?"

Well, Marguita tells herself, didn't I promise Mamá I'd do just that, keep my family together, at whatever the cost? And isn't that woman, Loló, now a part of *my* family? Do I want my little Renzo to grow up not loving his own aunt? She sighs. Mamá is probably right. Loló may not be as bad as I have made her out to be. And even if she were, people can change, can't they?

She remembers that barely a few moments ago she had seen Loló stepping out of the bathroom, her eyes red.

From crying? an astounded Marguita had asked herself then.

She remembers that for a brief second she thought she had seen in Loló's eyes something other than the insolent gypsy stare she has always seen there, a softness, a hidden sadness, even a vulnerability Marguita had never noticed before. As if that woman stepping out of the bathroom had indeed been a woman different from the one Marguita had always known and even feared.

Have I been mistaken about that woman? Marguita asked herself then.

The idea that Loló was perhaps not as evil as she thought had briefly crossed her mind, but just as quickly she had discarded it. No, that woman *is* evil, she told herself then.

But was I right? she asks herself now, as she listens to her mother's words.

Maybe the woman who stepped out of the bathroom is the real Loló, Marguita thinks. Maybe the real Loló is very different from the one I thought she was. Maybe the real Loló is truly not as evil as I made her out to be. Maybe.

Dolores hands Marguita a little tray filled with a couple of tiny cups brimming with freshly brewed Cuban coffee that smells heavenly.

"Here, take this," Dolores says. "Go find Loló, and when you see her, offer her some coffee. Then sit by her side and speak to her as civilized people do. *La gente hablando se entiende,*" Dolores says, quoting a Cuban proverb, "People get to understand one another by talking." "Try it, Marguita," Dolores adds. "Don't be so stubborn, child. Just try talking to her. I'm sure she won't bite."

Torn by the recollections of that painful night—even now, after almost two years, a night still very much present in her mind—and yet remembering the promise she made to her mother about becoming the peacemaker in the family, Marguita replies, her voice no longer argumentative but plaintive: "But Mamá, I've already told you a thousand times, I don't think Loló and I have anything to say to each other. We have absolutely nothing in common. Not a thing! What can the two of us talk about?"

"How can you say that, Marguita?" Dolores says, pleasantly surprised, for this is the first time she has heard Marguita refer to "that woman" by her given name. "Loló is a woman. Just as you are. How can you say that you and she have nothing in common? You probably have a lot more in common than you think. But you'll never find out unless you talk to her. So go, please. Talk to her."

"What if she doesn't want to talk to me?"

"Well then, my love," continues Dolores, "that will be her loss, not yours."

Carrying a small tray holding two tiny, steaming coffee cups, Marguita is looking for Loló when Lorenzo rushes to her, and, jumping up and down with unbelievable excitement, like a child at play, embraces her tightly to him.

"Lorenzo, what do you think you're doing?" Marguita asks,

her voice sharp. "You're going to make me spill this coffee and burn myself! Are you crazy? Let go of me, Lorenzo. I said, let go. Let go!"

But he will not let go of her.

Instead he gets closer to her and lowers his voice.

"I got great news. Incredible news. For you. For us." He embraces his wife's belly. "For *all* of us!" He won't let her say a word. "You know that Loló got a promotion at work and that she got a raise, too, don't you? Well, guess what? She's giving all that extra money she'll be making to Mamá, so . . . don't you see?" Marguita shakes her head. "Mamá just came to me," Lorenzo goes on, his voice excited, even urgent, "and she told me that they won't be needing the ten pesos we give them every month anymore, because Loló is going to give all of that money to Mamá! Isn't that great?"

He sees Marguita look at him, a strange look in her eyes.

"Don't you see?" Lorenzo adds. "It's like us getting a ten-peso raise. With that extra money we'll be able to afford our new baby, just the way we both wanted, so we won't have to go to Doctor Manuel Monday morning. Thanks to my sister Loló, my dear, dear sister Loló. Isn't that great, isn't that great?" He pulls Marguita even tighter to him. "Isn't that almost unbelievable?" He sighs. "If Mamá hadn't told me tonight, just a few seconds ago, by this time Monday, you and I . . . Well, that other thing was never meant to happen, I guess." He kisses her. "I'm so happy, so happy that tonight I think—no, I don't think. I know. With no doubts—I know that tonight I'll be able to sleep all night long, like I used to. And so will you, my love, and so will you!" He kisses her again. "I already told Manuel to cancel Monday's thing. When I told him, he sighed. You should've seen his face. I think that even *he* will be able to sleep all night long as well! Just like us. Isn't that incredible?"

Moments later, Marguita is still shaking her head in total disbelief.

It all seems so silly, so ironically silly to her, now that she looks at it all in retrospect, the unbearable pain, the insufferable agonies she has lived through in the last few days. How could I ever think that ten pesos, ten measly pesos a month, were more important than the life of this child growing inside of me? she asks herself. How could I think that keeping Lorenzo going to the university, and saving every penny we can so we can buy a house or secure a better education for Renzito, how could I ever think that any of that was more important than the life of this child growing inside of me? How could I equate any of those chimerical dreams with the reality of my child's life? Sooner or later those dreams will come true, she assures herself. Lorenzo will graduate, and he will get a better position at the bookstore, and he and I will have a house of our own, and we will give our children the education they need, and we will get our children out of this barrio. Those dreams will come true. We will make them come true, Lorenzo and I. Of that I am totally certain. But, once we put a stop to the life of this child growing inside of me, that life is totally gone, forever, never ever to be created again. How could we have even entertained that silly idea, Lorenzo and I? How could we have been so stupid? What were we thinking?

By now, even the most intimate friends are already gone. And that includes Renzito's godparents, Manuel the doctor and Celina his wife, who left just seconds ago. Marguita was still holding her tray with two tiny cups of that heavenly smelling coffee—the coffee she was taking to Loló—when Manuel and Celina came to say good night to her. Seeing them look at the coffee on her tray with such avid eyes, Marguita smiled at them and offered it to them. Now she is back in the kitchen, waiting for more fresh coffee to drip down the flannel filter Cubans use to make coffee, and into the two tiny cups she has placed underneath.

Only the last few members of the family have remained, to help out with the chores of cleaning the house and putting into a semblance of order what is otherwise a huge mess. Asunción is in the kitchen cleaning up, even though Marguita has told her time and again not to do a thing. Dolores and Carmela are busy picking up trays and platters and taking them to the kitchen. Lorenzo, Padrón, and Maximiliano have gone out, hoping to find, at this late hour, a cab that can take Lorenzo's family back to Old Havana, at the other end of town where they live, for the streetcar service running on La Calzada Avenue stops at one o'clock in the morning, and it is already way past that time.

As soon as the two tiny cups are filled, Marguita breathes deeply and then, with tray in hand, goes around the house until she finds Loló in the living room, sitting in one of the cane rocking chairs.

She notices that Loló looks tired. Even more than tired, Marguita thinks. She looks listless. As if she were lost in a world of her own.

I must have been wrong, Marguita tells herself, as she remembers the hidden sadness she thought she had briefly seen in Loló's eyes earlier as Loló stepped out of the bathroom, and how quickly she had dismissed that thought from her mind. The sadness I thought I saw in Loló's eyes then must have been there, Marguita asserts to herself, for it is still there now as Loló's eyes keep staring emptily into the distance. And then Marguita wonders if those red eyes she saw earlier are somehow related to the dejected, almost disconsolate way Loló seems to be right now.

"Here, Loló," Marguita says, her voice echoing the kindness and gentleness that is always present in her own mother's voice, "have some coffee. It'll wake you up."

Startled by Marguita's words, Loló looks at Marguita, her dark, gypsy eyes asking a silent question. These are the first words she has heard Marguita say to her not only all night long but ever since that night, that embarrassing night, when Loló's eyes met Marguita's, right after Marguita had made love to her husband in the not-so-private privacy of their own room.

"Thank you," Loló says, as she takes the tiny cup of coffee Marguita is offering her and begins to sip it.

Marguita sits by her side, in the other rocking chair.

This is a very difficult moment for her. The dishonored criollo woman inside Marguita keeps reminding her of what this woman opposite her did, telling Marguita over and over that this woman opposite her is the same woman who made her feel as if she had been raped by those very same eyes that are looking back at her right now. And the outraged criollo woman inside Marguita keeps insisting and insisting that this woman opposite her pay—and dearly—for that horrible and vicious affront.

Avenge yourself. This is what her criollo heart keeps telling Marguita she must do.

Avenge yourself.

And yet, how ironic it all is, Marguita thinks, that it is thanks to this woman that I can keep alive the life of the child growing inside of me.

She remembers her mother's words quoting the Cuban saying. *La gente hablando se entiende.* "People get to understand one another by talking." Isn't it time Loló and I tried to understand each other? she asks herself. Isn't it time we talked to each other? But before Marguita can say a word, Loló places the now half-empty cup of coffee on the little tray Marguita is carrying and then words begin to pour out of her mouth.

"Marguita," she says, "for the longest time I've been meaning to talk to you. To ask for your forgiveness." She shakes her head and looks away from Marguita. "I was, well, crazy when I did what I did. I'm so sorry. There are no words to . . ."—she shakes her head again, but this time her eyes look for Marguita's—"You have no idea how bad I have felt ever since . . . well, ever since *that* night. I haven't been able to forget what I did, and I don't know how I can make up for it. All this time, ever since, I've been meaning to ask you, to beg you for your forgiveness. I know that perhaps you'll never be able to forget what I did"—she quickly adds—"for I know that I won't, either. But perhaps . . . perhaps you'll be able to forgive me. One day. I hope you will."

This woman opposite me is not the woman I used to know, Marguita tells herself. That other woman would have never said anything like this, Marguita thinks. Or was I always totally wrong about Loló?

Marguita sighs, as her eyes look questioningly at Loló.

Not really knowing what to say, how to react to a confession such as this of Loló's, to make time, Marguita places the tiny tray in her hands on top of the wide flat surface of the arm of the mahogany and cane rocking chair Loló is sitting in, and takes the other tiny cup of coffee to her lips. But then, unexpectedly, even before she realizes it, she decides to open her heart to Loló.

She never meant to do that.

She had planned to come to Loló, sit by her side, and have a civilized talk. That's what she had promised her mother, Dolores. That was all she had meant to do.

But as she sat next to Loló, something happened. Like a dam overflowing, Marguita felt a strong need to tell the truth, her painful truth, to someone. And who better than the person who saved the life of the child she is carrying in her womb, even if she did it unknowingly?

"Loló," Marguita says as she places the tiny cup of coffee in her hands on the tiny tray by her side. "I came here to thank you."

"Thank me?" a puzzled Loló replies. "What for?"

There's a long silence that is finally broken by one of Marguita's sighs, a long, deep sigh that seems to come from the bottom of her heart.

"For saving the life of my child," Marguita finally says. Seeing Loló's puzzled eyes, Marguita quickly adds, "No, Loló, it's not Renzito I'm talking about. But"—Marguita takes Loló's hands in hers and places them on her belly—"but the life of this other child, inside of me."

Loló raises her questioning eyes to Marguita.

Marguita goes on.

"No one knows anything about it yet. You are the first one to know. You see, I . . . I mean we, Lorenzo and I, we were going to . . . to terminate this pregnancy. This coming Monday." She looks at her watch. "Tomorrow, because it is Sunday already." She looks back at Loló. "Lorenzo and I, we didn't think the time was right for . . . a second child. We just didn't have the money to . . ."—she shakes her head—"I know it sounds stupid to even think of doing what we were planning to do just because of a few pesos. But . . . now that you're giving that extra money to your family, you know, the extra money you'll be making with your promotion, well, now we . . . Lorenzo, I mean, he won't have to give your family the money he was giving them every month, and now . . . now, well, we'll be able to keep this baby." Marguita gently embraces her waist. "So . . . it is because of this child that I thank you. For even though you knew nothing about it, you saved his life."

Suddenly aware of what she has just said, words that painfully remind her of what she herself has been going through, of the horrible and interminable days she has lived through while considering terminating her pregnancy, Marguita finally realizes that what her mother has been telling her all this time is absolutely true. Because all of a sudden Marguita feels the healing power—the miraculous healing power—of forgiveness and love. Forgiveness and love that come from the bottom of Marguita's heart, just as her mother told her it should be.

Feeling at last totally liberated from the fear and the desire for revenge that had been crowding her heart with hate, and almost without thinking about it, Marguita adds, words honestly pouring out of her, "So, Loló, once this baby is born, I would love for you to be the child's godmother."

An astounded Loló looks at Marguita.

Can it be true that Marguita has just offered her, Loló, the honor, the *immense* honor, of being the godmother of Marguita's yet-unborn child?

Then, embracing her own waist, Loló begins to cry, weep, the moment she realizes that it is because of her being with child—a child she will not keep, a child no one in her family will ever know anything about; that it is because of that child inside of her—a child she is giving away, a child she is losing forever; that it is because of that child that she is able to save the life of another child who will get to see the light and whom she will be able to call her godchild. A child who will be able to call her god*mother*.

Shocked by Loló's reaction, something she was not expecting in the least, Marguita embraces Loló, who will not stop crying.

And as she looks at Loló, Marguita can see in Loló's weeping eyes that, as unbelievable as it may seem to Marguita, Loló seems to understand exactly the agonies that she, Marguita, has felt; the agonies that tore at her heart night after night, the agonies that she has been going through for days, weeks, debating whether to keep or to lose the child in her womb.

After a long, long while, Loló raises her eyes and smiles at Marguita, a gentle, kind smile. The kind of smile the other Loló, the one she used to be, would never have smiled, for that other Loló didn't believe that kind of a smile was ever possible for her.

But Loló knows better now, thanks to Father Alonso, who taught her how to smile.

That, Loló will always treasure.

Just as she will always treasure the life of that child whose heart is already beating inside of her—even though no one in her family will ever know about it.

"I'll be more than honored to be your child's godmother," Loló finally manages to say, as she erases her tears. Then, still teary-eyed, she picks up her cup of coffee, which is still steaming, from the little tray by her side, and smells its heavenly aroma.

"This is really good coffee," she adds, taking it to her lips, and sipping it. Delicately, she places it back on the tray and smiles at Marguita. "Thank you, Marguita. I really needed this."

Marguita places her little cup of coffee on the tray by Loló's, and smiles back at her sister-in-law, soon to be the godmother of her next child.

"So did I, Loló," she says and then adds. "May I get you something else?"

Loló shakes her head.

"How about some cookies?" Marguita asks.

Loló shakes her head again.

"Loló, let me tell you. Mamá's old cook, you know, Lucía, makes some cookies that are this side of heaven. How about it?" Marguita smiles. "Doctor Manuel told me to stick to my diet, but since he's already gone"—she looks around—"and since Lorenzo is still looking for a cab . . . what do you think? Should we dare?" She touches her belly. "After all," she adds, "in my condition, I'm supposed to eat for two, you know."

When Loló hears this, her eyes brighten up and glitter. After all, Loló tells herself, mimicking Marguita, I am also in the same condition as Marguita, so maybe I should be eating for two as well.

"I guess I could have one or two," Loló says.

"Or even three or four," Marguita replies. "I won't count. Wait till you taste them. I tell you, I never liked the taste of milk alone. But these cookies . . . they go great with a glass of cold milk, believe me, they really do."

Marguita stands up. "Come," she tells Loló, "let's go to the kitchen."

Marguita grabs the tray with the now empty cups of coffee and as she starts for the kitchen, she confides to Loló, "I confess I hid those cookies. I didn't want people to know about them during the party. But, please"—she lowers her voice—"don't tell anybody, all right? And especially Lorenzo. You know how he is. He gets raving mad at me when he sees me stepping off my diet!"

Under the amazed eyes of Dolores, who manages to smile broadly at the two of them even though she can hardly believe what she is seeing, Marguita and Loló walk almost hand in hand into the kitchen. There, Marguita gets a tin can she had carefully hidden by the coalbin, opens it, and proceeds to place several of those out-of-this-world cookies of Lucía's on a plate, which she hands to Loló. Followed by Loló, Marguita then goes into the dining room, opens her Free-hee-dye-reh, and pours out two large glasses of milk, which she takes to the table.

Once in the dining room, the two women—each of them with child—two women who, as Marguita assured her mother barely minutes ago, have absolutely nothing in common with each other—there the two of them sit at that famous table carved by a Cuban criollo man, the one who did exactly as the Cuban criollo code demanded and avenged himself and cleansed his stained honor by stabbing his wife and her lover to their death. The same man who ever since has not been able to sleep, for despite how brave and manly people may think him, he knows himself to be nothing but a coward. A man who was not able to face standing up to his world and do as he really wanted to do: forgive his wife, the woman he loved beyond reason, and give her—and himself—another chance. But forgiveness is not part of that criollo code that used to control—and that *still* controls—his life and the lives of many others like him.

As Loló and Marguita sit at the dining table—under the approving gaze of Dolores, who, standing in the kitchen doorway, is pretending to dry yet another dish with a kitchen towel—and as they begin to taste those out-of-this-world cookies of Lucía's that indeed go so well with a large glass of cold milk, a breathless Lorenzo rushes back into the house, followed by Maximiliano and Padrón. Finally, after waiting and waiting for what they thought were hours, they were able to locate a cab, which is now standing at the corner of La Calzada and the Street of the Bulls, right in front of Hermenegildo's bodega.

The smell of freshly brewed coffee coming from the kitchen is so strong and so enticing that the men have no choice but to follow it.

As Maximiliano and Padrón are offered tiny cups of coffee by Dolores, Lorenzo—who was about to shout, "We got a cab waiting at the corner"—sees that Marguita and Loló are sitting side by side at the dining table.

"Hey, don't you dare move!" an astounded Lorenzo shouts instead. He is so happy, seeing that his wife and his sister seem to have made their peace, that he can scarcely believe it. He rushes into his bedroom only to come back a second later, his little Kodak in his hands, its flashbulb already attached to it, for he has been taking photographs all along during his son's birthday party.

"Now, the two of you," he says, as he looks through his viewfinder, "you gotta get closer together." Marguita and Loló get closer together. "More, more," Lorenzo adds, still looking through his viewfinder.

"If we get any closer we'll be sitting on top of each other," Marguita says jokingly, as she and Loló pull their chairs even closer to each other.

"That's good, that's good," Lorenzo says as he moves back and forth, framing the picture through the viewfinder. "Now, the two of you, look at—oh, like that. Just like that. That's perfect, that's perfect," an excited Lorenzo shouts.

Lorenzo snaps the photograph.

This is the same photograph that a week later can be seen, enlarged, nicely cropped, and beautifully framed, in the display window of the photographer's studio where Lorenzo has his film developed; a photograph that seems to have soul, for it makes people stop and look at it as they go by.

The photograph is a very simple one. It just shows two women sitting side by side and looking at each other. That is all.

Except that these two women are as diametrically opposite from each other as they can be.

One of them is slender, perhaps even too thin, with an elongated horselike face that is almost pure white, a long, narrow nose, thin lips, dark, gypsy eyes, and dark glossy hair pulled back and tied in a tight bun at the back of her neck—while the other one is pleasantly plump, with an oval face that is deeply tanned, a tiny nose, full sensual lips, light eyes, and long light hair falling in loose curls down to her shoulders.

And yet these two women, who seem to have absolutely nothing in common, have been captured alive by the photographer in a moment of great intimacy, as everybody who looks at the photograph will tell you. Because everybody can see that there is a special kind of love being shared by those two women as they look at each other; a very special kind of love—a mixture of understanding and gratitude—that permeates the photograph and that makes everybody go, "Aaahhh!" as they look at the photograph and smile.